LOST BONDS

BINDING WORDS BOOK SIX

DANIEL SCHINHOFEN

1

Complete and total darkness engulfed Sean. *Is this what death feels like?*

"No, not death," Morrigan spoke softly. "You'll survive, though, in truth, you pushed yourself past your breaking point."

Sean spun around to find Morrigan seated in his front room, the manor appearing around him. "Odin—!"

"Didn't break any accord," Morrigan said bitterly. "The Einherjar were invited."

"Just *happened* to be invited?"

"No. One of the Asgardians accessed rarely-used channels to arrange it. I don't know who or why, but the obvious answer would be Thor, because he was brought to task for killing you."

"My wives!" Sean cried out suddenly as his memory of the fight hit him.

Morrigan's lips turned down. "Most of them are fine."

"Most?" Sean choked.

"Sean..." The soft voice from behind him was filled with sadness.

Turning to see who had called to him, Sean's heart clenched. Chastity and Lilly stood side by side at the foot of the stairs.

"No..."

"We're sorry," Lilly sniffled. "We tried."

Sean lurched toward them, tears spilling from his eyes. "No...!"

Both women rushed to him, grabbing him and sobbing.

Morrigan watched them, her face impassive. "They died doing what had to be done, Sean."

Sean's anger flared and he let go of his wives to spin on Morrigan. "What had to be done? What had to be *done*?! That fight never had to happen!"

Morrigan sat in the chair, unmoving. "That fight was destined the moment you placed yourself against Denmur. Maybe not on a field in front of the city, maybe not with your wives beside you, but a battle would have come, regardless. If they'd not been there, you'd be the one dead on the field now, and they would all be dying in the manor."

"Sean," Chastity said, grasping his arm, "we *chose* to stand beside you."

"We knew what might happen," Lilly said, taking his other arm.

Sean's anger turned to ash as his two dead wives stopped him from attacking the goddess in front of him. "I... I got you both killed."

"No," Chastity said firmly before spinning him to face her. "You did your very best to protect us. Lilly gave her life to save Felora, and I gave mine to save Andie." Grabbing his face, she dragged his lips to hers, kissing him hard.

Sean was shaking, tears pouring down his face, when the kiss ended. He never got a chance to speak, because Lilly turned him around and kissed him just as passionately.

When she pulled back, her forehead rested against his, her eyes burning with emotion. "Never blame yourself for us, husband. We saved our wives. We both had a choice, and we made it. You will need to be the rock for them, now— they surely blame themselves for us. Help them, love them, and then avenge us."

"You'll never be without them," Morrigan said, pulling their attention back to her. "Both of them venerated you, Sean. This place is yours, and as such, you may bring those who worship you to it when they die. There is already one person here, in fact." She nodded to the hallway that led to the kitchen.

"Oh, Chas..." Marjorie whispered, stopping in the entryway to the room, her eyes wet.

"Momma!" Chastity exclaimed and rushed her.

Marjorie met her halfway, and the two of them sobbed as they held each other.

"How?" Sean asked Morrigan while Lilly held him.

"You've grown," Morrigan said softly. "Maybe you didn't fully comprehend what happened when we sent you off. Your memories of it might be fragmented."

"You held a party and then put me in the world."

"No, Sean. We had a wake."

Brow creasing, Sean tried to piece together the fragments of what had happened before he was dropped off into this new world. "I was on a table, and a party went on around me."

"You are recalling the very end of it," Morrigan nodded as she stood. "I need to go. You have a few moments with your loved ones yet. Cherish them, Sean, those here and those still alive. We'll talk again in time."

"Wait—!" Sean tried to stop her, but she vanished as if she'd never been there.

"Sean, where am I?" Marjorie asked as she and Chastity came over to stand near him.

"I'm not sure," he replied. "Did you... hell... did you pray to me?"

"Yes," Marjorie said. "You saved me from torment. I prayed to you every night, like my daughter did."

"I think... this might be the afterlife for whoever does so."

Marjorie inhaled sharply and her grip on Chastity's arm went white. "No... please, no...!"

Chastity covered her mother's hand with her own. "Yes. I'm dead, as are you."

Marjorie sniffled. "Oh, dear child... did that man get you, too?"

"Man?" Sean asked.

"I only caught a glimpse of his face while I bled out," Marjorie whispered. "Average height, brown hair, and black eyes... he exuded hatred."

Sean exhaled sharply— he knew someone who matched that description. "He came out of nowhere?"

"I was going to fix dinner when a sharp pain creased my neck and I was spun to face the couch. I saw that flicker of his face when I tried to struggle to save myself. As I grew colder, I felt my clothing being..." Trailing off, she shuddered.

"*After* you died?" Lilly asked in horror.

"Better than if I were alive," Marjorie swallowed.

"Wait," Chastity said, her eyes going wide, "wasn't he with them?"

"Yes," Lilly nodded, having made the same connection. "Myna killed him."

"Evan and Klein were behind it all," Sean said grimly. "Evan's dead."

"So is Klein," Lilly said. "I saw Myna kill him before..."

Sean pulled her tightly to his chest. "I'm sorry."

"No, Sean. I made my choice. We'll be here making your home ready for you and our wives. Take your time, though?"

"All the time," Chastity said, going to hug him, as well.

Sean exhaled. "I'm going to gut them."

"Do it right," Lilly said tightly. "If you just kill them, it will hurt our family. Make them attack you, force them into a corner, and make them lash out at you."

"When they do, bleed them out. Make it hurt," Chastity said.

"I will."

"Sean," Marjorie said from a few feet away, "thank you. For saving me when you did, for giving me a purpose again, and for loving my daughter as much as you do. I will only ever praise your name. You can do so much more for the world. I know you'll make things better."

Sean took a slow deep breath. Her faith in him was palpable. "I'll do my best."

"We know," Chastity mumbled into his chest.

A flash of silver caught Sean's attention, and his heart ached again when Omin landed on Marjorie's shoulder. "Tell Onim that I'll wait for them. The home will be ready for every member of the clan, as well."

"I will," Sean whispered before he felt something pulling on his heart. He pushed against it. "I think I'm going."

Both of his wives kissed him again and stepped back. Love filled their gazes, and Sean tried to save that image in his mind as the room warped, elongating and stretching.

* * *

A soft hand touched his face gently, as if afraid of breaking him. "He'll wake when he can," Fiona whispered. "He's breathing, and his wounds are healing. He used everything he had and refused to take any from us."

"When he hears, what will happen?" Aria asked.

"We don't know," Myna said with sadness. "He couldn't have helped even if he'd been awake... he had no energy, and we don't combine for even a tenth of him."

"Ven, is Onim okay?" Aria asked as she rested her hand on Sean's leg.

"Heartbroken, but we knew it might happen. None of us expected a barrier. We got them clear, but it was too late by the time we did."

"Their child?" Myna asked.

"Jutt is taking it a little harder," Ven replied, "but Onim is handling it well. Arla is there to support Jutt. The clan is in mourning, but they all look to what will come in the future. We're changing our tactics; we'll no longer be going close to our foes."

"That would be for the best," Aria agreed.

"They're asleep," Ida said, coming into the room, followed by Ryann.

"When we checked, Felora was holding Andrea close. Their cheeks were red, like they'd been crying," Ryann added. "Has he stirred yet?"

"No," Fiona sighed. "We'll have to try waking him soon, as much as I dislike the idea."

"I'm awake," Sean mumbled, forcing one bloodshot eye open.

His name was called out by all of his wives and Ven, with Myna using her nickname for him. Sean lay still as they piled on to hug him, letting their love start to thaw his heart.

Fiona was the first to pull away, her face grave. "Sean, we have terrible news."

"Chastity, Lilly..." Sean said, beating her to the news, "and Omin. I know."

"But how?" Aria asked. "You were out by the time we got to you. You haven't stirred since."

"I spoke to them," Sean croaked, his throat beyond parched.

Ryann picked up the glass by the bed and thrust it to Fiona, who was in the best position to help Sean. Water sloshed over her hand as she did. Fiona gave her a nod and helped Sean sip.

"How?" Myna asked softly.

"Since they venerated me, there's an afterlife for them," Sean replied, taking another sip. "A manor like this. Marjorie's there, too."

"She was reunited with her mother?" Ida asked.

"Yes. They asked me to not act rashly." Sean's eyes closed and tears fell, his voice thick, "They'll wait for us. They want us to take our time before we see them again."

The door to the room opened, and Felora stood there with Andrea. "I felt him wake," Felora said as they approached the bed.

Sean looked at his two wives coming toward him, and his heart clenched at the pain he saw in them— both of their lovers had died on the field. "I'm sorry," he said.

Andrea sniffled, but shook her head. "No, Sean. No. She died saving me."

"As Lilly did for me," Felora added.

"What happened?" Sean asked as they joined the family on the bed.

"You'd paired off against Evan," Fiona said. "Myna had to contend with Klein and one of the warriors, leaving the other four of them for us. We were badly outclassed, Sean. They were Darragh's equals or better in combat. I was pushed away from them and barely able to defend myself."

"The same for me," Aria nodded. "It left Lilly, Felora, and Ryann to face two of them."

Ryann looked away. "I didn't have the energy left to do what I should've been able to do. I'm sorry."

"No," Felora said, moving over to hold Ryann. "No one blames you. Lilly and I thought we could take the one warrior alone. We were fools." Felora looked at Sean, her eyes wet. "He was like a storm... we didn't even have a chance. When he knocked me and Lilly away, he went for Andrea, Chastity, and Ida."

"Chas lurched to her feet and flung herself at him to save me. I was closer and not able to move out of the way," Andrea cried.

"He ran her through without remorse," Ida added, her voice thick with emotion. "I tried to get up, but I had no energy left in me."

"I rushed back and was able to get there to stop him from going after the others, but he knocked my sword away, slicing my arm to the bone. I was done for in that instant, but Lilly knocked me away and he gutted her, instead. She went mad, stabbing him again and again, and finally got an eye. I almost went to her, but..." Felora's voice caught in her throat, "she gave me a smile and I saw her die."

"Felora hit the one on me like a runaway wagon," Ryann said. "She buried him and gave me the chance to finish him off."

"They split to help me and Fiona at that point," Aria said.

"When we looked at you, we saw you standing victorious, but then you fell," Fiona said. "We all feared, but the Bond was there to reassure us."

"The commander called the fight over and the shield was dropped," Ven said. "The clan rushed to protect you, just in case."

Sean finally understood why he'd heard the sound of wings when Ven told him that. It wasn't crows, but the Fairies that had flocked to him. Shifting so he was a little more upright, he held out his arms, and his wives all pushed into his extended embrace.

"I'm going to gut them," Sean said softly. "I'm going to destroy them and make sure everyone knows what hurting my family means."

"Sean—"

"I'll do it right," Sean said, interrupting Fiona gently, but firmly. "I won't risk hurting any of you by lashing out, but I *will* make them bleed. I'll make them feel pain for what they've done... For our wives waiting for us, and for us."

"We will aid you in any way we can," Fiona said when he finished. "Together, we'll make them pay."

A knock on the door came just before Tiska spoke from the other side of it, "Mistress, word came from the high magistrate. He requires Sean to attend his court tomorrow morning."

Fiona exhaled the breath she'd been holding when she heard that Jasper had sent word. "Thank you, Tiska. Please inform the cooks that we will all be down for some food shortly. Gather the others, as well, please."

Sean's stomach growled and he chuckled weakly. "I guess food is a good idea."

The others joined him briefly, but they still felt the loss of their loved ones too keenly to keep their smiles for very long. Everyone got out of bed to allow Sean up, but instead of getting up, he pulled Andrea and Felora back to him and held them tightly.

"Ladies, give me a moment with them, please?" Sean asked.

"Of course," Fiona said as she ushered the others toward the door.

Andrea hiccupped and clutched him. "I miss her."

"I know," Sean said, "but you two weren't here for what I told them."

Felora sniffled as she snuggled against him. "What do you need to tell us?"

"They're waiting for us," Sean said softly. "It appears that Chastity's insistence on worshipping me had an effect that spread with the rest of you and the Fairies. There's an afterlife waiting for all of us... it looked like home. Chastity, Lilly, Marjorie, and Omin are all there right now. They told us to take our time rejoining them, but that they'll have everything in order for when we do."

Felora stared at him as tears spilled down her cheeks. "You truly are divine, Sean."

"Oh, Chas...!" Andrea cried harder, burying her face in Sean's chest. "You get to be with your mother again... I'll keep him well, until I see you again."

Pulling Felora to his chest, he stroked both their heads and let them cry. His own tears fell on them as they mourned.

* * *

Sean followed Andrea and Felora into the dining room. He looked down the table to where the staff sat, and saw the worried eyes. "Once the cooks get here, I have some things to say."

The cooks weren't long, as they'd been leaving the kitchen when he entered the dining room. "It's a simple meal. We hadn't expected to make a full one before dinner," Glorina apologized.

"It's fine," Sean said. "You had no way of knowing when I'd be awake."

They put bread, cheese, meat, and fruits on the table. Sean served himself first, but he didn't start eating. He waited for everyone to take some before he addressed them all.

"You've noticed and heard of our loss," Sean said, his tone subdued. "Chastity and Lilly are both gone. Things here will be shifting some, but the important part is that we've made a serious enemy of Lord Sharpeyes. He and his ally, Otis Denmur, will both increase their efforts against us. I feel the need to offer you all the chance to step away from this. You don't need to be caught in the crossfire that is about to ensue."

Everyone looked at Sean in silence until Glorina cleared her throat. "Sir, do you wish us to leave?"

"That isn't my choice," Sean said. "I welcome you all to stay and work. While I'll do my best to keep you safe and happy, I can't promise it."

"You've given us so much," Cali interjected, "and asked for

nothing in return. We'd be ungrateful wretches to turn away from you now."

"She's right," Lona nodded.

"Do you think they'll attack here?" Quilla asked.

"Yes."

"Then we'll meet them and defeat them," Quinna snorted.

"Sir," Rumia said, "I've never known a person of your power who is as gracious or giving. I..." She trailed off and took a deep breath. "I'm with you, even if the Queens stand against you."

"Agreed," Mona said, echoed by Lona a moment later.

"The Queens is a tall order," Quilla said, "but against anyone in this city? Yes."

The rest of the staff at the table nodded in agreement with Quilla.

Rosa, Rumia's mother, shifted in her seat before standing abruptly. "Sir, we won't leave just because something might happen. We might not be fighters, but we aren't cowards, either."

Sean met her eyes and bowed his head. "So be it. I'll do everything I can to make sure you're all protected, and that starts by giving you more. Everything we can do, you can now do. My wives will help you understand what that means and train you to be prepared to use those skills if called upon."

"Sir," Xenta asked a bit hesitantly, "who do we report to now?"

Sean blinked slowly, his eyes closing as he tried to hold his emotions in check again. Before he could answer her, Myna said, "Me. I'll take over the duties of the house. Since I'm already training you and the cooks in other matters, it makes the most sense for me to oversee your duties, as well."

"I'll take up the oversight of the outside staff," Aria offered.

Sean swallowed hard and nodded, his voice thick, "Thank you, Myna. You, too, Aria."

"I will join Andie in handling the store," Felora said, "if she'll have me."

Andrea nodded, tears falling from her eyes again. "Please? I don't want to be alone."

"Sir," Ven said, coming down the table to stand in front of Sean, "we've assigned a contingent of five Fairies per house member and have a large number in reserve. I've made sure that extras have been sent to each of your allies, as well, and at least one at each location to stay with the cuon all the time. If they catch scent of *anything*, the people there will know swiftly. We won't let another incident happen."

Sean looked down the table at the empty spot where Omin and Onim usually sat. "Thank you, Ven. If I can do anything for Onim, please let me know."

"I'll be speaking with Fiona about ideas later," Ven said. "She's already told us that you need time to recover."

Sean glanced at Fiona, who was watching him with worried eyes. "Okay. No energy today."

"Thank you," Fiona exhaled.

A Fairy landed on the table. "Excuse me. Dame Mageeyes' Fairy, Pura, is here to deliver a message."

"They're always allowed," Sean said. "Any Fairy from a friend is."

"Yes, sir," the Fairy said.

Pura landed on the table a few seconds later. "Oh, you're okay, sir. I was asked to see if you were okay, and to ask if you or Fiona could make it to the Oaken Glen tonight."

"I'll come," Sean said. "I will have at least a couple of my wives with me."

"Yes, sir," Pura said, launching into the air. They hovered instead of leaving right away. "I'm glad you are okay, sir. All of us were worried." They bowed their head, then shot away.

"Sean, you need to eat," Fiona said gently.

Sean's stomach rumbled and he felt an ache in his gut. "Yes, dear."

2

rriving at the Oaken Glen, Ryann pushed Sean back into his seat. "No, we'll do this correctly. Your guard goes first to make sure it is safe."

Sean met her eyes and saw the determination in them. "As my shield wishes."

Ryann gave him a nod and got out. Looking around, she stepped forward. "*Now* you may leave."

Sean stepped out of the carriage, followed by Fiona. Ryann moved a few steps ahead of him, leading the two of them into the inn. Arliat watched them go before rubbing at the modified clothing Fiona had given her. Once they were inside, she got the carriage moving to the yard.

The inn went quiet when people saw who had entered, conversation dropping off quickly. Sean looked over the room, his expression grim.

One of the barmaids rushed over to them and curtsied. "If you'll follow me, the Dame is waiting."

"We're following," Sean said.

As they crossed the room, muted conversation started up in their wake.

"Took his head clean off—"

"Split 'im from navel to crown—"

"I heard every Messenger Fairy in the city went to protect him at the end. My cousin said they covered him entirely."

"Two of his wives died... You can see the pain in his face."

"Sharpeyes is going to have his head. Killing the only heir he had? That's bad business."

Sean snorted softly when they made it into the hallway. "Rumors and lies will always outpace the truth."

The maid knocked on the door before opening it. "Excuse me, MacDougal is here." She stepped aside for Sean and his wives. "Sir."

Ryann entered first, stepping over to the right and resting her hand on a throwing knife when she did. Sean followed her in, giving his friends a strained smile as he went to the open seats.

"Sean," Fredrick Gertihs was the first to speak, "our deepest condolences."

The others chimed in their agreement to the statement.

"Thank you," Sean replied, his voice tight. "You all saw the fight and the outcome. It's obvious what's likely to happen from here."

"Before we go down that road," Charie Flamehair said, "I have their bodies resting and waiting for your approval. I didn't want to do anything until you gave word."

Sean stared at her blankly, and Fiona cleared her throat. "We'll be by tomorrow to say our goodbyes, Charie. Thank you. Please put them in the best you have."

Flamehair bowed her head. "I will. Omin is also with them. You wished them to be honored similarly, right?"

Ven landed on the table. "Please, and on behalf of the clan, we thank you for that."

Flamehair met Ven's eyes. "You four fought as well as you could. It was saddening to hear that you had a loss."

"Thank you," Ven said before leaving in a flash.

"Sean, what are you planning?" Amedee Mageeyes asked into the sudden silence.

"To stamp out the problem," Sean replied, holding up a hand to stall her rebuttal. "I'm not going to be rash, but I will make them pay."

"What can we do to help?" Fredrick asked.

"It's time to push back, and hard," Sean said grimly. "Denmur tried to put the screws to us. Give it back to him, threefold or more. I didn't want this war, but I'm going to end it."

"He lost his mind last night," Ryan Watercaller said. "The guard had to escort him away." Ryan licked his lips when Sean looked his way, clearly uncomfortable with the intensity of his gaze. "When Myna killed Klein, he tried to go over the wall, screaming obscenities."

"It was shocking," Italice Stoneeyes added. "I would never have guessed he had any emotions before that."

"Sean, we took in the extra Fairies," Joseph Tackett said. "Do you think they'll come for us?"

"I don't know," Sean admitted. "I just don't want another..." He trailed off as memory of the bathhouse on fire filled his mind.

"We'll all be prepared," Sam Bronzeshield said evenly. "The guard is still asking questions about that."

"It was Zachary," Sean said quietly, the hatred in his voice making some of them lean away from him. "He snuck in using a Talent and killed them before he—" Sean cut off sharply as he again recalled that night.

"He killed them first?" Chester Knox asked, his tone dark. "Killed my son and his wife, and then raped her?"

"Yes."

"How do you know?" Torin Callon asked.

Sean exhaled slowly— he wasn't sure he should tell them. He was given a moment to think when the door opened and Tabitha came inside with drinks.

"Oh, my apologies," Tabitha said as she delivered everyone their drinks. "What can I get for you three?"

"Tea," Ryann said. "Any of them is fine."

"A glass of white wine," Fiona said.

"Ale," Sean added.

"Of course."

When she left, Sean looked at the others in the room. Every one of them had already agreed to hold his secrets, so he cleared his throat after looking at each of them. "You asked how I know, Torin? I'll tell you, but let's wait for Tabitha to come back so she won't interrupt."

"Sean," Winston Giralt said slowly, "take all the time you need. When you're ready again, my door is open to you."

"I'll be over after tomorrow," Sean said softly. "I need to work on something."

"Very well."

Tabitha came back into the room a moment later, carrying two mugs and a glass on her tray. She handed them off, then quickly left the room.

"While I was recovering," Sean began after taking a deep pull on his ale, "I had a dream, but it wasn't a dream. I spoke with Morrigan in a place that resembled my current home."

"The Morrigan?" Augustus MacLenn asked.

"Yes, but she isn't the important part here, though she thanks you all for the prayers. The important part is that Chastity and Lilly were there."

Everyone exchanged looks, thinking he'd lost touch with reality a little.

"None of you know, but my wives and the Fairies had started to offer prayers. Not to Morrigan or the Tuatha, but to me," Sean said, looking at his mug. "It seems that the Tuatha didn't just craft me a body, but they pushed their divine essence into me. That, along with the faith of my wives, created a small plane of existence for those who pass on while believing in me."

"Sean—" Fredrick began, stopping when Sean held up a hand.

"Chastity, Lilly, Omin, and Marjorie were all there. Each of them had prayed to me before. Marjorie told me what she remembered— she saw him as he slit her throat. It was the same Talent he used on the battlefield to commit murder. I have no proof besides her word, but I believe her."

"Sean," Joseph cut in, "we know you're special and blessed, but is that really possible?"

"Gods create demi-planes for their faithful to enjoy an afterlife," Mageeyes explained. "The men Sean fought were from one of those. Saret explained it to me last night."

"You believe him?" Italice asked her.

"Did you not watch his face?" Mageeyes replied. "He believes what he said is the truth. When you add his blessing by the Tuatha, I believe it is possible. Would that extend to any of us if we offered you prayers?"

"I don't know," Sean said. "I really don't."

"Not sure I'd want to live in your manor," Jefferson said, "but it's better than nothingness. Could I talk you into making an outbuilding for me to work on my leathers, and maybe a room of my own?"

Joseph laughed, and the others joined in. Sean's lips even twitched a little, as he had a hard time imagining the surly leather-worker living in his manor.

"I can't make any promises," Sean said when the laughter began to die down, "but I'd gladly give all of you a place of your own."

"Hmm," Mageeyes mused, "interesting. I can tell Saret this, yes?"

"She's mourning Delia's death?" Fiona asked.

"Yes. She was a little upset that Jasper put the hearing of her killer off, but she understands why."

"Give her our condolences, please?" Sean asked.

"Of course. You will see her yourself tomorrow, though, won't you? You were summoned to the court, I believe."

"Oh, right," Sean said, downing his mug. "I don't know why, though."

"So you can be found not guilty," Eva Silvertouch said. "It was trial by combat."

"Oh, yes... right," Sean said slowly. "I apologize, but I think I should go home."

Everyone stood up as he did. "We'll be there tomorrow," Fredrick said. "Forged Bonds stands by its members."

Sean looked at each of them, a small smile touching his lips briefly. "Thank you."

As he went to leave, each gave him a pat on the back, a squeeze of the shoulder, or a hug. The same treatment was given to Fiona and Ryann, as well.

The room went silent again as Sean and his wives entered the main room. Arliat jumped to her feet, her voice loud in the silence, "I'll bring it around, sir."

"Thank you, Arliat," Fiona said. "We'll be waiting."

As she hurried away to get the carriage, the muted conversations started up again. Sean met Ryann's eyes as he heard the first few. "I'd like to wait outside, Ry."

"Okay," Ryann said and led them across the room.

By the time they made it home, Sean felt exhausted. On autopilot, he followed Fiona and Ryann upstairs to the changing room. Stripping off his clothing, he stepped into the bedroom to find his other wives all speaking softly as they lay in the bed.

Heart aching, he crossed the room and crawled into bed with them. Andrea curled up on his right, and Felora on his left, while the others snuggled in next to them. No more tears were shed, but all of them felt the pain in their hearts.

Sean kissed Andrea's head. "Tomorrow, we'll see them one last time before we join them."

"Yes, Sean. Is she going to be happy?"

"I think so, Andie. She has Lilly there, and her mother."

"Lilly will keep her content," Felora whispered. "They'll ache as we do, but for them, we'll do our best to live well... to make them smile."

"Yes," Andrea sniffled, reaching across to take Felora's hand and placing them on Sean's chest. "We'll keep our love safe."

"As they would want," Felora agreed.

Sean kissed Felora's head. "Fel, we'll be seeing your mother tomorrow, too. Will she be okay?"

"She'll have been in mourning all day," Felora said. "Tomorrow, she will have set it aside and be looking to the future. It is our way. I might take a day or two longer, though."

"Take as long as you need," Sean said.

"We'll be here to help," Ryann said from behind Felora.

"All of us are," Ida agreed, echoed by the others.

"I can help us find rest," Felora whispered. "Dreamless sleep."

"Can I dream of Chastity?" Andrea asked.

"Yes... A dream of goodbye might be better," Felora said. "Does everyone want to?"

"Not goodbye," Sean said thickly. "A dream of waiting. They're waiting for us, not leaving us."

"As my husband wishes," Felora replied, kissing his chest. "Dream... dream the dreams of waiting, of love, and hope." Her words were tinged with sadness, but also a deep yearning.

Sean embraced the energy that washed over him, leaving tomorrow for later.

3

S oft lips woke Sean. After returning the kiss, he opened his eyes to find Andrea leaning over him. "Morning, Andie."

"Morning, Sean," Andrea whispered. "It's time to get up."

Blinking, he looked around to find only them left in the room. "Last one awake, huh?"

"You needed it more than we did."

Sitting up, he pulled her in for a hug. "How are you feeling?"

"A little lost," Andrea replied, leaning against him. "It wasn't long, but Chas and I... we just fit together. The dream helped some, and today should help more, but I still don't want to admit she's gone."

"It'll be rough for a long while," Sean said. "Luckily, we have loved ones around us to help."

"Yes. Our wives make it a little easier." She pulled back from him gently. "They're waiting for us."

"I'll get dressed and be right down," Sean told her as he stood up.

"Okay," Andrea said, stealing one more kiss before leaving him alone in the room.

Sean watched her go. *I'm sorry, Andie... I was too passive. Chas, Lilly, Omin... you three should never have had to pay for my mistakes.* Taking a deep breath, he went to get dressed. They had things to do today.

* * *

Breakfast was somber, conversation nearly nonexistent.

"Sir, we've put up a sign on the gate letting everyone know that the shop is closed for today," Rosa said as the meal ended. "I hope that was okay."

"Thank you," Sean said. "I hadn't thought of it."

"We know you've all had a lot on your minds," Rumia said. "We'll do our best to make things easier for you."

"And we thank you for that," Fiona said. "All of you. We'll be gone for a good portion of today. You shouldn't have any issues, but the Fairies can find us, if needed."

"We should get going," Sean said. "Arliat?"

"Yes, sir," Arliat said, hurrying off.

"Are you going to the summons first, or...?" Glorina started to ask before trailing off.

"We will be at the magistrate's first," Sean said.

"Umm..." Cali raised her hand hesitantly.

"You don't need to raise a hand," Sean said with a small smile.

"Would it be okay if we went over to pay our respects before you get there?" Cali asked.

"Yes," Sean replied, "of course you can. I'm sorry. I hadn't thought you'd want to."

"Lilly was kind to us," Tiska said.

"Very kind," Xenta nodded.

"We don't want to get in your way, though, either," Lona added.

"We'll have Arliat bring the carriage back to you after she drops us off," Fiona said. "We're happy you wish to pay respects to them. Thank you."

Andrea sniffled, nodding agreement. "Thank you."

"Lilly would be honored," Felora agreed.

"It's settled," Sean said. "Just have things ready to go when she comes back for you."

"Thank you," Glorina said. "We didn't want to overstep."

"You're family," Sean said, stopping by the door. "Maybe you're staff, too, but you're family. You may always speak your mind."

* * *

Myna sat on Fiona's lap to Sean's right while Ida sat on Ryann's lap to his left. Felora, Aria, and Andrea sat across from them. Everyone was absorbed in their own thoughts on the way to the magistrate building.

When the carriage came to a stop, Ida was the first one out, followed by Ryann. Once they said it was clear, Sean stepped out and helped his other wives down. Straightening his clothing, Sean followed after Ryann and Ida, flanked by Fiona and Myna, and trailed by the others.

The foyer had a large number of people milling around. One group of them was standing where Ryann led the group.

"Sean, it's good to see you, and your wives," Mageeyes greeted them. "We were told that High Magistrate Jasper will be opening his doors soon."

"Good," Sean said. "I hope this won't take too long."

"MacDougal," someone called out to him.

Sean looked over to see Carmady heading his way. "Sergeant, how can I help you?"

"I wished to tell you that Marjorie Bisset's body is with Dame Flamehair's people. We always inform the next of kin, and in this case, that is you. My condolences on the recent loss to your family."

Sean took a deep, slow breath, as the sergeant seemed to be sincere. "Thank you, sir. Is there an investigation for the murders?"

"We have a file open, but with no witnesses and all evidence destroyed in the fire, there's little we'll be able to do."

"There was a man in town. His name was Zachary..." Sean trailed off, looking at Myna.

"Zachary Shadowstep is what he took as his name after the academy," Myna supplied.

"He was with Velin Dykstra at the party," Sean went on. "If you trace his movements back, you might find similar crimes left in his wake."

Carmady nodded. "I'm not sure the commander will allow for such expenses, but I will ask." He gave Sean a salute before turning and walking off.

"Did he just salute me?" Sean asked.

"He sees you as a man to respect," Bloodheart said, walking their way. "Considering your fight, he isn't wrong." Bloodheart went over to stand by Mageeyes. "My condolences on your losses."

Swallowing hard, Sean gave him a curt nod.

"Do you think we'll be waiting much longer?" Joseph asked.

"The magistrates keep their own time," Knox snorted. "Never one for punct—"

"Those waiting for High Magistrate Jasper, the room is now open. Second floor, fifth door," one of the clerks in the room announced.

"Jasper is the exception," Fredrick said when the announcement ended. "He was willing to stand up to Lord Sharpeyes at the party. I do not envy him the task he has ahead of him."

"You shouldn't, as we're in the same boat," Ryan said, taking Italice's hand, "but we have more leeway than he does."

Making their way to the courtroom, Sean was a little surprised at the size of the chamber. It held the group comfortably with a lot of extra space, but that space was rapidly filling up with others.

Sean's eyes narrowed when Denmur entered the room. Denmur's nostrils flared when he spotted Sean. Carver started whispering to Denmur, but the conversations in the room masked what was being said. Fiona touched Sean's shoulder, stopping him from moving toward the other group.

"Leave them for now, Sean. We'll make them pay later, but here and now would cause trouble."

Sean exhaled slowly. "Of course."

His eyes were pulled from Denmur when Saret entered the room. The Succubus was clad in a red and black dress that hung loosely on her, shrouding her figure. Her eyes were dry, but looked slightly red, as if she'd been crying until recently.

"Saret, it's good to see you," Sean called to her.

Saret headed his way. "Sean, I'm glad you are alright. I was concerned for you."

"Thank you. If it's possible, may we speak later? I have questions about the afterlife for you."

"Of course," Saret said. "Charie, is it okay to stop by after this?"

Flamehair nodded. "I believe Sean and his family are coming over then, as well."

"We are. My staff was going there now. Is that okay?" Sean asked.

"It should be. I can send a message to my people so they're aware."

"Please?"

"Of course."

Conversation fell off suddenly, and Sean looked over to see Jasper, in black robes, heading for the high desk. Sean faced front again and sat with the others after Jasper sat.

Jasper rapped his gavel twice. "This room is called to order. I see two people are missing."

The doors to the room opened and Lady Sharpeyes came gliding into the room. "I apologize, your honor," she said. "My favorite horse turned up lame this morning. It delayed my departure."

"Lady Sharpeyes, please take a seat. We just called the room to order," Jasper said.

"Of course, and thank you, your honor," Lady Sharpeyes said, claiming the empty seat beside Saret. "Thank you for holding a place for me, Somnia."

Before Saret could reply, the door opened again, and Lord Sharpeyes stalked into the room. His eyes were locked on his wife, his anger on open display. "You—!"

"Order!" Jasper snapped, banging his gavel. "Lord Sharpeyes, this room has been called to order already. As you've just arrived after Lady Sharpeyes, we will overlook your lateness. Please take a seat."

Lord Sharpeyes turned his anger toward Jasper. "High Magistrate, if you know what's good for you, you will mind your tone when speaking to me."

Jasper raised his head slightly. "In this room, Lord, I am the highest authority. I will abide by the laws, as *everyone* here will."

Sharpeyes snorted and moved to take the remaining empty seat in the room, which was next to Denmur. Once he was seated, Jasper looked over the room, clearly noting people.

"As everyone called to be here is here, plus many others, I'll remind those not called to attend that you are here to observe only. Any disruption will not be tolerated, and the guard will escort you out. Sergeant, you may take anyone I wish removed straight to the cells for contempt and I will see them tomorrow."

Sergeant Ernest Carmady saluted. "As you wish, High Magistrate."

"Very well," Jasper said. "We shall move to the first order of business. Sean MacDougal, step forward."

Sean rose from his seat and went to the open space in front of Jasper. "Your honor."

"I'm glad to see you have recovered enough to attend. I need to pass judgement on the trial by combat."

The sound of splintering wood filled the room, and all eyes went to Lord Sharpeyes, who was holding the broken remnants of the railing that'd been in front of his seat. Sean met Sharpeyes' eyes, seeing the hatred in them, and returned it.

"Lord Sharpeyes," Jasper said tightly, "I know you are distraught over what transpired, so I am willing to look past this incident, but if you cannot contain yourself, I will have to ask you to leave."

"Get on with it!" Sharpeyes snapped, his eyes still locked on Sean.

Jasper exhaled slowly. "The prior day's trial by combat was called for, so you, MacDougal, could prove your innocence in the massacre of Oakwood. That combat pitted you and your Life Bonded against the servant of Lord Truestrike, Velin Dykstra; Klein Denmur; Knight Evan Sharpeyes; and their Life Bonded."

Sean exhaled slowly, his hands clenched tightly as he thought about his two dead wives. "Yes, your honor."

"You are found innocent of these charges, MacDougal," Jasper said. "The court extends its condolences on the loss of your wives."

Closing his eyes and swallowing the lump in his throat, Sean bowed his head to Jasper. "Thank you, your honor."

"The court further extends condolences to Otis Denmur and Lord Sharpeyes on the loss of their sons. This is why I detest trial by combat. Lives were lost that should never have been lost," Jasper went on.

Neither Denmur nor Sharpeyes replied to Jasper as they stared at Sean.

"That incident is directly related to two other items for today. MacDougal, please be seated. I need you here for another matter that I shall be having before me soon."

"As you wish, your honor," Sean replied, returning to his seat.

4

―――――

"Sergeant, have Dame and Knight Loplis brought before me," Jasper announced once Sean was seated again.

Carmady nodded, and stepped outside into the hall. He returned a minute later with Gaoler Henik, who led Dame and Knight Loplis into the room.

"Dame and Knight Loplis, your honor," Carmady said as he moved them to stand before Jasper.

Knight Loplis looked angry and glared at Jasper. When Dame Loplis caught sight of Saret, she blanched.

"Well, *your honor*, have you come to your senses?" Knight Loplis asked.

Jasper shook his head. "Knight Loplis, disrespect will be punished. I do not care if you hate me, but disrespect to the office will be handled harshly."

"You won't be on that bench past tomorrow," Knight Loplis sneered. "Lord Sharpeyes will see to that."

"Enough!" Jasper said loudly, banging his gavel. "I will have you muted if you insist on continuing."

Knight Loplis sneered, but closed his mouth.

"Dame Loplis," Jasper said, pulling her gaze from Saret to him, "you are brought before the court on the charge of murder. You did willfully kill another in front of myself. I offered you the chance to speak on your behalf at the time, but you refused. I believe you were afraid of reprisals from someone in the room at the time. I give you this one more chance to speak."

"She won't—" Knight Loplis started.

"No!" Dame Loplis shouted at her father. "No! Enough, Father!"

Blinking in shock, Knight Loplis stared at his daughter like she'd grown a second head.

"High Magistrate, I killed Delia Somnia. I have one question before I speak: is it true that Knight Sharpeyes died?"

"He died during trial by combat," Jasper replied.

Falling to her knees, she began to cry. "All for nothing..."

Jasper gave her a few seconds before clearing his throat. "Dame Loplis?"

Wiping at her face, the young woman looked up at him. "Your honor?"

"Do you wish to speak?"

"I killed Delia because Evan asked me to," she said, her voice slightly broken. "He promised he'd take me as his mistress if I did. I threw away my life because he promised to take care of me..."

"You killed Delia Somnia because Evan Sharpeyes asked you to?" Jasper asked.

"And because I hated her..." she whispered. "She took all of his time. He used to ply me with attention, until he had her. When he told me to silence her and said that I would be his new mistress, I acted without thinking."

"What are you saying?!" her father shouted at her. "To implicate—!"

"Silence!" Jasper shouted over him, banging his gavel. "Sergeant, take Knight Loplis back to the cells. I will deal with his contempt tomorrow."

Henik, who'd been standing there, grabbed Knight Loplis and started to drag him from the room. As he was taken past Sharpeyes,

Loplis called out to the Lord, "Lord, please! Have mercy! I disown her! She is no longer part of my house!"

The room went silent.

Sobs broke that silence a few seconds later when the former Dame huddled into a ball.

Sharpeyes didn't reply to Loplis as he was dragged from the room, nor did he look at the sobbing woman on the floor.

"Hmm," Jasper sighed, "we have had a member of nobility stripped of their family. This will be recorded, as the law demands. Miss, you are without a family and without a title, yet you are still on trial for murder."

"Kill me." Those two words were broken and tear-filled. "Just kill me..."

There was the sound of heels striking the floor before people realized Saret was moving. She stepped past Carmady and knelt beside her. "Your hell has come to pass, child," Saret said softly. "Do you really wish for oblivion?"

Jasper stared along with everyone else, entranced by the moment.

"Yes." Her voice was soft, but hung in the air.

Saret picked the young woman up and turned to Jasper. "Your honor, this child has been thrown out by her family and has committed crime against mine. I ask the court to grant her life to me. I will Life Bond her and give her something to live for. On this day, Cartha Loplis was killed by her own father, Knight Lavan Loplis."

Jasper blinked, free of the moment, and tapped his gavel to the bench. "Granted. Dame Cartha Loplis killed Delia Somnia, and her life was granted to Saret Somnia. The court shall reflect that she was ejected from her family, and was a commoner when she was sentenced."

"I'll take her and go, if you allow," Saret said, holding the young woman like a babe to her chest.

"Granted," Jasper said.

Saret turned on her heel and held her head high as she walked from the room. She looked at Sean briefly, giving him a small nod. Sean bowed his head to her before turning back to Jasper.

Clearing his throat, Jasper banged his gavel on the bench. "The second order of business is concluded. I now have the trickiest of today's cases to oversee— Sergeant, have her brought in."

Sean wondered what was going on, as he noted both Lord and Lady Sharpeyes tense.

A couple of minutes later, Henik brought someone else into the room. Sean stared at her in surprise. The last time he'd seen her, she'd been knocked from the sky.

Arms manacled behind her back and wearing tattered, muddy clothing, the Valkyrie's once vibrant blonde hair was now crusted with dirt and blood. She turned her head and met Sean's eyes. Remorse showed on her face as she was ushered past the crowd and brought before Jasper.

"How is she alive?" Aria asked in a shocked whisper.

"That's what we hope to find out," Lady Sharpeyes replied in the same hushed tone.

Jasper stared at the Valkyrie. "Name?"

"Helga Helsdottir," Helga replied.

"You Life Bonded to Knight Evan Sharpeyes, did you not?"

"I did."

"How are you still alive?" Jasper asked.

"A soul was required to be given when the Bond was called due," Helga said. "I gave a number of souls to satisfy it."

"Lying bitch! You still live while my son lies dead!" Lord Sharpeyes spat.

"Order!" Jasper pounded his gavel. "Lord Sharpeyes, we are conducting an interview. Contain yourself."

Sharpeyes glared at Jasper. "What is there to ask? Kill her and be done with it! Her life was forfeit when my son died."

"Your honor," Lady Sharpeyes said, rising to her feet.

"Lady Sharpeyes?" Jasper motioned her to speak.

"My husband is correct. She must be killed for the Bond to be settled. I ask the court to have her slain at once. Once she has been killed, this matter should be put to rest."

Jasper looked from Lord to Lady and sighed. "The law is clear— a

Life Bond must be balanced by a life. We cannot prove how you survived Evan Sharpeyes' death, Helsdottir. As such, I must decree that you to be slain in my presence."

"And then what?" Helga asked flatly. "Will I be freed, then?"

Jasper stared at her, not understanding. Sean cleared his throat and raised his hand. Jasper motioned to him. "MacDougal?"

"Your honor, she's a battle maiden. According to myth, she ferries the souls of the dead back to Valhalla, an afterlife for the followers of a particular pantheon."

"And...?" Jasper asked when Sean paused.

"Helga, how many other souls do you currently possess?"

Helga grunted. "Three, MacDougal, but they will never return to Valhalla. I have broken one of the oaths of my kind. If I did make it back, my life would be forfeit to Odin."

"Why?" Sean pressed.

"I spent the majority of the souls in my care to negate the Life Bond," Helga said. "I valued myself over their souls." She turned her head to see him and his wives. "Thor wronged you twice, and tricked me into coming here. I am sorry for your dead. I tried to collect them and preserve them for you, but they slipped away from me. It was then that I knew I had to repent for my folly."

"Kill her!" Sharpeyes snapped. "Kill her now! For my son."

"And mine!" Denmur shouted, standing up beside Sharpeyes. "Why should she live while my son lies dead?!"

Jasper banged his gavel hard. "Order! There will be order!"

"Your honor?" Lady Sharpeyes again waited to be called on.

"Lady?" Jasper asked tiredly.

"I would place before you this idea— let her be slain once by my husband, once by Denmur, and once by Knight Solanice, for Lord Truestrike's loss in Velin Dykstra. That should satisfy all of them."

Helga faced the judge again. "If I must die to them, I accept it."

"Your honor?" Sean asked, rising to his feet.

"MacDougal?" Jasper asked slowly, having a bad feeling about how things were going.

"If we're killing her for the deaths of loved ones, and since I am the last to speak, I will take her life for my own after they have had their turns."

Jasper exhaled. "I see. As the Lord and Lady are both in agreement, and Life Bonds do call for deaths, I reluctantly agree to this idea. I still have no idea how she is supposed to die more than once. Lord Sharpeyes, you may kill her."

Helga turned to Lord Sharpeyes and went to one knee, exposing her neck to him. Eyes filled with rage, he leapt the broken barrier between them, drew his sword, and slashed down with all his strength. The flaming sword swept Helga's head cleanly from her neck before lodging in the stone floor. The stump was instantly cauterized, so no blood spurted. Growling in anger, he planted a foot against Helga's torso and kicked her clean across the room. Her body slammed into Jasper's bench before he kicked her severed head, making it land in her lap.

"Enough!" Jasper called out, banging his gavel. "It is done. Sergeant, please remove the corpse."

"As you comm—!" Carmady began, cutting off in surprise as he stared at Helga.

The room was silent when Helga's body moved, placing the head back onto the severed stump of her neck. Twisting her head side to side, she levered herself back to her feet. "One death has been paid," she said softly, again going down to one knee.

Sharpeyes turned red in anger. "I'll make sure you stay dead!"

Sharpeyes made it two feet before he was suddenly locked in place, unmoving. Jasper was white in the face as he pointed an amber rod at him. "Sergeant, remove him from the room! The immobilization will not wear off for at least a quarter-hour. Make sure he is on his way home by then."

"Yes, sir," Carmady said slowly, clearly uncomfortable with what he was about to do.

The room was dead silent as Carmady went over to Lord Sharpeyes and, with a grunt, hefted the man from the floor and waddled him out the door. When the doors closed behind him, the room exploded in conversation.

"Silence!" Jasper commanded, his gavel snapping as he hammered it on his bench. "Denmur, you may proceed."

Denmur was seething as he drew a dagger from his belt, the blade dripping green and sizzling as he approached Helga. "Maybe fire and beheading won't kill you, but acid to the brain surely will." Yanking her head up and back, he stared into her eyes before slamming the blade into her eye socket.

Helga let out a brief scream of pain, her body spasming before she slumped to the floor. Denmur sneered as he yanked his dagger free, her ruined eyeball sliding off the blade as he stood back up.

"For Klein, you useless sow!"

Denmur started to go for the door when Helga let out another brief scream. He froze and turned back to see her fling her hair back to meet his eyes.

Her two unmarred, vibrant blue eyes showed her disdain. "He wasn't even a good shield," Helga said as she went back to one knee. "That is two."

Denmur cocked his arm back and threw the dagger. A second before it could reach her, it was deflected away with a metallic clang. Everyone blinked in confusion except Jasper, who was staring at Ryann.

"I thank you for the help, but drawing weapons without approval of myself in this room is a crime," Jasper said, looking at Ryann.

"I apologize, your honor," Ryann said. "I reacted without thinking."

"Very well. Do not do it again," Jasper said, turning his attention back to Denmur. "Otis Denmur, you are hereby under arrest for contempt. Gaoler Henik, place him under arrest and collect that dagger. It is eating my floor."

"Why me and not that bitch, too?!" Denmur snarled, staring at Ryann with hatred.

"Because she didn't attack anyone. She defended someone," Jasper replied stiffly.

Henik blew a quick call on a whistle and two men came rushing into the room. "Arrest that man! Contempt charge."

The two guards grabbed Denmur and hustled him from the room.

"Your honor, since Knight Solanice is not in attendance, I shall take her life for him and inform him tonight so he knows that we tried to settle things for him," Lady Sharpeyes said evenly.

"I will allow it," Jasper said.

Lady Sharpeyes moved to stand in front of Helga. "Raise your head."

Helga did as instructed, meeting Lady Sharpeyes' gaze without fear.

"Drink this," Lady Sharpeyes said, holding out a small vial.

Helga took the vial and downed it in one go, then passed it back to Sharpeyes. A few seconds later, she began to choke and spasm. She fell to the floor, twitching for nearly a minute before growing still.

"All done," Lady Sharpeyes said, going back to her seat.

Another couple of minutes passed before Helga grunted, then shifted back to kneel once more. "Three."

"MacDougal," Jasper said.

Sean got to his feet and looked at his wives one by one.

Andrea sniffled, bowing her head. "Chas wouldn't want her death."

Ida shook her head. "No, she wouldn't."

Felora met Sean's eyes and nodded. "Lilly always believed in you."

"Sean, we will back you," Fiona said softly.

"Yes," Myna agreed.

"She didn't want to fight," Aria said, "but she gave her all when she had to."

Ryann was the last and her hands flexed open and closed as she stared at Helga. "I hate her for what happened, but you know my feelings. You've done it twice already, but she'll have a lot to make amends for."

Sean exhaled when they finished. "Very well."

Going up to stand before Helga, Sean looked at Jasper. "Your honor, I have accepted Life Bonds in place of someone's death before. I ask the court to allow me to do so again."

"But she already broke a Life Bond once," Jasper said.

"She is out of lives to spend," Sean replied. "Helga, what happens if I kill you now?"

"I die. My soul would be trapped in this world, as I have broken oaths and have no right to return to Valhalla."

"I don't know," Jasper said slowly.

"Helga Helsdottir," Sean said when Jasper hesitated, "I, Sean MacDougal, offer you a Bond— a Soul Bond. Your soul will belong to me. I will treat you as I do my other Bonded, but upon your death, your soul will be mine, never to know Valhalla or any afterlife other than the one I give you. You shall listen to my wives as if they speak with my voice and do everything you can to do my will."

Helga met Sean's eyes, and hope sparked in them. "I knew when I first met you that you had a soul worthy of knowing. I, Helga Helsdottir, accept your Soul Bond, Sean MacDougal. I shall follow your word as law and tie my soul forevermore to yours. Today, my old name dies, and I ask you to name me as your own."

"Rise, Helga Oathsworn," Sean said.

Helga rose to her feet and, when she did, her entire neck and forearms, from elbow to wrist, became blackened. White Celtic knotwork appeared on the inky canvas of her newly marked flesh. "As my master wishes," Helga said softly.

Jasper coughed, shaken from his trance as she stood. "Uh... I mean, very well. Helga Helsdottir died. Let the record reflect that. MacDougal now has a Life Bonded named Helga Oathsworn."

"Your honor, can you have my Bonded freed? I have a viewing to attend," Sean asked Jasper.

"Of course. With the cases settled, we are done for today," Jasper said. "Henik, free the Bonded."

Henik removed Helga's manacles and gave Sean a small nod as people began to file out of the room. "Never got the chance to thank you for your help with the cart, MacDougal."

"It really was hurting my ears," Sean said lightly. "I'm glad it helped, though."

Henik got her leg cuffs off and gave Sean another nod before walking away.

Helga turned to Sean, going to one knee before him. "What is your command?"

"Attend my wives. We'll speak more later today."

"As you command," Helga said. She stood and went over to his wives, who were all watching her.

"I wasn't sure you'd do it, but I had a feeling you might," Lady Sharpeyes said when she approached Sean. "You do seem to love saving people." A small, vicious smile touched her lips. "My husband will be most wroth over this turn of events."

"Fuck him," Sean said bluntly.

Lady Sharpeyes blinked, her eyes a little wide. "My goodness, MacDougal. You are speaking to a Lady."

Sean met her eyes. "I am, but I don't care. Two of my wives lie dead, and the ones responsible are still breathing."

"I offer my condolences to your family, MacDougal."

"Thank you. If you'll pardon me, I'm on my way to see them for the last time."

"I apologize for keeping you," Lady Sharpeyes said before turning and walking away.

"Tonight, at the inn," Sean said to the others. "I'll see you all there."

"Of course," Mageeyes said. "We will have the private room. Please, do not let us keep you from your family."

Flamehair nodded. "I have room in my carriage, if some of you would like to come with me."

"Thank you, Dame," Fiona said, "but we have private things to discuss as a family."

"Very well. I'll see you there."

5

Sean was glad to see Arliat waiting for them when they left the building. Getting to the carriage, he turned to Helga. "You'll ride with Arliat." Sean pointed at the driver's bench. "Arliat, this is Helga. She's Bonded to me."

"A moment before we go, Sean?" Fiona asked. She came over to Helga, who was still in the tattered and muddy clothing she'd been wearing during her trial.

"Understood," Sean said, climbing into the carriage.

Helga watched him, her expression stoic. When Fiona placed a hand on her shoulder, she turned her attention to her. "Yes, mistress?"

"Your appearance reflects on him," Fiona said as she used her energy and Talents to fix and clean Helga's clothing. The blood, mud, and filth that had been caked onto the fabric flaked off and fell to the ground while the clothing mended.

Helga stood perfectly still. "I apologize for my clothing, mistress."

Fiona and Myna were the only ones still outside the carriage when Fiona finished fixing Helga's clothing. "You have a hard road ahead of you," Fiona said, not unkindly. "Because of your allies, two of our wives died."

"I will submit to the punishments you all see fit," Helga said, bowing her head.

"We'll see," Myna said. "We leave now."

Helga climbed up to sit beside Arliat, who gave her a worried smile.

Myna was the last one into the carriage, closing the door before taking her place on Fiona's lap. "Master, why?" she asked as Arliat got them moving.

"Because she's remorseful," Sean said. "I saw it in her eyes. She never wanted to fight us... she was merely doing as her god demanded of her. She didn't strike at us, either, though she did aid her allies."

Aria frowned for a moment. "You're right. She never attacked, but I still had to chase her, and that ended up with me getting shot multiple times."

"It was her healing them that cost us Chastity and Lilly," Ryann said stiffly.

"She did heal them, but that's just one of the things battle maidens do," Sean said. "I was being selfish when I asked her to Bond."

"Because she can collect souls," Felora said.

"If she'd been with us, then maybe she could've held their souls for me until I could try to bring them back."

"Oh..." Andrea said, seeing what he had in mind. "She said she tried."

"Yes," Sean nodded. "That was one of the reasons I Bonded her. I wouldn't have done it if any of you had objected."

"I almost did," Ryann said, "but you once gave me a second chance when I deserved none. I can't sit in judgment of another when our places were so similar."

"Sean," Ida said softly, "you made the best decision. Neither Chastity nor Lilly would've asked for her death. Both would see the wisdom in your logic."

"She'll have a lot to make amends for," Ryann said stiffly. "She might not have attacked us, but she helped them. With that said, I'll give her a chance. For you, Sean, and for our family. I don't want to lose another of us."

"Agreed," Fiona said. "You don't have to embrace her, but try not to be antagonistic. Aria, might I ask you to be her guide to our family? You and she fought in the sky, and you two have more in common than the rest of us do."

Aria nodded. "I'll shepherd her."

"Why did she fail to gather them?" Andrea asked.

"She didn't seem to know," Sean said. "I believe it's because she can only gather those who believe in her pantheon, but that's only speculation."

The carriage slowed, and Myna looked out the window. "We're here."

"Fiona, what's the custom?" Sean asked as the carriage came to a complete stop.

"We'll be shown to the room where they are. When we finish saying our goodbyes, one of the staff will show us to a waiting area. After a little bit of time, they will bring their urns to us."

"How long do we get?" Sean asked as Ryann and Ida got out.

"As long as we want," Fiona said. "I know of some people who spent the entire day with their departed, while others spent only a few moments."

"Okay. There's one tradition from my world I'd like to observe."

"We'll be glad to observe it with you, dear."

Sean exhaled, following the others out.

"Sir," Arliat called down to him, looking past Helga, "I paid my respects before coming to get you. Would you like me to take Helga back to the manor with the others?"

Sean frowned, not understanding until the manor staff came out of the building they were parked in front of. "Oh, yes. Helga, go with them." Sean turned to Tiska. "Please see her settled into a room. Her name is Helga Oathsworn."

Tiska curtsied. "As you wish, sir."

"Glorina, we'll be here for a while. Training is probably off for tonight, so please have dinner ready for when the sun goes down."

"Of course, sir."

"Thank you, Sean," Rumia said as she waited to get into the carriage. "It felt right to say goodbye."

Sean's heart suddenly ached, and he had to close his eyes to hold his emotions tight. "You're welcome. It makes me happy to know that they were loved by you all."

Sean stepped away before anyone else could speak to him. His wives fell in around him, forming a protective bubble, but Sean didn't notice, his thoughts on the viewing.

When did I last pay my respects? James' girlfriend's funeral? Yeah, that was it. And before that, my parents. Those were rough, on both of us... I wonder how he did with my funeral?

Lost in his thoughts, Sean collided with Ryann's back when she came to a stop and he didn't. "Sorry!" he apologized on reflex, his arm going around Ryann to make sure she didn't fall.

"It's okay, Sean," Ryann said, patting his hand on her waist.

"MacDougal?" a member of the staff asked when they got inside.

"That's us," Fiona answered.

"Please, follow me," he said.

The hallway was long, but their door wasn't far down it. Opening the door, the man stepped aside. "When you are done, just use the bell pull and one of us will come to assist you."

"Thank you," Sean said softly.

Entering the room, Sean didn't know what to expect, but what he found wasn't it. He'd thought they might be laid on flat slabs of metal or stone, or perhaps in coffins. What he saw were single beds. Lilly was laying on one of white and blue, while Chastity was on a bed of yellow and orange. Omin was on a smaller bed off to the side, atop pure white bedding.

Swallowing the lump in his throat, he moved fully into the room so everyone else could enter. *They look like they're asleep, but they aren't...* Closing his eyes, Sean let the dam of emotions break, and tears poured down his cheeks.

Warm hands touched his back, soothing him as he stood there, silently crying. Sobs of anguish came from his right, where Andrea stood near Chastity. Softer hiccups came from the left, letting him know that Felora was near Lilly. Three new sobs made him open his eyes, and he saw Ven, Venn, and Onim perched beside Omin, touching them softly.

Looking right, he saw Andrea hugging Chastity's body as she leaned over the bed. Unable to bear the sight, he looked away to find Felora kneeling beside Lilly's bed, her hand resting on Lilly's folded hands.

"We'll make them pay, as Velin paid for Oakwood," Myna said softly, her voice a mixture of sadness and anger.

"Yes, we will," Fiona agreed. "Oakwood still has one more to pay back for what transpired, though. Velin was Truestrike's lackey. She couldn't have put that into motion without his approval."

"Why?" Sean asked softly as he throttled his emotions down. "Why would he have wanted to do that?"

"Darragh," Fiona said. "There was a rumor before we set out into the wilds. Darragh lost his sight because of breaking an Agreement, an Agreement with Lord Truestrike. Maybe Truestrike wasn't satisfied with just his eyes? The rumor was that Darragh sired a son with Truestrike's daughter, but I don't know if that's true or not, as he never told me himself."

"It's the rumor that Whelan spoke of," Myna said. "He mentioned it at least once in my presence."

"After Sharpeyes, we'll see about Truestrike. I would have anyway, because it was his people who made the deal with the Einherjar." Sean was no longer crying when he finished— he was pissed.

"Yes," Myna nodded. "We will gut them, and Denmur."

"They will pay," Ida said, looking over from where she was rubbing Andrea's back.

"Threefold," Ryann said, gently stroking Felora's hair.

"Threefold," Aria repeated from near Omin.

Taking a deep breath, Sean went over to Lilly first. The person who'd arranged her had placed just enough makeup on her to give her a semblance of life. Going to one knee, he placed his hand over Felora's and Lilly's. "Lilly, I'm going to miss you. You were persistent, but reserved in your pursuit of me. You showed me your true spirit, and for that, I will always cherish you. I'll do my best to keep your dear Felora happy until we all meet again."

Felora hiccupped as she spoke, leaning into him, "She loved you as much as I do... as much as we all do. Thank you. Thank all of you for bringing her happiness before the end."

"I'm sorry I was such a bitch to her for so long," Ryann said, kneeling down to hold Felora. "I'll do my best to make it up to you in her place."

Felora leaned back into Ryann's arms, and Sean rose to his feet. Going over to Aria and the Fairies, Sean felt an ache in his chest. Onim looked up at him with tears falling from their eyes.

"I'm sorry, Onim."

"No. We all knew it was possible when we joined you in the fight," Onim sniffled. "I'm upset we could do nothing of import for you. Omin was excited for the fight... they expected to do so much more than we did. They died doing what they wished, and we mourn for our loss. I'll give you everything I have so when I rejoin my pair, I can tell them of all I did for you."

Sean swallowed hard and placed his hand beside Onim, palm up. "If you need anything, you just tell us and it will be done."

Onim laid their palm on Sean's. "As you decree, Sean."

Ven and Venn nodded and placed their hands with Onim's. "You will be told, Sean."

Sean gave them a sad smile as they withdrew their hands and huddled back around their friend. Moving with heavy feet, he finally came to a stop next to Ida and Andrea. Chastity had been placed in a yellow sundress that Sean thought looked lovely on her.

"Wish she'd worn that," Sean said.

"She had it made by her mother," Andrea sniffled, looking up at him. "She got it the day before Marjorie..."

Sean felt his anger spark, but he suppressed it and sat on the bed beside Chastity, gently pulling Andrea onto his lap. "They'll be waiting for us. I'm going to miss her smile and her bubbly nature. I know that it'll be harder for you."

Andrea pushed her face into his chest, her voice muffled, "It hurts so much, Sean. My heart aches so much..."

Swallowing, Sean felt the tears slip again and fall on her head. "I know. She wants us to do the best we can while we're still here."

"I know. She always talked of being beside you, helping you achieve all your dreams. I will do twice as much now, for me and her, so she'll smile and praise me when I see her again."

"Don't push too hard," Sean said softly, kissing her head. "She'd want you to try to be happy, to laugh, and to love."

"I will. All the love for you, for our wives, for our children..." Her last word trailed off. Pulling back, she looked at him, her eyes red and with snot starting to drip from her nose. "Can we? Please? I'll name the first daughter Marjorie, in honor of her mother."

Sean stared into her eyes. He wanted to agree, but the thought of death coming for their children froze his tongue.

"Andrea, if he agrees, we'll change what we agreed upon," Fiona said from behind Sean.

Myna rocked back and forth for a few seconds before she hung her head. "It's too late. I broke that accord... I apologize."

"What?" Fiona asked, turning to her. All the women looked at Myna in shock.

"The morning of the fire, I had my cycle. I wanted to make sure I was ready for next year," Myna said morosely. "While I was cleaning myself, Sean came into the bath. I convinced him a little fun would be okay, and we did. I don't know for certain yet, but... I might've broken it."

Fiona's eyes glinted. "Myna, I'm disappointed in you."

"As am I," Ryann huffed.

"And me," Ida added.

"No," Andrea said gently. "No... I'm not. I understand. I forgive you, Myna."

Everyone looked at Andrea, who got up and hugged Myna. "Chastity would laugh and tell you how angry she was, then ask if we should plan for a boy or a girl. I know about wanting to have his child, so I can't be angry."

Fiona sighed. "All of our talk... None of us is immune to the intox-icating thought of having his children. I'm still disappointed, but I can't stay angry when I almost broke it the very day he accepted Andrea and Chastity into our family. I was so close to allowing myself to be fertile in that moment. We'll discuss a new plan tonight, but yes, Andrea, I approve."

"Approved," Ida nodded.

"Approved," Felora said from near Lilly.

One by one, the others all agreed, and Sean felt the tension of Myna's admission drain away. He was still staring at Myna, his eyes going to her belly. Myna saw his face and blushed, looking away first.

"I didn't mean to, Master. My hormones—"

"Boy or a girl?" Sean asked.

"I'd hoped for a boy," Myna admitted. "I was going to name him after my grandfather."

"It's dangerous, but I won't deny any of you what you want," Sean said. "I only wish I could do the same for them." Rising to his feet, he went to the middle of the room and opened his arms.

His wives came to him, hugging him, as they felt sorrow over the loss of their loved ones, and joy that soon they'd have the chance to have children. Sean kissed each on the forehead and felt his own heart lighten a little.

Minutes passed and, in time, the hug came to an end. When it did, Fiona looked at Sean. "What tradition did you wish to observe, Sean?"

"It's a song," Sean said. "I sang it at my parents' funerals, and James sang it for his girlfriend. I'll sing it twice. Join in the second time, if you want."

All eyes were on him as he closed his eyes and took a calming breath. Three seconds slipped by before he began to sing *Amazing Grace*.

The second time through the song, the others joined him for bits and pieces, but they all joined him for the last chorus. As the last note died away, not one of them had a dry eye.

A knock on the door startled them and they turned as one when it opened to reveal Mageeyes, Bemin, Tabitha, Allonen, and a dozen others. "We don't mean to intrude," Mageeyes said. "I had come to ask if we might pay our respects to Lilly. We hesitated outside for the last few minutes, as your song enraptured all of us."

Sean's cheeks burned red, but he nodded. "Lilly would love it if you paid your respects. Please."

6

---

ndrea and Felora both sat with crystal urns on their laps on the way back to the manor. Onim had already left with theirs, after thanking the staff who'd presented them the small urn. Sean felt a lessening of his grief, but his anger still burned hot, even being locked as tight as he could keep it. He held Marjorie's urn— it was more simple than the others, but he knew how much it would have meant to Chastity to have her mother with her.

The sun was setting as the carriage rolled into the yard. Quilla shut the gate behind them, locking it up. Sean was the third one out of the carriage and helped Andrea and Felora so they could keep a firm hold on the urns.

"Bathing, then dinner," Sean said. "Let's put our wives in a place of honor, first."

"Where did you have in mind?" Fiona asked.

"We're all in the dining room most often," Sean said. "There, the bedroom, or the bath would be where we would see them most often. Or, we can create a special place in the front room, so everyone who comes over will see them."

"The front room or dining room," Andrea said.

"In the front room, please?" Felora asked.

"Alright, let's go," Sean said.

Looking over the room with a critical eye, Sean nodded. "There." He went to the archway leading into the hall. "Fiona, please Shape two shelves beside the archway? Andie, Fel, if you two want to create likenesses of them, we can place them below the urns. We can put another one next to Chastity's for Marjorie."

"I'd like that," Andrea nodded. "I'll work on it tomorrow. I want to craft it with a few different materials."

"Yes, I'll work with Andrea on it. She has more skill with Shaping than I do," Felora said.

"We can do it during the slow times tomorrow."

Fiona smiled as she motioned them to place the urns on the two shelves she created on either side of the arch. "There you go."

Andrea placed hers on the right, kissing the urn before stepping back. Felora held Lilly's for a few seconds longer before doing the same. Once both of them were on the shelves, Fiona touched the wall and made sure the urns were stable and not going to fall.

"Let's go bathe and have dinner," Sean said softly after he put Marjorie's urn next to Chastity's.

They were just about to the bathroom when the door opened. Helga and Tiska left the room, pausing when they saw the group.

"Sir, we are bathed. Everyone else went before us," Tiska reported.

"We'll join you all shortly," Sean told her. "We'll just be showering."

"I'll let Glorina know," Tiska said.

"Ten minutes," Sean told her before he entered the bathroom.

* * *

True to Sean's prediction, they were seated at the dinner table in just under ten minutes. No one had dawdled in cleaning up, and there'd been almost no conversation during their showers.

"Sean," Onim called from their spot at the table with Jutt, "would it be okay to include Omin with your wives?"

"Of course," Sean replied. "They'll be given the same treatment. If you want to craft a likeness, it will be added with their urn."

Onim bowed their head. "Thank you. I know we're like family, but some things still take some getting used to."

"Thank you," Jutt added, bowing as their parent had.

"Did you want to wait to discuss things?" Ven asked.

"Now is fine," Sean said just before Glorina and the cooks brought dinner in. "During dinner is fine," he amended.

"It's just salad, steak, and vegetables, sir," Glorina apologized.

Ven waited for the food to be placed before they spoke. "About us being useful in a fight... We learned a painful lesson, but we have a solution: crossbows and poisoned bolts."

A few of the staff shifted uneasily, and Helga's lips twisted in distaste, but she didn't speak.

"I'm not sure about the poison," Sean admitted. "I'd hate for an accident to happen with them. Crossbows and bolts I'll agree with entirely, though. I think I can craft one for you that'll cause harm to anyone. More so if you can learn to shoot on the fly."

"We'll practice a lot," Venn said.

"Us, too," Arla said. "We can protect the manor, if nothing else."

"Small metal bolts," Sean mumbled around a bite of food. "If I enchant the crossbow, it'll definitely be different..."

"Sean, swallow before talking," Fiona said gently.

"Huh?" Sean blinked, swallowed hard, and coughed once. "Sorry. Didn't realize I was speaking out loud." He looked back at Ven. "Give me a day or two, and I think I can have the prototype made up."

"Sean, please use as little energy as possible tomorrow," Fiona asked him. "You exhausted yourself entirely during the fight. I worry about you."

"I'll try," Sean conceded.

"Thank you, Master," Myna said, touching his left hand.

"I have a question," Helga said.

"Go ahead," Ryann said coldly.

"The staff calls him sir or Sean, most of you call him Sean or husband, but she calls him master. How should I address him?"

"Sean is fine," Sean said before Ryann could respond. "Sir is acceptable, but I prefer Sean."

"So only she calls you master? Is that because of her heritage?" Helga blinked at the looks she got from the table and raised her hands. "I see I have asked the wrong question."

"Easy," Sean said lightly to his wives. "She's trying to find her way. I also realize that we haven't fully introduced ourselves to you, Helga. Myna," he nodded to Myna, "calls me master to be a brat. I allow her to do so because it amuses her, and it does make me smile. I will not answer to that title to anyone else."

Felora coughed into her hand.

"Outside of special situations," he amended with a roll of his eyes.

"Thank you," Felora smiled softly.

"I'm assuming you all introduced yourselves to Helga already?" Sean asked the staff.

"We have, sir," Tiska replied.

"Okay," Sean nodded, "let's do the rest of the introductions, then. Helga, these are my wives; Fiona, Myna, Ryann, Ida, Andrea, Felora, and Aria. They each excel in their own areas, and I would be lost without them."

Helga bowed her head to each as they were introduced. She looked at Aria longest. "You fly very well. Not many can match one of my kind in the air."

Aria gave her a sidelong look. "Not many can dodge my arrows. If we'd met differently, I would've been glad to fly with you."

Helga's eyes clouded and she looked at the table. "Yes... That might have been wonderful. I can never undo what has come before, but I will do my best to be useful going forward."

"No one can undo the past," Felora said. "In time, we might be more understanding, but right now, the wound is raw."

"I understand, mistress," Helga replied. "I mean no disrespect."

"Felora," Sean said, changing the topic when he recalled something, "can you summon wings, like your mother?"

"Sadly, no," Felora replied. "None of us can. We can summon the tail and horns, but that's all. It's why I hope to use Aria's talent to summon some."

"Oh, that would be nice," Andrea said, "to fly like a bird."

"I can show each of you the basics," Aria offered. "It'll take some practice to learn how to use them."

"We can add that after training," Myna said. "A little cross-training every day could be useful."

"Agreed," Sean nodded. "We need to make sure we're ready for anything."

"Sir, are you going to the inn?" Arliat asked.

"Yes," Sean said. "Go ahead and get the carriage ready again, please. We'll be out shortly."

"Yes, sir," Arliat said, having finished her meal.

"Who's going with me tonight?" Sean asked.

"I am," Fiona said.

"I am, too," Ryann added.

"I'm going to work with the staff," Myna said.

"I should go," Ida said. "I'm sure the apprentices will have a lot to talk about."

"I'll be staying home, Sean," Andrea said.

"I'm staying with her," Felora smiled softly, placing her hand on Andrea's shoulder.

"I thought about going for a night flight," Aria said.

"Okay. Stay safe, Aria. Andie, Fel, if you need me to come home, just send word."

"We will," Felora replied.

"As safe as I can be," Aria nodded.

"I hope the rest of you have a good evening," Sean said, getting to his feet.

"Sir, what should I do?" Helga asked.

"Rest and recover," Sean told her. "I'm sure you didn't get a lot of either in the cells."

"As you decree," Helga replied.

* * *

"She's going to take some time to fit in," Fiona said as they got closer to the Oaken Glen. "Her bands are distinctly odd."

"Yeah, I noticed that. There's a tree of life on her neck and knot-work on her arms..." Sean paused for a moment his lips pursed. "I'm not sure why it did that. I can only think it's because of what she is."

"'Battle maiden,' you called her," Ida said. "What does that mean?"

"Valkyries are the choosers of the slain in the Norse pantheon. They select valiant fighters and transport them to Valhalla. In Valhalla, they would train every day for Ragnarok, which was their version of the end of the world. The maidens, besides transporting the fallen, were supposed to be fearsome fighters in their own right."

"How did they transport them?" Fiona asked.

"I don't know. We can ask her tomorrow," Sean shrugged. "It's all guesswork on my end."

The carriage slowed and Ryann touched the door. "I'll let you know when it's clear."

Sean met her eyes. "I know, and I'll wait."

Ryann's eyes grew cloudy for a moment and she shook her head. "I'll do better, Sean."

Before Sean could speak, the carriage stopped and Ryann was out the door.

"She blames herself some for them dying," Ida said softly. "She thinks she should've been better at defending them."

"She didn't have much chance against someone who trained for decades," Sean sighed. "None of you did. I had to take wounds to put down the one I faced, and that was with Darragh's knowledge in my head."

"It's clear," Ryann said from outside.

"We know," Fiona said as she moved past him. "We'll help her."

"Focus on what you can do, and let us do the rest," Ida said, kissing his cheek as she climbed out.

Taking a deep breath, Sean stepped out of the carriage last. "Thank you, Arliat."

"Of course, sir."

"Ryann," Sean motioned to the doors, "we're behind you."

The inn was packed with people who all went quiet and looked at them as the group entered. Sean looked over the room and saw the regulars, but also a lot of new faces. The silence was broken by Hans Tackett.

"Ida, we have a mug waiting for you," Hans called out.

"I'll see you when it's time to go," Ida told Sean.

"Yes," Sean agreed, kissing Ida's cheek before following Ryann toward the hallway.

Whispers sprang up as they crossed the room.

"One of his wives, Ida Bronzeshield. Yeah, from the smithing family."

"Openly kissing her cheek like that? Disgusting."

"I heard they all had to Life Bond to marry him. Not surprising—he's powerful enough to take on a Knight in single combat."

Sean shut out the voices as he trailed Ryann. Fiona took his hand when they entered the hallway and gave him a soft smile. Sean gave her a strained one back.

"It's okay, Sean. None of the rumors bother us."

Ryann rapped on the door to the private room before opening it. She gave the association a nod, then stepped aside for Sean. Sean thanked her and entered the room, giving his friends a strained smile.

"Glad you could make it," Fredrick said.

"It's been a tiring day," Sean replied, "but there are things to discuss."

"A few things," Fredrick agreed.

"Oh, MacDougal and wives," Tabitha said. Ryann was still in the doorway when she got to the room. "What can I bring you?"

"Cider," Ryann said.

"Red wine," Fiona replied.

"Dark ale," Sean added.

"Let me drop these off and I'll be right back," Tabitha said as she had refills for the table.

"Sean," Mageeyes said as Tabitha served the table, "the song you sang earlier, is it from your old world?"

"Yes. It's sung at a lot of funerals."

"Might I have the lyrics to it?" Mageeyes said.

"I'll see about writing them down for you," Sean shrugged.

"Thank you."

"First order of business," Fredrick said when Tabitha left. "The first bathhouse. I want to rebuild it to prove that we won't be cowed."

"Agreed," Mageeyes said. "We need to show that when challenged, we pick ourselves back up."

"We can do it," Fiona said. "If the pipes are still good, then it's just the shell and interior items that need to be replaced. A tenday at most, if we get what we need supplied. I also want to touch up the other two and make the walls nearly impossible to burn. We'll need a good amount of lumber so I can make the walls dense enough for all three."

"I'll arrange it," MacLenn said. "You should have some delivered in the afternoon tomorrow, and it'll keep coming until you're satisfied. I'll give Fredrick the bill."

"Change the layout," Sean said. "Make it identical to the second bathhouse. That mix of public and private is best."

"As you wish," Fiona replied.

"Second order of business. Eve?" Fredrick asked, nodding to her.

Eve Blackhand gave the group a long look. "The coal is being cut off to all of Denmur's allies unless they publicly denounce him. Sean, you asked us to start squeezing. We're starting now."

"Same with me," MacLenn said. "If they work with Denmur and won't denounce him, they won't be purchasing anything from us. That includes anyone in Westpoint."

Sean gave MacLenn a smile. "Ballsy, and I appreciate the gesture. Won't it hurt you?"

MacLenn laughed. "Not at all. Compared to before joining this association, we'd still be up two hundred percent in profit. If I tried to do it without you, yes, it would hurt a great deal. One needs to stand by their friends, and this is, truthfully, a small step for what could be asked."

"It'll get cold on both sides of this conflict," Joseph said. "We're all in agreement though. Nails are going to be in short supply for anyone who wants to stay in Denmur's good graces."

"Thank you. All of you," Sean said.

"Third item," Fredrick said, trying to pull the conversation back on track, but pausing when Tabitha came in with the drinks. Once she was gone again, he spoke up, "I've found people to act as guards for our businesses. Trustworthy people," he assured the room. "If you want to have one on hand during business hours to deal with any trouble, just let me know. All of the association buildings will have two all the time, both day and night."

"You expect trouble," Sean said.

"Of course," Fredrick nodded. "Denmur will try strongarm tactics next. I want to be ahead of him. Also, Fiona, can we have the icehouse reinforced?"

"Of course. We'll be glad to touch up each of your homes, one at a time, if the supplies can be found."

Sean gave her a concerned look and she placed her hand on his. "We'll be careful and not press ourselves, Sean."

"Okay."

"The last item," Fredrick said, looking at Italice.

Italice placed her hand on Ryan's. "We're making our courtship official tomorrow. Criers will be sent through town, letting everyone know."

Sean's lips creased upward as he watched the two of them. "That's good news."

Everyone congratulated the new couple.

Mageeyes cleared her throat. "I'll be glad to hold a feast for your families tomorrow eve."

"I accept," Italice said.

"Good. There was one other piece of business, though, Fredrick."

Fredrick frowned. "There was?"

"I didn't bring it forward officially, but yes. Pura, have her bring it in."

Pura flashed away, returning a couple of seconds later. "She is coming."

"Thank you."

"Is Saret okay?" Sean asked while they waited. His eyes went to the empty seat at the table.

"She's helping her new child," Mageeyes said. "There's a lot for her to do there."

"Okay. Ven, please send her a message and let her know we're available if she needs help," Sean said.

"I'll make sure it's delivered, sir," Ven replied from the chandelier.

Sean looked up at the wisps and exhaled. "How much for that, Mageeyes?"

Mageeyes looked up and frowned. "The wisps?"

"Yes."

"I'll deduct it from the bet winnings. I can have it delivered tomorrow."

"What do you want it for?" Giralt asked, interested in what Sean had in mind.

"I'm going to free them," Sean said.

Shocked inhales filled the room and Sean looked down from the wisps. "I'm killing them. It's the only way to free them from their eternal suffering."

Mageeyes looked shocked. "You can do that?"

"Yes."

"That's Sean," Sam commented. "Always helping the people who need help the most."

A knock on the door announced Tabitha, who was carrying a leather satchel that was causing her some strain. With a muffled grunt, she set it on the table in front of Mageeyes. She gave Tabitha a smile before shoving the bag to Sean.

Sean reached out and dragged the satchel closer to him, his eyebrow going up slightly at the weight. Unbuckling it, he opened it to find it filled with coins. "Huh?"

"No one but us bet on you," Mageeyes said. "That's ten percent of what I won. Several houses lost a sizable sum on your fight."

Sean looked at the money and his eyes clouded with emotion—

all he wanted was his wives alive, not this. Throat tight, he closed the bag, still not saying anything.

"I know you'd rather have your loved ones, Sean," Mageeyes said. "I felt that you could use this money far better than the people who lost it. The majority of my winnings is going to the improvement of the association's buildings."

Sean swallowed, his throat tight as he looked up. Fredrick, Italice, and the others all agreed they were doing the same. Sean pushed the bag to Fredrick. "I'll do that, too, then."

They broke up soon after, the mood having stayed somber.

7

S ean took his seat at the table a few seconds before Glorina, Lona, and Mona brought breakfast in. "Thank you, ladies."

"You're welcome, sir," Glorina said. "We have one of your favorites again— pancakes, along with the syrup you preferred. To go with them, we made scrambled eggs with cheese and the thick-cut bacon you said you liked."

"Every meal is a feast from you three."

"Thank you, sir. We try," Glorina replied as all three cooks smiled broadly.

"What is this syrup you speak of?" Helga asked as the plates were put out for everyone to serve themselves.

"It's made from the sap and nuts of the penko tree," Lona explained as she moved to take her seat. "It's very sweet." She lowered her voice to a whisper, but Sean still heard her say, "It's incredibly expensive."

Helga nodded sagely. "I understand. Thank you."

Sean paused with the one small jug in hand. "Who else would like to sample it, at the very least?"

"I'd like some, Master," Myna said. "Just a little bit for one of my pancakes. It's too cloying if more is used."

"I'll use the jam," Fiona said. "I prefer fruit over the nut flavor."

Felora coughed hard, having been sipping her water when Fiona spoke. All eyes went to her as Ida slapped her back. "Sorry!"

Fiona blinked, and her cheeks turned a light pink when she put together the reason why. She gave Felora a raised eyebrow, and the Succubus gave her a slight smirk.

"I've never had any, so I'd like to try it," Ryann said.

"I'm not a fan," Aria said. "It makes me too jittery if I have more than a single spoon of it."

"I'd like some as well, Sean," Ida commented.

Sean looked at the staff and held the jug slightly out to them. "Ladies, please? If you want to sample anything on the table, it's fine."

Rumia raised her hand. "If it's really okay, sir?"

Sean gave her a smile. "Thank you, Rumia."

"I'd like to—"

"Me as—"

"If it's—"

A chorus came from down the table and Sean's smile grew. "Coming down shortly," he said as he poured as much syrup as he used last time onto his food, then passed the jug to Myna. "And it's okay to use all of it, but make sure everyone who wants some gets to sample it. Glorina, budget a little more for it in the future, please."

"As you wish, sir."

Helga waited for the jug to be passed down to her and looked at Sean. Her intent gaze caught his attention, making him look toward her. She sighed and looked back down at the table, clearly lost in her head.

"Helga? Is there a problem?" Sean asked.

She jolted at his question. "Not a problem... but an oddity, sir."

"You can call me, Sean. It really is okay," Sean reminded her.

"Sean," Helga said. She took a deep breath before looking up to meet his concerned gaze. "I visited a new place last night while I slept."

The idle conversation at the table dropped to nothing, and everyone gave her their full attention.

"I visited a place much like this manor. It extended to the walls, but not beyond. Past the walls was only a night sky in all directions, even beneath it."

Sean inhaled slowly as he put his fork down. "And?"

"I was greeted first by a mature woman. She was shocked to see me. The other three were even more surprised, and angry to start with. I do not blame them for their anger. Once I explained my markings," Helga paused and held up her arms, showing everyone at the table her arm bands, "they gave me a chance to sit with them."

The clatter of a fork brought all eyes to Andrea, who was staring at Helga with a mixture of hope and rage. "Chas?"

"Yes," Helga said softly. "Chastity, Lilly, Omin, and one I had not seen before, Marjorie."

"You can speak with them when you sleep?" Felora asked, her tone a little distant.

"I've never had a dream like it before," Helga said slowly. "It was unique and different, but I believe that place to be your realm, Sean."

Andrea rose to her feet, her conflicting emotions clear to everyone. "No..."

Sean stood and had Andrea in his arms before anyone knew he'd moved. "Easy, Andie... easy. She might very well be telling the truth."

"But why should she be able to see her and not me?!" Andrea hiccupped. "I said goodbye, but the pain doesn't fade."

Sean stroked her hair when she spun and buried her face in his chest. The others got up to hold her as well, so Andrea and Sean were in the middle of a group hug.

"I didn't mean to hurt anyone," Helga said softly. "I'll go. Excuse me."

"Stop," Sean said softly, but his word was iron. "Sit. Please."

Helga felt the command in her very core and sat without thought. Her eyes were wide as she stared at Sean.

"Felora, if she dreams again, could you connect her to others?" Sean asked.

"I don't know, Sean. I could speak with Mother. She'd have more knowledge on plane walking dreams than I do. But if it's happening while she dreams, then there's a chance."

Andrea's crying slowed. "Really?"

"I can't promise, Andrea," Felora said softly, "but I can try. I'd like to go speak with my mother first, though."

"Take all day," Fiona said. "It's for our loved ones, including you. I can still see the pain in your eyes."

Felora met Fiona's gaze and gave her a sad smile. "You would. Very well. As soon as breakfast is done, I will go."

"And the rest of us will be heading off for our own projects," Fiona added. "Andrea, do you need to take the da—?"

"No," Andrea cut her off, before saying softer, "no. I want to do what I can. Chas would want me to."

"I'll be home all day, too," Sean said, kissing the top of Andrea's head. "I've been told to use as little energy as possible. I'll come sit with you once I finish a simple task."

"I'd like that," Andrea sniffled. "Thank you. All of you."

"Come on," Sean said, kissing her head again, "the food's getting cold."

"Yes."

The hug broke apart and breakfast continued, but conversation was muted as everyone at the table had food for thought.

* * *

Sean sat at his desk, looking at the wisp orbs that'd been delivered an hour prior from the Oaken Glen. "I know what you're all waiting for," Sean told the glowing points of light. "Can you reassure me that this is what you want?"

All the lights bobbed up and down before centering on him again.

"Okay," Sean said, standing up and drawing Dark Cutter.

The sword pulsed in his hand, and Sean gave the weapon a puzzled look.

"Didn't you take Evan's life?"

An image of a healthy man appeared in Sean's mind, but the figure was slowly being sucked dry, then became filled out again. That image repeated, but when it refilled the second time, the man was still emaciated.

"Oh. You were using your energy to Shape to my will during combat?"

The blade hummed gently in his hand.

"Thank you," Sean said softly. "I should've realized it, but I was busy at the time."

The image of a puppy with big eyes slowly wagging its tail came to him.

"I can give you a little," Sean smiled, taking a seat again and resting the blade across his knees.

Picking up a shard of bronze, Sean nicked his hand and held it over the flat of the blade. Fat drops of blood splashed onto Dark Cutter, but instead of throwing flecks of blood when impacting, they sank instantly into the blade.

The emaciated man of the image sat at a lavish feast and began to eat in a dignified manner.

"Glad you still enjoy my blood," Sean laughed. "You've been alive a long time, haven't you?"

An image of a calendar with months flying off it gave Sean the clear idea of hundreds or even thousands of years passing.

"Besides Darragh, how many have you enjoyed having as your wielder?"

A handful of people sat at the table with the feasting man. One of them was Darragh, and the others were sharp-featured individuals, clearly with Fey blood. The only exception was a hard-faced woman with dirty red hair.

"One of the first?" Sean asked, focused on the woman.

The man held up three fingers.

"Grandchild of the first. Then you've been alive a very long time, indeed."

The man pointed at the woman and held up a single finger.

"She was the first to wield you?"

Nodding, the man sighed as the food vanished from the table.

Sean realized the cut had healed over. "Sorry about that." Gashing his hand again, he let more blood fall onto Dark Cutter.

The food reappeared and the man smiled broadly, going back to his feast.

"When you're done, can you shift into a hammer for me? I need to free these wisps, and I'm not supposed to use energy if I can help it."

The man nodded as he chewed the meat off a turkey leg.

"Thanks. I'll give you a few minutes."

After the third cut healed, Sean stood up again. "Ready?"

Dark Cutter changed into a war hammer.

"Okay, we'll start on the left," Sean said, picking up the first wisp orb and setting it on the metal strike plate he'd made.

* * *

Sean left his workshop to find the staff forming up with Myna. "Midday training?"

"Yes," Myna replied. "Did you want to join us?"

"It'd be good. I have a feeling that we'll have a lot more fighting in the near future."

"We're working on unarmed combat still, but we're going to switch to fighting until one gives up," Myna said.

"Yeah, people don't stop just because you hurt them a little," Sean agreed. "Are you dividing them into pairs?"

"I was going to," Myna said. "Did you want to pick someone to start with?"

Sean looked at the women before motioning Quinna out. "Come on. Don't hold back on me."

Quinna grinned as she moved to the side. "You will for me, though, right?"

"If I didn't, your chest would cave in on the first punch," Sean said. "I don't honestly think about it. I stay in normal Human ranges unless it's life-threatening or if I stop paying attention."

"Yes. You losing your focus hurts," Quinna grunted, rubbing her shoulder.

"I'll be focused today," Sean said.

"Helga, you're with me," Myna said. "The rest of you, pair off. Winners will spar against each other. Losers will do the same."

Sean faced Quinna and bowed his head to her before setting into a defensive posture. "Ready when you are."

Quinna didn't rush— she moved forward with slow measured steps, her balance nearly perfect. Sean smiled, knowing Myna had bludgeoned all of them repeatedly so they'd learn to move correctly. Just short of what he thought her range was, Quinna lunged forward, her front kick going for Sean's chest.

Dodging to the side, he slapped her leg away with his left and pivoted into her as he slid down, going to sweep her planted foot. He hadn't expected her to push off the back leg, jumping his sweep as she went further forward.

Landing, she spun and gave another powerful kick toward his back. Her leg brushed over his chest when Sean dropped flat to the ground, having realized her intent. As her leg went past, he kipped up and spun to face her.

"That was good," Sean said as he backed off a few feet.

Quinna stayed silent, but she stamped one of her feet, giving away her frustration. She stalked in again, her hands up to block or attack.

Sean waited again. He knew if he exerted even a small percentage of what the Tuatha gave him, he could just overpower her, but that didn't train them to fight, nor did it help him integrate the knowledge Darragh had given him.

She closed and went for a punch. A flurry of powerful blows rained at Sean, forcing him to focus more on defense. Sean smiled slightly as he redirected her attacks— he knew that Quinna and Quilla with their Bovine Moonbound heritage could overpower a lot of people. Their size and heritage would probably make them an even fight for Angus Angusson. Against him, though, they couldn't just brute their way through the fight.

During her flurry, Quinna made a mistake. One of her punches was not balanced, and when Sean forced it aside, she overextended. Nodding, Sean grabbed her arm and yanked her into his hip. He twisted and sent her over him, slamming her onto her back. Holding her arm still, he brought his heel down onto her chest, but checked the blow so it hit as if Myna'd done it.

"Your chest is caved in," he said evenly, "against me, but not against others."

Quinna winced at the blow, but she was built strong and used that to work through the pain. Yanking with all her strength, she pulled him off balance. Sean let her take him, resisting the urge to plant his feet and not move, as most people would have difficulty against Quinna's sheer physicality.

Dragging him down, Quinna clamped a hand to the back of his neck, pulling his head to her armpit. Sean let go of her arm to help control his fall, and that allowed her to grab the leg of his pants as he came down. Using those points to control him, she moved him into the position she wanted.

Sean grimaced when she maneuvered him into a chokehold, with him on her chest. Luckily, he'd been able to get his chin into her elbow, so he wasn't in danger of going out quickly.

"Submit," Quinna said, tightening her grip.

The strain on his neck was immense, but Sean just grunted as he rocked in place. He felt bad for what he was going to do, but if it'd been a real fight, she'd need to know to be ready for it. Quinna smiled, clearly thinking she had him.

Sean stopped prying at her arm and instead, used his open palms to slap the sides of her head. Missing the first time, he did it again while Quinna tried to understand what he was doing. The second strike was on target and Quinna winced, her arm loosening slightly as her eyes watered from the overpressure in her ears.

Using that moment, Sean was able to free himself from the chokehold. Instead of trying to scramble away, he spun his legs over her hips and drove his fist down. Quinna covered her face, thinking he was going for it, but he wasn't. Driving down just under her sternum, Sean forced the air from her lungs.

Quinna wheezed as she got winded, her eyes watering more. Huddling up, she tried to get her breath back, but Sean didn't give her the chance. He clamped a hand to her throat, squeezing her arteries as he punched her again.

Her eyes started glazing over when she couldn't get air, the blood flow to her brain being cut off. Quinna feebly tapped the ground. Sean stopped instantly, pushing himself to sit on the ground beside her as his body healed the bruises he'd received.

"An ear strike. Effective to disorient your foe," Myna nodded.

"She had me, if not for that," Sean said. "You let me get my chin into your elbow, too, Quinna."

Quinna sat up, breathing easier. "Why did slapping my head do that?"

Sean took a moment to explain what he'd done and why it worked. By the time he finished, he realized he had everyone's attention.

"It's a desperate attack or one to use against an unwary foe," Myna added. "Now, let's continue. Helga, you'll fight Sean."

"Fight Sean?" Helga asked slowly.

"No Talents. Just skill in unarmed combat," Sean said as he got up and dusted his clothing off. "Come on."

"I've never fought a divine being before," Helga said.

"I'll be Human enough for this," Sean reassured her. "I expect you to win. I'm only thirty-three, even if I do have combat knowledge shoved into my head. You've had how long to train?"

Helga stared at him. "Thirty-three?"

"I'm Human, or I was," Sean shrugged. "I'm far removed from the Einherjar in terms of skill."

"Yet you slew one of Thor's chosen?" Helga asked.

"I used everything I could in that fight," Sean replied. "I had to let him gut me to have a chance."

Helga took a deep breath. "Very well. May I request a fight against your full strength after this bout?"

"Physical strength? Sure. I'm not using Talents today, though, so maybe you want to wait until tomorrow for that."

"I will wait," Helga said.

"Okay."

8

S ean entered the shop and saw Andrea speaking with a customer.

"If you want a custom image on the kettle, we can do that, too," Andrea said with a professional smile in place.

"Hmm... the price goes up in that case, I'm sure," the man said. "No, I'll take just the one plain kettle." He placed the money on the counter and took the kettle in hand. "Good day."

"Good day," Sean said, holding the door for the customer.

The man gave Sean a look of distaste as he passed him. Sean didn't blame the guy in the least— Myna had removed the grime from him and his clothing, but they were still pretty disheveled.

"Sean," Andrea said, her professional smile fading, "what happened?"

"I joined the afternoon training. Since I shouldn't use energy, it felt like the thing to do."

"You could've taken the time to straighten up before coming to see me," Andrea said, her lips tugging up slightly.

"Could have, but I wanted to get here, instead."

"Step into the back and fix your clothing, please?" Andrea asked.

"You're the master of the shop; your appearance reflects on everything here."

"Okay," Sean agreed, moving to the door that led to the back.

A minute later, Sean came back out and took a seat next to her, behind the counter. "There, all better."

Andrea nodded. "Yes."

"Been busy?"

"No," Andrea sighed. "They've been very spaced out today. If not for Caleb, things might've been bad." She reached down and petted the cuon by her feet. "He's been a good boy."

"Wondered where he was," Sean said. "How you been, boy?"

Caleb rolled onto his side and waved a paw in the air with a huff.

"Been enjoying the belly rubs, huh?" Sean chuckled.

"He's helped keep me calm," Andrea said, bending over to give Caleb's belly a vigorous scratch. "Such a good boy."

"I'm glad he's been here to help."

Andrea's hand slowed, and she looked up at Sean. "Do you think she's telling the truth?"

"Helga? Yes. If anyone could easily touch that plane, it'd be her. Does that bother you?"

"Yes..." Andrea whispered. "I just want to hold Chas and have her tell me it's going to be okay. She was always there with me, and I thought I'd be able to step past it with the viewing. I might have, if not for hearing what I did this morning."

"Now, you just want to see her and hold her one more time."

"Yes," Andrea sniffled. "I keep telling myself 'just once more will help'."

"It might not," Sean cautioned her. "Seeing and feeling her again might make it hurt all the more."

"I know," Andrea sobbed. "I know, and that's why I hate her right now. To give me this hope and fear all balled together? If not for her, we might not have lost them at all. Those men were badly wounded before she healed them."

"She was doing as she was honor-bound to do," Sean said. "It was only after she was ordered that she got close enough for them to heal.

On top of that, she never once raised a weapon against Aria." Sean trailed off, his brow furrowing. "I'm missing something important here, and not the least of which is the how and why she was even in this world."

Andrea took a shuddering breath when Caleb pushed his head under her hand. She gave the cuon a broken smile and petted him again. "Who's a good boy, hmm?"

Caleb's tail hit the floor twice, and he gave her a doggy grin.

"Thank you," Andrea said, bending over to kiss his head.

"Done that a few times, has he?"

"Yes. I promised him a treat later, after the first time."

"Won't argue against that," Sean said.

The jingle of the bell attached to the door had Sean on his feet. "How can I help you?"

"I can think of a number of ways," Felora grinned.

"You're bad, Fel," Sean smiled at his wife. "How did the talk go?"

"It was very different," Felora said. "She treated me like an equal instead of a child. That's a first, especially when it comes to matters of my lineage."

"Did she say you can do it?" Andrea asked, wiping at her face.

"She wasn't positive either way," Felora said. "The long and short of it is that I'll just have to try. Since Helga is no longer what she was and is tied to Sean, it changes things. Even she couldn't guess what might've changed, though she was interested in the bands from the Bond on Helga."

"Can we, Sean?" Andrea asked.

Andrea's pleading tone squeezed Sean's heart. "Fel, can you?"

"Tonight, yes. I'll take from everyone but you for it."

"Thank you," Andrea said, surging to her feet and rushing to hug Felora.

Felora caught her in a hug and kissed her cheek. "You're welcome, Andie, but please save the thanks until we know if it's possible? I don't want to disappoint you."

Andrea gave her a smile. "Just trying is enough."

Sean moved over and held them both. "That'll be after the inn."

"Can you miss it for tonight?" Andrea asked.

"Ven?"

"I'll send word, sir," Ven replied from the rafters.

"Thank you." Andrea turned in the hug and kissed him.

* * *

Sean was bemused when he entered the manor. *Really does live up to her bloodline,* Sean thought as he closed the front door. *Andrea was all for her idea, too. If it hadn't been a slow day, it might have gotten tricky.*

Heading upstairs, Sean knocked on Helga's door. "Helga?"

A few seconds passed before Helga opened it. "Yes, sir?"

"I was hoping to speak with you."

Helga lowered her head. "As you wish, sir. Please, come in."

Sean was glad there were two chairs in the room. He took one and waited for her to sit. Helga took the other reluctantly, looking worried.

"I'm sorry, sir," Helga blurted out before he could say anything. "I know you said to fight you to my utmost, but I knew it was wrong."

"Easy," Sean said, holding up his hand. "This isn't about you thrashing me during sparring."

"It's not?" Helga asked, surprised. "Oh. Did you come for—?"

"Stop!" Sean said quickly when she reached for the ties at the front of her clothing.

Helga's body locked up at his command.

"I'm not here for sex, either. I have plenty of wives for that."

Helga felt his will relax, and she took a deep breath. "I'm sorry. I am trying to understand my place here. I do not mean to cause offense."

"I'm not offended," Sean assured her. "I wanted to talk to you about you being here, as well as why you didn't attack us during the battle."

Looking away from him, Helga looked ashamed. "That was the only time I have not drawn steel to kill someone when I should have."

"It struck me, especially after your show of martial prowess, that not once did you attack during the battle. You fly as well as Aria does. At the very least, you could've closed the distance with her and made her defend, but you never did. Why?"

"I couldn't. Not against you, not as it was."

"We only met once at Odin's table, when he had you flirt with me," Sean said, "so why not against me?"

Helga jerked slightly as if he slapped her. "He didn't have me flirt with you. He was upset that I showed interest in you at all, though he surely offered me up like a morsel to pique your interest after I did."

"So you flirted with me just because?"

"I am, or was, a Valkyrie, Sean. I can sense souls... the depth of them, their purity. Your soul was unlike any I had felt before. I wanted to know more about the Human who fought Thor and sat at Odin's table without cringing in fear. Beyond that, your soul resonated like a chime that made mine shiver in echo. When I heard Odin all but promise me to you, I was upset, and yet deeply grateful, but then you turned him down and went with the Crow of Battle."

"Don't think I would've enjoyed it there, present company excluded," Sean said with a shrug.

"No, you would not have, and Thor would have made your life torment. He hates you." Helga smiled slightly as she took on a mock voice. "'A mere human would dare stand up to me? I will make him pay for eons.'" She laughed. "How he raged when you chose the Tuatha."

"Yeah, sounds like the Thor I met. Giant, petulant child with anger issues."

Helga laughed harder. "Yes, exactly." She sobered quickly. "And yet Odin dotes on him. I was moved from Odin's ranks to Thor's after your decision. That was unpleasant. But Thor gave me a chance... all I had to do was go with his chosen and help them in a single battle. If I did that, he would gift me back to Odin."

"Thor isn't smart enough to figure out where I went, much less make a pact with Truestrike," Sean said.

"It bothered me how everything worked so smoothly," Helga

agreed. "I came to understand why— one of Thor's brothers hates him, and loves to embarrass and make a mockery of him."

"Loki?"

"Indeed. Loki must have put things into motion, then tricked Thor into going along with it. In the end, it cost him a champion, twenty Einherjar, and me. Moreover, it cost him all their souls, too."

"Because you broke rules," Sean said.

"Yes. I didn't keep their souls safe. I spent them like coppers to preserve my own life."

"But if you died, wouldn't they have perished as well?"

"No. If I return to Valhalla, they return with me and are remade. If I die, my last sparks carry them to Valhalla to be remade. Instead of doing my duty and letting myself die so they could return, I used them to stay alive. My sisters would be appalled at what I have done. Odin will be furious that I broke the first law of my kind."

"He can suck a dick," Sean snorted. "If he cared at all, he'd keep Thor on a fucking leash." Shaking his head, he grabbed his anger and throttled it back under control. "Then again, if he had, I wouldn't be here."

"Yes."

"So why didn't you attack us and just return with them?" Sean asked, pulling the conversation back on track.

"I should have," Helga said, looking into the distance. "Any of my sisters would have... probably. But I had felt your soul, and when I saw you again here and knew why I had been sent, I felt a fury in my own soul. To be used to strike down a soul as pure as yours? One that seeps into everyone around it, making them better? I would rather have cut my own throat. I knew when I saw you that you would not back down from the trap they had set. I made a vow of my own to do as little as I could to assist them."

"Can you still feel souls?"

"Yes. Being this close to you makes my soul hum with resonance." Helga took a slow, deep breath, her eyes closed. "I have never felt as alive and as free as I do now. I know that my very soul is changing, and I want to see what I will become." Exhaling slowly, she opened her eyes, and a deep sadness lived in them. "Your family hates me, and I cannot blame them. That is the punishment I deserve for not doing more when I could have. If I had struck at the start, your wives would still live. No one would have expected me taking his head and condemning all of us to death. How just it would have been, a snake beheaded by his own machinations."

"You'd have died, as well. You wouldn't have had their souls in time."

"Yes," Helga whispered. "That is possible."

"We're going to try having Felora connect your dream to my wives. They want to see if they can touch the afterlife like you did. Are you willing to do it?"

Helga looked at him, searching his face. "You can just command me to do it."

"That isn't me," Sean said.

"They would surely despise me if I did not," Helga said. "Andrea, especially."

"It's possible."

"No. I have caused her enough pain. I am willing. I do not know how I did it or if I can do it again, but my very soul is changing, and I find myself welcoming it. There is no saying what I will be able to do or not do with you as my foundation."

"We'll find out together," Sean said, rising to his feet. "It's about time for evening sparring. Want to come thrash me again?"

Helga stared at him with curiosity. "How do you not care about losing to me?"

"Because I'm not an ass," Sean laughed. "Training is so we can grow and improve. Can someone truly improve if they never lose? Besides, I got you good a couple of times."

Helga's lips quirked up. "You are much stronger than you look, and quick, too. It is difficult to account for what you can do."

"Until you fight me enough, then I'll *really* get thrashed," Sean laughed as he opened the door. "Come on. Everyone should be back."

9

Sparring was lively— all of his wives went up against Helga one by one, and as no Talents were used, each was handed a resounding defeat. Sean got his ass kicked after they did, but it took Helga longer than it had the first time.

Quinna and Quilla were both impressed by Helga's ability to defeat their strength. Rosa, Rumia, and the maids all declined to fight her, though talk of how formidable Helga was dominated their conversation on the way to the bath.

Sean hoped that seeing how skilled she was would drive home the point of how much worse things could've been for them during the battle. Sean trailed the entire group, glad that Ryann was talking with Helga.

"That combination you used on me, can you show me how to do that tomorrow?"

"If that is what you desire, mistress," Helga nodded, "but it isn't the combination that matters. It is learning what works best for you and at what moment you can chain your moves together. That takes a lot longer to learn."

"I understand that," Ryann said, "but as Sean's shield, anything I can do to improve now is needed."

"His shield?" Helga asked. "I don't recall seeing you with a shield."

"I don't carry one normally," Ryann was starting to explain when Sean split off from the group.

When he entered the bathroom a few minutes later, all eyes went to him. "What?"

"We thought you were doing what you do," Fiona said with a glance toward Helga, who was under the shower.

Sean looked where Fiona did and shook his head. "No, I'm not doing that. I just had to make a quick stop."

"That's good," Fiona said as she made her way to the tub, which already had several people in it.

Sean sat down to get his boots off when Andrea was suddenly in front of him. "Andie?"

"Please," Andrea said softly, not moving.

"Just tonight," Sean replied.

"Thank you." Andrea stripped off his boots and his socks. She tossed the socks into the washtub before setting his boots on the shoe rack by the door. "I'll be waiting to wash your back."

"As you wish, Andie," Sean replied as he undressed.

Dropping his clothing into the washtub when he made his way to the showers, his pace slowed slightly as Helga passed him. Her scars were noticeable on her naked body, but none of them detracted from her beauty. *Like Ryann and Ida had a love child,* Sean thought. *All that hard muscle on a taller frame, and with blonde hair.*

Shaking his head, he got to the shower. The image of Helga was driven from his mind by Andrea washing her hair. Wetting himself down briefly, he grabbed the soap and got a lather going. When Andrea stepped out of the spray of water, he began scrubbing her back.

"Oh, I was going to get yours," Andrea said.

"After I get you first," Sean said.

"Ah, so it really is a family thing," Helga nodded from the tub. "It wasn't surprising when Tiska washed my back yesterday, but you washing my back I had not expected."

"We all help each other," Aria replied. "We normally wash whoever is there at the time."

"That is good to know. I will not be as awkward next time. I thought briefly you were preparing me for him."

Fiona laughed lightly. "No, Helga. Sean only sleeps with his wives."

"Your turn," Andrea said, pulling his attention away from their conversation.

"Sure," Sean said, turning his back to her.

"It's his way," Myna said, catching his attention again. "That's just the way it is. He's much better about being seen naked now, though."

Fiona laughed lightly. "Oh, yes. That first time in a bath? Oh, he was so awkward." Sean sighed, and Fiona giggled. "Sorry, husband, but it's true."

"Yeah, still awkward," Sean grumbled. "I'm getting better."

"That's true," Ryann said. "After giving all of us a complex about it being us and not you."

Andrea giggled as she rinsed her hands off. "You're done, Sean."

"Thanks, Andie," Sean said. He stepped under the water to cut off the conversation for a moment.

"My sisters would fight over him," Helga was saying when he came out from under the spray. "While not as physically imposing as many in Valhalla, he is still very attractive. With the soul added onto that, he would need a *very* large stick to..." Helga trailed off when Sean turned around to head for the tub.

Seeing where her gaze was, he turned red. Clearing his throat, he gave Fiona a look. "What was that about it being rude to stare while in the bath?"

Fiona snickered and nudged Helga. "It's rude to stare."

Helga looked at Fiona, her ears red. "Yes." Looking back at Sean, she kept her eyes on his face as he crossed the last few steps to the tub. "My apologies."

"Happens," Sean said, sliding into the water.

"These water things are very nice," Helga said, clearly trying to move past her gaffe.

"Thank you," Sean said. He leaned against a couple of the jets and closed his eyes. "They are nice, but they're just a small stone on my path."

"The supplies for the first bathhouse are still coming in," Fiona said. "We managed to reinforce the second and third one today."

"Tiring?" Sean asked.

"With five of us, it was fine," Fiona replied. "The association is gathering supplies for their businesses and homes, as well. I asked Augustus to have some delivered here, along with copper."

"Reinforce the building, top to bottom?" Sean asked, his eyes still closed as he let the hot water and jets relax him.

"Yes."

"I'm going to go to Winston's tomorrow," Sean said, "which means you'll be missing Ry."

"Hmm, that's a good point," Fiona said. "I'll have Helga come with us. I'm assuming you gave her access to everything?"

"Yeah."

"She'll be clumsy and slow to start with, but I'm sure she will adapt quickly."

"Adapt to what?" Helga asked.

"Shaping," Myna replied. "We'll explain and show you tomorrow."

"I'm skipping going to the inn tonight," Sean said. "I'm going to do the dream with Felora and Helga tonight. You all want to join, right?" All of his wives answered affirmatively. "That'll be after dinner."

"That brings us to another point," Fiona said. "Andrea, tomorrow night is for you."

The sudden swirl of water almost made Sean open his eyes, but he kept them shut.

"Thank you," Andrea said, her voice coming from his left now.

"You're welcome," Fiona replied. "Ladies, we need to discuss who and when a little later tonight. Ryann, you're still okay with being opposite Myna?"

"Yeah," Ryann said, but there was frustration in her voice. "One of us needs to be his shield."

"We know how hard it is, Ryann," Felora said. "If you want, I can take your place so you don't have to wait as long."

"No," Ryann said tightly. "This is my duty. I'll be okay with Myna taking over for me, but otherwise, it's my job."

"It is not my place," Helga said, "but I can be his shield while you bear his child. I am skilled and will gladly put myself between him and all danger."

Tension filled the air, and Sean wondered which of them would break it.

"Maybe," Ryann said. "Tomorrow, we'll go all out, *with* Talents. If you can prove you can do the job, I'll consider your offer."

Sean opened his eyes and noticed the surprise on his wives' faces at Ryann. Closing his eyes again before they saw him looking, he was glad that maybe Helga was being accepted at least a little.

"I was curious," Xenta asked, "why are your bindings so different?"

"I do not know," Helga said. "Is it that unique?"

"We're all Life Bonded to Sean," Ida said. "You see how different our marks are to yours? They're just Bonded for a set period of time, and theirs is lesser still."

"Maybe that's why?" Aria offered. "He said he was Soul Bonding her."

"Master," Myna said, "I wish to Soul Bond."

Sean opened his eyes and sat up, meeting her gaze. "Okay. I, Sean MacDougal, offer Myna MacDougal this Soul Bond. Everything her Life Bond is, but to her very soul, instead of her life."

"I accept," Myna said quickly.

Everyone was still as they watched the mark on Myna's neck, but after a couple of seconds, a collective sigh of disappointment filled the air.

"That wasn't the—" Ryann began, cutting off as her eyes grew wide.

Sean watched as the black circle on Myna's neck faded bit by bit. Myna pulled her arms out of the water and everyone watched as those bands faded away, as well. Another few seconds of nothing, and the tension climbed to new levels as everyone waited for what would happen next.

Gasping breaths came when people remembered to breathe, not having realized they'd been holding their breaths, but no large markings appeared on Myna. Myna looked at Sean. Her eyes were wide and fearful— it looked as if her Life Bond was gone and nothing had taken its place.

Sean was the first to spot it, and his dreams came to mind. He took her left hand and held it up between them. A half-inch wide black band encircled her ring finger. There was a white tree of life in the center of the band, with knotwork coming from its roots and working around the back of her finger.

"My wife is Soul Bonded," Sean said softly, meeting her eyes.

Myna tackled him, plunging them both underwater as she kissed him passionately. A confused babble of voices came from all around Sean, but the distortion under the water stopped him from understanding what was being said. Gasping when they came up for air, Sean was trying to get his bearings while Myna beamed like she'd won the world.

"Husband," Fiona said, grabbing his attention, "the rest of us would like to do the same now."

"Of course," Sean smiled at her. "I..."

Conversation was energetic all through dinner. The cooks expressed shocked delight for his wives. As they showed off their new Bonds, they noticed that each wife had a different symbol hidden in the knotwork on the backs of their finger.

Fiona had a staff with leaves, Myna was marked with a dagger, Ryann's held a bullseye, while Ida's was an anvil. Andrea had an oven for hers, Felora a pair of lips, and Aria's was a bird.

Aria heavily inspected Helga's markings, but she couldn't find anything hidden in them. Her markings were obviously different in size and placement, and, as Glorina pointed out, she wasn't Sean's wife.

"That's true," Sean said, "and that's likely why there's no hidden mark."

"What do they mean?" Prita asked.

"I think they tie to how I see them," Sean said. "Shaper, hunter of the night, sharpshooter, smith, housewife, seductress, and as free as a bird." All of his wives smiled, but Andrea's was the broadest of them all.

"Since dinner is done, shall we retire and try our experiment?" Felora asked.

"Yes," Andrea said, jumping to her feet.

With dinner done, people said good night, and the family went upstairs, with Helga behind them.

* * *

Sean was the first one into bed— he wanted to be covered before Helga was brought into the room. His wives all wore their nightgowns when they joined him. Fiona was the last one into the room, leading Helga in. Sean was surprised they had an extra nightgown for her. The black gown covered her enough that Sean wasn't feeling awkward about it.

"Helga, you'll be on that edge of the bed," Fiona said, pointing to the far side, away from Sean. "That does mean you'll be close to Ida. Do forgive her if she hits you. She twists and turns in her sleep."

"It is fine," Helga said. She got into the spot designated for her and looked at Felora. "What do I do now?"

"I'm going to push you to sleep," Felora said. "I'd like you to focus on going back to Sean's plane. Intent is important. Once you're there, someone will knock on the closest door to you. It'll be us, so open it and let us in."

Helga nodded. "I understand." She closed her eyes and breathed slowly. "I am ready."

"Everyone else?" Felora asked, getting nods from them. "Very well. Embrace the dream, step across the threshold, and find the place of belonging. Your master's home beckons you."

Sean didn't fight Felora's energy as it covered him. Instead, he embraced it, welcoming it deep into him.

* * *

Blinking, Sean sat up in bed. He was alone. "What happened?"

No one answered him, so he got out of bed. Looking down at his naked body, he visualized clothing on himself, but nothing happened. Frowning, he went to the dressing room. A few minutes later, he was dressed and heading downstairs.

"I missed you so much!" Andrea's cry was clear from the first floor, and Sean rushed to get there.

Everyone was in the main room. Sean went a little red— everyone who'd gone to bed with him was naked, including Helga. His sudden arrival caught their attention, and Fiona gave him a shaky smile.

"We didn't know what happened to you," Fiona explained.

"I appeared upstairs," Sean said. "I, uh... got dressed first."

"Yep, that's him all over," Myna snickered.

"Come on, ladies, we should go get dressed," Fiona said. "Lilly, Chastity, you don't need to get dressed, but please come with us? We might not get Andrea to go, otherwise."

Chastity was holding Andrea tightly. "Do we have to? None of us cared about being naked in front of each other before."

"Please, daughter?" Marjorie asked from the far side of the room. "For me."

Chastity sighed. "Come on, Andie. It won't take long."

Andrea sniffled and nodded, letting go of Chastity long enough to grab her hand. "Okay."

That motion got Chastity's attention. She noticed the new band on Andrea's finger, and the lack of marking on her wrists and neck. "Andie, what happened?"

"We'll explain," Fiona said, starting to usher the others toward the stairs. "Come on. Helga. You, too."

It took a minute, but soon, only Omin, Marjorie, and Sean were left in the front room. Sean gave them an apologetic smile. "Sorry about us all showing up like we did."

"No. This is your place, Sean," Marjorie said. "Gave us a real fright that something bad had happened. Fiona explained it was a dream, but not a dream, before you showed up. Can I get you some tea?"

"Yeah, we might be here for a little while," Sean said. He looked at the archway that led to the kitchen and froze. The urns were in place, just as they were in the waking world.

"Yes, we were surprised when they showed up," Marjorie said. "It was flattering to know that you valued me so much to enshrine me, as well."

"Everyone," Sean said as he looked at the urns. "Everyone will have a place."

"Yes. That's who you are," Marjorie smiled.

"There will be likenesses added soon. That way, everyone will know who we loved and cared for."

"That'll be interesting. They might be a while, from what little I heard about the rings. Shall we get the tea?"

"Oh, yes," Sean said.

They were back in the front room with a couple of kettles of tea. Sean had been surprised at the magic kettles for a moment, but then he wasn't. This place was identical to their normal manor.

"Even the bath?" Sean was asking when the others came down the stairs.

"Yes, though the bath here is a great deal more relaxing than the ones at the bathhouse."

"Sean, do you think we can do the same as they did?" Chastity blurted.

Sean turned to her, chewing his lip. "I don't know, but we can try."

10

Sean woke to the sound of happy voices. Prying his eyes open, he saw his wives all getting out of bed. Andrea was wearing a sad smile on her lips as she spoke with Helga.

"Thank you. It was so good to see her again..." Andrea explained.

"It is my pleasure to serve, mistress," Helga replied respectfully.

"Time to get up already?" Sean asked, sitting up.

"It is if you want to accomplish anything today," Fiona said. "Andrea and Felora will be holding down the shop, and Myna's going to be helping the staff hone their Talents. The rest of us will be working on reinforcing buildings again."

"I'm going to head to Winston's," Sean said, "so you'll be missing Ry."

"Right. Helga will be coming with us, instead," Fiona corrected. "I forgot."

"I am ready to serve," Helga said, having caught the conversation.

"Ladies, can I have a moment with Sean?" Felora asked the room.

"Of course," Fiona said. "Breakfast will be waiting if we dawdle too much."

Andrea looked back at Sean and gave him a smile before

following the others. Sean watched her go, recalling her telling Chastity about what tonight was going to mean. Sean hadn't been sure what to expect about that, but he figured she'd be angry that she wouldn't get the chance herself. He'd been completely surprised when Chastity squealed happily and nearly dragged Andrea out of the room to talk.

"Sean?" Felora asked with a smirk.

"Huh?"

"If you can stop ogling our wife for a moment?"

"I wasn't ogling," Sean said, but his cheeks were burning slightly as he got out of bed.

"Of course not," Felora laughed, then grew serious. "About last night... I want to talk with my mother about it, but I don't want to let others know. What do you think is best?"

Sean scratched his chin for a moment. "She's my mother-in-law, which means she's family. If you trust her, Fel, then I trust her, too. Do what you think is best and I'll support you."

Exhaling her held breath, she gave him a strained smile. "That wasn't a yes or a no."

"It's a yes, unless you think she can't be trusted," Sean said.

"Okay." Felora looked toward the dressing room door that Andrea had gone through. "I'm glad she got a little more closure."

"Me, too. I didn't expect Chas to be as okay with everything as she was."

"I believe part of it was the rings showing up for her and Lilly. That was everything to them in that moment."

"Yeah. I was so damned worried," Sean admitted. "I know they would've been hurt if it didn't work."

"Luckily, it did," Felora said softly, looking down. "I'm going to need more from you, Sean. I'm sorry. I know it's not what you prefer. Lilly helped stabilize me with our play, but—"

Sean took her into an embrace and, with a hand tangling into her hair, pulled her head back as he dipped her. Felora's eyes went wide before they closed, and she moaned into his mouth. The kiss was demanding and passionate, and Felora melted into it.

Moving just as quickly, he got her upright and stepped a few feet away from her. Felora gasped, her breath coming fast and shallow. Her pupils were dilated when Sean met her gaze and gave her a smile.

"I'll give you what you need, Fel. It'll be a little awkward to start with, but if you help me, I'm sure we can find our own balance to satiate your needs."

Felora's eyes glowed with energy and she shuddered in place. She let out a small whimper before slumping to her knees a few seconds later. She looked up at him, her eyes still glowing. "From three feet away, and with just your words? Your love is almost too much..."

Sean just stared at her. "Uh... that was different."

Felora giggled as she rose to her feet. "Yes, it was, dear husband, but I enjoyed every second of it. I'd drag you back into that bed right now, but Fiona would be disappointed and Andrea would be upset with me. Tonight is her night, and I shouldn't spoil it for her." A devious smile crossed her face. "Maybe I'll just wind her up a little while we work..."

Sean laughed. "You are definitely your mother's daughter. Let's get dressed and go downstairs."

* * *

"Sean, it's good to see you again," Giralt grinned. "Did my wife take yours off to talk?"

"Of course," Sean replied.

"Are you sure you're up for working today?"

"I'm not fully recovered, but good enough to do some work. It'll be okay to get back to the nuts and bolts of things."

"I've been tinkering with rune improvements, since I wasn't sure where you wanted to go next."

"I want to make sure we've killed the overflow problem. I've had a few thoughts on a water erasing rune."

Giralt took a deep drag on his cigar, exhaling slowly before smiling broadly. "Sounds intriguing. Tell me more."

"Putting water into the reservoir is easy. We can just place runes down there, if needed, and that should stop anyone from saying it'll run out. We could use a simple fill rune— one that works when it's not being touched by water— and we'd be good to go. The opposite is still a problem that some people might be worrying about, though... Even with the ice and steam, I've been thinking that it might not be enough to keep it from overflowing."

Giralt set his cigar down and took a sip of the cognac he had on his desk. "Hmm... With more of the faucets being sold every day, I can see where there might still be some concerns. You think a rune will be the solution?"

"Easiest way," Sean said. "Well, easiest to implement, once it's created. Creating one is going to be the tough part."

"Indeed. Runes are not simple to create to start with, and one that is so different from any I've ever heard about?" Giralt shook his head. "But if there is one thing I've learned, it's that you have unique ways of viewing problems. Where do we start?"

"Well, we could try just reversing the rune for creating water, but if it were that simple, someone would've done it already."

"Doesn't work," Giralt said. "No rune works just because you reverse things. It's been tried hundreds or thousands of times."

"Okay, but I'd like to eliminate possibilities, myself. We'll start there, then work on other ways water can be made to change or vanish."

"Heat will change it into steam," Giralt said, picking his cigar back up. "Cold turns it to ice, but I've never heard of water just vanishing."

"True, but if water can come from nothing, then it can be sent back to nothing?" Sean suggested. "We'll try different things, but first, we start from the beginning." Grabbing a small square of copper, Sean began to Shape the rune onto it.

* * *

Sean stretched as he got out of the carriage. "It was nice to do some theory-crafting again."

"I'm glad you had fun with Winston," Fiona said.

"Wasn't fun," Sean replied. "It was frustration given form."

"He had fun," Ryann said, leading them to the door of the Oaken Glen. "He was all smiles, even when he was complaining all the way home."

"We'll just have to accept that he's a crafter at heart," Fiona said.

"Just what I always wanted my husband to be," Ida added.

"Glad I didn't disappoint you, then," Sean chuckled.

Conversation in the inn muted when they entered, but didn't die off. *That might be because the association is sitting in the main room tonight instead of in a private dining room? Or maybe people are finally letting the sensational rumors die,* Sean thought.

"Sean, it's good to see you," Angus Angusson greeted him when they passed the large man.

"Angus," Sean smiled, "how's the wife?"

Angus' grin grew wider. "Best she's ever been, and to top it off, we found out today that she's carrying our next child."

Sean laughed and clapped him on the back. "Grats. I hope they grow up to be as healthy as you and as smart as your wife."

"And as pretty, if they're a girl," Angus laughed. Laughter dying off, he met Sean's eyes. "We thank you. Everything turned around when you showed up. I'm not saying you're the reason, but I believe you are."

Sean grimaced. "We'll be getting the bathhouse up and running again. I don't know what you're doing in the meantime, but just give us a little time?"

Head cocking to the side, Angus stared at him for a few seconds. "Gertihs has us working at the second one right now. You didn't know?"

"Been busy," Sean frowned.

"Aye, I've heard. If you need me for anything, you just say, and I'll be there," Angus said seriously. "My wife says we owe you everything, and I listen to what she tells me."

"I'll keep it in mind," Sean said. "You just keep her happy and your children healthy."

"Aye, that I'll be doing."

"Sorry for disrupting your evening," Sean told the other three men sitting with Angus.

"No trouble," one of them laughed. "We work for the association, all thanks to Angus and you. Best jobs we've had, eh, boys?"

The other two cheered and raised their mugs.

"As Angus said, things have been better since you showed up."

Sean shrugged, aware of everyone nearby listening in. "I'm just me. Nothing special." Ida coughed loudly, and Sean looked at her before correcting himself, "Well, to some, I am." That earned him laughter from the four at the table, and Sean said goodbye before moving further into the inn.

"I'll be over shortly," Ida said.

Sean's brow furrowed as she went to the apprentice table. "What?"

"She's going to join us," Ryann said, then lowered her voice, "She feels bad sitting with them now. They all defer to her as if she's better than them, and it's been wearing on her slowly."

"Oh."

"Sean, it's good to see you," Joseph grinned. "Winston was telling us about your mad plan."

"*Ingenious* plan," Italice corrected the smith. "If he can manage it, there will never be worry about too much or too little water for the city. Our families," she squeezed Ryan's hand, "will be set for easy work for the city and would be able to start pushing out to do more."

"I'm betting on you," Ryan told Sean. "I'd say it was all a fantasy, but with you... with you, anything seems possible."

"The second bathhouse is done," Fiona said, interrupting them before too much could be said. "We'll be starting on the third tomorrow."

"Everything will be in place for it, so you shouldn't have to wait for the supplies," MacLenn said. "Two days, and supplies will start arriving to rebuild the first."

Sean looked at the table and noticed they were missing three. "Where are the Dames, and Saret?"

"Charie was called to task by Lord Sharpeyes today," Fredrick said. "Some homes were starting to smell enough for their neighbors to petition the Lord."

"Ugh," Sean grimaced.

"Mageeyes is with her, I believe," Fredrick continued. "Saret is still with her new concern. I don't know how that's progressing."

"Well, I hope," Eva said. "That whole situation is horrible, and yet none of the nobility even blinked at it." She turned to Sean quickly. "Present company excluded, of course."

"Oh, right. I forget about that," Sean shrugged. "It's all just part of her game. I feel as noble as I did two tendays ago."

"It's one of your charms," Sam smiled.

"Very relatable," Eve Blackhand agreed. "Most would have their noses in the air and look down them at the rest of us."

"But not him," Jefferson chuckled. "Knew I liked him the first time he came into my shop."

"Can I get you something to drink?" Tabitha asked, coming over to the table.

"Cider," Ryann said.

"Just some tea tonight, please," Fiona replied.

"Dark Delight," Sean said.

"Make that two," Ida added, taking the empty seat next to Ryann.

"Joining us now?" Sam asked her daughter.

"Yes. I felt like I was stifling them, and this way, I get to spend some time with you."

Sam gave her daughter a soft smile. "That's very sweet of you."

"I was wondering about the cuons, Sean," Eve said, getting his attention. "Are you going to be getting more of them?"

"I'm not sure. Why?"

"I was thinking I'd like to have one at my home," Eve said. "Just to add some extra security."

"Hmm... I'll ask Aria if Schin has more, or if she knows where we can get some."

"No rush," Eve said. "I was only putting it forward, just in case."

"I'll ask Aria later tonight," Fiona said. "I should have an answer for you tomorrow or the day after."

"Oh. Thank you, Fiona."

11

S ean swallowed, his nervousness high. *Just relax. This isn't any different than the other dozen times you've slept with her,* he tried to tell himself. *Yet... it is... it's completely different. This will change so much... Myna might already be pregnant, though, so this would be the second child.* His internal pep talk calmed his nerves, and he took a cleansing breath before walking into the room.

Andrea sat in the single chair in the room, a glass on the table in front of her. When he entered, she gave him a tentative smile. "I was wondering if you were going to stay late."

"Nope. I had someone waiting for me."

"I was getting worried," Andrea admitted. "What if you didn't really want kids, but didn't want to hurt us by telling us no?"

"I'm a little nervous about the idea of kids, honestly," Sean replied. "Will I be a good dad? Will we be safe enough for them to grow up without fear?"

"You'll be a wonderful father," Andrea said, standing up.

Sean's mouth went dry when he got a clear view of her. The night-gown she was wearing was similar enough to her other one, so he'd thought it was one he'd seen before. It was sheer, letting him get a good idea of her body without her being completely exposed.

"I'm glad you like it," Andrea giggled and walked slowly toward the bed. "I wasn't sure if it was too forward for me."

"You look amazing," Sean said as he followed her.

Glancing over her shoulder, she gave him a sultry smile. "Felora and I worked on it earlier. She can be difficult to work with."

Sean recalled Felora saying she was going to wind Andrea up for tonight, and his mind started to supply a number of ideas of what might've happened. "Yeah," Sean said absently, "she can be intense."

"Oh, yes," Andrea agreed, reaching the bed. Instead of climbing onto it, she turned to face him. "We need to get you stripped first, husband."

Sean came to a stop a few feet from her. "Oh, right. Just give me—"

He never got the chance to finish. Andrea was on him, her soft lips pressing to his, as her tongue slipped into his open mouth. His arms went around her automatically, one sliding around the back of her neck while the other wrapped around her waist. Sean was so intent on meeting her passion with his own that he failed to notice what she was doing. He found out a few seconds later when his pants dropped to his ankles.

Andrea giggled when he broke the kiss in shock. "I told you we need to get you undressed, and no, you won't be doing it. I will."

Sean thought about objecting, but laughed instead. "I'm at your mercy."

"Good," Andrea said as she turned him in a slow circle, then pushed him backward.

Knees hitting the bed, Sean sat abruptly. "Yeah, Felora *definitely* gave you ideas."

Andrea hesitated, uncertainty clear on her face.

"Andie, it's fine. It's different, but it's nice."

The uncertainty vanished and she smiled. "Good. Now, I'll start with the boots that you always try to stop me from removing."

Sean raised one foot slightly. "As you wish."

Andrea knelt in front of him and deftly removed his footwear. His socks were quickly stripped off, followed by his pants. When she slipped his pants free, she looked up at him through her lashes, giving him a heated smile. "I need you to stand for me."

Sean didn't have a lot of room to work with— not with her kneeling in front of him— but he was able to do what she wanted. As soon as he was standing, his underwear was pulled down to his knees, and Andrea gently pushed him back onto the bed.

With no more words spoken, she slipped his underwear completely off. In doing so, she leaned forward and took the tip of his cock into her mouth. Sean's happy inhale made Andrea smile, and she slowly began to bob her head on the first few inches.

Surrendering to what Andrea wanted, Sean let out a moan and leaned back on the bed, resting on his elbows. Using the extra space, Andrea rose onto her knees and put her hands on his thighs before taking more of his hardening length into her mouth.

Moaning again when Andrea's tongue traced the head of his engorged cock, Sean slumped back on the bed. She'd never done that to him before, but he enjoyed the hell out of it and he silently offered a "thank you" to Felora.

Sean was lost in the moment. He wasn't sure how long Andrea had been alternating between taking as much of his length as she could and teasing the head of his cock, but he wanted to return the favor. "Andie, I want to taste you, too," he managed to say.

Her mouth popped free of his rigid shaft and she replied, "Not tonight, Sean. I'm about to do what I truly wanted to do tonight."

Lifting his head off the bed, he saw her stand up, the nightgown slipping from her body to pool at her feet. As she straddled him on the edge of the bed, an odd thought distracted him for a second. *Did she use Shaping to defy gravity?* That thought was pushed aside when Andrea sank onto him.

"Damn, that's amazing," Sean murmured as he pushed off with his legs, shoving them both a little further onto the bed.

Andrea let out a pleased sigh as she sank fully onto him. "Yes, but it always is with you, Sean." She leaned forward enough that she could see him over her breasts. "Just let me set the pace, please?"

"As you wish," Sean replied, his hands going from her hips to her chest. "I'll just give you a helping hand." Thumbs grazing her nipples, he smirked.

"Yes," Andrea agreed and sat upright, beginning to slowly ride him. "I want to make sure I get everything you have to give tonight. Be ready for a long night."

"As long as you need, and as often as you want," Sean replied as his nerves sang with pleasure.

Andrea came often enough that neither of them could keep track, but she made sure he filled her every time he could. Sweat-covered, exhausted, and a little sore, Andrea finally asked him to stop.

Sean cuddled up next to her, being the big spoon to her little spoon. His arm went over her waist and he kissed the back of her neck. "If that didn't work, we'll have to try again."

"Hmm, now I'm not sure if I want to catch the first time or not..." Andrea murmured.

Sean chuckled. "We can always try again in a couple of days, just to be certain."

Andrea nodded, but Sean felt her muscles tense. "Yes." The word was soft and held an edge of sadness.

"Andie?"

"It's fine, Sean."

"You're crying. That isn't fine," Sean said, tightening his arm slightly and kissing her neck again. "What's bothering you?"

"I was just feeling bad for Chas. I know she agreed and encouraged me, but at the same time, I feel bad for her not getting the chance too," Andrea sniffled.

"I understand," Sean said. "I wish she could've had the chance. She'd be upset if you didn't follow your heart, though."

"Yes, she would," Andrea agreed, letting out a small hiccup-laugh. "'Andie, don't be so dense. It's okay.' That's what she'd say."

"Sounds right."

"I'm a mess," Andrea said, sniffling as she tried to regain emotional control. "I'm elated that we're trying for a child, I'm depressed over Chas not being here, I want to kill anyone involved with the fight, and I want to just hide in a cave with our family."

"I get it," Sean said. "I feel the same. We do the best we can. Our loved ones need us to be there for them as they are here for us."

"Okay," Andrea whispered. Turning over, she held him back. "Maybe we can try one more time?"

Sean gave her a soft smile. He leaned in and kissed her gently and with all the love he had.

12

Three days passed by without incident. Fiona and the others managed to shore up both bathhouses, the icehouse, and their home. Sean poured himself into trying to find a water-erasing rune with Giralt, but they hadn't had any luck. His attempt at making small crossbows for the Fairies had been more than successful, though.

Pushing his empty plate away, Sean gave Fiona a smile. "Working on rebuilding the bathhouse today?"

"Yes, that was the plan."

"Sean, we're going to Schin's today, right?" Aria asked.

"Yeah. I told Winston yesterday."

"We've been getting more business the last couple of days," Andrea said.

"Same with the others," Sean nodded. "Denmur and Sharpeyes are losing the war of pressuring us."

"Master, before you go, will you do something for me?" Myna asked.

"Anything."

"Check me with your Flesh Shaping? You see the body differently, and I want to know if I'm pregnant."

"Huh... hadn't thought of that," Sean said and got up. "Sure."

Going over to Myna, he felt every eye on him. He touched her head, closed his eyes, and used his Talent to find out what she wanted to know. He smiled happily when he felt the beginnings of a baby inside of her, then faltered when he remembered something.

"Myna," Sean asked as he stopped his energy, "didn't you have a cycle the morning of us... uh... you know?"

"Yes," Myna nodded. "As it should be."

"Huh?" Sean asked. "But your body shouldn't be ready for a child if you just bled."

"Sean, maybe your old world is different than ours," Fiona said. "Here, women refresh their womb just before they're ready to conceive. It doesn't mean that she will be with child right away. It just means that it's possible."

"Oh, huh... So, you don't have a few days of cramps and bleeding every few tendays?"

All the women looked shocked and disgusted. "No," Fiona said simply. "That's not how this world works."

"Okay. I apologize if my question offended any of you. Outsider, so I know things are different. And Myna, yes, you *are* pregnant."

Her smile grew wide and she nodded. "I'd hoped it was so."

"Uh, I have other uncomfortable questions," Sean said slowly. "Aria, do you think you can answer them for me while we walk?"

"Of course," Aria said, getting to her feet. "That would be for the best."

"We'll see you tonight," Fiona said. "And Sean? Tonight, you're mine."

"Ah, okay. Didn't realize we were going to have as many as possible right now."

"Is that okay?" Fiona asked at his sudden uncertainty.

"It's fine!" Sean blurted. "I'm just getting used to the idea, still. I mean, I want kids, and knowing that Myna is already carrying our first and that Andie is probably also carrying... it's amazing. I just wasn't expecting to have a lot of them all at once, but it makes sense, too."

"Good. We're spreading out some, but we felt it would be good for our children to have siblings they can grow up with."

Ryann's smile faded a little before she made it bright again. Sean caught the slip, and wondered if he could do anything to let her be with the others for this.

"Okay, we all have tasks," Fiona said, getting up. "Ryann, since Aria will be his shield, will you come with us to work?"

"Yeah, I was planning on it," Ryann said. "Sean, be careful. Aria, he's in your care."

"I'll keep our husband safe," Aria said. "I can switch with you once we get back, if you wish."

"No, it's okay," Ryann said. "I don't Shape as often as you all do, so this will be good for me."

"Ladies," Myna said, looking at the cooks and maids, "in an hour, we have our little game. I look forward to your efforts."

Sean wanted to ask what she was planning, but instead, he kissed her head and headed for the door.

Aria and Sean were walking when Aria coughed. "You had other indelicate questions?"

"I don't know about indelicate, but since I'm wrong about other things, I was wondering about the pregnancy stage and birth."

Aria nodded. "Yes, I'd thought so. The child will grow inside the woman for eighteen tendays. She will grow rounder in the belly, will have some emotional outbursts, and possibly want odd foods. Birth is simple, normally. Every woman normally knows a few days before on what day they will give birth to their child. Hot water, clean clothes, and a sharp knife are needed for the event. On rare occasions, something will go wrong, and a healer is needed to help the mother and possibly the child. If a healer isn't available, it's possible to lose the mother, child, or both."

"Six months, not nine," Sean mumbled, suddenly remembering Giralt mentioning the length of time when he asked him to be the guardfather to his child.

"It was different?" Aria asked, looking at the people nearby to make sure no one was eavesdropping on them.

"Twenty-seven tendays, give or take, and it was almost never as straightforward as what you just said. There's a whole profession dedicated to helping with childbirth."

"Hmm... I think this is better," Aria said.

"Undoubtedly," Sean agreed. "I feel bad for Ryann," he said, changing the topic slightly.

"Because she is your shield and has to wait?" Aria asked.

"Yeah. I think it bothers her more than she's letting on."

"That's possible," Aria agreed. "I could offer to become your shield so she may go sooner? I don't mind waiting for a child of my own. It's odd... I hadn't really thought of having children of my own before marrying you. I knew I would eventually, but it wasn't at the forefront of my mind."

"Now it is?"

"With all of them being so eager, I find myself looking forward to it more each day."

"All of them? Even Felora?"

Aria laughed lightly, the sound high and happy. "Oh, dear husband, she is *especially* eager. She might have been even more eager than Myna, but Myna stole the lead on the rest of them. Now, she waits as patiently as she can for her turn. I do hope you're ready for when that day comes. She might not let you get any work done at all."

"Yeah, now that sounds like her," Sean agreed.

* * *

Reaching Schin's farm, Sean grinned when he saw a cuon running around, jumping after a butterfly. "That's a happy one."

"Indeed," Aria laughed.

Her laugh got the attention of the cuon. She stopped jumping after the bug and headed their way at a trot. Coming closer, the cuon chuffed and beelined for Sean.

"Good morning to you, too," Sean said, holding out his hand.

The cuon sniffed his hand before pushing her head into it. Sean chuckled as he gave the big beast a scritch behind the ears.

"I'll go find Schin," Aria said, "since you're occupied right now."

"Sounds good."

The cuon chuffed at Aria and pulled her head reluctantly from Sean's hand. With a shake, she started to trot away, looking back at them.

"We're coming," Sean assured the cuon. "She'll lead us right to him."

"I'm a little envious of that gift," Aria sighed. "To be able to understand them so easily?"

"Wish I could share it," Sean replied.

The cuon led them to the same barn-like building they'd visited last time. Aria opened the door and they entered to find Schin kneeling before a cuon, checking their legs.

"Is something wrong?" Aria asked.

Schin inhaled sharply. "Wish you wouldn't sneak up on me."

"Didn't think we were sneaking," Sean commented.

Schin looked over his shoulder. "You might not have been," he conceded. "I was surprised when Aria asked about more cuons the other day. You need more for your manor?"

"We only have one," Sean said. "The others went to friends to safeguard them."

"Heard you and the Lord were having trouble," Schin said. "You plan on using the hounds against him?"

"No," Sean replied. "I'll be giving these few to more friends. You heard of the bathhouse burning down nearly a tenday ago, right?"

"Yes. Terrible."

"If a cuon had been there, what're the odds that someone using a Talent could've snuck in unseen?"

"Nearly zero," Schin replied. "Cuons are damned good hunters and protectors."

"Exactly. So all my friends are getting a protector to keep them safe."

"You expect more of that?" Schin grimaced.

"No. Those assholes died," Sean shrugged, "but I want to be prepared for anything."

"Smart. I have four, like I told Aria. Three are bad off— I have them sedated and sleeping. This one," he reached back and patted the one he'd been checking, "is okay, except he has a limp I can't figure out."

"We'll handle it," Sean said. "Can you give us some time with them?"

"Yeah, yeah I can," Schin replied, unmoving. "I'd like to see this for myself. You have to have some Shaping Talent, but I've never heard of one that can replace lost limbs."

Sean met the farmer's stare and exhaled slowly. "Everyone who knows that much has taken an Agreement."

"Fine. I'll take it," Schin said.

"It's balanced by your life," Sean said bluntly.

Eyebrows rising, Schin turned to Aria, but instead of talking, his mouth fell open, his eyes locked on her throat. "Bu... wha... huh?"

Aria laughed lightly as she watched his expression. "Yes. It's worth your life, Schin."

"Life Bond..." Schin managed to get out before trailing off. "You were Life Bonded...?"

"Part of the Agreement," Sean said.

Schin tore his eyes away from Aria to look back to Sean, then at the two cuons that were sitting and watching them. "Uh, okay. Aria says it's balanced with a life. I want to hear it."

* * *

Aria was chuckling when they left the farm behind. "His face was priceless."

"His world was turned upside down," Sean said. "I don't blame him."

"Turned upside down?" Aria laughed. "Inside out, is more like it." She gave Sean a happy smile. "And then you gave him even more."

"He helps them," Sean said, motioning to the four cuons

marching along in front of them. "That'll let him help them better, though I do feel bad for what he went through."

"I never knew it could be that bad for someone without energy," Aria said, her mirth fading. "For the staff, it was different, since it wasn't pain, but poor Schin."

"I tried to give as little as possible, too. I think my fine control needs work."

"How would you even do that?" Aria asked.

"Not sure. I can Shape in minute detail, but giving energy is just difficult for me. It feels like a pipe. I can narrow the opening, but I can't seem to narrow it as far as I used to."

"Trying to tap an ocean, one drop at a time," Aria mused.

"Yeah," Sean agreed, then looked off at nothing when a different idea came to him. "Maybe if I separated out energy before giving it to others...? Then I could maybe make it work..."

Aria gave him a sideways glance and shook her head, knowing he was lost in his thoughts.

13

M yna let the staff move onto training blades during sparring. Sean felt bad for them, as she'd not been easy in rebuking them for mistakes. Thankfully, the healing they got from him eased the pain of their fading welts.

Quinna and Quilla had the most difficulty with the training blades, as the wooden blades clearly did not belong in their strong hands. The cooks earned a lot of respect from the others— they moved with grace, and the blades looked natural in their hands. The maids and gardeners were mixed in handling the new weapons.

Helga defeated everyone that went up against her with ease, including Myna. She was even able to push Sean hard before finally beating him, as well. She gave him a bright smile as she helped him back to his feet.

"You are a match for the lesser Einherjar. With more practice, you should be able to hold your own against the captains. Without taking grievous wounds, that is."

"Thanks," Sean said ruefully.

"I think we're going to do a few extra rounds," Myna said. "Every-one, move back. Helga, to the middle. All Talents, minus Flying, are viable. When you face Aria, you may both fly."

Sean stepped back and wondered why she wanted to push this now.

"Sean will go last," Myna added. "The rest of us will line up and fight you in random order. Staff, stay back. You're not even remotely ready for this."

Quilla and Quinna had started to move, but stepped back when she said the last part. Neither of them were happy at being dismissed so lightly, but they knew she wasn't wrong.

Andrea was the first one to step forward to fight Helga. She used Camouflage to give herself a chance, but when Sean saw Helga's eyes glow white, he knew it wasn't going to work. Two seconds later, Andrea was on her butt and rubbing her chin.

"You can use Mage Sight that easily?" Andrea asked.

"Mage Sight? I used my ability to look at souls," Helga replied. "You might mask yourself from sight, but your soul is always where you are."

"Hmm... this might be even more difficult than I'd thought," Fiona said, stepping forward with her staff.

Helga bowed her head to Fiona and set herself to attack. "I will do my best to win, mistress."

"Yes, I know."

The fight lasted marginally longer than their first bout, but only because Helga was taken by surprise when the staff turned into a spear, then a sword, and finally, two smaller blades. In the end, while she might've been wounded, she was never hit in the right spots for a kill. When she understood what Fiona could do, the fight was over quickly.

"Yes. I figured it wouldn't give me an edge for long," Fiona sighed. "Well fought."

"Thank you, mistress," Helga smiled.

Ida sighed as she stepped forward. "My chances are non-existent, but you only fail if you never try."

"No, you can fail," Helga said, "but not trying is horrible."

Ida frowned at her. "You don't understand Sean, not with that attitude." Her weapon changed into a hammer and she picked up a plank, Shaping a quick shield. "I'll make you regret that sentiment."

Sean was surprised at how furiously Ida attacked Helga. *Almost like she was personally insulted. I mean, I don't agree with Helga, but damn, she's mad.*

The sound of training weapons clacking against each other filled the air as everyone watched the fight. Because she had the shield, Ida had given herself enough defense to drag it out a little longer. In the end, Helga just had more experience and got Ida into a bad position. With a grunt, she slammed her shoulder into Ida's shield, shoving it back into the shorter woman and knocking her off balance. With a quick thrust, the fight was over and Ida dropped to the ground, wincing at the impact on her breast.

"Heart thrust," Helga said, bowing her head to Ida. "Thank you for the workout."

Felora helped Ida to her feet. "I'll step in here."

"Give her everything you've got," Ida grumbled as she went over to Ryann, who hugged her.

Felora gave Helga a bright smile and held a spear in her hand. "This will be entertaining."

Helga hefted her sword and waited, understanding that Felora had a trick up her sleeve. "I am ready, mistress."

"Let's begin," Felora said, her eyes glowing red. "Suffer."

With that word, everyone listening felt a twinge of pain. Helga grunted and staggered back, her sword arm dropping. Her eyes flared white and she brought her sword up just in time to deflect Felora's spear from a killing thrust, pushing it out to graze her left arm.

"Pain is momentary," Helga gritted as she pushed back into Felora.

Felora was quick to give her ground, still smiling. "It is, but what of the opposite? Bliss."

Everyone around the pair swayed in place as intense pleasure brushed them. Sean shook his head as he pushed the edge of pleasure off. His eyes widened when he saw Felora on the ground with Helga's blade to her throat, the Valkyrie kissing the Succubus.

"Stop!" Myna shouted.

Helga jerked back and away from Felora. Backing up, she bowed to Sean and his wives. "I apologize. I had not intended to do that."

Felora coughed as she got to her feet. "No, that was my fault. Sean, I'm sorry. Helga, I violated you. I'm deeply sorry."

"I was not violated, mistress. I broke one of the rules of the home, and I apologize for that."

"To be fair, you were forced into that," Sean told Helga. He turned to Felora, who looked ashamed. "Maybe don't use that one on anyone here without consent? And no one outside of those here. Okay, Fel?"

"Yes, Sean."

Fiona moved out and took Felora by the arm, leading her out of the ring. "We all make mistakes. Maybe not as grand as that one, but we do."

Ryann stepped forward, her face grim. "I will not lose."

Helga turned to face Ryann. "I will not lose, either."

Ryann's hand drifted to the wooden throwing knives on her hip. The first came fast, followed by the second, third, and fourth in rapid succession. Helga turned sideways and held her sword out, defending her narrow frame. The sound of the training knives hitting the sword echoed briefly before Helga rushed at Ryann.

Ryann cursed under her breath. Her hand went to her back and one more training blade came flying out. Helga slapped it down with her left hand, hissing in pain as she did.

The clack of wooden swords being crossed lasted for only a moment before Helga backed off. "Your clothing stopped my blade like steel."

"Yeah," Ryann said, breathing hard. "You managed to stop them all."

"Your skill is known to me," Helga said. "One of my sisters has something like it. If you know and prepare to take minor hits, you can survive and have the advantage once they run out. I did not know you had one more at your back. That would have cost me my hand."

"You still would've gotten me even if I hadn't Shaped my clothing."

Helga nodded. "Will you show me how to do that?"

"We will," Fiona said. "Ryann, do you want to yield now?"

Ryann looked at Sean, and he saw the disappointment on her face. "Yes." Dropping her eyes, she moved away from Sean and went over to Ida.

Sean's throat tightened up— he knew that admission hurt her. Aria stepped forward to fight Helga next as Sean worked around the circle toward Ryann. The murmurs from the staff got him to look toward the two fighters.

Aria's golden-brown wings were spread out behind her, and her feet had the talons he recalled. Helga looked uncertain as she looked at her own energy wings. Where her wings had been pristine white before, now they were black at the root, fading through dozens of shades of gray to become brilliant white at the tips.

"My lord?" Helga asked, her eyes wide as she stared at him.

"I don't know, either," Sean said, "but damn, those look awesome. Do they feel normal?"

"Lighter," Helga said as she started to rise off the ground. "They move easily."

Aria shot into the air, a bow in her hand and with a quiver of padded arrows on her hip. The quiver had a spring mechanism built in to bring just a single arrow to the front at a time, similar to a gun's magazine. Aria could draw without a problem no matter where she was in the air— the quiver had a switch, allowing an arrow to be pulled while keeping the others in place.

"Begin," Myna said.

Helga looked up before shooting away at an angle from Aria. The two women climbed into the air, higher and higher. Their energy wings were dim in the dying daylight, but still visible. They both vanished from sight a moment later, and everyone released held breaths.

With the distraction gone, Sean hurried over to Ryann. "Ry?"

"Yes, Sean?" Ryann asked sadly, not looking his way.

"It's okay."

"No, it's not. How can I be your shield if I can be so easily defeated?"

"Easily?" Sean asked, putting his arms around her waist from behind. "I don't think it's easy to have hundreds or more years of battle experience."

"There will be those we have to face who do," Ryann said. "I won't be what you need in those moments."

Gently turning her around, Sean looked directly into her teary eyes. "You'll always be what I need, Ry. You're a wife who loves me and does as much as you can for me. That's more than any man can ask for."

Ryann sniffled and shook her head. "I won't be a good enough shield..."

"Maybe it's time, then," Sean said. "Maybe it's time to put down the shield, Ry, and pick up something else, something you love. Perhaps a child?"

Blinking tears from her eyes, she stared at him. "But who'll protect you, if not me?"

"All of us," Fiona said, having edged over to them. "One of us can and will always be at his side, Ryann. All of us will worry about being the one there, but we will each give everything we can when we are. You love Shaping— I've seen your smile when you do. Maybe you should join me in doing that, and let that love grow?"

"Yes," Myna said softly, her hand resting on her belly. "You should be a part of this, Ry. Do you know why I pushed for this tonight? This display? Aria asked me to. She said she wanted to give you a chance to let her be Sean's shield, so you could carry a child with the rest of us."

Ryann sniffled and looked up just as the glowing aerial battle came back into view. "She wants to be his shield?"

"Yes, but not because she doesn't think you can do the job," Fiona said. "She wants to give you the chance to be with us for the first children. I'll give up my spot tonight, in fact, if you wish to do so."

Ryann looked to Fiona. "No. That isn't fair at all. You deserve it more."

Fiona gave her a loving smile. "But I do like to spoil all of you, and you deserve a bit of extra spoiling." Fiona looked at Sean. "Husband, will you take our darling wife to bed tonight and give her the child she wants, but can't ask for?"

"I'd like that, but only if she wants it," Sean said. "You don't need to have kids with me if you—"

Ryann kissed him hard, her arms tightening around him. Sean held her back, returning the kiss with even more passion. A small cough got their attention and they broke the kiss.

"The fight is over," Felora said, "and I'm happy for you, Ry."

Helga and Aria landed and looked at them. "I was defeated," Aria said lightly.

"Made me work at it," Helga grinned. "So much flying and needing to be aware of what you might try... You would have made an exceptional Valkyrie."

"Thank you, but I prefer to be Sean's wife more," Aria laughed. "Myna, it's your turn."

"I'll pass. She can defeat my best, and I know my Talent will not stop her. Aria, you are now Sean's shield."

"Oh." Aria looked at Ryann, seeing the tears and her sad smile. She moved over and kissed Ryann's wet cheek. "I'll do my very best to be half the shield you are, Ryann. They're big shoes to fill, but for you and our husband, I'll do everything I can."

Ryann giggled as she shook her head. "I know a fib when I hear it. You're a better fighter than I am without question, Aria. My trick is my only strength, but I will work on getting better, and after the child is born, I will take my place once more."

"Very well. I'll make you earn the spot back, so don't get soft while you let me take this important duty."

"I won't."

"It's your turn," Myna said, touching Sean's shoulder. Her voice dropped softer, and she spoke intensely, "Do not lose, Master. She needs to know you can be her match or more."

Sean gave her a look, his voice pitched equally low, "You say that like it's a given that I can."

"You can," Fiona said, her voice brooking no objections.

"Kick her butt," Ryann said, wiping her cheeks dry.

"You can do this, Sean," Aria said.

"Well, fuck. Can't let you all down, can I?" Sean asked as he let go of Ryann.

Sean drew Dark Cutter and made sure the wood was Shaped over the metal. Stepping into the open area with Helga, he took a deep breath. *Okay, you can do this. Just focus and use everything you have at your disposal.*

Helga watched Sean step away from his wives and took a steadying breath. She'd never faced Thor, Odin, or the others while she was in Asgard— they didn't spar with the Einherjar or Valkyries. Sean had faced her repeatedly, but she'd been the victor each time, even winning handily in some cases. *What becomes of me if I overpower that which I am supposed to serve?*

Taking up a stance across from her, Sean closed his eyes and cleared his mind of the doubts and worries. When he opened his eyes, he saw Helga watching him with conflicted emotions reflecting on her face.

The faith of his wives behind him was nearly palpable, and he set his feet. "Helga, this time, I'll win."

Helga squared her own stance. "I take no joy in defeating you."

With that said, she rushed him, intent on beating him quickly. Sean shifted a foot fractionally and waited for her to come closer. Just as she closed, he brought Dark Cutter out. Helga grimaced and went to bat the sword to the side with her own blade, but his sword was no longer there. He had Shaped it into a dagger.

Stepping in, he stabbed at her gut, hoping to end it. Helga managed to get her unarmed hand down to knock his attack away, taking what should've been a bad cut. She kicked out and knocked him back, springing away while she shook her hand.

"As I showed Fiona, those tricks don't work well in the long run," Helga said tightly.

"I know," Sean replied evenly just before he vanished.

Eyes glowing white, she shook her head. *Did you not learn from the others?* Tracking his glowing soul, she turned with him as he went wide. She frowned when he didn't move toward her, instead, just circling. When he suddenly stopped and touched the ground, her head canted sideways fractionally before she leapt into the air, her new wings taking her high above the small pit that'd opened under her feet.

"That would never have done much to me," Helga shouted down at him, her disappointment growing.

Sean reappeared and he wore a small smile. "I know."

Wings of brilliant white energy appeared behind Sean, and Helga's breath caught in her throat. His wings were more majestic than any she'd ever seen in Asgard, and they glowed with the purity of his soul. Helga was shocked when he launched off the ground, faster than she'd expected. Barely managing to deflect his attack, she spun away and tried to gain distance on him.

"Too slow!" Sean said as he dived down at her.

Helga's heart hammered as she spun, a dull pain hitting her in the side as she did. *So fast, but how? Even Aria, who was born to fly like I am, could not fly like this.* Helga tried to use nearby buildings to gain distance. Glancing back, Sean was still right on her heels, and her heart began to soar along with her.

Helga soon realized that while Sean could outfly her, he was still not her match in combat, especially in the air. The next two clashes left her untouched and with Sean flexing his foot where her sword had clipped it.

As they came close again, Helga's eyes snapped shut and she turned to the side as fire engulfed the very air in front of her. Face blistering, she wasn't prepared for Sean to grab her arms and wrap his legs around her.

"I can do that again, and at this distance, you'd burn badly," he whispered in her ear. "Give up."

Helga exhaled, her heart pounding as his breath tickled her ear. "My lord, it's improper to grab a woman from behind," she said before dismissing her wings and twisting.

Unprepared for her sudden weight, his grip loosened and Helga was able to slip out of his grasp. Her wings reappeared a second later as she flew backward, her sword coming out between them.

"It was stupid to not use your blade when you could have," Helga said angrily. "You should have just ended it."

"Maybe, but I didn't know if your wings fail if you drop unconscious."

Looking down to see how high they were, Helga missed the moment his arm moved. She looked up just in time to catch a wooden throwing blade in the throat. Gagging, she clutched at her neck, as the wooden knife had been thrown hard enough to crush her larynx. Wings vanishing as she started to fall, she tried to get her throat to heal enough to breathe.

Sean caught her as she fell and floated them both down to the yard. He gave his wives a grin as he landed, and they all gave him broad smiles back. Looking down, Helga was staring up at him, since he had her in a princess carry. Her eyes shone now— not with confliction, but with happiness.

"Told you I'd win," Sean said.

"As it should be," Helga breathed as he set her on her feet.

"It's time for our bath," Myna said. "Dinner will be late, otherwise."

"Sean," Helga asked, "when did you get a throwing blade?"

"When I Camouflaged and circled you. I knew you'd be waiting for a trick, but thought you might miss me pulling the knife out if I gave you something else to focus on, hence the ground." Sean looked over to see the ground was fine. "And thanks for fixing that."

"You're welcome," Andrea said. "Will you wash my back?"

"Gladly," Sean said.

Helga watched them all go, her gaze thoughtful. She was snapped out of her introspection by Aria, who touched her shoulder. "Hmm?"

"Will you get my back?" Aria asked.

"If you return the favor."

"Gladly," Aria said. "Tomorrow, if you would be willing to help me learn how to better use a sword, I'd be grateful."

14

S ean looked at Aria beside him as the carriage rolled down the road. "You haven't come with me before."

"I have not," Aria replied, "but that will change tomorrow."

Sean frowned before her meaning sunk in. "Oh, shit."

"I'm glad to see you are sorry for neglecting me," Aria said.

"Why didn't you...? No, never mind. This is my fault."

"I was hesitant to ask. After losing Chastity and Lilly, it just didn't feel right, and then with the talk of children, I grew hesitant again, as they've all been waiting. Fiona approached me last night and asked if I was holding back. When I explained, she just hugged me and told me I'd have you tomorrow. Everyone else apologized. They felt bad for not thinking about us being able to consummate our marriage."

"I still feel like shit," Sean said, covering her hand with his. "We need to have your wedding feast, as well. I mean, what kind of dick forgets his own wife?"

She gave him a soft smile. "The one who just lost two other wives and is trying to console the rest. It made me happy to know that you feel that deeply for all of us, even if I was a little upset that I was forgotten. And, before you say something even more stupid, tonight is Ryann's night, so don't even think about it."

Sean clamped his mouth shut. "I must be glass. You all see right through me."

"Decorative glass," Aria giggled.

"Stained glass?"

"No, you are simple to see through, remember? Not even frosted."

Leaning over, he kissed her. Aria let out a happy sound as she returned the kiss.

The carriage slowing down got their attention and Sean coughed. "First, we see the association, then we head home."

"Yes."

Aria preceded Sean out of the carriage and into the inn. She gave the room a hard glare, which made a few people look away from her. The association table was surprised to see her, but not as surprised as Sean was to see Cartha, the woman who had been Dame Loplis, sitting with the apprentices.

"Evening," Sean said as he sat Aria, then himself.

Mageeyes stared at Aria. "Aria, it is good to see you."

"Amedee," Aria smiled, "thank you for having me." She gave the others smiles and nods, even though they looked at her in shock. "Is there a problem?"

"You're... you're not Life Bonded?" Saret asked. "I would have sworn that you had the markings."

Sean snorted. "Oh, yeah. None of you mentioned it the last few days... probably haven't noticed it since Ry's been wearing high-necked shirts because of the chill."

All eyes went to Sean.

"Hang on," he said as Tabitha came over. "Dark Delight for me, and...?"

Aria grinned. "Cider. Hot, please."

"Ryann drinks those," Sean said.

"I know. It's something we have in common," Aria replied.

"Be right back. Does anyone need refills?"

Once everyone had asked for what they needed, Tabitha left and

Sean lowered his voice, "All of their Life Bonds are still in place, but they've changed."

Aria extended her hand so the band on her ring finger was easy to see.

"How did that happen?" Mageeyes asked.

"They Soul Bonded with me. Unlike Helga's giant bands, their Bonds changed to this. That's all I know."

Mageeyes pursed her lips, clearly giving it some thought, but Joseph just laughed. "That's Sean. He just *does* things."

"True," Fredrick said.

"Most of the time," Giralt agreed. "We're almost there for the rune."

Sean nodded. "Feels like it, right?"

"Your drinks," Tabitha said, dropping off beverages.

"Saret," Sean said after taking a swig, "welcome back. How is she?"

Saret looked at Cartha and smiled sadly. "Doing better. We had a lot to break down before we could build her back up. I'd forgotten just how twisted most of the nobility is. All she cared about was finding a powerful noble to wed— that's what her father had drilled into her since she could remember. Now, she has a goal of her own."

"Oh?"

"To run a successful business," Saret said fondly. "She wants to be known as someone who succeeded."

"Isn't that what we all want?" MacLenn asked.

"No," Flamehair snorted. "Not someone of station." The last word had a bitter edge to it.

"How're you?" Eve asked her. "It's been a few days since we've seen you."

Flamehair sighed. "I've been ordered, by my own family, to service those I cut off. It appears that Lord Sharpeyes sent them a message. I'm sorry I can't continue to do as I have."

"We understand," Sean said. "Once we grow stronger, your family will relent, right?"

Flamehair nodded. "Yes. The rumors of what's being produced

are just starting to spread in Westpoint. I believe Madam Archlet is behind that."

"I met her once," Sean said. "Is she trustworthy?"

"Hmm... yes. She can be trusted to serve her own ends, but she adores making friends with any who are loyal. Having her on our side could help," Mageeyes said. "I'll approach her in the next few days."

"That'd be good," MacLenn chuckled. "She has a long reach, and people listen when she talks."

"Sounds—" Sean began when the door of the inn opened loudly and an angry-looking man strode in.

"Where is the ungrateful wench?!" the man bellowed as he scanned the room.

Mageeyes rose to her feet, her voice cold, "Knight Loplis, this is a peaceful est—"

"Be silent!" Lavan Loplis cut her off. "I'm here for her." He pointed at his daughter.

"Here for my Life Bonded?" Saret asked standing up.

"Tramp! You're not nobility," Loplis sneered. "I'll pay the fine once I take her head."

"Like fucking hell," Sean said, his chair sliding back as he got up and turned to face the knight. "You've just insulted a Dame in my presence and threatened a friend. The only head that's going to end up on the floor tonight is yours, unless you apologize."

Loplis snarled at Sean, "*Aspirant.* You were given the lowest rank for licking Lady Sharpeyes' boots. You'll regret crossing the *truly* powerful."

"Insulting myself and Lady Sharpeyes, as well?" Sean tsked. "A fine reason for a duel. Mageeyes, I apologize for the violence that is about to happen. Knight Flaccid, I challenge you."

Loplis' nostrils flared, and his hand went to his sword hilt as a cruel smile touched his lips. "As he thought. Accepted. Swords, no champions, and outside, right now."

Aria sighed and shook her head. "Ryann is going to have my head for this..."

Sean touched her shoulder, giving her a smile. "I'll be fine, but come watch. If she gets angry, it's *my* fault for issuing the challenge, not yours."

"Is there a problem?" a guard asked, poking his head into the room.

Sean recognized the guard as the one who gave testimony during the party and nodded. *Of course, they set me up.* "Amedee, can you send for one of the Carmady brothers? I'd rather have a guard of integrity on hand."

Three silver blurs left the room in a flash and Sean chuckled. "Thank you, Ven."

Ven dropped down to the table behind Sean. "Of course, sir. We have scores to settle, ourselves."

"Let's go," Loplis sneered.

"Sure, as soon as I finish my ale," Sean said. He picked up his mug and took a sip. "Are you sure you don't want one last drink? I'd hate to kill you without giving you a last request."

Loplis glared at him. "Are you refusing to have the duel as stated?"

"Not at all," Sean said. "I'm just being civil. A drink before dying seems like something the nobility would do."

A few awkward chuckles filled the room, and Sean tipped his mug at them. Loplis was turning red in the face as he continued to glare at Sean.

"Coward!" Loplis snapped.

A single female laugh filled the room, and all eyes went to Cartha. "Coward? You would call another a coward? That is the funniest thing I've ever heard, Lavan," she laughed.

Loplis turned his hate-filled eyes to Cartha. "Quiet, you!"

"Or *what*? I'm not your daughter anymore, now am I? She was killed in court, by your own hand," Cartha said with a smile. "Now, I am Cartha Somnia, a practical woman who has dreams and aspirations, not a mindless puppet to do your or Evan's bidding. You were happy to whore me out to him to maybe raise your own station. Now that he is dead, what will you do? Do you whore yourself to the Lord?"

Loplis had grown whiter and whiter during her speech, but when she finished, he snapped and rushed her. He'd made it two steps before Sean's now-empty mug broke his nose and sent him to the ground. Everyone in the room looked at Sean.

"Hmm, seems my drink ran out," Sean sighed. "Guess I can't wait any longer. You ready, Flaccid?"

Loplis shook his head, trying to clear it, as he staggered back to his feet. His broken nose was mending as Sean watched. "I'll gut you and hang you by your own entrails!"

Self-healing? Good to know, Sean thought. *This might be a little trickier, but I doubt his head coming off will help him with that.*

"*What* is going on here?!" a commanding voice boomed, coming from behind the guard in the doorway, who'd watched the whole thing.

"Sergeant, sir," Guard Wolen said, giving Sergeant Carmady a salute. "I just witnessed an assault, sir."

"Oh?"

Loplis snarled. "Be quiet, you idiot."

Wolen's mouth snapped shut, and he looked away from Carmady.

Carmady gave Wolen a disapproving look. "Return to your station, and I'll be along to speak with you later."

"Sir," Wolen said tightly before he left.

"Now, what is going on that I was summoned by a Messenger Fairy?"

"Sergeant," Mageeyes spoke up, "there is about to be a duel outside. A neutral party was needed to officiate."

Carmady gave Loplis and Sean a level look. "The guard is not to be summoned to settle your disputes. However, since I am here, I will do as the Dame has asked. What are the rules?"

"Swords, outside, and no champions," Loplis said tightly. "Myself and... that person."

"MacDougal," Carmady sighed. "I think the commander is right. Trouble follows you."

Sean shrugged. "People should stop messing with my friends when I'm present."

"Are you both ready?" Carmady asked.

Loplis just sniffed and walked out. Sean gave his friends an apologetic shrug and followed him. As he was reaching the door, the sound of people getting up filled the room, and everyone went for the windows and doors to watch.

Aria walked out of the inn, followed by the entire association, and Carmady gave them a level look before pointing at them. "Stop there. If any of you interfere with a legal duel, I will come down hard on you."

"We only want to make sure that the duel is fair. We know you will be, but this whole thing feels contrived," she said.

Carmady looked thoughtful for a second, then blew his whistle. After a couple of seconds, other whistles replied, and Carmady gave a return blast. Nodding, he gave Loplis and Sean a hard look. "We will do this in just a moment. First, let me see your swords."

Loplis scowled, but produced the sword he planned on using, making Sean laugh. Carmady leaned back from the blade, as the fire coming off it was hot.

"Using Lord Sharpeyes' sword?" Sean asked. "Don't trust your own sword to get the job done?"

Loplis snarled, "I'm using the best tool to get the job done!"

Sean drew Dark Cutter and held it out to Carmady. "Be nice," he said.

Carmady gave him a strange look, then took the sword, his eyes growing wide at the metal of the blade. "Adamantine?"

"Yes."

Carmady handed the sword back. "Expensive. My brother mentioned it when he arrested you, but it was hard to believe."

"It was a gift," Sean said sadly. "The price was much too high."

Several guards came jogging down the streets toward the inn, and Carmady nodded. "Excuse me, gentlemen."

Sean moved back and waited. Mageeyes gave the sword a long look before her eyes went wide. Saret and Flamehair both saw her reaction and gave her questioning looks, but she just shook her head and glanced at the onlookers. Saret frowned and squinted at Sean before her eyes went wide, too.

Sean gave them a knowing look, then turned toward Carmady again, who was coming back. "I'm ready, Sergeant."

"Good. My men have secured the square. Anything inside of them is fair for the duel. Is this to blood or—?"

"Death!" Loplis snarled.

Sean shrugged. "Sure."

Carmady shook his head. "The paperwork..." he sighed. "Very well. Go take your starting places. Do *not* attack until I call for it."

Loplis moved back ten feet and brought his sword up in front of him. Sean looked at the inn, then moved around Loplis to stand with his back toward the crafter hall. Making sure no one was behind him, Sean nodded.

Carmady gave both men a few seconds, then cleared his throat. "A duel to the death. Begin."

Loplis slashed with the sword and a wave of fire flew out from it. Sean brought Dark Cutter up and swung it around. The fire wrapped around the blade and he flung it up, giving Loplis a shake of his head.

Loplis glared and growled, "No? Fine! I'll use the other."

Sean wondered what he was referencing, but he had his answer when Loplis let out a grunt of pain. His clothing started bursting off him as his body grew larger, and Sean took a step back, the image of Whelan coming to him.

"Troll!" someone shouted.

Sean took a deep breath and he adjusted his stance. "You think I can't take you because of your Trollish Talent?"

"I'll pull you apart!" Loplis snarled as he advanced.

Sean smiled and rushed forward to meet the giant man. Loplis swung down hard to bisect Sean, but he just caught the flaming sword with his own, directing the attack to land beside him. Loplis was shocked that Sean had deflected the blow, and his shock grew when Sean slammed Dark Cutter into his chest.

Gurgling, Loplis dropped the flaming sword and staggered back, clutching at the blade buried in him. The fire went out the moment it left his hand, but when Sean caught the falling sword, the flame reignited. With a grin, he brought it around and removed the hand

Loplis had used to grab Dark Cutter. The wound was cauterized instantly, and Loplis' pain-filled bellow made windows rattle.

Sean moved smoothly, hamstringing the Knight. As Loplis toppled to the ground, Sean darted around and, with a hard swing, tried to take the man's head off. The sword bit deep but didn't sever his head, making Sean chop at his neck twice more. As the head rolled over to Carmady's feet, Sean snorted and dropped the flaming sword to the ground. Pushing the body over, he yanked Dark Cutter free and cleaned it on the tattered remnants of Loplis' outfit.

Sheathing his sword, he turned to Carmady. "We good?" Carmady just stared at him. Sean waited, then coughed loudly. "Ernest?"

Carmady shook his head. "What? Yes... uh... this duel is over."

"Thank you. Sorry about the paperwork."

"Right..." Carmady said, still shocked as he looked back at Loplis' head.

"Shall we step into a private room?" Sean asked Mageeyes. "I'm sure you have questions."

"Yes. Please," Mageeyes said.

15

"Sean?"

Sean jolted upright, breathing fast. It took him a moment to recognize where he was. "Oh. I'm sorry, Ry. Nightmare."

"We realized," Ida said from his other side. "Are you okay?"

Sean took a shuddering breath. "Yeah. Last night was just a bit much."

His wives exchanged a look before Ryann said, "You're not talking about us, are you?"

"No. It was at the inn," Sean said. "I was going to tell everyone at breakfast. You two were a wonderful surprise."

"It just felt right for us both to be together for it," Ida said. "We were happy you didn't object."

"Not that we expected you would," Ryann smiled.

"I'll rarely tell any of you 'no.' If you both want to try having a child at the same time, I'm fine with that."

"Thank you," Ida said, kissing his cheek and climbing out of bed.

"Yes, thank you. Now, tell us what happened?"

"Ry, he'll tell all of us if we just get up and go to breakfast," Ida told her.

"Fine," Ryann sighed, getting out of bed.

"Speaking of breakfast," Sean said, "there's another thing that needs to be discussed, then, too."

"Aria?" Ida asked.

"Yeah. I felt like an ass when she brought it up."

"It's partially our fault," Ryann said. "We all wanted to comfort you, Andrea, and Felora, and then children were brought up."

"Yeah. She's not mad," Sean said, sliding out of bed, "but I'm going to do what should've been done already."

"Good," Ida smiled, already dressed. "I'll go let them know we're up and moving."

"Thanks," Sean called after her.

* * *

Taking his seat at the table, Sean noticed that Aria was on his right. "Morning, Aria."

"Morning, Sean." Her smile was bright.

"As soon as the cooks serve us," he told her.

As if his words were a summoning charm, Glorina, Lona, and Mona came into the room with the meal. The three cooks wore their own bright smiles as they deftly served everyone. "Breakfast, since today is a special day, is a fruit pancake. There will be no syrup, as the topping is a fruit compote."

Sean looked at the stack of six pancakes, covered in a multi-berry topping, on his plate. "Didn't skimp at all."

"We know you have a big appetite, sir," Glorina said, a hint of laughter lurking in her words.

"Yes, he does," Felora snickered.

"Felora..." Fiona sighed.

"I didn't start it," Felora was quick to defend herself. "I am what I am. Some things are hard to resist."

"I apologize," Glorina told Fiona as she put a plate before her. "It was inappropriate of me."

"It's fine," Sean said. "I barely even blushed that time."

"A pity," Myna said. "You turn a lovely shade of red, normally."

"With everyone here," Sean said, "there are a few things that need to be talked about. First off, we will have our wedding feast for Aria tonight. It's been delayed and I don't want it put off any longer."

"I understand and agree," Fiona said. "I'm glad to wait so you can welcome our wife properly."

Aria gave Fiona a soft smile. "Thank you, Fiona."

"I know it must have hurt you to see us clamoring to have him to ourselves."

Aria shook her head. "No, I understand. It's why I offered to take Ryann's place as his shield for now. I'm fine with waiting for that moment, but being fully welcomed as his wife is something I truly wished for."

Ryann looked down at the table. "Thank you, Aria. It was hard to let go of what I thought of as my place. Knowing that he wants to have a child with me makes it worth it."

"Glorina, can you put together a feast for tonight?"

"Yes, sir. Will there be any extra guests, or just family?"

Sean looked to Aria. "Did you want to have someone come?"

Aria looked thoughtful for a second. "Maybe one person. I'll send them a message and let Glorina know."

"Okay," Sean said, but his smile slipped and he looked at everyone at the table. "The second topic isn't pleasant at all. Last night, I ended up in a duel, and Ry, champions weren't allowed," he added quickly when Ryann's head snapped up.

"That was the nightmare?" Ryann asked.

"Yes. I killed Knight Loplis last night," Sean said. Taking a deep breath, he tried to shove the emotional turmoil down. "He came into the Oaken Glen, looking for his daughter. Turns out that it was mostly a ruse to trap me into a duel."

Myna snorted. "He caught a tiger by the tail."

"I think there was supposed to be more to it," Sean said, giving Myna a bemused look at her expression. "He had the same guard who'd testified at the party there to act as proctor. Luckily, Amedee sent for one of the Carmady brothers. If there was supposed to be an extra twist to the duel, it never happened."

"How did you kill him?" Helga asked.

Sean gave a brief retelling of his duel with Loplis. His voice was even as he spoke, but it was also flat and devoid of emotion. The range of reactions to his story was wide— Myna looked smug, Helga smiled happily, Quinna and Quilla were impressed, Rosa looked horrified, and Ryann was upset.

"Trolls-blood," Ida said. "A talent he must've gotten from someone."

"Reminds me of Whelan," Fiona said.

"Me, too. Velin was behind that, so I think that Knight Solanice was behind this," Sean said.

"Which means Truestrike," Myna said with a feral smile. "We have more to pay back yet."

Sean met her eyes and nodded. "Yes, but first, we have other, closer problems to deal with."

"Denmur, Sharpeyes, and Solanice," Fiona agreed. "I doubt they'll try that same tactic again. This is twice you've killed a knight in a duel."

"Which means they'll try something different," Sean nodded. "We all need to be aware of that."

"Sean, do you want my help?" Felora asked, seeing the strain in his eyes as he told of the duel.

"It would be welcome," Sean admitted.

"After breakfast, before you go to Winston's?"

"That works," Sean said, picking up his fork. He hadn't had a bite of food yet, while the others were at least half-finished. "Breakfast first."

* * *

Giralt looked up from the workbench when the door to his shop opened. "Sean, I thought you weren't coming today."

"Sorry, I had a few things to take care of first. I should've sent a message, but I didn't think about it."

"It's quite alright," Giralt said, putting his cigar down. "I was sure you'd miss today, because of last night."

Sean shrugged. "That wouldn't stop me."

"I noticed," Giralt said. "You slew a knight in a duel while he was using Trolls-blood. At the time, I was shocked at what happened, but once you explained your sword, it made more sense. May I?"

Pulling Dark Cutter out, Sean set it on the desk. "It doesn't like others using it, so I wouldn't recommend picking it up."

"I just want to see the famed blade of Darragh Axehand. The fact you can Shape it is even more amazing."

Sean reached out and Shaped it back into the axe-shape it'd had been when he'd first picked it up. "There you go. As for Shaping it, half of that is Dark Cutter agreeing to do so. There's a consciousness in there."

Giralt's eyebrows shot up and he took a drink of cognac. "Hmm... The rumors might be true, then."

"Rumors?"

"That the enchanter was sucked into the weapon when he enchanted it. It was the only time adamantine was ever enchanted. Everyone else stays well away from trying to do so now."

"Doesn't feel like that," Sean said, taking a seat. "It's more like it gained sentience when it was enchanted. It recalls everyone who it thought of as its owner. If it was that enchanter, I don't think it would view itself that way."

Giralt picked his cigar back up and puffed on it. "That's a good point. Thank you for letting me see it, and thank you, as well, Dark Cutter."

Sean reached over and picked the axe up. It reshaped itself back into the sword, and Sean sheathed it again. "Back to work on this new rune."

"Yes. I must say, this is proving quite frustrating. The concept is so simple, and yet it's so difficult."

"If there was just an easy way to drain the water off, it—" Sean cut off, his face blank.

Giralt sat back, shaking his head, and waited.

"Are you *fucking* shitting me?" Sean breathed out a few minutes later. "It can't be that damn simple."

"I don't know. You haven't explained."

Blinking, Sean looked at Giralt and sighed. "Drain. Why don't we just drain it?"

"To where?" Giralt asked.

"Where did the extra water come from, to begin with?" Sean asked.

Giralt paused, taking a minute to consider it as he smoked. "That's an intriguing question. The theories around how and why the world allows items to be created from nothing is a topic of debate in the halls of knowledge."

Sean got to his feet, going to the mocked-up reservoir they'd made. "Okay, how do I imagine a rune like this looking?"

* * *

"It was so nice of you to come," Clara was telling Aria as she opened the workshop door. "I wish Ryann the very best on her pregnancy. Are you two done in here?"

Giralt wore a large smile. "Ah, there she is. The light of my life."

"Having a good day, dear?" Clara laughed.

"We figured it out," Sean said from next to the model. "Finally."

"I can't wait to see Ryan and Italice's faces tonight," Giralt laughed.

"Agreed," Sean said as he got to his feet. "Winston, do you mind if I register this one?"

Giralt blinked. "Of course not. You've let me register all the others."

"Thanks," Sean said. "I need to do what I never wanted to do—putting myself out into the public."

"You were already there," Clara said. "The duel with Evan saw to that."

"Yeah."

"Are we going to do that before going home?" Aria asked.

"Yes. Ven, can you let them know we'll be delayed a little?"

"Already sent, sir," Ven said from the rafters of the room.

"Sean, thank you for bringing Aria to keep me company, and congratulations on all the children in your future."

"Thank you, Clara. Oh, Winston, I'll be missing the meeting tonight. Would you tell the others, please?"

"I can, but what're you going to be doing, instead?"

"Welcoming my wife with her feast," Sean said, taking Aria's hand. "Good night."

* * *

"MacDougal, how can we help you today?" Agatha asked.

"I need to patent a rune," Sean said. "I see the hair clip is still being used."

Agatha touched the clip in her hair. "Yes, thank you. I'll go see if Gertihs is in. Pardon me."

Sean and Aria went to the side of the room so others could get to the reception desk if they came in. They didn't wait long, though, as Agatha was heading back to them with quick steps.

"He's ready for you."

"Thank you," Sean replied, returning her smile.

Reaching the right door, Sean knocked before entering with Aria. "Evening, Jackson."

"Sean," Jackson Gertihs smiled. "It's odd using the familiar name, but my brother did impress upon me that you prefer that."

"It's just the way I am," Sean said. "I have a new rune to be patented. Forged Bonds is to have full use of it."

"Of course. Can you show me the rune and how it works?"

Sean placed a copper disc on the desk. The single quartz in the center gleamed dully in the lamplight. "It removes water. If you get a bucket of water, it'll be easy enough to show you."

Jackson had a staff member bring some water and Sean demonstrated how the rune worked. Jackson looked impressed as he pulled down a tome and leafed through it. After he'd gone through the whole thing, he got to a blank page.

"Very well, I'll register it. I'm surprised to see you, though. You've gone out of your way to stay out of the records as much as possible."

"You haven't heard about the last duel, have you?" Sean asked.

"Your duel with Evan Sharpeyes is the talk of the town still," Jackson said.

"I meant the one last night in the square outside this building."

Jackson glanced up before he focused on his task. "I saw the blackened cobbles and heard that a duel had taken place, but that was all."

"I'm sure that more about it will make the rounds tonight."

"I'll have to keep my ears open, then," Jackson said. "All done."

"How much is it to register a rune again?" Sean asked, reaching for his pouch.

"For you? Nothing. My brother made sure that Forged Bonds pays for any rune they have the right to use. This will cost you nothing."

"I'll have to thank him," Sean said, getting to his feet. "Thank you."

"My pleasure," Jackson said, shaking hands with Sean and giving Aria a bow of his head. "I hope you have a good night."

"We will," Aria smiled.

"Time to get home for dinner," Sean said. "Probably missed all of the sparring."

"Yes, but a missed night isn't horrible," Aria said as they were leaving.

"True. It's dinner and later tonight that are important."

"Agreed," Aria grinned.

16

"You won't even give me a hint?" Sean asked, sitting with Aria in the front room to wait for her one guest to show up.

"No. It's a surprise," Aria replied.

The jangle of harnesses and the crunch of wheels on cobbles caught Sean's ear, and he stood up. "Well, the surprise is over. I hear a carriage coming up the drive."

Aria stood and placed her hand on his chest. "Please wait here, husband. I will bring them inside."

"As my wife wishes," Sean said with a theatrical sigh.

Aria shook her head. "So put upon."

Sean didn't sit down, as he knew he'd have to stand again to greet the guest momentarily. Listening intently, he caught the muffled voice of someone greeting Aria, but the voice was masculine. *Is it a family member?* Sean wondered. *She hasn't really talked about her family.* The door opening caught him by surprise, as he hadn't heard anything past that one muffled greeting.

Blinking, Sean coughed to recover from his shock. "Lady Sharpeyes. It's an honor and pleasure to have you in our home."

Lady Sharpeyes gave him a smile. "It is my honor to be invited. Some might question me for coming to the home of my son's killer, but my friend invited me to her wedding feast and it would be rude not to attend."

Sean's jaw clenched at the mention of him killing Evan. "We lost two of our wives during that fight."

Lady Sharpeyes held up a hand. "I understand and sympathize, Sean. I was not meaning to cause distress. I only mention how some will view my being here."

Aria went to stand by Sean's side. "We understand, Lady. Thank you for coming."

"Won't this further divide you and your husband?" Sean asked.

"Hmm, yes," Lady Sharpeyes replied with a bright smile. "Do you mind if my maid attends as my servant?"

Sean's eyes went to the open door where Nola was waiting, coiled on her tail. "Nola, it's good to see you again. You're welcome in my home as a guest and a friend," Sean greeted her in Naga.

"I am honored, Sean MacDougal. I shall call you friend and treasure that you invited me with such grace," Nola replied. She came through the door and shut it before going to rest behind Lady Sharpeyes.

"Not many know their tongue," Lady Sharpeyes said. "The only other person that I know of was Darragh Axehand."

"He was a good man," Sean said.

"One of the better men who ever stood near society," Lady Sharpeyes agreed. "He might have become an Aspirant himself, but he had a habit of being too blunt to the people who might have spoken for him."

"I knew I liked him."

Lady Sharpeyes laughed. "Yes, you did have that in common. Since I am here as a friend of your wife, please, call me Saranita. For tonight, at least."

"That's quite the honor," Fiona said, coming into the room. "Welcome to our home, Saranita. Dinner is just about ready. Would you please follow me?"

"Of course," Lady Sharpeyes replied.

"Nola, would you like to join us at the table?" Sean asked.

Nola's tail quivered and she shook her head. "I am my Lady'sss maid. It would be improp—"

"Nola, you may have the next few hours off," Lady Sharpeyes said, cutting her off. "I have heard that Sean and his family usually treat their staff as family, letting them eat meals with them. If he invites you, it is your decision, since you are off-duty."

"The other ssservantsss will be there?" Nola asked.

"Yes," Aria said, "as they are family in their own way."

"I accept," Nola said, bowing deeply to Aria and Sean. "I regret that I did not bring a gift."

"Your presence is a gift enough," Sean said, giving her a smile. "Shall I show you the way?"

"Pleassse," Nola replied.

Entering the dining room, Fiona led Lady Sharpeyes in first, and conversation in the room cut off abruptly. "Our guests tonight are Lady Saranita Sharpeyes and Nola...?" Fiona trailed off, looking at Sean in the doorway.

Sean gave Nola a questioning look and she just shook her head. "My people do not have sssurnamesss."

"And Nola," Fiona said.

Lady Sharpeyes smiled, taking note of the tight expressions worn by Sean's wives and the fearful looks from the staff. "Tonight, please call me Saranita, as that is the custom of the house. Do not think you have to stand on formality, either."

"Surprised that it's you," Ryann said tightly. "If our wife invited you, we'll do our best."

Andrea got to her feet and stared at Lady Sharpeyes directly. "My Chas would've welcomed you with a smile and been as gracious as she always was. Since she can't be here, I will do my best in her stead."

Lady Sharpeyes bowed her head fractionally. "Which is more than I should get. Your wife was a very understanding and gracious woman, if she was so kind."

"Your seat will be here," Fiona said, leading her around the table to sit beside Aria.

Sean entered the room then, with Nola following him in. A sharp inhale got him to look at Rosa, who'd turned a little pale. "Nola, this is my family. You've met my wives previously. The staff are also family." He introduced them one by one before showing her to a seat beside Tiska. He quickly Shaped the chair into something Nola could use more comfortably.

Nola was silent as Sean Shaped for her, but her tongue flickered a few times. When he finished, she bobbed her neck before speaking in her native tongue, "My thanks, Shaper. Few think of my kind's needs."

"Darragh had a lover named Misa. She was a Lesser Naga, as well. She was a kind soul who helped me when I first met them. To have met and befriended two of you is a blessing to me."

Nola's tongue flickered again. "Thank you."

"Sean, if you'll sit, we can begin," Fiona said.

"Oh, sorry," Sean said, going to his seat. Once he was seated, he used the bell pull. "Let the feast begin."

A minute later, Glorina led Lona and Mona into the room, each pushing a cart that was fully laden with food and bottles. Glorina pushed her cart to the head of the table and began to set out the serving dishes. "We have a wide variety of foods for tonight. First, we have…" Her voice trailed off when she saw who their guest was.

"I'm just a guest," Lady Sharpeyes said with a smile. "Please, continue."

"Glorina, it's okay," Sean said, touching her arm. "Treat her like you would Amedee."

Glorina cleared her throat. "Very well, sir." She looked at Lona and Mona, who'd both gone still when they realized that Lady Sharpeyes and Nola were there. "As I was saying, we have a variety of foods."

* * *

"That was exquisite," Lady Sharpeyes said happily. "My cook would have been hard-pressed to match your skills tonight."

Glorina blushed and bowed her head. "You honor us, Lady."

"Lady Sssharpeyesss isssn't one for needlessss flattery," Nola said. "Thisss meal wasss exquissite."

"Thank you," Lona said. "I wasn't certain that the food would be to your liking."

Nola laughed, or at least Lona hoped that hissing sound was a laugh. "We eat the sssame food asss you. We jussst eat it differently."

"I apologize," Lona said, her cheeks burning. "I didn't mean to insult you."

"No, it isss fine," Nola said. "That wasss the politessst way I have been asssked. I am glad that you relaxed, asss well," she finished, looking at Rosa. "You were afraid when I came in."

Rosa looked away. "I don't like snakes. I know you aren't, but..." She trailed off, embarrassed.

"We have a lot of sssimilaritiesss to sssnakesss. I take no offenssse."

"I'm glad that she is doing well," Lady Sharpeyes said, looking at the far end of the table. "Oh, on an unrelated note, that icebox has been wonderful, Sean. I do believe that Forged Bonds is going to be getting a lot of orders from Westpoint in the future."

"Oh? Do you expect word to travel quickly?"

"Archlet will see to that," Lady Sharpeyes said, "just as word of what transpires over the next few tendays will be known."

"You expect things to happen?" Sean asked.

"My husband is still quite beside himself that his heir was cut down. Evan was going to be his tie to Lord Truestrike, after all."

"Truestrike's daughter?" Fiona asked.

"The one who has had a child," Lady Sharpeyes replied. "Her bastard child is being raised above the others to take over the family, eventually."

"Bastard children are rarely viewed kindly by society," Fiona said.

"True, but Truestrike has named this one his heir, already," Lady Sharpeyes said. "Do you know who the father of the child is?" Seeing the blank expressions, she smiled. "Darragh Axehand."

"What?" Sean asked.

"You do not know the Shame of Darragh?" Lady Sharpeyes asked.

"Only that he was blinded and sent to establish the outpost," Fiona said.

"Since he is dead, there is no harm in telling you," Lady Sharpeyes said. "Mind you, this is rumor, but it comes from a reputable source."

"Go on," Sean said.

"Darragh Axehand was fresh off of his fame in the arena when Lord Truestrike approached him with a request to keep his family safe. It was a large request for someone outside of nobility, but Darragh was a mighty man. Years passed with Darragh doing his duty— he killed a score or more of Knights and Aspirants who challenged Truestrike. That all came to an abrupt end when Darragh slept with Dame Trisha Truestrike."

Sean's lips pursed as he thought of Misa and Darragh. "Why did he?"

"Unknown," Lady Sharpeyes replied. "What is known is that Truestrike had Darragh brought before Queen Summer. She took his sight and ordered him to set up a village as far south as he could."

"That was when he came to see me," Fiona said softly.

"Why would he sleep with Truestrike's daughter? He had Misa," Sean said bluntly.

"You would have to ask them, but that is no longer possible, from what we have heard," Lady Sharpeyes said. "I do have one question, though, Sean, if it is not too imposing— I heard tale that your sword is adamantine. Is this true?"

"Yes."

"Hmm, how interesting," Lady Sharpeyes smiled. "Well, I do thank you for having me." She rose gracefully to her feet. "I need to return to the manor, or else my *dear husband* might try to claim the entire place as his own."

Everyone stood up, and Nola moved to open the door for her.

"Thank you for coming, Saranita," Aria said, escorting her toward the door. "I hope that you find freedom yourself one day."

"That is my hope," Lady Sharpeyes said. "I do think I found the right key to that lock, but only time will tell."

"Thank you for inviting me into your home, Sean," Nola said in her native tongue.

"Thank you for being a good guest and being kind to my family when they were clumsy."

"They didn't mean insult and were talking to me as a friend. That is rare enough that minor mishaps should be forgiven. If they had malice in their hearts when they said those things, it would have been different."

"Excuse me," Tiska asked, having followed them, "Nola?"

"Yesss?"

"If you get more time off, we'd like it if you would come by to talk with us," Tiska said. "We usually take a small break for tea after our afternoon sparring."

"Sssparring?" Nola asked.

Tiska looked at Sean, wondering if she misspoke. Sean covered for her, "Our staff has been learning how to better defend themselves. We have enemies, and I would hate for them to come to harm."

Nola's tongue flickered for a moment. "Would joining thisss sssparring occasssionally be okay?"

Sean looked down the hall at Myna. "Myna is the one who's been in charge of it."

"If you would fight with me, I would allow it," Myna smiled. "Your kind is known for their ability to avoid attacks."

Nola's tongue flickered and a small hissing sound came before her words, "Yesss. I ssshall asssk the Lady."

"Granted," Lady Sharpeyes said from near the front door, "when I have nothing else for you to attend to during those times. Now, it is time for you to attend your duties, Nola."

"Yesss, Missstressss."

"Thank you for having us, Sean," Lady Sharpeyes said. "I am sure that you shall accomplish more that will please me in the future."

"I'll do what I have to, Saranita."

"Excellent," Lady Sharpeyes smiled as Nola opened the door for her.

17

———

Sean shut the door behind them and gave Aria an awkward smile. "So, uh... here we are."

Aria laughed lightly and sat in the only chair in the room. "Awkwardness. It fits you, Sean. It's charming, but I do hope that it doesn't continue for too long."

"No, no. I'll be fine. It's just nerves."

"Nerves? You face down nobles like they are nothing but common brigands, but you're nervous about taking your ninth wife to bed?"

"When you say it that way, it seems stupid," Sean replied. "All I see is a beautiful woman waiting for me."

Aria gave him a bright smile as she pulled her boots off. "Thank you. We've both been with others before tonight, though, so what's making you this way now? Surely you aren't this way *every* time you sleep with one of us?"

"No, I'm not," Sean replied. Scratching his chin, he tried to find the right words. "It's odd, and maybe it'll sound cliché, but I just want you to have the best wedding night. My mind keeps trying to tell me 'what ifs,' and I get nervous that I might fuck up and ruin tonight for you."

Aria's head tilted to the side as she stripped her socks off. "From any other man, I would laugh. I can see your worry... the corners of your eyes are tight and your forehead is creased. I'll just have to call you sweet, instead. Truly, Sean, you could do very little to make me hate tonight. My whole world was turned upside down from the day I met you, and I thank you for it."

Sean frowned slightly. "Thank me? For turning your world upside down?"

"Yes... I'd lied to myself for so long. I insisted that I was happy and all I wanted was to be with the animals. When you showed up, I saw what someone free of society could be. The cuons and birds reacted to you even more than they did for me, and I was jealous." Aria shook her head as she stood up, taking her vest off. "I asked about you and heard mostly bad things, but I knew better, considering who was spreading the rumors. I asked Saranita about you and she told me what she'd heard from Amedee. I could hardly believe it, that anyone could be so free with their life."

Sean watched her, his breathing slowing, and the fear falling away from him.

"Then, I had to make a decision. I chose to save Prita, knowing it would probably cost me my life. Even when I was put in chains, my heart felt light. The hounds still respected me, and I know that they believed in what I'd done."

Dropping her vest, Aria went over to the bed. Her hands moved without thought, and the buttons on her shirt popped open.

"I was kept locked in the dungeons for days with little food and a lot of harassment. I still felt good about what I did... then, they came to get me. Told me I was going to fight for my life. I was fine with fighting... until I saw you."

Dropping her shirt, Aria unbuckled her pants. Sean's mouth went dry as he watched her strip, and he moved to get his boots off.

"When you spoke to Cuander, I knew— knew to my bones— that he wasn't going to listen to me, but I had to try. I never wanted to hurt you or Ryann, but I knew if I didn't fight, they wouldn't accept your win, and..." Aria giggled, "I wanted to see what you could do. I had no idea how dangerous you were. I tried to get Ryann to give up, but she's a fighter. When she hit me with that rock the second time, I knew I'd have to drown her at least a little to get her to stop. Even then, you didn't try to hurt me. You forced me to flee back into the air."

Her pants hit the floor and Aria stood in just her underwear, her back to Sean. With a sigh, she dropped those and climbed onto the bed. Sean yanked his socks off, his eyes locked on her as he hurriedly undressed.

"You tried to reason with me, but I was so full of myself. I'd never been bested when in the air, but I should've known better. Ryann took me out of the air once that fight. When your stone hit me, I gave myself up for dead, welcoming the release. Instead, you caught me, held me, protected me, and took my hurt for your own."

Shifting so she was leaning against the headboard, she smiled as she watched him fumble with his clothing.

"You chose to give me life, even though I feared it might be another, tighter, chain. How foolish I was about you. And now, here we are, on our wedding night."

Sean stumbled and fell onto the bed, his pants tangled around his ankles. "Uh... yeah."

"Since you're so hapless, maybe I should assist you?" Aria giggled as she leaned over his head.

"Thank you?"

Aria's eyes sparkled as she leaned down and kissed him softly.

Sean forgot about his pants and returned her kiss. Her soft lips parted and her tongue met his as the kiss deepened. It was a little strange, with their heads one hundred and eighty degrees from each other, but neither minded.

Aria broke the kiss first and climbed over him, her hands going to free his legs from the confining clothes. Sean found a delightful distraction and was quick to raise his head to partake. Aria let out a surprised trill as Sean's tongue traced her sex.

"Sean, I was just trying to help you," Aria said, lowering her hips to give him better access.

"And I *am* helping you," Sean replied, glad Aria was receptive to him pleasuring her.

Aria moaned lightly, letting him distract her for a few more seconds before she tore his pants off. Breathing fast, she tugged his underwear down. Her eyes lit up when his rapidly-swelling cock popped free of them. Not caring if she got his underwear all the way off, she focused on returning the pleasure he was giving her.

Sean moaned into her sex as Aria's tongue traced along his rigid flesh. Eyelid twitching when Aria took the tip into her mouth, Sean redoubled his efforts to bring her pleasure.

Aria let out a muffled squeal of pleasure when Sean's tongue found her clit. Using her right hand to get the correct angle, she tucked her left hand into a fist, squeezing her left thumb tightly. She then went from tip to base in one go, her gag reflex subdued by the pressure point in her hand, but it was difficult to suppress completely with how large Sean was.

Sean felt his body start to tense when Aria took him deep. Intent on making her orgasm before he did, he tried to think of anything else but the wonderful sensation of her mouth. Muscles tightening, Sean licked her faster and with more pressure.

Aria's breath hitched as Sean pushed, her moan around his shaft signaling her own impending orgasm. When she felt Sean's muscles clench, she knew he was close, but she still wasn't prepared for him to orgasm when he did— her moan had been enough extra sensation to push him over the edge before her. Swallowing as fast as she could, she did her best to take everything, but she had to abandon that and pull up to breathe.

Sean's head fell back to the bed, and he panted as his body slowly relaxed from the orgasm. "Fucking hell, that was quick."

Aria coughed as she came free of his shaft. "I wasn't expecting it, either. I guess I found the right spots for you."

"Yeah... yeah, you did," Sean laughed. He raised his hand, grabbing her ass to pull her back down to him so he could ravish her sex with his tongue.

"Oh, Sean..." Aria moaned as she rested her head on his thigh. "Almost there...!"

True to her word, it was less than a minute later when her body went rigid. An almost musical exhale of air, not too unlike a small bird call, escaped as she went limp atop him.

"Hmm... now *that* was very nice," Aria sighed.

"And we're just getting started. If you give me a moment to get rid of these," he said, wiggling his feet where his underwear was tangled, "and lay back, I'd like to spend a bit more time learning your body."

"Hmm, I do like the sound of that, but I want to do the same."

"I won't stop you from doing that," Sean was quick to agree.

"Since I won our first bout," Aria said, sliding off him, "I'll go first."

"Bout? Didn't know we were in combat," Sean chuckled.

"It's one of the few times I've bested you in some way."

"Very well," Sean said, sitting up long enough to kick his underwear off. "How would you like me?"

"Such an open-ended question," Aria laughed.

Sean chuckled, "Yeah, I guess it is."

"Let's start slow," Aria said, shifting on the bed. "Lay back, close your eyes, and just let me explore."

"As my wife wishes."

18

Sean smiled at Aria sleeping beside him. The soft feathers where her hair should've been were almost tickling him. *Funny... when I think about it, it's barely been over three months since I came here. So much has happened since my first day. Morrigan is right—I* am *a nexus of change.*

One of Aria's red eyes opened and a smile formed on her lips. "Good morning, Sean."

"Morning to you, dear," Sean murmured, leaning in to kiss her lightly.

"That was quite the evening," Aria said when the kiss ended. "Is it your innate healing gift from the Tuatha that lets you keep going like that?"

"Probably," Sean chuckled softly. "I never had that kind of stamina on my old world."

"I was so proud that I'd bested you first, but then you went on to be on top of every other thing I try to beat you at. I'd be sore if not for the healing you give us all."

"And I'd be just as bad, or worse."

"True. You do have seven of us to keep happy, after all."

"Thankfully, you're all understanding."

Aria started to say something, but stopped.

Sean kissed her cheek. "What's bothering you?"

"Nothing's bothering me, but it's a little silly."

"I promise not to laugh."

"Fine. You gave Myna a tail, repaired whip marks on Ryann, and even took away Fiona's Shame. I was wondering... if you could do a small favor for me?"

"Anything at all."

"It's silly, but my feathers..." Aria said, touching her crown of small white feathers, "could you make them into hair? I've always wanted to be able to do what other women do and make elaborate coiffures."

Sean touched her head gently and looked at her with his Flesh Shaping. After a couple of seconds, he nodded. "Yeah, it's doable. Are you sure? I think your feathers are beautiful."

Aria shifted in bed, clearly giving his question some thought. "You really like my feathers more?"

"I'm sure I'd like you just as much with hair, but your feathers are unique," Sean said.

"Okay, then I'll leave them alone for now. Maybe I'll ask Felora to dream with me so I can see what having hair on top of my head is like."

"That's a good idea. If you still want hair after, I'll give it to you."

Aria's eyes misted and she leaned into him, kissing him passionately. Sean was more than willing to return her passion. He let out a surprised sound when she slipped her leg over his waist, intent on straddling him.

The knock on the door interrupted them from going further. "Breakfast is being served in a few minutes," Fiona's voice announced.

"Okay!" Sean called back.

"Hmm... we should get going," Aria said, slipping her leg off him.

"Yeah," Sean sighed. "It's time to get up."

"You have that covered already," Aria giggled, her hand snaking down his waist to make her point obvious.

"Mind of its own..." Sean exhaled slowly.

"She *did* say it would be a few minutes," Aria said. One of her eyes looked down at the tent in the bedding while the other was up at his face. "If I work my very best, I can help you with this and we can make it to breakfast."

"Felora is corrupt— oh gods." Sean shuddered when Aria dove under the blankets like a striking hawk.

* * *

"Good morning," Sean greeted everyone as he took his seat.

"Good morning," Fiona replied with a knowing smile.

The cooks coming in with breakfast saved Sean from replying. Glorina placed the large dishes on the table in front of Sean, full of eggs, grilled ham, fresh biscuits, and a boat of gravy. "I hope you enjoy it, sir," Glorina said.

"I've enjoyed everything you three make for us," Sean said.

"They are better cooks than I am, and I am a good cook," Andrea said. "You should all be very proud."

The three curtsied to her, and Glorina was the one to speak for them, "We thank you, mistress. We will continue to do our very best for the family."

"And we appreciate it," Fiona smiled.

"They're also becoming adept in moving without sound and hiding," Myna added. "The maids, as well. Very adept."

All seven of the interior staff wore broad smiles at her praise, but the maids seemed to be especially happy. "We thank you, mistress, and we will work harder," Tiska said, getting nods from Cali, Xenta, and Prita, a second before Glorina, Lona, and Mona joined in.

"Sir," Ven called from further down the table, "I wanted to let you know the other Fairies have made friends with the cuons. They've even taken to allowing riders."

Sean laughed as he imagined one of the cuons festooned with Messenger Fairies, all armed and armored. The image changed to a war elephant with a howdah, and archers aboard it. "That must be a sight for the others."

Venn laughed. "It's different. We tried it with Caleb."

"And I missed it? Darn."

"We ride him often," Jutt said.

"We could show you after breakfast!" Arla was quick to add.

"Before I go to Winston's," Sean agreed.

* * *

Sean was still chuckling when they got to Giralt's house. "That was priceless."

Aria was shaking her head. "Was it really that amusing, Sean?"

"It was to me. It looked similar to something from my old world."

A small smile touched her lips as she watched him looking into the distance. "It must be a good memory."

"Huh? Oh, yeah. I was never one for movie theaters, but some movies on the big screen were priceless. Lord of the Rings— all three of them were in that group."

"Movie theater? What's a movie?"

Sean rubbed his chin for a second. "Not sure how to describe it... You know what a theater is, obviously?"

"A place for watching plays and other dramas or comedic pieces of work," Aria said.

"Well, a movie is the short name for a 'motion picture.' Motion pictures were a way of preserving a play so it could be watched again, whenever you wanted, without needing to put on a whole new show."

Aria's brow furrowed. "Wouldn't that put the actors out of work?"

"Not at all. If anything, it caused an increase in them. You see, motion pictures were a dominant form of entertainment for years. All different types of stories became movies."

"How did they preserve the play?"

"They were recorded onto film. It's a long explanation, and I don't know how all of it worked."

"Very well. It does sound fascinating, though, being able to watch a play whenever you want."

The carriage slowed, and Sean could hear Arliat speaking to the guard at Giralt's manor. "It was. How are you getting along with Clara?"

"She is a very forward person. If Fiona was more outgoing, they might be alike. Fiona helps guide our home. Clara dictates theirs."

"She does seem to be the one in charge."

The carriage lurched forward, and after a hundred yards, it stopped again. "We're here, sir," Arliat called.

Aria was out of the carriage first, and Sean followed her out once she cleared the doorway.

"Thank you, Arliat. We'll be ready at the usual time."

"Yes, sir."

"I'm glad you could make it," Clara said from the porch. "He's been eager to start on a new project."

"I'll go get started on something difficult," Sean chuckled.

"Please do," Clara said, waving to him as he walked around the manor. "Aria, it's good to see you again. Are the others still focused on their tasks for the association?"

"They should finish Fredrick's home and business today," Aria said. "I believe they're slated to start work here tomorrow."

"I was the next on that list," Clara nodded. "Not sure we need it, but best to be safe."

Sean got too far away to hear more, but he agreed with her last statement. *Better safe than sorry... Mom always said that.* Knocking on the shop door, he waited to be told to enter before walking in.

"Sean, it's too bad you missed last night," Giralt laughed. "If you had seen Ryan and Italice's faces when they saw the new rune."

"I bet," Sean chuckled. "Did they already move to get them made and installed?"

"I'll be making a dozen of them over the next tenday so they can get them installed in the reservoir."

"Going for safety, are they?"

"No one can give them grief if they have a ton of redundant safeguards."

"True enough."

"Now, what're we going to work on next?" Giralt asked, taking a drink of his cognac.

"A car," Sean said. "It'll be more a Model-T than a sports car, but it's the best place to start."

"A car. This is connected to why you wanted the smallest heat rune you could get?"

"Yup. Okay, a lot of this is going to be Shaping to get the thing into the right form. The hardest part will be getting the steam engine small enough and light enough that it can do the job without bogging it down."

"Hmm... Okay, what am I going to be working on?"

Sean grinned. "The runes for the engine, to start with. I'll be working on the engine first— it's the most important part for us. Let me give you a quick sketch of what I'm talking about."

"Please do," Giralt said, passing over charcoal pencil and parchment.

* * *

"Guess that's all for today," Sean said, stretching.

"This is trickier than I had thought it would be..." Giralt sighed.

"Good. It'll give you something to work through," Clara said.

"They're both smiling, so it's obviously still going well," Aria added.

"That's very true," Clara nodded. "If it wasn't, they'd both be bent over something, complaining."

Sean and Giralt exchanged a glance, but kept their mouths shut.

"I'll see you tomorrow," Sean told Giralt.

"Of course."

The couple escorted Sean and Aria to the front, where Arliat was waiting for them. With one more set of goodbyes, Sean climbed into the carriage, and Arliat got them moving.

"What was it you were working on?" Aria asked. "It looked odd."

"An engine. A small steam engine, to be precise. The problem is going to be getting it to produce enough power to move a car, but not have it weigh a ton."

"If I've learned anything in my time with the family, it's that you'll make it work," Aria said.

"I don't make *everything* work."

"Maybe, but you do enough that the successes eclipse the failures."

Sean just shook his head and looked out the window. Aria let him ponder what he was thinking about, and just watched him with a smile.

19

Sparring was different that day— Myna was not fighting, nor were Andrea, Ida, and Ryann. When he asked about it, Sean agreed with their sentiment that they might be carrying children and should refrain from getting hit. Helga stepped into Myna's role, leading the sparring session.

Fiona pulled Sean aside during one of his breaks. "Sean, tonight, I will be waiting for you, and Felora will be joining us."

"Uh, are you sure about that?" Sean asked, glancing at Felora, who was in the middle of a match with Aria. "Her tastes are a little... masochistic."

"I've talked with her," Fiona reassured him. "Tonight, she will do as I say if she wants the outcome we both want. Trust me."

"I do."

"Good. Myna would like to go with you to the inn tonight. She wants to announce the good fortune of our family, about how we're all planning on expecting."

"That'll be interesting," Sean chuckled awkwardly.

"I'm sure you'll manage," Fiona giggled. "I have cigars waiting for you in the carriage since we know that Myna and Andrea are pregnant. In another few days, you should be able to verify Ryann and Ida."

"Yeah," Sean said softly, his voice and eyes distant.

"I'm glad you're looking forward to them as much as we are," Fiona said, touching his chest.

Blinking, he met her eyes and smiled. "I'm nervous as hell, actually. What if I'm terrible at being a dad? What if our troubles hurt them?"

"Then you'll kill the ones who hurt our children, and we'll help you."

"Yeah... yeah, I would," Sean exhaled, pulling her into a hug.

"Sean, it is your turn," Helga called out. "The twins will be against you. Weapons only."

* * *

Arriving at the Oaken Glen, Sean snagged Myna's hand when she tried to leave the carriage before him. "Aria goes first, then I will, and finally you," he told her.

"I should go ahead of you," Myna said as Aria left the carriage.

"Our child is more important th—"

"Exactly," Myna cut him off. "If you die, we *all* die, even the unborn. That means me going next is the right thing to do."

Sean closed his mouth and sighed, motioning her to the door. Myna gave him a smile, kissed his cheek, then got out. Sean rubbed at his face and took a deep breath before finally stepping out.

Following Aria into the inn, Sean chuckled and waved to Joseph, who'd called out to him when he entered the building. *Fucking Cheers,* Sean laughed internally.

"We missed you last night," Italice said as Sean reached the table.

"Sorry, but it was Aria's wedding night," Sean said.

"There's no need to apologize. Congratulations to you, Aria," Eva said.

"Thank you," Aria smiled.

"Do you need another round? And drinks for the MacDougals?" Tabitha asked, coming over to their table.

Sean tossed her a silver. "Dark Delight."

"Cider," Aria said.

"Berry tea," Myna added.

The rest of the table ordered, and Tabitha went to go get their drinks.

"Before business takes over," Myna said, "I would like to inform our friends that, not only am I expecting our first child, but Andrea is as well, and Ryann and Ida are both hoping to be joining us soon."

Everyone congratulated them, and Sean passed around cigars, wondering how that tradition started in this world. When Tabitha came back to the table with his change, Sean told her to apply it to the table for the evening.

"Sam is going to be upset she stayed home tonight," Brendis laughed. "Oh, I can't wait to see her face when I tell her that Ida might soon be expecting!"

"Children are a blessing," Joseph said, looking over at the apprentice table where his oldest son was sitting. "They make you proud."

"They can cause you a lot of concern, as well," Brendis said, thinking back to Ida Bonding to Sean originally.

Sean could see Brendis' distant look and recalled that same moment. "I hope my children don't give me a heart attack like Ida did to you."

"I was so mad," Brendis chuckled. "Looking back, I feel short-sighted."

"No, you were right to worry."

"Maybe, but look at all of us here," Brendis said. "All of us have seen life become better, and it's because of you."

"I don't kn—" Sean began, cutting off when a silver blur turned into a Messenger Fairy that landed on Sean's cup.

"Sir, the Bronzeshields! Hurry," the Fairy blurted out, clearly agitated.

Sean didn't question it— he was up and running before anyone else could even process what was happening. The doors to the Oaken

Glen flew off their hinges when Sean hit them without pausing to open them. Sean bounced off a large man that'd been by the door, sending the man sprawling, as he made the turn for the old smithy.

The newly-modified building came up fast. Sean rushed for the stairs that led up to the second floor, where he could hear a cuon baying. His blood ran cold— he feared the worst as he hit the door with his shoulder, sending it flying into the main room.

Sam was standing in the far corner, clutching a hammer in her hand. Brendan stood behind her, tears streaking his face as fear was etched on his features. Standing protectively in front of both of them, the cuon had its hackles raised, teeth bared, and was growling at the empty air. A Fairy was perched on the cuon's back, holding a small crossbow in their hands.

"Shit...!" The word was nearly lost under the growl of the cuon.

Sean spun toward the sound, his left eye summoning Mage Sight. A person, clearly covered in energy to not be seen, was standing near the back-hallway door, holding a knife in their hand. They took a step back when they noticed Sean looking directly at them before turning and bolting.

"No!" Sean hissed as he leapt over the sofa between him and the man, rushing after him.

"Sean?" Sam asked in confusion. The front door had just come off its hinges before Sean appeared a second later, so she was still processing what was going on.

The fleeing man had only made it to the hallway when Sean grabbed the wall, tearing a chunk of wood from it and forming it into a ball. With a hard toss, the wooden ball hit the man in his lower back. A scream of pain echoed in the hall as he went tumbling to the floor from the impact. Sean was on him a second later, yanking him up as he glared into his wide and fearful eyes.

"You made a mistake!" Sean hissed as he tightened his grip on the man's head. "Talk, and I'll consider letting you live." The distant sound of whistles touched Sean's ears, but he didn't care about them.

The man's eyes went even wider and his pupils dilated before he passed out in Sean's grip.

"Fuck!" Sean yelled. He wanted to pulp the attacker, but he needed information.

"Sean?" Sam asked, looking into the hall.

"He's unconscious," Sean said, dropping the man to the floor.

"Can you help Esmerelda?" Sam asked, her voice tight.

"Who?" Sean asked as he got to his feet.

"Esmerelda, our cook and maid," Sam said. "She's in the kitchen."

Sean hurried to the kitchen and found the older woman moaning feebly as she tried to stop the flow of blood from the stab wounds. Sean was quick to help stabilize her and make sure she wouldn't die. By the time he finished, the guard had come pounding up the stairs to the front room.

The cuon growled and the guard stopped in the doorway, clearly not expecting the hound. "City guard!" the man yelled, announcing his presence.

Sam let go of Esmerelda's hand and went to the front room. "The attacker is in that hallway," she said, pointing. "Ang, let them by."

The cuon huffed and moved to her side. More voices could be heard outside, a few of them loud and angry. As the guards went to the hall, Sam stepped outside to find her husband standing nose to nose with a Dwarven guard.

"Brendis, stop! We're fine!" she yelled down to him.

Seeing his wife and hearing her voice, Brendis deflated some, his voice catching, "Oh, thank the heavens..."

The guard looked up at her, then to Brendis, and stepped aside. "Sorry, sir. I was just trying to secure the scene."

Sean came out behind her with Brendan in his arms. "Sam, you three should stay at my home for tonight. I'll make sure that Esmerelda is okay before we get her over there."

Sergeant Eugene Carmady came rushing up to the scene. "Mac-Dougal? What happened?"

"Sergeant, the Bronzeshields were attacked. I can explain things if you're fine with the distraught family going to my place for now. You'll be free to talk to them tomorrow."

The two guards who'd entered the house stopped behind Sean. "Excuse us, sir, you're in the way."

Sean looked back to find them carrying the attacker. "He was the assailant."

"Maybe, but he's unconscious," the guard said flatly.

"MacDougal, let them through. I'll have him checked at a healer, then taken to the magistrate's hall."

Sean nodded and stepped aside. Sam and Brendan went down the stairs before the guards, moving to the growing crowd. "Sergeant, their maid was attacked, as well. She was wounded."

"We'll have her seen to." Turning to Sam, his voice softened, "Ma'am, I'd like to speak with you about the attack. Tomorrow will be fine."

Sam nodded, her calmness starting to crack. "Of course."

Brendis was beside her, holding her and Brendan in a blink of an eye. "We'll be at MacDougal's," he informed Carmady. He patted Ang on the head, giving the hound some praise.

"Very well. MacDougal, you were here for the attack?" Carmady asked as he climbed the stairs.

"I got there at the end," Sean said. "Come on up and I'll explain."

* * *

Sean's explanation was interrupted briefly when Esmerelda was taken out to see a healer. She stared at Sean with wide eyes as she went past, and Sean felt a small thrum of energy from her.

Carmady had Sean walk through the account three times, taking notes the entire time. "A Shaper who might be the most dangerous man in the city... Things have been very busy since you've arrived."

Sean almost took offense to his words, but he heard the tiredness behind them and the lack of accusation. "All infections come to a head."

"Which makes you the lance?" Carmady asked.

"I'd rather just be a crafter," Sean shrugged.

"And I just want to keep the people safe," Carmady sighed. "That looks like everything I'll get tonight. I'll be by tomorrow to speak with the Bronzeshield family."

"Yes, sir. Do you mind if I put that door back on and lock up for them?" Sean asked.

Carmady shook his head as he looked at the room. "You took it out of its frame."

"And I'll have it back up in a moment."

"Go ahead, MacDougal. I'll have a man posted on the building tonight, regardless."

"Thank you, Sergeant."

"If you want to thank me, stop giving me paperwork," Carmady said.

"I'll try," Sean replied as he picked up the door.

* * *

Arliat was waiting for Sean with the carriage when he came downstairs. Aria was sitting beside Arliat. "Sean, we're taking you home," Aria told him.

"Need to stop by the inn," Sean said, reaching for the carriage door.

"No, we took care of it," Fiona said, opening the door before he could. "Please, husband, get in?"

Doing as she asked, Sean climbed in and sighed when Fiona hugged him. "I'm sorry."

"No. *Never* apologize for doing the right thing, Sean. I would've been disappointed if you hadn't done what you did. Ida is making sure her family is settled in the manor. Now, tell me what happened, please?"

Sean finished his telling as they arrived home. "If she hadn't asked me to help Esmerelda, I might've cracked his head open."

"You wouldn't have been wrong to do so," Fiona said, "but leaving him alive gives us a chance to have the magistrate force him to tell us why he was there."

"Yeah. That was the reason I tried to capture him."

Fiona opened the carriage door when it came to a stop. "That's for tomorrow, though. Tonight, you will lay with me and Felora and give us the children we wish."

"But—"

"No buts," Fiona cut him off. "Our lives might be in flux and uncertainty, but that doesn't mean we will give up our dreams. It'll just make us embrace them tighter to make them real."

Sean exhaled, watching her get out. "Okay."

20

Sitting down for breakfast, he gave Sam, Brendis, and Brendan a smile. "I wish you were here under better circumstances."

"As do we," Sam replied. "Ida told me last night that she's expecting her first with you, so at least there was some positive news last night."

"We're not positive on her carrying yet," Sean said, "but we're optimistic."

"Thank you for saving Momma and me," Brendan spoke up.

Sean gave the younger boy a nod. "Ang and your mom would've saved you without my help."

"Sir," Onim said from their spot, "I talked with the family that lives with them. They apologized for not doing more. They couldn't see the attacker— all they had was a general direction because of Ang."

"Make sure you all carry some flour or other fine powder," Sean said. "It was an old trick to break invisibility... hmm, but I think we should test it first."

Glorina came in the door as he spoke, her cart holding several covered platters. "Breakfast is served."

"Thank you, Glorina. Can I get you to bring me a quarter cup of flour, please?"

"Of course, sir," Glorina said slowly, clearly not understanding.

"He wants to test something," Fiona explained.

"Shall I serve first?"

"Please," Fiona replied.

"Did they give you any trouble after we left?" Sam asked Sean as the food was set out. "What of Esmerelda?"

"No trouble. They took her to a healer, but I don't know after that. I had your front door fixed and things locked up before I left."

Sam exhaled. "Thank you for coming for us. With Ang, I'm sure I could've gotten Brendan to safety, but I didn't want to risk him."

"What happened? I know the end, but not how it all started."

Glorina left the room and Sean served himself so the others could.

"Brendis went to the inn after dinner, and Esmerelda was cleaning up," Sam began as she took the serving spoon her husband offered her. "I was in Brendan's room, asking if he'd like to have me read to him, when Ang started barking outside. I heard the back door splinter. I could hear him in the front room, so I grabbed Brendan and snagged the hammer I had just finished making for Brendis, then went to find out what had happened. When I got into the main room, Ang was facing the kitchen, growling, and the Fairies were shooting at the air, but they didn't seem to be hitting anything."

"Here you are, sir," Glorina said, coming back into the room.

"Thank you," Sean said, taking the measuring cup of flour. "I'll use it after we eat."

"One of the Fairies left in a flash and I put Brendan behind me in the corner, figuring it might be like the bathhouse. A few moments later, the door crashed in and you were there, then you were over the couch and into the hall. I went to check on Esmeralda and found her..."

"It's okay," Sean said softly when she trailed off. "She won't die— I made sure of that. Ang must've picked up the attacker's scent, which got him to warn you. This is exactly why I made sure everyone has a cuon."

"It has to be Denmur and Sharpeyes," Brendis said grimly.

"Of course it is," Aria said, "but proving it enough so that they can be held accountable is a different matter. This might turn very bloody."

"Only if it's *them* bleeding," Sean said with leashed anger.

"The food is going to get cold," Fiona said, touching Sean's arm.

"Sorry, dear," Sean said, picking up his fork.

When the meal ended, Sean picked up the flour. Focusing on his Talent, he turned his arm up to the elbow invisible. He looked up and found everyone watching him intently as he sprinkled the flour over his missing arm. It took on a slight form, coated in flour, and made it just visible.

"It's an old trick to beat invisibility," Sean said. "Cover them with a fine powder. I should've thought of it sooner, but it really only works if you have an idea of where they are."

"I'll spread the word," Onim said seriously.

A bell chimed and Tiska jumped to her feet. "Excuse me. That's the front door."

"We're done eating and we all have things to do. I'm surprised Carmady hasn't shown up yet," Sean said, rising to his feet.

"We'll go home. Maybe the guard there can— Sergeant," Sam said, greeting Carmady when Tiska brought him to the dining room.

"Looks like breakfast is over," Carmady said, the dark circles under his eyes speaking of a long night. "If I can speak with you about the attack, please?"

"Fiona, I'll catch up with the rest of you," Ida said.

"Of course," Fiona replied. "I'll have the carriage come back for you. Sean?"

"Hmm? Go ahead. I'll wait for Arliat to come back. I think it's best if I stay while we have company."

Fiona's eyes darted to Carmady, who'd stepped aside to let the women leave. "Yes. Of course."

"Sergeant, would you like some tea?" Glorina asked before she left.

"As black as you can brew it, please," Carmady replied, stifling a yawn.

"We also have some odds and ends in the kitchen," Glorina offered. "Would a snack be okay?"

Carmady gave her a bow of his head. "I will accept. It's been a long night, and I haven't supped."

"Very well."

"Have a seat, sir," Sean said, motioning Carmady to take the seat to his right.

Sam, Brendis, Brendan, and Ida all sat on Sean's left. Aria took the seat to Carmady's right when he sat down. Carmady pulled out a notebook and pencil, looked for the first empty page, and set his pencil down next to it.

"The attacker will be seeing the magistrate tomorrow," Carmady said. "He's currently being held in isolation on the order of High Magistrate Jasper. The similarities between your attack and the bathhouse have been noticed."

Sean's lips pursed, but he kept his comment to himself.

"Now, if you can tell me what transpired last night?" Carmady asked Sam, picking up his pencil.

Sam gave him the same retelling she'd already given to Sean. Carmady stayed silent, taking notes until she was finished.

"You were going to read a story to your son when the cuon started barking?"

"Yes."

"The back door was broken in. I can verify that," Carmady said. "My men noticed it last night. You believe the cuon did that?"

"Yes."

"What made you grab a weapon and go to the front instead of taking your son to safety?"

"Esmerelda," Sam said without hesitation. "She was in the kitchen cleaning. I wanted to make sure she got out."

Carmady nodded as he jotted down another note. "Do you have any enemies that would go to these lengths?"

"I can say without question that Otis Denmur has disliked my family ever since my daughter became Sean's apprentice."

"I see," Carmady said, writing it down.

"Are we allowed to go home now?" Brendis asked, his patience thinning.

"Yes," Carmady said, finishing off the tea Glorina had brought him during Sam's retelling. "You will need to be at the magistrate hall tomorrow morning. Other than that, we're done. Thank you." Carmady closed his notebook. "And on a personal note, I'm sure Jasper will make sure the attacker pays."

"I hope so," Sam said, getting to her feet alongside Brendis.

"Sean, I'm going to go with them and fix the door before meeting up with Fiona," Ida said.

"That's fine, Ida. If we wait for Arliat, we can all ride together. She'll drop Aria and me off, then take you all home."

"I'll go see if she's back," Ida said, heading out.

"MacDougal," Carmady said, "you'll be required to attend the magistrate, as well."

"I figured, Sergeant. I'll be there."

"Thank you. Thank you for the hospitality, too. The tea and food were very good."

"I'll make sure Glorina knows you're appreciative," Sean said. "Thank you for being understanding last night."

"I'm just doing my job. It was obvious that a family had been attacked in their own home. We had a man in custody— there was no reason to trouble them further. I just needed a statement for the magistrate, and this morning is just as good as last night."

"We still thank you," Sam said.

"And I'm sorry for yelling at your man," Brendis said.

"It's fine, sir. If I'd been in your place, I would've attacked him and tried to get to my wife," Carmady said. "Thankfully, you didn't, so I didn't have to bring you in."

"Almost..." Brendis sighed. "If she hadn't come outside when she did..."

"I'll be on my way," Carmady said, pocketing his notebook and pencil. "Good day to you all."

Sean walked Carmady out, catching sight of a line at the front of the manor. "Ven, what's going on?"

"Lots of customers. They're here mostly for kettles, but a few want faucets and hair clips," Ven replied.

"Business seems to be doing well," Carmady said. "I wish you the best, MacDougal. I know you have a lot to deal with at the moment."

"Yes. I'm sure things will be resolved soon."

Carmady nodded and walked off. Sean shook his head and went back inside to find out if Arliat had come back yet.

* * *

The day went by without incident, for which Sean was glad. Entering the Oaken Glenn, he was surprised that the group wasn't at the central table. Allonen waved to Sean as he crossed the room.

"They're in the private room, sir."

"Thank you, Allonen."

"Of course."

Aria led Sean to the room and entered after knocking once.

"There he is," Fredrick said.

"Did something else happen?" Sean asked as he shut the door behind him.

"Nothing like last night," Mageeyes said.

"Thank gods," Sean sighed.

"Let's wait a moment before we start," Mageeyes said. "Pura, tell Tabitha to bring two rounds for everyone, plus whatever Sean and Aria want. We don't want to be disturbed after she delivers them."

"Yes," Pura said, landing on the table.

"Hot cider, please," Aria said. "The chill of Winter is strong."

"She's likely on her way to Westpoint," Flamehair said.

"Does she come through the city?" Sean asked.

"No. We're further out than the Queens travel," Mageeyes said.

"Sir?" Pura asked.

"Oh, hmm... hot cider for me, please."

Pura flashed away.

"How goes the work on your steam engine?" Joseph asked Sean.

"Slow. I can get the engine to work, I'm fairly certain, but the transmission and differential are going to be the problems. I might be able to make the bronze dense enough and hard enough to take the torque, but honestly, steel would do the job better. It's unfortunate that iron can't really be found here... at least not enough to be useful. The easy answer would be to use adamantine, but that would make the vehicle cost more than people can afford."

"It would, except for the richest nobility," MacLenn agreed.

"The problem with making the bronze better is the increased weight, but we're working on it," Sean said.

"*He's* working on it," Giralt pointed out. "There isn't much I can do for it besides helping him refine the engine as much as we can."

"You've been invaluable," Sean said. "Everything you do makes it easier."

There was a knock on the door before Tabitha came in, pushing a cart. She distributed the drinks quickly and took her leave.

"Now that we won't be interrupted, go ahead, Fredrick," Mageeyes said.

Fredrick took a deep breath. "The pushback has begun. Besides the attack on Bronzeshield last night— and we're glad you and your family are okay, Sam— there have been reports from both bath-houses and the icehouse that people have tried to strong-arm the workers and drive off customers."

"It's true," Leith Werrick said. "I was glad for the cuon and guards. They ran when Judil started growling, and the two guards stayed out front, stopping the harassment after that."

Knox nodded. "They tried to strong-arm the bathhouse. The guard took him away after I knocked him cold."

"Try not to do that again?" Fredrick asked. "That's why we have the guards there."

"Yeah, they were keeping the front clear so people could come and go without being bothered. That one thought he'd come inside and get cute."

"Well, no one is cute around you," Joseph said deadpan.

The table laughed.

"Your wives are moving fast with rebuilding the bathhouse," Fredrick went on, looking at Sean. "They think they'll be done on Fourday."

"Then they will," Sean said. "Any trouble there?"

"Not likely," Jefferson said. "I went past there today and, between the two guards, the cuon, and Angusson, I doubt anyone is mad enough to try something."

"We do need to find people to run it once it's open again," Fredrick said.

"If I might," Ash Botrel, one of the two quietest men at the table, said, "the wife and I will step in. She wants me to stop working as much, so I think this would allow her to get that. She was a little upset that I missed my chance with the icehouse."

"You are more than welcome to," Fredrick said.

"We should have Angusson and his wife split the top floor with them," Sean said. "As has been pointed out, not many will go after him, and he works there already, anyway."

"Ash?" Fredrick asked.

"I won't say no. Angusson has always been good to me," Ash replied. "Wife might like that, since I hear that Angusson is expecting a child. She'll be thrilled to help them."

"That's settled, then," Fredrick said.

"I've started to hear complaints from the other smiths," Eve Blackhand said. "They're threatening to go to the Lord about us cutting them off."

"That'll be interesting," Fredrick said, "as our own troubles were given to him and he said he didn't care to meddle with the 'lesser crafts.'"

The smiths stirred at those words, but didn't say anything.

"I'll be sure to remind him," Fredrick said. "Politely, of course."

"One of them has given me an Agreement that they will cut ties with Denmur," Eve said. "I told him I'd have a shipment for him tomorrow."

"Speaking of Agreements," Jefferson laughed, "Goldentouch Merchants came to me to get some armor made for their new guards."

MacLenn snickered, but waved Jefferson to continue.

"When I told them the cost, they complained, but started to agree," Jefferson smiled broadly. "Then, I told them they had to cut ties with Denmur. I haven't seen someone look so stunned in years. They tried to argue, and that's when Bix came out of the back. One look at that hound and they backed to the door, promising to ruin me. Ah, it was a good day."

"Hmm, that reminds me... I need to get my men refitted," MacLenn said. "I'll have them stop by to be measured and fitted. I'd also like to get a few dozen sets to take on the next shipment to the outliers. I'm sure some of the guards out there would love your armor."

"Gladly," Jefferson laughed. "Besides, they can't ruin me. I have Agreements for all my materials, and breaking them would ruin the people who work with me. As for stopping me from selling, at this point, I can make more from our association than I can doing my work. I work because that's what I do, and if I ever find a wife, it'll be what my child will do."

"The pushback has begun, but we are stronger," Fredrick said.

"I'll be at the magistrate hall tomorrow morning," Sam said after a moment of quiet.

"Me, too," Sean added.

"To talk about the attack," Fredrick nodded. "Those of us who are free will come."

"No need," Sam said. "It'll be over with quickly, and I doubt there will be problems. High Magistrate Jasper has the case."

"Very well."

21

S ean stepped out of the carriage after Aria and Ida. "I hope Jasper throws the book at him..." Sean muttered.

"Why would he throw a book at someone?" Ida asked puzzled.

Sean looked at her before he snorted. "An idiom that didn't translate. It means I hope he gets the worst possible punishment."

"Jasper is a man who values the law," Aria said. "We saw that at the party."

"True."

Entering the building, Sean called out to Sam and her family, "Sam, Brendis, how are you?"

"We're good," Sam said. She lowered her voice, "The healer said that Esmerelda was out of danger when she came in. She was wondering who'd seen her first."

"I'm certain it'll come out in time," Sean sighed. "I'm glad she's okay."

"Is Brendan with her at home?" Ida asked.

"Along with a few friends," Brendis replied.

"Someone get the healer! Quickly!" someone shouted from further in the building.

Sean looked up, as the voice sounded familiar. One of the jailers was standing at the top of the stairs, looking worried.

"I wonder what's happening..." Brendis said.

"One of the guards is yelling for a healer," Sean said, going that way.

"Someone get the commander, and hurry with the healer!" Henik said, rushing to the top of the stairs. "I'll go inform the High Magistrate."

Sean grunted— he had a bad feeling about what he'd just heard. Stopping, he watched Henik go to the magistrate's office. He was about to turn away when he realized who'd yelled for the healer. Guard Wolen met Sean's eyes and quickly looked away.

"Fucking hell..." Sean muttered.

"What is it?" Aria asked from beside him.

"I think the assailant is being killed," Sean said.

"What? While in custody?!" Sam asked from Sean's other side.

"One of the head jailers just went to inform the High Magistrate, and they were sending for Commander Babbitt. I think it kind of speaks volumes."

"What does that mean for us?" Sam asked.

"If he dies, then the case is likely going to be closed, but a new one is going to be opened," Sean replied. "If he lives, the new case will likely take priority."

"Cutting off ties," Aria said coldly. "The tool was not useful, just a liability."

"Where does that leave us?" Brendis asked.

"Waiting for the judge to tell us that we're not needed anymore," Sean said.

Sam rubbed her face. "Which means that it *was* Denmur or Sharpeyes," she muttered.

"We knew that, but the doubt, if there was any, is gone now," Ida agreed.

"I'm here," a man said, rushing forward. "You sent for me?"

Wolen nodded. "This way, sir. He needs a healer badly."

"With you there, it's probably already too late," Sean muttered as he watched the two men go into the cell area.

The group was silent for a few minutes as they waited to be summoned. Henik came rushing downstairs and spotted them. Heading their way, he looked serious and worried. "Bronzeshields, MacDougal, if you will come with me, please."

"Of course," Sam said.

"The High Magistrate wants to see us ahead of the trial?" Sean asked.

"I can only say that he wishes to speak with you."

"After you, sir," Sean replied.

They weren't taken to the courtroom, but to another door. Henik knocked once, waiting for a voice to tell him to come, before he opened the door and announced them. He stepped aside to let them inside, then followed them in and closed the door.

Jasper looked angry, but he did his best to hide it as he asked them to sit. "Thank you for coming. I need to apologize— it appears we've had an incident."

"How did he get injured or killed?" Sean asked.

Jasper stared at Sean. "What are you referring to?"

"The guards were calling for a healer, but both the Commander was going to be told and Henik came to inform you before he came to get us. We were in the lobby when the commotion started."

Jasper's eyes went to Henik, who shifted uncomfortably. "It has yet to be determined what happened, sir," Henik said.

"As you can see, the expected trial isn't happening today. I can waive you needing to be there when the trial happens, if you'd like. We have your statements on record."

"I'd rather see him face judgement, your honor," Sam said.

"Very well. I'll schedule for it tomorrow aftern—"

A hard knock came on the door before Carmady entered, pausing when he saw everyone. "Apologies, sir. I came to inform you of news regarding... the incident."

"They've already heard enough to know there's a problem, Sergeant," Jasper said tightly. "Just say it."

"The healer was unable to save him, sir."

Jasper exhaled and looked hard at Henik. "Lockdown the entire cell block. I want a full accounting."

"Yes, sir," Henik said before leaving.

"Sergeant, is the Commander in yet?"

"No, sir. He was being informed, though."

"You may take your leave," Jasper said.

Carmady saluted and left the room.

Jasper rubbed the bridge of his nose before looking back at Sam. "I must apologize for what has happened. Your assailant has died while in custody. I will do my best to find out what transpired to stop this from coming before me."

"He's dead," Sam said, rising to her feet. "I don't blame you, nor those who tried to make this matter come to light. I know that you will be very busy, your honor. Thank you for trying to find the truth."

Jasper rose as the others did. "Thank you for understanding."

As they reached the lobby, a commanding voice could be heard booming from the front of the building, "I want a full account of *everyone* who came in and out of the entire building from when I left last night to this morning."

Babbitt came striding into the room, anger written large on his features. His eyes found the group and his pace slowed. Shaking his head, he marched across the room for the stairs to the cells.

"Someone's going to get reamed," Sean said. "I hope it isn't Henik. He was a decent guy when I was in there."

"It has to be one of the gaolers," Brendis said.

"Maybe," Sean replied, thinking of Wolen, "or someone who was filling in for one."

Seeing Carmady near the front door, Sean went straight up to the sergeant with the others trailing him.

"Sergeant, can I have a moment?"

"MacDougal. What can I do for you?" Eugene Carmady asked.

"I just want to point out something that seems odd to me. I'm not making an accusation, nor implying anything."

Carmady's eyebrow went up, but he stayed silent.

"Guard Wolen was on duty in the cells this morning. He was also at the party, giving testimony that ended up with me in a duel with Knight Sharpeyes. On top of that, he was the guard who just *happened* to show up first when I had a duel with Knight Loplis. It seems odd that he keeps turning up the way he has."

Carmady's lips pursed. "Hmm... That does sound like a string of coincidences. I'll need to verify that he was there for the duel with Knight Loplis. My brother recorded the duel for the city, so his report should state if Wolen was there."

"Thank you," Sean said. "I hope you find out who is behind the attack on the man who assaulted one of my family."

"The Commander is going to be turning over every rock," Carmady assured him.

"Good. I trust him," Sean said, turning to leave, "and you and your brother, as well."

"Sean, that was dangerous," Aria said softly. "He could've taken that as you implying that a guard was corrupt."

"He might have, but that fucker is tied to it somehow," Sean said as they stepped outside. "Ven, is Arliat on her way back?"

"She'll be back as soon as she drops the others off at the bathhouse."

"Guess we wait," Sean said.

* * *

Having decided to not go to Giralt's, Sean stayed home to tinker in his workshop. His mind was on how to prove Denmur and Sharpeyes were behind the attack on Sam and the death of the attacker, so his work didn't go far.

"Sir, you wanted to know when sparring was going to start," Ven said.

"Huh? Oh, right. Thanks, Ven."

Putting his stuff away, Sean left his workshop and paused. "Hello, Nola."

The Lesser Naga turned to look at him. "Good afternoon, MacDougal."

"Sean is fine," Sean said. "We're informal."

"Myna wasss apologizing for not being able to ssspar with me," Nola said.

"Being pregnant, it's best that I not fight unless I have to," Myna said. "I should've thought of that when I asked you before, but I was excited and didn't think of it."

"It isss fine," Nola said.

"While I might not fight you, I can at least let you fight them," Myna said, nodding to the cooks and maids.

"Us, too," Quinna said as she and her sister came out of the barn.

"We'd like to join in," Rumia added.

"Ssso many," Nola said. "I look forward to the fightsss."

"Split up as normal. Everyone who wins can get a match in with Nola," Myna said. "Unarmed and weapons only."

"Do they normally ussse Talentsss?"

"Not so much, yet," Sean said. "They're working on the basics. I can give you a match while they fight, if you'd like?"

Nola's tongue flickered before she nodded. "I accept."

Sean gave her a grin and stepped away. "Unarmed and weapons, or do you want to add in Talents?"

Nola's tongue flickered again. "Unarmed only?"

"An advantage for you," Sean said, "but I'll go along with it."

* * *

Sean coughed as he sat up. "You're faster than I expected."

"You held back," Nola replied simply in her native tongue. "I watched your fight with Knight Sharpeyes. I know you can do more."

"I try to limit myself to human normal."

"Yes, and normal Humans almost never beat my kind because they're too slow."

Sean dusted himself off when he got back up. "We can have another match, if you'd prefer."

"Yes. One where you give me your full strength," Nola said as she moved away and coiled herself again.

"Sean?" Myna asked.

"One more match. She wants me to be more than Human," Sean told her. "Sorry for disrupting your plans."

"It's fine," Myna said, coming over to give him a kiss on his cheek. "Now win."

Sean gave her a smile. "Well, now I have to."

Everyone else had finished their first set of fights and watched the second match between Sean and Nola. Sean set his feet and exhaled before meeting Nola's eyes, extending a hand to beckon her.

Nola took the invitation, launching like a coiled spring released from tension. Sean slid to the side, pushing her attack past him as he caught her body midway down and pivoted. Nola let out a startled sound as she was thrown across the yard and landed in a heap. Shaking her head, she started to get herself untangled when Sean pounced on her. Nola whipped and bucked, trying to loop around him, but Sean just wove past her thrashing body and got ahold of her arms. With another heave, she was flying again.

Nola tapped out after the third throw— her head was spinning, and she collapsed on the ground. When Sean appeared above her, she was afraid he hadn't seen her tap, but his hands gently touched the side of her face and her head stopped spinning.

"Good fight," Sean said earnestly.

"No. You controlled the entire thing. I've never been so humiliated. How can you manage that?"

"Not Human," Sean said as he helped her upright. "I'm just as fast as you, but much stronger."

Nola's tongue flickered and she nodded slowly. "Yes. I've never been thrown before. That was frightening. I tried to wrap you, but you were never still long enough."

"Yeah, I knew what you were trying to do. I had to use everything to not get caught."

"Mollifying," Nola sighed.

"Nola, do you still wish to spar with the maids?" Myna asked.

"Yesss, but maybe not asss roughly."

"We'd appreciate that," Tiska smiled. "We can have tea afterward, after our bath?"

"Bath? You bathe in the middle of the day?"

"Some of us bathe twice a day," Xenta grinned. "The bath is amazing."

"I'm going to go back to work," Sean said, not going to get roped into bathing with Nola. "You all have a good day."

Myna watched him go, her lips twitching as she suppressed laughter when she guessed why he was suddenly so eager to be elsewhere.

22

S   ean was deciding what kind of transmission would work best for the vehicle when a Messenger Fairy landed hard on his desk. "Sir, quickly! Rebecca Angusson needs help!"

Sean didn't think— he rushed for the door. As soon as he stepped outside, his energy wings sprang into being. "Show me the way!" he said when Ven appeared in front of him.

"Sean?" Aria called out from the barn where she was talking to Quilla.

"Need to go!" Sean said, suddenly airborne and following Ven.

Aria took off after him, but Sean wasn't going slow.

Ven led him toward the outskirts of the city. When Ven dove, Sean did, too, and could see that one of the small homes had a door broken in. Sean pulled up hard, letting his wings go, and rolled into the room.

Coming to his feet, he found the front room had been nearly destroyed, and there were pieces of furniture everywhere. What caught his eye was the heavily-muscled man who'd just shattered a door down the short hall.

Sean's energetic entry made the man turn away from the door.

Seeing Sean, the man sneered. "Just stay out of it and you won't get hurt." With that said, he turned and entered the room.

"Fuck that shit," Sean said, bull-rushing him.

The thug was turning when Sean hit him under the left arm, driving them both into and across the room. The crunch of flesh meeting the wood wall brought a feminine scream from the corner of the room. Sean pushed himself off the man and turned to find Rebecca.

Aria came rushing into the room at that moment. "I've got her!" she said.

Sean nodded, giving his attention back to the attacker. The man lay unmoving on the floor, his neck bent at an impossible angle. Kneeling down, Sean checked to make sure he was dead.

The sound of crying faded as Aria led Rebecca from the room. "Serves you right," Sean muttered. Getting to his feet, Sean followed the women outside.

The sound of whistles was getting closer. Sean exhaled, thinking of how things would likely go— none of his thoughts were happy ones. There were two guards, then four, that came running their way while neighbors looked on with interest from their own homes.

"What's going on?" the first guard demanded.

"Her home was broken into and she was attacked," Sean said flatly. "The attacker is still inside."

Both guards went running into the home. When the second pair arrived, they checked on Rebecca. Aria was speaking to the guards, so Sean stepped back.

"Ven, did anyone go tell Angus?"

"Yes, sir," Ven said. "The Fairy who brought you the message went to Angus. They knew you'd make it here first."

"Thank them for me," Sean said. "I barely made it."

"Yes, sir."

"Excuse me," one of the two guards said, coming out the doorway and giving Sean a hard look. "That man is dead."

"Yup. His neck broke when we hit the wall."

Both guards exchanged a look before the pair separated to flank Sean. "Not many people could manage to do that."

"My name is Sean MacDougal," Sean said, "and I'm someone who could."

Both guards stopped and backed away from him instead. "Sir, we... we, uh, apologize. Who is the woman, and how do you know her?"

"Rebecca Angusson. She's a friend. A Messenger Fairy told me she was being attacked, so I came right here. When I arrived, that man was breaking into the room she was in. He was turning when I hit him."

"A Messenger Fairy?" the guard asked. "One of them that covered you on the field?"

"Ven?" Sean asked.

Ven dropped onto Sean's shoulder. "Yes, it was. We keep an eye on all of his allies, since people are trying to hurt him and them."

Another man came jogging up to the scene, and Sean nodded to him. "Sergeant. Sorry about the paperwork."

Sergeant Ernest Carmady sighed. "MacDougal... What happened?"

"Well, someone attacked Rebecca Angusson. One of Ven's friends told me, and I came here. Got here in time to save her."

"Angusson?" Carmady said. "As in Angus Angusson's wife?"

A loud bellow echoed down the street. "Becca?!"

"Yeah, that'd be him," Sean said, looking past the guards to where the very large man was barreling toward them. "I'd get your men out of his way. He's probably not thinking clearly."

Carmady turned and yelled to his men, who were watching Angus coming at them like an avalanche. Angus saw only his wife and he swept her up, holding her tightly once he'd reached her.

"What happened?" Angus asked when he saw the guards all around them.

"Brutus attacked me..." Rebecca sniffled. "Said he was being paid."

Angus stiffened and his nostrils flared. "I'll kill him."

"Too late," Sean said. "His neck is broken already."

Seeing Sean, Angus exhaled. "You saved her?"

"The Messenger Fairy came to me first, since I could get here faster. I got here just as he broke into the back room."

Angus kissed the top of Rebecca's head. "You saved the only thing that matters to me... I'll repay this."

Sean gave the guards a glance. "We can talk later."

"MacDougal," Carmady asked, "if you have a moment to tell me everything?"

"Of course, Sergeant."

* * *

"How are you all tonight?" Sean asked as he took a seat at the table.

"We're fine," Fredrick said. "Better than the guards right now, at least."

"Oh?"

"Sam told us about what happened this morning," Fredrick said.

"Oh. Yeah."

"That's going to end badly," Flamehair said. "I got a look at the body before we ashed it. The man who attacked Sam had his wrists slit."

"They're claiming he committed suicide," Saret said.

"He was supposedly alive when the healer got there," Sam said.

"The healer didn't do anything, if that's true," Flamehair said. "There was no sign of healing on the wounds."

"Wolen took the healer down," Sean said, thinking back to the morning. "I don't think the healer was supposed to help."

"A serious accusation," Fredrick said, looking around casually.

Sean nodded and gave Tabitha, who was heading their way, a smile. "Dark Delight, please?"

Tabitha's smile went wooden. "I'm sorry, sir, that beverage is currently out of stock."

"Darkfoam hasn't come around yet," Mageeyes said.

"I doubt he will. He's a toad," Eva sniffed.

"Anything dark, please," Sean corrected his order.

"Hot cider?" Aria asked. "Winter is here, and the heat helps."

"And a round for the rest of the table, as well," Mageeyes added. "It's on me."

"At least she isn't raging," Eve said. "Our workers feel the brunt of it when she does."

"Makes the tanning hard, too," Jefferson nodded. "I have enough leather in stock currently for Augustus' order, plus a little more. Tanners are running behind for me."

"Glad you do," MacLenn laughed. "Will you make the deadline?"

"Unless something happens, I'll make it easily. I've put a closed sign up on my shop so that I can work without interruption. It's been nice being able to craft and not having to deal with idiots."

"How's the Shaping?" Sean asked.

Jefferson's smile grew wide. "Oh, so nice. It's hard to recall what it was like to have to scrap a piece if I made a mistake."

"Oh, Sean, are you going to get Helga some armor?" Aria asked.

"Probably should. Jefferson, can you get a set of leathers made for me if I bring her by?"

"The one from the trial?" Jefferson asked.

"Yeah."

"I can. I'll put it through before I finish Augustus' order."

"I'm fine with that," MacLenn said.

"Thank you." Turning his head to Sam, Sean smiled. "I'll see you after the leather is done. She's used to metal armor."

"I'll make sure to give you our best," Sam replied.

"Mithril, please?" Sean asked. "I can help with the exact fitting, if you do the harder part."

"I'll need to get mithril first," Sam said. "It's not common for me to make armor like that."

"I'll have it delivered," Fredrick said. "I'll deduct it from Sean's next payout."

"Thank you," Sean nodded.

"Your drinks," Tabitha said, coming back to the table to drop them off.

"I am a little worried for Commander Babbitt," Mageeyes said once Tabitha had left. "Sharpeyes is looking to remove him from his position. He has been for some time. The death of someone in custody might be enough for him to force him out."

"Lady Sharpeyes would object, wouldn't she?" Sean asked.

"Yes, but things are strained, and she already pushed for Jasper over his choice for High Magistrate. She might not be able to stop it, if it comes to that."

"That'll be a terrible thing for the entire city," Saret said. "He's always been fair and honest. It explains why he's so disliked by some."

"How does the position get filled?" Sean asked.

"The Lord will appoint a new commander," Mageeyes said. "The replacement has to be a captain, at the very least. Of the four in the city, I don't like what is likely to happen."

Flamehair's nose wrinkled. "He'd choose Lomar."

"Yes," Mageeyes shook her head.

"Distasteful," Saret sighed. "That man is a pig."

"Ah, I recall him," Fredrick said. "He has purchased a number of items from my shop. I wondered how he could afford them on a captain's salary."

"I'm surprised he wasn't ousted when the corruption investigation went through the guard," Saret said. "It's well known that he's willing to turn a blind eye for the right price."

"There's not enough evidence," Flamehair commented dourly. "He might be a pig, but he is a careful one."

"Wait, I remember him," Sam said. "I did a breastplate with silver and gold trim for him two or three years ago."

"That isn't good at all," Italice said. "He attended one of Darkfoam's parties. He was elbow to elbow with Denmur just last year."

Sean exhaled slowly. "Fun..." Taking a deep drink of his mug, he addressed the other topic he thought had to be talked about, "You've heard what happened to Angusson, right?"

"No," Fredrick said.

"His wife was attacked this afternoon," Sean said. "I got there just as the man, uh... what did she call him? Brutus? Was breaking into the bedroom."

"What happened?" Knox asked.

"His neck got broken. The Messenger Fairy that lived with them told me, then Angus. I got there just in time."

"She's safe?" Eve asked.

"Yes. They're staying at my place tonight. Fiona thinks she can have the upstairs done tomorrow so they can move into the bathhouse."

"How did Angus take it?" Jefferson asked.

"He was grateful, but that just made me feel worse. That attack had to be because of Denmur."

"Sean, it's not your fault," Sam said. "Denmur will attack *anyone* he thinks might hurt us."

"Yeah," Sean said darkly, taking another deep drink.

"She'll be safe now, with Angus always being beside her," Eva said.

"Until the next thing happens," Sean exhaled slowly. "I need to get a cuon for the bathhouse. Ven, please send Schin a message? Ask if he has one or can get us one by Fiveday."

"Yes, sir," Ven said from above them.

"I'm going to head home," Sean said, getting to his feet. "It's been a long day."

"Sean," Fredrick said solemnly, "please be careful."

"I will be."

"I'll make sure he is," Aria added.

23

Sean gave Angus and Rebecca a nod when he came into the dining room. "Good morning. I hope you slept well."

"As well as we could," Rebecca replied. "The bath helped, but..." She trailed off, looking down at the table.

"Nightmares," Angus said softly, covering her hand with his.

"If you'd like, I can help with that," Felora offered gently.

"You can?" Angus asked.

"It's a family secret," Felora said, "but with a small Agreement of secrecy, I'd be more than happy to help."

"Anything that'll stop the dreams..." Rebecca whispered. "Thank you."

"After breakfast. It won't take long, and Angus can be with you, if you'd like."

"How?" Angus asked, his brow furrowed.

"I'll put you both to sleep, and then we'll break apart the nightmare so you'll no longer fear it."

"Okay," Angus said, clearly not understanding.

"It's hard to explain," Sean told him. "It works, though."

"Breakfast," Glorina informed them when she came into the room. "Today, we have cheese-covered eggs, bacon, and pancakes."

Sean saw that each cart held a bottle of syrup and smiled. "Thank you, Glorina. Angus, Rebecca, you should try the syrup."

The guests looked at the bottle Mona set on the table before them and their eyes widened. "Sean, that's too much," Rebecca said.

"Everyone here will likely have some," Sean said. "Everything on the table is there for anyone to use."

"It's very sweet," Rumia said. "Delicious, but sweet."

"I have to use jam with it," Prita said. "Just a few drops mixed with the jam is how I prefer it."

Angus shook his head. "Your staff eats with you and gets to use syrup? It's as odd as the Messenger Fairies at the table." Seeing the sudden frowns that dominated the table, Angus spoke on quickly, "It's just different. Everything you do is that way, though. Most importantly, you're always there for friends."

"I'm just me, and yeah, I do tend to turn societal norms on their head."

"I'd like to try a small bit of the syrup," Rebecca said.

"Have as much as you like," Sean told her as he picked up the bottle in front of him.

* * *

Fiona let Sean know they'd be going over with Angus, so the carriage was his.

"I'm going to take Helga to get leathers made for her," Sean said. "I'll let Giralt know I'll be a little late. We'll drop Helga off at the bathhouse on the way to his manor."

"Okay, husband," Fiona smiled.

"Armor?" Helga asked.

"Leather to start with, though I've already told Ida's mother that we'll be looking to get some plate for you, as well."

Helga bowed her head to him. "Thank you, sir."

"I was surprised they didn't have you in your normal armor for the fight," Sean said as they left the dining room.

"We had to leave our gear behind," Helga said tightly. "Iron is forbidden here."

"It is," Sean agreed. "We'll be getting better than iron for you."

Helga's eyes widened. "Sir, I'm honored, but I'm not sure you should give me such exp—"

"He has spoken," Aria said, cutting Helga off. "You're used to a certain type of armor, and it's best for his allies to be as equipped as he can make them."

"Of course, mistress," Helga said, bowing her head.

"Also, what weapons do you prefer?" Sean asked.

"A short spear and shield," Helga said. "A curved shortbow is also useful."

"Aria, you know the best bowyer. Can you get her a bow?"

"Of course, Sean."

"I'll work on the spear," Sean said. "The shield can be done with the armor, I'm sure. Ven, can you send word to Sam about adding a shield, please? Helga, could you give them instructions on the type you'd prefer?"

Ven landed on Helga's knee, listening as she described what she needed.

* * *

Arriving at Jefferson's, Sean waited for Aria to confirm that he could step out. "We shouldn't be too long, Arliat," he told the driver.

"I'll pull into the alley and wait there," Arliat said.

"Thank you."

Jefferson opened the door to the shop. "You'd have been out here knocking for ages. I just ignore people if I have the sign up." His thumb hooked to the closed sign on the door. "If you hadn't sent one of the Fairies ahead of you, that is."

"Glad I thought of it," Sean said wryly, making a mental note to thank Ven. "Helga, this is Jefferson. He's the leatherworker."

Helga bowed her head to him. "A pleasure, sir. I always hold the crafters of armor in high regard."

"I do all kinds of leatherwork, not just armor," Jefferson said. "Come on in. You can wait inside, Sean."

The group went inside, and Sean took a seat in a chair that hadn't been in the front room the last time he'd been there. "Making the place more conducive to waiting?"

"Got tired of people complaining they couldn't sit while I was with a customer," Jefferson said. "Even *I* have a limit."

"Good to know," Sean laughed.

"Come on," Jefferson said to Helga. "In the back, we'll get you measured and talk about what you'd prefer."

"She's going to have pieces of plate over the top of it," Sean told him. "Keep that in mind, Helga."

"Yes, sir," Helga said.

When the two of them stepped into the back, Aria asked, "Mithril, Sean?"

"Going to enchant it, too," Sean said. "I know she's still earning goodwill with all of you, but she'll be the best fighter we have. I'd rather keep her going as long as possible."

"I see. She is very formidable in the air and on the ground. Armor would make that even more true. Toughening our clothing is good for minor things, but we'd all be best served to have leather armor for if we end up in another battle."

"I agree. We could have armor today, if needed. Shaping it is something we can do. Having our friends help, though, is better for now."

"Tightening the bonds," Aria nodded.

"And this gives the impression that we need outside help, if our enemies are paying attention."

"Ah, a surprise for them to fall for."

"Yes. Ven? Thank you, by the way."

Ven landed on Sean's shoulder. "You're welcome. We try to help as much as we can."

"You do a lot. I'm always grateful."

"As are we," Ven replied.

"Let Winston know I'm going to miss his shop today. After this, I want to go home and work on her spear. Aria, take her to see the bowyer, please? I'd like her weapons at least squared away."

"Okay, husband," Aria said softly, bending to kiss his cheek.

"Battle!" Helga's voice echoed from the back and Sean was on his feet instantly.

A second later, the door to the back flew open and Helga was standing there. "Outside, in the alley!"

Sean was out the door first as he rushed around the corner. Arliat was bleeding out on the carriage bench and the horses were stamping their feet, but unable to move with the brake set. Three arrows were sunk deep into Arliat's chest. Sean hardened his clothing, and just in time, as he felt the impact of an arrow on his back.

"There!" Helga shouted as she flew off.

Aria hesitated, her wings glowing behind her. "Sean?"

"Go. I'll try to save her."

Aria took off after Helga, who was chasing the two men running across the rooftops. Sean hurried to Arliat, who was grimacing in pain, her hands feebly holding the arrow shafts.

"Sean..." Arliat whispered as blood began to trickle from her mouth.

Sean reached out for the Bond between them and poured his energy into her, forcing her body to heal. "Fight, Arliat! Fight, dammit!"

Her eyes started to glaze over, and her hands fell away from the arrow shafts. Sean leapt, landing on the carriage and making it rock in place. He pulled the first arrow from her body, knowing that it would heal faster without the impediment. The Bond between them fluctuated, and Sean mentally wrapped his mind around it, refusing to let it go.

"What in the Queens' names?" Jefferson asked, looking into the alley.

Sean pulled the next arrow free and tossed it aside as he ignored the leatherworker— his mind was focused solely on Arliat. The first wound had closed up, and the second was closing fast. Grabbing Arliat's chin, he opened her mouth, leaned her forward, and made her lungs heave. Blood gushed from her mouth as it was forcibly expelled.

Gasping, Arliat would've fallen over if not for Sean's firm grip on her. When he pulled the third arrow from her, she screamed in pain.

"Fight!" Sean hissed as he continued to heal her. "Don't let some cowardly assassin do you in!"

Arliat panted as she grabbed his arm weakly. "Alive...? But..."

The last wound closed up, and Sean focused on her marrow, tasking it to replenish the lost blood. "Because you're family, and my family won't die... not if I can help it," Sean said as he leaned her back against the bench. "Just rest. The weakness will pass in a moment."

"She's going to live?" Jefferson asked, shocked as he looked at all the blood.

"Yes," Sean said as he watched Arliat. "She'll live."

"They would not surrender," Helga said, landing beside Sean. "I tried to subdue one." A gash on her left arm was healing.

The sound of whistles grew closer, and Sean sighed. "This seems familiar."

Aria landed beside the carriage. "Arliat?"

"I'm alive," Arliat whispered, looking down at her blood-soaked clothing. "I..." Trailing off, she looked at Sean.

Sean gave her a worried smile. "Hang on." He forced her clothing to Shape so the blood ran off her and to the carriage bench. "There you go."

Arliat looked from the blood to Sean. "You... saved me?"

"Can't let family die," Sean repeated.

"Over there!" someone shouted.

Sean jumped off the carriage and moved to the alley's mouth just in time to see two guards running toward them. "Over here."

"There's a disturbance?" one of the men asked, but his mouth fell open when he saw the blood dripping off the carriage.

"We were attacked by two men," Sean said. "Helga, can you show them where their bodies are?"

"Of course," Helga said.

"Wait a minute!" the guard snapped. "What about all this blood?"

"It was hers," Sean said, motioning to Arliat, who was still sitting on the carriage. "We've got her patched up. Did you want the dead or not?"

More guards came running their way, and Sean sighed. "I guess your fellows can have Helga show them. Jefferson, can we step inside the shop to explain things?"

"Of course," Jefferson said, his voice a little distant. He'd been told what Sean could do, but seeing it was completely different than just being told.

"Hang on. We need to check the carriage first," the guard said. "Make sure nothing's being hidden from us."

Sean stared at the guard for a few seconds before he motioned Arliat down. "Feel free. Aria, please take her inside and see if you can get her something hot to drink? She might be in shock."

"Of course, Sean."

The other guard was about to object before his eyes widened. "Huntress?"

"Aria MacDougal now," Aria said. "Excuse me. Our driver needs to go inside."

Frowning at his fellow guard, the first one went to the carriage. Neither of them moved to stop Helga, who stepped into the street to speak to the next two guards. Sean stood outside with the guards as Jefferson, Aria, and Arliat went inside.

It took the guards over ten minutes to finish inspecting the carriage and the immediate area. One of them gathered the arrows, making notes about where each was found as he did.

"Tell us what happened," the first guard said warily.

Helga came flying back, landing next to Sean and startling the two guards. "They are making notes and examining the scene," she informed Sean.

"I'm sure they'll talk to these two eventually."

"MacDougal," a tired voice sighed. "I should've known."

Sean looked over his shoulder to see Eugene Carmady heading

his way. "Sergeant, it's not our fault. Speak with my enemies and maybe this will stop."

"Did you get the scene noted?" Carmady asked.

"Yes, sir," the first guard said. "We were about to question the suspect."

Sean exhaled slowly. "I'm the employer of the victim."

Carmady shook his head. "You two get your notes in order. Where are the others?"

"They are with the bodies four streets over," Helga said.

"Bodies?" Carmady asked.

"Two men with crossbows attacked Arliat, my driver," Sean said. "Helga and Aria went after them. They'd have to explain what happened at that point."

Carmady's eye twitched and he looked at the drying blood. "And the driver?"

"Inside, recovering," Sean said. "We got her healed as best we could. I still have to get her to a healer after this."

"Sir, the driver wasn't wounded at all," the first guard protested.

Carmady looked to Sean. "Then whose blood is that?"

"Arliat, my driver's. As I said, we got her healed as much as we could so she wouldn't bleed out," Sean replied.

"Lying to the guard is a crime!" the first one snapped.

Sean stared hard at the guard. "Is it? You seem awful intent on trying to make my driver or me look like the bad guys here. Why is that?"

"Easy," Carmady said, moving between them. "Get your notes in order, Private. MacDougal, where is the driver?"

"In Jefferson's," Sean replied.

"Shall we go inside, and you can tell me what happened?"

"Fine by me," Sean said.

"But, sir! He's a suspect," the first guard said.

Carmady turned slowly to the guard. "Do your job, and I'll find out who the suspects are. Unless you suddenly became a sergeant and I got demoted?"

"Sir, yes, sir," the first guard spat.

"We'll talk later," Carmady replied. "Until then, you might want to consider how close to insubordination you are."

Sean left the two of them to argue and went inside with Helga trailing him.

24

Arliat was sitting in the chair Sean had been in before. She looked distant, and Sean touched her shoulder, making her jump and tense up.

"Easy," Sean said gently. "You're safe now."

"Sean, how did they even know you were here?" Jefferson asked. "You haven't been here long enough for them to have followed you and ambushed her."

"No idea, and unfortunately, we can't talk to the dead."

Helga shifted in place and she shook her head minutely, glancing at Jefferson when Sean looked her way. Sean's lips pursed, but he let it go for the moment.

"Can you go ahead and finish measuring Helga, Jefferson? We'll be here for a while talking to the guard, but we can at least get that done."

"I can do that," Jefferson nodded. "Come on, Helga. This time, try not to run off on me?"

"I make no promises if Sean or the others are attacked."

The front door opened to admit Eugene Carmady, who exhaled as he shut the door. "Things are tough enough right now, MacDougal. More incidents with you will not help matters."

"I'd rather not have my family injured, either," Sean said tightly. "What can we answer for you?"

Carmady took out his notebook and looked at Arliat. "Miss, let's start with you. What can you tell me about the attack?"

Arliat looked at Carmady blankly for a few seconds. "Umm... I dropped them off at the front, then went around the block and came back up the delivery way before turning into the alley and setting the brake. The next thing I knew, I was in pain, as I had two bolts in my chest." Arliat's hands moved to where the quarrels had pierced her, and she looked down at her uninjured front.

"How long was it between parking and you being attacked?"

"A minute, maybe?" Arliat said questioningly.

"We hadn't been here long," Sean said.

"After you were injured," Carmady said, not looking at Sean, "what then?"

"I looked up and saw two men across the street, kneeling on the roof. The taller one fired again," Arliat winced and her hand moved to the third spot she'd been hit. "I was in so much pain..."

"Did you cry out in pain?"

"I... don't know," Arliat said, her eyes beginning to water. "I don't know..."

Aria was beside her in an instant, holding her as Arliat cried. She stared at Carmady reproachfully.

Carmady sighed and looked at Sean. "MacDougal, how did you know she was being attacked?"

"Ven," Sean called out.

Ven landed on Sean's knee. "Yes, sir."

"Sergeant, I always have Messenger Fairies near me. I thought this was known by now."

"Ah, right, the field. You were informed by the Fairy that she was attacked, and then what?"

"I rushed out to help her, and a bolt missed me. Helga and Aria went after the two men, and I went to help Arliat."

"By her own account, she had three bolts in her, and I saw the blood," Carmady said, looking at Sean with curiosity. "How did you help her?"

"Use of my Talents, and that's all I'll say on it."

Carmady hesitated before making a note. "You aren't registered in the city as a healer, are you?"

"No."

Carmady grimaced. "That might be a problem."

"I don't see how," Aria said flatly. "He isn't operating a business as a healer. Surely those laws are only for those conducting business."

"Hmm... could be," Carmady said, making another note. "Go on. You healed her somehow, and then what?"

"The guards showed up," Sean shrugged. "The one was being argumentative and an ass right from the start."

"Noted," Carmady said. Turning his attention to Aria, who was still soothing Arliat, Carmady bowed his head slightly. "Huntress, I—"

"*MacDougal*," Aria said firmly. "Aria MacDougal is my name, Sergeant."

"Ah, my apologies. What can you tell me of events?"

"We followed Sean out the door and saw two men with crossbows running away. Helga and I took to the air to apprehend them. When we caught up to them, they refused to surrender and attacked us. Helga took an injury to her arm before I got there. Seeing that they were using weapons, we had no choice but to counter their force with our own."

"You cut them down?" Carmady asked, looking to the short blade on Aria's hip.

"No, we pushed them," Aria said. "They broke their necks on impact."

Carmady stared at her for a second before making a longer note in his book. "You pushed them off the roof?"

"Nudged them as they ran after we called for them to surrender multiple times," Aria said again. "That was also after they hurt Helga."

"Very well. I might need to talk to you again later. Where is Helga?"

"Being fitted for leather armor, which is why we were here to begin with."

"Ah, very well. I'll just go get her statement."

"She's with Jefferson," Sean said.

Carmady didn't move. "Hmm... I can wait a few minutes."

Sean's lips ticked up at the corners briefly. "Probably for the best."

Fortunately, it wasn't long before Helga came back out with Jefferson. Carmady stopped leaning against the wall and straightened up, his eyes focusing on the large bond marking on her neck.

"All done, Sean," Jefferson said. "It'll be a couple of days, at least. I'll send them along as soon as they're done."

"Excuse me," Carmady asked, "Helga, right? I need to question you about the attack."

Helga looked at Sean. "Do I answer him?"

"He knows that Ven told us about the attack, and Aria told him how the attackers died. He just wants to hear your story."

"Very well," Helga said, turning back to Carmady. "I followed Sean out the door, and upon seeing two men with crossbows, I went to chase them. Aria and I called out many times for them to stop and surrender, but they did not. I tried to capture one, but he pulled a dagger and cut me." Helga showed the partially healed wound on her arm. "When he struck me, I pulled back and Aria caught up to me. Together, we tried again to convince them to stop, but as they were not, we tried to nudge them off course. Instead of making the next jump, they fell and landed on the ground."

"I see," Carmady said, writing in his book. "That wound looks older than today."

"And Arliat is healed, or mostly healed," Sean said. "What's your point?"

"You healed her, too?"

"Not fully, obviously. Even a master healer would have had trouble with Arliat's wounds."

Carmady gave it a few moments of thought before nodding and

closing his book. "Very well. I am asking you to leave the carriage with us until we are done. I'll make sure it's returned to you."

"If you need to, Sergeant," Sean said, standing. "We'll be heading home."

"Sean, we should hire a carriage to take us home," Aria said. "We need to take Arliat and Helga to see a healer, remember?"

"Thank you, dear," Sean said. "Ven?"

"I'll send for one now," Ven said, blurring away.

"Thank you for understanding, MacDougal."

"I try to assist the guard," Sean said. "You, your brother, and the commander have shown me what the guard is truly made of."

Carmady gave Sean a nod of his head. "Thank you for that. I'll be in touch if we need more information."

* * *

Sean was glad when the carriage began to roll. "That was a fucking mess."

"I'm sorry, sir," Arliat said, looking depressed.

"No, Arliat. It absolutely wasn't your fault," Sean said quickly. "I meant the guards. That first one..."

"Sean," Helga said, "about your comment earlier. I... collected the souls of the dead. It is possible that you can talk to them, somehow."

"You *what*?" Sean asked.

"When the men died, I felt the rush of their souls, and I instinctively grabbed them," Helga said.

"If they end up with my wives, I will be very upset," Sean said tightly.

Helga shook her head. "No. I do not know how I know, but I know this is different."

Exhaling a shaky breath, Sean nodded. "Okay... You don't know how to speak with them, though?"

"No, sir. I'm sorry."

"Maybe Felora will have an idea," Sean said. "Arliat, are you okay?"

Arliat blinked, looking up from her lap. "Sir?"

"Are you okay?"

"I think so."

"I'm sorry you were attacked," Sean said. "If you want to leave, I—"

"No!" Arliat blurted, before her cheeks heated. "No, sir. I don't want to leave. It wasn't your fault, sir."

Ven landed on the seat next to Sean. "If anything, we're sorry. The two I left outside got distracted by a commotion down the street. They went to investigate it together. I've since talked with them both. We're sorry, Sean."

"The truly dedicated will find a way," Sean said. "If the attack had come from the commotion, we'd have thanked them. They know better now than to leave no one behind, right?"

"Yes."

"Then I don't fault them."

"Did you still want me to take Helga to the bowyer, Sean?" Aria asked.

"Yes, please," Sean replied. "After that, take her to Sam's and have her measured for her armor. We need to get it done soon. We'll get some leather and make armor for the rest of us at home."

"Do you want me to let Fiona know?" Ven asked.

"Please, Ven."

Sean lapsed into silence, thinking about what he could do to stop these attacks.

* * *

Back at the manor, Sean stopped at the shop. Two people were being waited on by Andrea and Felora. When he entered, both of his wives smiled brightly at him, and the customers turned to see what had caught their attention.

"Don't mind me," Sean said. "I just need to have a few words with you when you're done, Felora."

"Of course, husband."

The click of nails on wood made Sean smile as Caleb came out from behind the counter. "Hey, boy. How're you doing?"

The female customer let out a startled exclamation when Caleb passed her.

"He's harmless, as long as you are," Sean said. "Aren't you?"

Caleb chuffed and bumped his head into Sean.

"Yeah," Sean said, smiling and scratching Caleb's neck.

Caleb sniffed, then let out a soft growl, which stopped everyone in the shop.

"Stop it," Sean said softly. "Arliat was injured, but she's fine now. You're scaring the customers."

Caleb stopped growling and chuffed again.

"She's back. Go find her and give her some love. She could use some," Sean said, opening the door to let him out.

Turning back to the shop, Sean stepped aside as the man who'd been speaking with Felora gave him a smile and went out the door. "Have a good day, sir," Sean told the man.

"You, as well, MacDougal. You have quality goods. I'm sorry it took me so long to come buy them."

"Thank you?" Sean said with a questioning lilt to his voice, as he had no idea who the man was.

"Good day," the man chuckled as he left.

"Who was that?" Sean asked, going over to Felora.

"I don't know," Felora said. "He said his name is Cole Fuller."

"Hmm," Sean shrugged. "Andie, I'm going to take her into the back for a few. You good?"

"Yes," Andrea replied, taking a moment from making a deal with the woman to answer him. "Do you need me, as well?"

"No. Just a question or two is all."

"Okay."

Felora followed Sean into the back room and, as soon as the door shut, she pushed into him, kissing him. Sean accepted the kiss, but after it began to turn heated, he broke away from her.

"Easy, Fel," Sean murmured. "I really did have questions."

"Oh. I thought maybe you were just using an excuse to bring me into the back."

"Not this time, at least," Sean replied. "Let me explain what happened earlier, and what I'm asking for help with. I think you'll have to talk with your mom about it, but maybe not."

Felora stepped back and took a seat in one of the padded chairs. "It sounds serious."

"Yeah... it was nearly a disaster," Sean sighed as he took his seat.

25

Sean smiled when he finished crafting Helga's spear. The mithril weapon gleamed in the light of the workshop. The inset rubies were flush with the haft, and wouldn't hinder the movement of her hands at all.

Moving into the open space of his workshop, Sean spun the weapon through a simple attack and defense sequence. As he finished, he leveled the spear and pushed a fraction of energy into one of the rubies his hands touched. A burst of fire fanned out for five feet from the head of the spear.

"Nice," Sean grinned.

The door to the workshop opened, admitting Fiona. "Sean? Are you okay?"

"Yeah," Sean said, still grinning before his lips dipped. "Huh... I should be tired, though."

"Why do you say that?" Fiona asked, looking at the spear.

"Between healing Arliat and working on this, I should've tapped myself out. Hell, just healing Arliat would have before. Making this thing wasn't exactly light on my energy."

"Why a spear?" Fiona asked.

"It's for Helga," Sean said. He spun it again before it shrunk down to forearm length, the edges dulling enough to be safe to carry. Sean clipped the carabiner, attached to the butt of the spear, to his belt and smiled. "It's a damned good weapon, too."

"Will she be able to handle it?" Fiona asked. "It looks to be made solely from mithril."

"She should be fine," Sean said, unclipping it and tossing it to her.

Fiona caught it, her eyes widening as she felt the weapon. "Sean... this is filled with your energy."

"Yup. Go ahead and Shape it."

Fiona barely thought about making it full size and the spear was already fully formed. "Interesting. How did you manage that?"

"I had help," Sean said, tapping Dark Cutter on his waist. "Most of today was spent studying, and then doing. I'll be making all of you a similar weapon over the next few days. Once I figure out how to do the siphoning that Dark Cutter can, I'll add that to them. I do realize that it might be because of the metal, and I'm not ready to try enchanting adamantine yet. I don't want to end up like the one who made it."

"Please be careful," Fiona said, shuddering at the thought.

"These, though, being made out of mithril... they shouldn't be a problem. I might be able to form them down into innocuous items like rings that can take a weapon's shape. I'll be working on it."

"You always do the impossible," Fiona said with a small laugh, shrinking the spear back down. "It's time for sparring."

"Right on time," Sean said. "I want to see her face."

"What happened to Arliat?" Fiona asked, recalling he said he healed her.

"That's a long story," Sean sighed. "Might as well tell it to everyone. Can we put it off until dinner?"

"If that's your wish, my dear husband."

"Yeah, best to just tell it once. Things are going to get worse quickly, I think."

"I fear you may be right," Fiona agreed.

Sean found everyone but the cooks waiting for them. Taking the small weapon from Fiona, he threw it to Helga. "Catch."

Helga grabbed the small spear with a frown. "Sir, I am honored you would bestow a weapon upon me, but..." She trailed off, giving the small thing an uncertain expression.

"Any gift from him should be treasured," Myna said pointedly. "Besides, knowing Master, I'm sure that it's full of surprises."

"Easy, Myna," Sean said. "I don't blame her for being under-whelmed."

"No, sir, I—" Helga started to protest.

She cut off when Sean held up his hand. "Just imagine it being a spear of your desired length."

Felora snickered, her eyes glittering at his choice of words.

Sean rolled his eyes, but no one saw— they were watching the spear. Helga's eyes were wide as she stared at the now six-foot-long weapon. Her hands slid along its haft, not believing that the rubies were so firmly set.

"It is beautiful..." Helga whispered. "Almost as beautiful as Gungnir..."

"That's high praise from you," Sean said, recognizing the name of Odin's spear. "There's another trick to this one. Make sure it's pointed up, please, but while your hand touches one of the rubies, feed it a trickle of energy."

Helga looked up at the tip of the weapon for only a second before a five-foot fan of fire blossomed into the air. Her mouth fell open, and she did it again and again. Everyone else in the yard was watching just as raptly as she was.

"You might need to infuse some energy into it eventually," Sean said, breaking the moment, "but it should be good for a long time. That is your spear."

"What is her name?" Helga asked, looking at Sean with eager eyes.

"It's your weapon, Helga. It's yours to name."

"I... must consider carefully," Helga said in awe.

Sean looked over to Myna, who was looking a little envious. "I'll be making each of you something," Sean said. Myna's eyes snapped to him, and he gave her a smile. "Two for my dual-clawed kitty."

Myna's cheeks heated, and her lips curled into a pleased smile. "Thank you for thinking of me, Master."

"I am sorry," Helga coughed as she shrunk the spear back down. "We are sparring."

"Clip the end to your belt," Sean said when she gestured with it.

Looking at the carabiner, she played with it, then clipped it to her belt. "Thank you, sir."

* * *

When sparring and bathing were over, Sean heard from everyone what weapon they would prefer— all of them asked for the same weapons they'd been training with. Myna washed his back and sat beside him all through bathing. Her hands had wandered once, but when Sean gave her a raised eyebrow, she stopped.

Sitting down to dinner, Sean took a slow breath, knowing it was time to tell them all about what had happened earlier in the day. He waited for Glorina, Lona, and Mona to bring the food in before speaking.

"Thank you, Glorina," Sean said, making sure to serve himself so the others would.

Once he had done so, he didn't start to eat, but cleared his throat to get their attention. "You can all start, but before I do, I have to tell you all about today."

All eyes went to Sean while they dished up their food.

"We took Helga to Jefferson's. While Arliat was waiting for us, two men ambushed her..."

* * *

It took a while to explain everything, but he made sure the full story was told. When he finished, he began to eat.

"Well, that is disturbing..." Fiona said. "From now on, we'll have to be especially vigilant, and have our clothing toughened. I will work with you," she looked at the staff, "to make sure that your clothing can at least resist such an attack."

"I'll be speaking with my mother tomorrow," Felora said. "Hopefully, she has some insight into what we can try. I could try a dream with Helga and see if that works?"

"Carefully," Sean said. "I don't want either of you injured."

"She knew the attack happened," Andrea said, looking to Helga, "which is what saved Arliat."

Helga blinked. "I only—"

"No," Andrea cut her off. "Your warning is what let Sean get there in time. You had a direct hand in saving her life."

"She's right," Sean said. "Another half minute, maybe less, and she would've slipped away. Granted, I might've been able to do something about that, but I'm sure I would've been done for the rest of the day, too."

Helga bowed her head. "I do not mean to argue. I merely felt the fight and knew she had been outside. I grew concerned. I feel that Sean is the one who saved her— all I did was inform him."

"We understand," Ryann said. "The fact still remains; without the warning, it might've been much worse. All of us would be somber tonight if not for what you did."

"I understand, mistress. I shall accept some credit, but only a small portion."

"And the two who were supposed to look after her take some of the blame," Ven said. "They will not fail like that again."

"Helga, thank you," Arliat said. "You helped save me. From what I understand, if you and Aria hadn't gone after them, they might've taken another volley at me. Both of you have my thanks." She looked at Sean. "As do you, sir. If you hadn't been there..." Arliat trailed off, overcome with emotion for a moment.

"I understand," Sean said. "You're family, and we protect our family with everything we have." His eyes went to everyone at the table. "If you're here, you are family. Period. I would do the same for any of you, but I hope I never have to. With things getting even more bloody and dangerous, I understand if any of you'd like to leave. We'll terminate the Agreements and—"

"Never," Glorina was the first to speak.

The others all spoke up a second later, and the hubbub made it hard to discern who said what. As the noise grew, Aria let out a high-pitched whistle and they went quiet, though Myna, Fiona, Prita, and Sean all winced at the sound.

"Sean was speaking," Aria told them.

"As I was saying, if you want out, it's fine. None of us will hold it against you," Sean said.

"Sir," Glorina said, the first one to speak again, "no. I've spoken at length with Lona and Mona before this incident, and all three of us agree— we are your cooks. If you'd let us, we'd Bond for longer."

Lona and Mona both nodded and said in unison, "She's right, sir."

"Sir," Tiska said, "all three of us," she motioned to herself, Cali, and Xenta, "are also with you. Not only do you treat us better than we'd ever thought, you've also given us so much, even empowering us to be your unseen blades, if needed. You'd have to send us away, and even then, we wouldn't go far."

Cali and Xenta nodded vigorously in agreement.

"Me, too," Rumia said. "I'll not leave willingly."

Rosa glanced at her daughter, then nodded. "I will stay, as well."

Quinna snorted. "As if we'd leave."

"Right?" Quilla laughed.

Prita licked her lips, the last to speak. "Sir, Aria saved my life, and you gave it back to me. I'm with the maids— even if you forced me away, I'd be nearby to help."

Sean felt a spike of energy from everyone who'd spoken, and he closed his eyes. "I see. I will shoulder your faith in me." Opening his eyes, he met each of theirs in turn before speaking again, "Family... If you're determined to stay, I will make sure you are given everything I can give. It's the best I can do to keep you all as safe as possible."

"I agree with you, Sean," Fiona said. "You're going to the inn tonight, aren't you, Sean?"

"We don't have the carriage, so—"

A blur of silver announced the Messenger Fairy as they landed in front of Sean. "Sir, there's a guard driving the carriage into the yard."

"I'll go check on it," Arliat said, getting up.

"We'll come with you," Quinna said as she and Quilla followed her.

"Guess I can go," Sean said.

"Aria, make sure he stays safe, please?" Fiona smiled. "Have a good evening, husband."

26

Arriving at the Oaken Glen, Sean took a deep breath. As he followed Aria out of the carriage, Sean looked toward Arliat. "Are you sure you're okay?"

"Yes, sir. This is my job, and I will see it through."

"Okay," Sean said, still worrying for her.

"She'll be okay, Sean," Aria said softly as she led him to the door. "Ven has a dozen sets of eyes watching her. We'll know if trouble happens."

Sean exhaled and nodded. "I know, but it doesn't make me feel any less uneasy."

"Because you're a good man," Aria said, opening the door and stepping inside the inn.

Sean saw that the table was empty and followed Aria toward the hall to the private dining rooms. Crossing the floor, he felt the eyes watching them, and heard snippets of their conversations.

"I'd hoped it would be one of the Carmady brothers."

"They'd never last as a captain under Lomar. We both kn…"

"Still can't believe it. Things are going to get worse, much wor…"

"At least he had the last word on it. I can only imagine the look on Lord Sharpeyes' face," a man snorted.

Sean glanced back at the last bit, but as he kept following Aria, the conversation was lost to him. Giving Allonen a nod, he got one in return from the bartender.

When they reached the private dining room, Aria knocked, then entered. "Sorry for the delay."

"We heard," Fredrick said. "I'm glad she survived the attack."

A round of agreement came from everyone at the table.

"Us, too," Sean said. "We got the carriage back, or I might not have made it."

"That would have been problematic," Mageeyes said. "There has been a shift in power."

Sean hesitated before sitting. "Okay?"

"Commander Babbitt was removed from his position," Joseph blurted out.

The snippets Sean had heard in the main room suddenly came into focus. "Fuck. Who replaced him?"

"It'll be one of the four captains," Mageeyes said, giving Joseph a put-upon look. "Considering that Sharpeyes dismissed Babbitt, it'll likely mean Lomar will become commander."

"How he survived the sweep of the guard, I still don't know," Saret said. "He must've burned a few people or made deals to not get turned on."

"Regardless, it means things will get worse," Flamehair said. "He obviously will not be understanding about our fight."

"Less than fair," Eva said pointedly.

"He's attended a few of Denmur's parties," Italice said. "The deck is being stacked against us again, just as we were gaining momentum."

"I remember him now," Ryan said with a frown. "Didn't he try to get you to dance last time?"

"Yes. I turned him down," Italice said tightly. "Not listening is his strongest point. I had to wind him before he stopped asking."

Fredrick laughed, recalling the scene. "Oh, yes. When he was able to speak again, he was quite upset. You left at that point, didn't you?"

"Right after I hit him," Italice sniffed.

"Yes. Denmur had one of his staff 'console' him," Fredrick said. "Poor girl didn't deserve that."

"No one does," Italice snorted.

"What does that mean for us?" Knox asked.

"That every little thing the guard can cause grief for us will be called into question," Mageeyes said, "which will make things even more difficult for Sean."

"Because I always end up in situations," Sean said.

Tabitha knocked and entered the room. "Oh, I was right. What can I get for you? Refills?"

"Hot cider," Sean said, and Aria nodded her agreement.

"And another round for everyone here," Flamehair said, handing over the money.

"I think someone knew there was a change coming," Jefferson said with a frown when Tabitha left. "That guard that was acting odd, Sean, the one who wanted to search your carriage. After you left, he got into a disagreement with Carmady. Normally, a private wouldn't argue with a sergeant in public."

"Hmm... what was the reason given for Babbitt being asked to step down?" Sean asked.

"None of us were there," Mageeyes replied, "but I have it from a good source that Lord Sharpeyes used the corruption and spike of violence in the city as the reasons."

"All of which probably ties back to Sharpeyes and Denmur," Joseph snorted.

"This is going to be rough," MacLenn sighed. "I move so many things in and out of the city. If they're targeting the association, I can bet my people will get grief from the gate guards."

"That's petty, so it's likely," Sam sighed.

Sean picked up on a commotion coming from the hall and he looked at the door. A moment later, the door flung open and a Rabbit Moonbound came stumbling into the room.

Fredrick's eyes went wide when he saw her. "Bonnie? What is it?"

The woman fell to her knees short of his chair. Her voice was cracked and raw as she said, "Jackson... Bond...! Gone!" With one last gasp, she fell face down on the floor.

Sean jerked out of his seat, rushing to her side. Touching her, he tried to find what was wrong, but all he found was a dead body. Her soul was gone— he had no chance of even trying to save her.

"She's dead," Sean said.

"Brother..." Fredrick whispered, his face paling. Chair shooting back, Fredrick rushed for the door.

Tabitha had just been returning to the room when Fredrick ran into the hall— he barreled into her, sending her and the drinks flying backward. The room rapidly emptied as everyone went after Fredrick. All eyes were on them as they crossed the main room. They were clearly waiting to see what was happening.

Sean beat Fredrick across the room and had the doors open before anyone else could get there. The cold night air felt colder than he recalled it being when he arrived, and the quiet was suddenly split by distant whistles.

"That way!" Sean said, pointing as wings appeared behind him. "I'll go see what's happening."

Aria grimaced as her own wings appeared behind her and she shot into the sky after him. Glancing down, she could see the others following on foot. When she looked forward, she caught sight of a few dozen silver streaks in the air with them. One of them was close enough for her to see the leather armor and crossbow that the Messenger Fairy was carrying.

Sean aimed for where a group of men with lanterns was standing, angling so he touched down a few dozen yards away from them. His glowing wings caught the attention of the guards, who all turned to face him.

"This is a restricted area," one of them said, stepping forward.

"Why?" Sean asked.

"Not your concern," the guard said, coming close enough that Sean could make out the sergeant insignia on his uniform. "Oh. Of course it's you, MacDougal," Wolen sneered.

Sean frowned. "Sergeant? That's new."

"The guard is changing for the better," Wolen snorted. "Now, move along or you'll be arrested for interfering with a crime scene."

"So there *was* a crime committed?" Aria asked, having landed beside Sean.

"Not your concern," Wolen growled.

"But it might be," Sean said. "We heard that Jackson Gertihs died and are trying to find him."

Wolen frowned. "How did you find out he's dead?"

"His Life Bonded came to the Oaken Glen and told Fredrick," Sean replied.

"Be that as it may," Wolen snapped, "you aren't family, and this is a crime scene!"

The sound of people rushing toward them caught Sean's ear. "I'm not, you are correct. I will not bother you."

Wolen's chest puffed up. "Good that you understand, MacDougal."

"He is, though," Sean continued as if Wolen hadn't spoken, hooking a thumb over his shoulder.

Wolen looked past Sean and his lips drew tight.

Fredrick's steps slowed as he approached, clearly dreading what was coming. "Sergeant, have you seen my brother?"

Wolen's lips twisted, but he nodded. "Come with me, Gertihs. The rest of you, stay back."

"Gertihs, maybe you need a friend along, to support you?" Sean said.

Fredrick blinked at Sean for a few seconds before nodding. "Yes. Please, Sean?"

Wolen's frown was clear to everyone. "Very well. You two *only*."

Sean walked side by side with Fredrick as they followed Wolen. "We'll find out who, and make them pay," he said softly.

"We *know* who," Fredrick said tightly. "Right now, it's proving it so they can get what's due them that will be the hard part."

Sean didn't argue the point, as he was certain who it'd been, as well.

Getting closer to the building, Sean took in the structure with a curious gaze. "Warehouse?"

"This whole area is," Fredrick said. "Merchant warehouses."

Wolen motioned the guards aside. "Make sure those gawkers stay back."

"Yes, sir," one of the guards said, saluting Wolen and giving Sean a sneer. "Sir, you should be careful. This one was already involved in a few deaths today."

Sean stared at the man— it was the same guard who'd given him grief outside of Jefferson's. "You mean when my driver was attacked? Odd that I saw you there, and now, you're here."

The guard's gaze shifted away from him, and Wolen stepped chest to chest with Sean. "Are you implying something about the guard?"

"Only that they're doing their jobs," Sean said evenly, making a note about how brazen Wolen was. "If you don't mind, Sergeant, my friend just wants to see what happened."

"Of course," Wolen snorted, turning to enter the building while the guards all went toward the growing crowd.

Only a single lantern illuminated the dark, cavernous room. The light was pointed directly at Jackson's body. He was laying on his back with his eyes wide open, and dried blood staining his face and clothing. A pool of congealing blood radiated out from the corpse. Something about the body was bothering Sean, but he couldn't figure out what it was.

Fredrick's breath caught, and his hands curled into fists as he stared. Tears trickled as he continued to stand there.

"That's your brother, right?" Wolen asked bluntly.

Fredrick nodded, taking a step forward. "Jackson Gertihs, my younger brother. Mother doted on him so much."

Wolen's hand shot between Fredrick and the body. "Stop there. This is an active scene."

"It's dark for an active scene," Sean said, bringing his wings back into existence.

The increased light flooded the area around the body, and Sean spotted a bloody footprint a handful of feet away from Jackson. There was a knife on the ground, a dozen yards further away, in line with a second door that might lead out the far side of the building. The most telling thing was the coin pouch still attached to Jackson's belt.

"That's interesting," Sean mumbled.

Wolen glared at Sean. "Do *not* contaminate the crime scene."

Sean gave the man an incredulous look, but let his wings fade. "They are pure energy. They can't contaminate anything."

"This is currently an unknown crime, possibly a robbery gone wrong," Wolen said.

Sean's lips thinned. "Robbery?"

"Possibly."

Sean wanted to retort, but knew it wouldn't do him any good. "Ven, did you see everything?" Sean asked.

"Yes, sir," Ven replied, landing on Sean's shoulder.

"What is that *pest* doing in here?" Wolen growled.

"Ven is Bonded to me," Sean said flatly. "They go everywhere I do, so they can run messages for me."

"Well, it needs to leave. Now!" Wolen snapped.

"Ven, go ahead," Sean said. "You have the idea, right?"

"Yes, sir," Ven replied.

Fredrick swallowed and rubbed at his eyes. "Sergeant, you'll make sure his body is handed over to Flamehair's people. Correct?"

"Once we're done," Wolen said coldly.

"My brother always left the guild hall on time and went straight home," Fredrick muttered. "There was no reason for him to be here."

"Maybe he had unlawful reasons to be here," Wolen said. "This warehouse is owned by the Darkfoam family. Last I heard, your family and theirs weren't on the best of terms."

Fredrick's face became expressionless. "Are you suggesting my brother was committing a crime?"

"All possibilities are being investigated."

Exhaling slowly, Fredrick turned on his heel, heading for the door. "I'll be lodging a complaint, sergeant."

"Of course you will," Wolen snorted. "He's leaving. Now you are, too, MacDougal."

Sean stared at Wolen for a long moment. "The other sergeants I've dealt with had more decorum than to insult a victim's family. Pity. I had respect for the guard until just now."

Wolen's lip curled up. "Move, or be arrested."

Sean shook his head and followed Fredrick.

Sean didn't speak as he fell into step with Fredrick. The two of them moved to their friends, who were waiting at the front of a growing throng. Fredrick shook his head and kept walking. Eva took his hand in hers, as she took his left side and Fredrick's impassive face cracked. He swallowed hard, but kept moving.

Once they were away from the crowd, Fredrick stopped and hugged Eva tightly. She held him, stroking his hair and hoping to soothe him.

"It was him?" Jefferson asked.

Fredrick nodded, his face in Eva's chest.

"He'd been stabbed repeatedly," Sean said. "The bloody knife was still there, along with a footprint. Jackson's coin pouch was still on his belt."

"Not a robbery," Joseph grunted. "But why would he be here?"

"He wouldn't," Fredrick croaked. "There was no reason."

"The warehouse belongs to Darkfoam," Sean added.

"Think they lured him here, then killed him?" Knox asked.

"Or they grabbed him and brought him here," Sean said, thinking about the body. What had bothered him finally clicked into place. "His wrists had abrasions."

"Bound?" MacLenn asked.

"Rope," Sean said. "He left at the same time every day?"

Fredrick pulled his face away from Eva. "Yes."

"Maybe Agatha, the clerk at the hall, saw him?" Sean suggested.

"I'll speak with her tomorrow," Fredrick said. "Charie, please hold his body for me. I'll be hiring an investigator to look into his death."

"I wouldn't trust them, either," Eve said. "Those guards were very... aggressive."

"Indeed," Mageeyes said, "as if they hadn't expected to have people show up."

Fredrick wiped his eyes and looked at the group. "I'm going to go inform my family."

Goodbyes were said as the group broke apart, all of them thinking about this latest tragedy that had, yet again, hurt one of their own.

27

Sean was quiet when he came down to breakfast. He paused in the doorway and looked over his family before closing his eyes— he'd made his decision.

"Husband?" Fiona asked.

Sean gave her a soft smile. "I'm fine, Fiona." Looking at Ven, he spoke again, "Ven, after breakfast, please let Winston know I won't be over today."

"What are you planning on doing today?" Fiona asked him.

"Reading. I need to learn some things, and I haven't looked at the books at all."

"A day relaxing might be best," Ryann said.

"It'll be good for you," Ida added.

"Aria, you can go with them," Sean said, taking his seat. "Since I'm staying home, there's no reason to keep you here, too."

"We could finish earlier if you come with us," Fiona said.

"Very well," Aria said.

"Breakfast," Glorina said, leading the cooks into the room.

* * *

Sean walked into the library, taking in the shelves of books. *Odd that I haven't spent any time here. I used to read all the time... well, listen mostly. One of the few downsides to this world I guess— no more audiobooks.*

"Can we help?" Jutt asked, landing on the desk near Sean.

"We've been reading the titles," Arla said, landing beside Jutt.

A smile touched Sean's lips. "How about writing and math?"

"We're working on them, too."

"Hmm... which books are about nobility?" Sean asked.

Arla streaked across the room. "This row has a lot of books with nobility in the title."

"Thank you," Sean said, going over to where they were.

Looking over the titles, he pulled one off the shelf. "I'll start with this one. Did you want me to pull one down for you to read?"

"Yes, please," Arla replied. "I know just the one."

Arla flew to a different shelf and touched a book. "This one, please."

Jutt landed beside them. "'The Huntsman'?"

"I want to know what it is," Arla said.

Sean snagged the book and took them over to the desk. He placed theirs down on one side and took the seat behind it for himself. Pausing, he watched the two Fairy children manhandle the cover open so they could start reading.

* * *

Sean sighed as he put the book back. *Three books and nothing that I want to know was covered. I could just go ask Mageeyes, but I'd rather not... If people knew what I had in mind, they might object.*

"Sir, there is a Toivo Bloodheart asking to speak with you," Ven said, fluttering in front of Sean.

"Odd," Sean said. "Send him up, please, and have the maids bring us something to drink."

Jutt and Arla were closing their book when Sean turned around. "Done already?"

"We don't want to cause problems," Jutt said quietly.

"And you never will," Sean replied. "You can stay and read. It'll help me see who he is."

They exchanged a glance. "We want to help, too," Arla said as the two of them opened the book again.

There was a knock about a minute later, right before Tiska opened the door and showed Bloodheart inside. "Sir, your caller, Knight Toivo Bloodheart."

"Thank you, Tiska," Sean said.

"I'll have the drinks brought right up. Did you want the cigars, as well?"

Sean hesitated, not knowing they even had cigars in the house. "Yes, why not? The best we have please."

"Of course, sir." Tiska curtsied before leaving.

Bloodheart took in the room, pausing on the two Fairies reading. When Tiska left, he looked away from them. "I shouldn't be surprised, not after the end of the battle. Mageeyes did tell me that all of those Fairies were in your employ. Never thought I'd see two of them reading, though."

"Why's that?" Sean asked as he motioned Bloodheart to have a seat.

"It's unusual. Most barely give them a glance, but that's short-sighted. I'm sure you don't know, but Messenger Fairies have long been allies to my family. When fighting, their intelligence gathering and clear communication are vital."

"All I did was offer them a place to call home," Sean said. "Jutt, Arla, this is Knight Bloodheart. He is a friend to Dame Mageeyes."

"It is nice to meet you," Jutt said.

"A pleasure," Arla added.

"Jutt?" Bloodheart said slowly.

"Yes, sir?"

"Hmm. Would you be interested in meeting a Messenger Fairy called Jott?"

Jutt flew up, stopping an inch away from Bloodheart's face. "Can I?"

Bloodheart's eyes crossed briefly and he chuckled. "Yes, of course. MacDougal, would you mind if Jott came over?"

"Not at all," Sean said.

"Wesa?" Bloodheart called.

A Fairy landed on the desk in front of him. "Yes, sir?"

"Let Jott know they should visit this home."

"Yes, sir," Wesa saluted before zipping off.

"Wesa's line has been with my family for a few generations. Like you, we learned that treating them like people was the best thing to do."

"Glad I'm not the only one who could see that," Sean said.

A knock on the door announced Tiska with a tray. She crossed the room on silent feet, placing a humidor, a bottle of cognac, and two glasses on the table. "Are these to your liking, sir?"

"Yes," Sean said, not knowing if he was supposed to do something with them.

Tiska took the cognac and poured for both of them before deftly setting the glasses on the table, placing the decanter to the side so Sean could easily reach it later. Opening the humidor box, she put a crystal ashtray next to them, then selected two cigars. After handing one to each of them, she gave Sean a small silver knife.

Sean took the knife and cut the head of his cigar off before passing it to Bloodheart. Tiska had the ignitor in hand, ready for him. Having seen Giralt light a number of cigars, he understood that he wasn't supposed to engulf the end in flame, but warm the edges of the cigar until it lit gently. Taking the ignitor, he got his lit, then handed it to Bloodheart.

Bloodheart did the same, taking a moment to light his. Exhaling a stream of smoke, Bloodheart nodded. "A very fine smoke. Are these the same ones that Giralt uses?"

Sean's eyes darted to Tiska, whose head bobbed a fraction. "Yes, I believe they are."

"Do you wish me to stay and attend, sir?" Tiska asked, her eyes going to the two Fairies.

"That would depend on Bloodheart. Do we need privacy?"

Bloodheart switched hands with the cigar and took a sip of his cognac before answering, "If it's not any trouble, I would feel better about it."

"Very well. Please excuse me and my guest," Sean said.

Tiska curtsied. "If you need anything, sir, I will be nearby."

Jutt and Arla got the book closed, and took to the air. They hovered between the two men, bowing to both, before they zipped off.

Once everyone was gone, Bloodheart exhaled slowly. "MacDougal, I know this is a bit odd... We have barely talked at all, but I had to come to find out something."

Sean's lips twitched at the corners. "I have no plans on Amedee. I'm happy with my wives."

Bloodheart stared at him. "Am I glass?"

"It's obvious," Sean said, "which, coming from me, is kind of funny. My wives all say I'm oblivious."

Bloodheart set his cigar down on the edge of the ashtray and rubbed at his face. "So she does know, then?"

"You made it very plain at the party," Sean said. "Why do you even question it?"

"Because she doesn't return any of my small advances. I had thought that maybe—"

Sean cut him off by raising his hand slightly. "No. It's not me or anyone else." Sean hesitated, as her secrets weren't his to share. "She might not be ready for a relationship."

Bloodheart considered things, picking the cigar back up and taking a puff. "Does Knight Solanice have anything to do with it?"

Sean stared back at Bloodheart, who was watching him intently. "I can't say."

"I see. I'm a Knight, as he is... I could find a reason to challenge him easily enough. It would put my family into conflict with Lord Truestrike, though," Bloodheart murmured. "While I have no problems with this, my father might."

"I was looking for information on how the nobles settle disputes, or if they just issue legal duels that can go to the death," Sean said. "Do you have a few moments to explain that to me? I take it I couldn't just outright challenge Lord Truestrike."

"If it were only that easy," Bloodheart snorted. "No. One may only duel those of equal rank or below, unless offense has been given by the higher-ranked noble."

"If I wanted to fight another Aspirant, I can just march up and challenge them?"

Bloodheart nodded slowly. "Yes, but it looks bad for you. That isn't how things are done."

"I don't care about that," Sean said. "I have family and friends being injured and killed."

"And no proof as to who is behind it," Bloodheart said. "It is obvious, but without some kind of link, it'll reflect badly on you and those who associate with you."

"How badly?"

"In the case of Denmur, since you've been in conflict for at least six tendays, you mean?"

"Theoretically."

"I'm not sure it would affect you much, honestly," Bloodheart said slowly. "Those who might shun you are already with him. It might raise questions for outside observers, though."

"Madam Archlet?"

Bloodheart nodded. "She is a shrewd woman, and yes, her above others. Just dueling and killing your opponent is gauche."

"I'm sure Fredrick can find a way to overcome my misstep," Sean said.

"Gertihs could overcome that, but that won't end your problems."

"I'll get to him, eventually," Sean said.

"Removing a Lord is not easy," Bloodheart cautioned. "That would draw many eyes to you. From what I've heard, you prefer not to be noticed."

"I did, but it wasn't working." Sean sighed, looking up at the ceiling. "I'll give Fredrick's investigator a few days to work, but if nothing comes of it or something else happens..." Sean's face became stony and cold. "That'll be the end of it."

"I do not blame you in the least."

"I never did thank you for that duel during the party," Sean said, shifting the topic.

"You're welcome, but that wasn't for you, so much."

"It was for her," Sean smiled.

"Mostly," Bloodheart agreed. "It was also because I hated the idea of that weasel as a high magistrate."

"It would've been disastrous for me, which is why I thanked you."

Bloodheart bowed his head. "I should thank you. Evan would have pushed to try to repay my win against him, and that would have left me with few options. Even his father doesn't look to repay me anymore. Lord Sharpeyes has his eyes set on the one who scattered his son's brains on the field of battle."

"I was so mad," Sean said, looking into the distance. "I couldn't allow him to be saved and have to deal with him again."

"Don't leave an enemy who hates you alive."

"I'll try not to," Sean said. Shaking his head, he met Bloodheart's eyes. "You'll keep my inquiries to yourself, I hope?"

"I wouldn't spoil the surprise for Denmur," Bloodheart chuckled darkly. "He is upsetting Amedee, and that deserves to be paid for in pain."

"Cheers to that," Sean said, picking up his drink.

A knock on the door came after they drank. "Sir, it is time for midday sparring. I will be down with the cooks unless you need me," Tiska said, poking her head into the room.

Bloodheart blinked and turned in his seat. "Sparring?"

"Sir wants us to be able to defend ourselves," Tiska said.

"Hmm, much like our staff," Bloodheart nodded. "Do you spar during these times?" he asked, turning to Sean.

"I normally spar during the evening session," Sean said.

"Ah, well," Bloodheart sighed. "I had half-hoped to cross training blades with you."

Sean set his cigar in the ashtray. "I do owe you for you dueling Evan. I'll consider this even."

Bloodheart grinned. "This will be fun."

"For you," Sean snorted. "Try not to bruise my ego too badly?"

28

S ean looked up when the door to his shop opened. "Time for sparring?"

"Almost," Fiona replied. "I came to check on you. The maids were talking about you sparring with Bloodheart."

Sean rubbed the back of his head. "That was embarrassing..."

"That isn't how I heard it," Fiona said.

"I only won one match out of five," Sean sighed.

"Yes, but you *won* one. Bloodheart is a master swordsman."

"Oh..."

"Yes. Evan was an idiot to think he could fight Bloodheart and win. The only reason he even had the slim chance he did was because Bloodheart was blinded twice. If not for the knowledge Darragh gave you, you'd not have won the one match."

Sean thought about it— he'd stopped having to blank his mind to fight like he had to before. Through the fight in the field and the matches with Helga and Nola, he'd been fully in the moment. It'd been the same with the duels with Bloodheart— in all five bouts he'd fought, he never once unfocused his mind.

"I think I've integrated all that knowledge."

"It was going to happen in time," Fiona said.

"I should say the knowledge is second nature, but I still need to work on my execution."

"Which we do all the time."

"Fair enough," Sean said. With a smirk, he pulled her onto his lap and kissed her.

Fiona let out a happy sound as she kissed him back. The kiss lingered, soft, sensual, and full of love. Fiona was the one who broke the kiss after a moment.

"I didn't give enough time for more, Sean. However, you can always have me later tonight."

"I'd like that, my lovely wife."

"Now, what else have you been doing today?"

"I did some reading earlier. After Bloodheart left, I started work on these," he motioned to the desk.

Fiona looked at the desk and smiled. "Weapons for us?"

"They're not done yet. The enchantments still need to be done."

Fiona touched the forearm-length, ruby-studded, mithril staff. "This one is mine?"

"Yeah. I'm working on a lance of flame for it instead of the fan that Helga's has."

"That will be a surprise to any who attack me."

"That's the point."

"What are these clips?" Fiona asked, tapping the one end.

"Carabiners. They're something from my old world. Great for attaching things together. The non-bladed weapons will have them so they can be carried all the time."

"Interesting. Most won't think they're real weapons in their smaller form."

"That's my hope."

"The hammers look like hammers, though," Fiona giggled.

"They aren't hammers when they expand. They become mauls."

"Oh, yes, that does suit the sisters."

Sean nuzzled Fiona's neck. "You need to get off my lap, please."

"Yes, I can feel that," Fiona giggled, wiggling slightly before getting up. "It's nice to know that you still find me attractive."

"I always will," Sean said.

They both heard voices gathering in the yard, and Sean sighed as he stood up. "Time for sparring."

* * *

Sean cracked his neck as he took a seat to pull his boots off. The women were all talking about the various matches that had taken place during the sparring. *That match with Helga was different,* Sean thought. *She was surprised as hell when I beat her. Frankly, I was, too, but everything just felt natural and fluid.*

"Can I get those for you, sir?" Prita asked, coming over to kneel next to him.

Sean shook his head. "No thank you, Prita. I can handle my own boots and clothing."

Prita bowed her head. "As you say, sir."

"Prita, that was a good fight," Rumia called from the showers. "You're getting better."

"Thank you," Prita smiled as she stripped her clothing off. "I'm doing my best to get better."

"And you are," Myna said from the bath, the first one to climb into the tub. "You move the quietest of the maids, too."

"Thank you, Myna," Prita blushed.

"You need to work on your Talents, though," Myna said. "The others are better able to hold their energy and move without shimmering."

Tiska grinned. "Can we have another game tomorrow?"

"Possibly," Myna said.

"Sean," Ryann asked, coming to a stop in front of him, "can you check me and Ida?"

Pulling his boot off, he looked up at his two naked wives and his mouth went dry. "Gladly." He reached out and touched their stomachs. Ida and Ryann watched him with hopeful expressions, and Ida took Ryann's hand in hers as they waited.

Sean's smile was bright when he pulled his hand back. "Yes, for both of you."

"A father of four, at least," Felora murmured as she strolled past them, her hips swaying. "I'm betting six by next tenday."

Sean coughed, pulling his eyes away from Felora's ass. "Never thought I'd be a father really. Now, I'm going to have half a sports team."

"Do you think you'll be able to tell the sex of the child before it's born?" Ida asked Sean.

"I don't see why not. I think that was during the third trimester on my world, so maybe the last six tendays?"

Andrea nodded. "I'd like to know. It'll make picking a name much easier."

"We'll try," Sean said.

"Thank you," Ida said, going forward to kiss him.

Sean returned her kiss, then Ryann's. "Go on, you two. I still need to get undressed."

"We could help," Ryann said with a smirk. She continued before Sean could reply, "But we know how you feel about that."

"Just wanting to make me blush..." Sean grumbled, his cheeks pink.

"It's such a lovely color on you," Ida giggled as she pulled Ryann toward the showers. "Get my back, Ry?"

"Of course," Ryann replied.

Sean shook his head and got to his feet, doing his best to ignore all the eyes watching him. By the time he was done, he was the last one to the shower.

Fiona stepped away from the one she'd been using and offered it to him. "Here you go, Sean."

"Thanks."

"Prita, make sure you get his back, and he'll get yours," Fiona said as she walked to the tub.

Sean blinked when he realized that he and Prita were the only ones not heading to the tub or already in it.

"Will you get mine first, sir?" Prita asked, facing away from him.

"Yeah, I can do that."

* * *

When dinner was over, Sean brought up the subject that he knew he'd have to address, "Before I go, there's something I wanted to discuss with you."

Everyone quieted down and gave him their attention.

"I'm giving Fredrick's investigator, whoever that is, help to figure out what happened to Jackson. We all know this is going to lead back to Denmur, but I'll give them a chance to gather proof to make what I'm going to do less painful."

Fiona's lips pursed. "You mean to go after Denmur?"

"I'll challenge him, and keep doing so until he lies dead or proves he's not worth anyone listening to," Sean said. "I'm done letting them come after our family and friends. I'd do the same to Sharpeyes, too, but according to society, I can't. I'll be looking into how to deal with him, even if it means working with Lady Sharpeyes."

"Fiona and I should be there if you're going to approach her," Aria said.

"I'm going to deal with Denmur, first," Sean said.

"If you don't have proof, your reputation will suffer and, by association, Forged Bonds' will, too," Fiona said. "Are you going to speak with them about this?"

"Yes, tonight. I'm telling all of you first because I'm going down a path I never wanted to walk. I don't see any other way, though."

"We're with you, Master," Myna said, her eyes narrow. "Please tell me that Knight Solanice is also on your list? He was with them."

Sean looked at her and nodded. "Truestrike will be after Sharpeyes. They cost us our friends in Oakwood... I promised you retribution, and I will make sure it happens."

"Thank you," Myna said, her eyes shining. "If Fiona hadn't claimed you tonight, I would, just for that statement."

Fiona covered her hand. "Share him, like old times?"

"Hmm... yes."

Sean's face flushed, and he coughed. "Back to the topic. Does anyone want to speak up?"

"Isn't Truestrike going to become a High Lord?" Rosa asked.

"Not when I'm done with him," Sean said. "His pawns are being removed, and his association with Sharpeyes will hurt him."

Rosa looked uncertain, but the others all looked determined.

"Sir," Tiska said, standing up and looking at the other staff members, "if it's okay, we'd like to amend our Bonds. We talked with Fiona the other night and now seems like the best time to ease your mind about where we stand."

"Okay. What did you have in mind?"

"It'd be easier to have you offer it to everyone in the room," Fiona said. "They can accept as they wish, if you state it that way."

"Fair, but what kind of time frame are we talking? Five years? Ten? More?"

"Life," Tiska said.

Sean froze for a second. "That's a lot to go to from a single year. You might regret doing that."

"No," Tiska said, shaking her head. "We know what we're asking for, and it would be up to us to accept or not."

Sean looked uncomfortable, and Fiona touched his hand. "It would be their choice, Sean. Is that so terrible?"

"Their lives would depend on me staying alive," Sean said.

"Ours already do," Fiona said gently.

"I, Sean Aragorn MacDougal, offer this addendum to the Bonds to any in this room who wish to accept it— the Bonds will become Life Bonds, and they will get access to equal amounts of energy, access to all Talents held by those in the family, and keep the jobs they currently have." Sean exhaled once he'd finished.

One by one, the staff all accepted the new status. Even Rosa, who had hesitated before, did so while holding her daughter's hand tightly. Everyone was wearing wide smiles after they said the words and their bands thickened, taking up both their wrists and neck.

"Sir," Onim asked, rising to their feet, "may we Soul Bond?"

"What?" Sean asked, still off-balance from the sudden shift in the house.

"May those of us who want to Soul Bond do so?" Onim asked. "Maybe you can have Omin do so when you see them next?"

"Ah," Sean said, then nodded. "You three, and when I see Omin, I will ask them, too."

* * *

Sean was still trying to wrap his mind around what had happened when the carriage came to a stop outside of the Oaken Glen. *Now they all depend on you living...* he reminded himself. *Can't stop doing what I've planned, but they all believe in me so fiercely... Definitely didn't expect Jutt and Arla to jump on that Soul Bond, too.*

"It's clear, Sean," Aria said.

Shaking his head, Sean got out and took a deep breath of the cold night air. "Sorry for the delay."

"Still thinking about what happened?"

"Yes. I probably will be for a few days, at least. They all just gave their lives over to me... I'm in a little bit of shock. If I wasn't who I am—"

"Then they wouldn't have done so," Aria cut off his sentence. "It's because you are who you are that we love you and that they're willing to tie themselves so firmly to you."

"I guess that's true," Sean said.

"Sir, she's not wrong," Arliat said from the driver's seat of the carriage. "More so for me. You saved my life."

Sean exhaled, looking up to her. "Which was only in danger because you work for us."

"Are you sure of that?" Arliat asked.

"No," Sean grimaced. "Felora and Helga are trying to see if they can contact the souls of the two men tonight. I might have an answer tomorrow."

"Until then, I'll see it my way," Arliat nodded.

Sean chuckled as she got the carriage moving. "All the women around me are strong-willed."

"We have to be," Aria said.

Sean wondered in what way she meant that, but wasn't about to give her a straight line.

Entering the private dining room, Sean greeted everyone and took his seat. Before anyone could speak, Tabitha was there to take their drink orders.

"Fredrick, how're you doing?" Sean asked.

The dark circles under Fredrick's eyes spoke of little sleep. "Tired," he said with a wan smile. "The good news is that I found a good man to look into my brother's death."

"Who?" Sean asked.

"That's what we asked, but he wouldn't say until you got here," Joseph said.

"Now that he is," Fredrick said sharply, "I'll tell you."

Joseph leaned back. "Easy, easy. I don't mean to anger you."

Exhaling a long breath, Fredrick nodded. "I'm sorry, Joseph. I didn't mean to snap at you."

"You have reason to be in a bad place," Eva said, covering his hand with hers.

"I hired Thomas Babbitt," Fredrick said after a second.

"What?" Knox laughed. "That's priceless. It'll piss the new commander off, without a doubt."

"I believe it will," Fredrick said grimly. "All he asked for in payment was a single copper coin."

"Ah," Saret smiled, "it's personal, then."

"Indeed. A way to strike back at what he views as a personal slight and help me at the same time."

"That'll be good," Sean said. "Ven, you know who to work with."

"Yes, sir," came the reply from the ceiling.

"Your drinks," Tabitha announced after knocking on the door.

Once Tabitha was gone, Sean spoke up, "I wanted you all to know my plans."

Everyone looked at Sean, curious about what he was going to say.

"I'll give Babbitt until Tenday. If he hasn't found any evidence that can be presented by then, I'm going after Denmur myself. I'll challenge him again and again until I break him. I'm done letting my friends and family be hounded, injured, and killed."

Aria covered his fist with her hand. "We stand with him," she told the room. "All of his house stands behind him. We'll take the repercussions, if there are any, but it was only fair to let you all know ahead of time."

"Denmur is a problem, but he's far from the worst of it," Mageeyes told him.

"I can't challenge Sharpeyes without cause, or I'd be going for him in the same way," Sean said. "I'll find a way to declaw or kill him, too."

The room went silent, and Flamehair spoke after a moment, "Sean, stating out loud that you intend to kill a City Lord is a good way to be brought before a magistrate."

"Which is why I'm saying it here with you," Sean replied. "This room is secure. Amedee would have seen to that, and as for small spies, Ven handles those."

"There are none present but those who know the truth," Ven added.

"So it was safe to say, but you all need to know," Sean went on. "After Sharpeyes, I have old business with Truestrike to put to rest. If you need me to step away from the association—"

"Never," Fredrick cut him off. "Everyone here knows that this is only because of you, Sean, though it is fair to see where everyone stands. You will not be criticized for feeling differently, but does anyone here think Sean should leave?"

"Leave?" MacLenn asked. "No, but we should start making sure we minimize any backflow from this."

"Indeed, we should," Mageeyes nodded.

"And we will," Fredrick said. "Does anyone disagree with Sean's plans?"

Jefferson looked up. "Two assassins nearly killed his driver outside my business. Just that alone has started rumors about how unsafe my shop is. I don't have anything against his plan."

"They tried to kill me and my boy," Sam growled. "Gut them, Sean."

The others all began to speak up— Knox and Ryan were right alongside Fredrick and Sam in their vehemence that he make them pay. Sean listened to his friends encourage him and bowed his head.

"I was worried, but it appears my fears were groundless," Sean said when it grew quiet again. "Tenday will be the start of it, unless Babbitt gives us something to work with. Fredrick, can you tell him?"

"Yes. Gladly."

29

The next morning, after everyone had finished with breakfast, Felora got Sean's attention. "Sean, I got word back from my mother last night. She had to dig through her archive to find any references at all. It *should* be possible, but she recommends you be there for it. Helga and I decided not to risk anything until we'd heard back from her."

"Okay, we'll do that tonight," Sean said. "I hope we get some answers."

"That would be good," Fiona said, "though nothing we get from them would be usable in court."

"I don't care," Sean said grimly. "If they say Denmur hired them, it'll just solidify what I plan on doing. I'll still give Babbitt his time, but Denmur will pay in blood."

"Babbitt?" Myna asked.

"Oh, right, sorry," Sean sighed. "You two scrambled my brain last night, and I forgot to mention it."

Myna grinned. "I can scramble it again right now, if you'd like."

"Myna, we chastise Felora for that," Fiona laughed, "though I love the shade of red he's turned."

"Okay, so pregnancy makes some women hornier, even on this world," Sean coughed.

"Some women react that way," Fiona agreed. Sean raised an eyebrow and she laughed. "Not me, husband. I've never been pregnant before. I've had friends who were."

"Odd breakfast conversations for a thousand, Alex," Sean muttered.

"What?" Ida asked.

"Something from my old world," Sean said, shaking his head. "I've told you about Babbitt being replaced as commander. Well, Fredrick hired him to investigate his brother's death. Babbitt took the job for a single copper."

"Oh, goodness," Aria said. "He must be very angry about being let go."

"I'd say so, if that's all he asked for," Fiona said.

"The bathhouse opens again today, so what're you all doing?" Sean asked.

"Working on our manor," Fiona said. "Are you going to Giralt's?"

"Told him I wouldn't be over today," Sean said. "I want to finish the weapons for everyone today."

The maids and cooks perked up at his words.

"Thank you, sir," Tiska said.

"We really do appreciate it," Glorina added.

"I want everyone to be prepared," Sean said. "I'm trying to tweak each one based on who they're for. I'll make no promises on anything, but I'm seeing what I can do."

"Anything at all is amazing, sir," Prita piped up.

"Since we're working on our home, everyone here can help us with the fortifying," Fiona said, getting to her feet. "Everyone but Sean and Andrea, that is. Andie, if you want to trade out with Felora or another of us later, just let us know."

"I will," Andrea replied.

"Everyone, meet by the front gate," Fiona said before she left the room.

* * *

Sean sat down at his desk and looked at the weapons laid out. Knives, staff, hammers, and swords, but no bows. *I don't know how bows work... I mean, I have the basic idea, but nothing about actually making one... Maybe I can take the bows they have and augment them?*

"Ven, will you ask Aria and Helga to bring their bows to me, please?"

"On it," Ven replied.

"Ranged weapons for two of them, at least," Sean muttered. "If I could work out a returning enchantment, that would make throwing knives amazing. Ryann would love it if she could just carry two or three instead of a few dozen." Picking up a throwing knife from the pile, he thought about how one would express the desire of returning.

"Sean," Helga said, coming into the workshop, "I have the bows for you."

"Huh? Oh, right. Just bring them on over, Helga."

"Why did you want them?"

"I want to see if I can enchant or enhance them, somehow. Any extra plus is better for us."

"That is true," Helga said, setting them on the desk. "I am just surprised to hear you say it."

"Why?" Sean asked, puzzled by her comment.

"Thor, and even Odin, to a lesser extent, never saw the need to enhance the gear of the Einherjar. The captains would get better gear, but not everyone."

"That's stupid, unless they just don't have the resources."

"They have resources they could use," Helga said. "Hel and Loki have no trouble using what they have to improve their allies."

"Hel," Sean said, thinking of the goddess. "Does she have a half-living, half-dead body?"

Helga's face scrunched up. "No. Why would you even think that?"

"Myth from my world," Sean shrugged.

"No. Hel is a dual-nature. She is the frozen queen of those who could not make it into Valhalla, but she is also passionate about the things she cares for."

"She doesn't have a father fetish, then?" Sean asked.

Helga's nostrils flared and she looked upset. "That is just sick."

"Easy, easy," Sean said gently. "I'm just picking apart myths, is all."

"That sounds like one of Thor's rumors. Hel slapped him numerous times for his vulgar language toward her."

"Sounds like my kind of woman," Sean laughed. "Your surname was Helsdottir. Any relation?"

"The Valkyrie are elevated by one of the gods. Hel chose me to become a Valkyrie, but when Odin lost one of his, he pushed Hel for one of hers. As I had just been elevated, she gave me to him. I do not blame her— I was the newest, compared to some who have been with her since her own rise."

"Huh. Never would have figured it that way."

"If there is nothing else, I should return to help them," Helga said.

"How're you doing?" Sean asked. "Are you feeling more at home?"

Helga hesitated, having turned for the door. "I am fine, sir. Thank you for thinking of me, but I shall be okay. Things have been getting better for me, but the cost was nearly Arliat's life."

"That helped make things easier?"

"I have a function that they can see the use of," Helga said. "Aria has been the friendliest of your wives, and Myna and Fiona have been welcoming, as well. The others are starting to thaw."

"I guess I should've seen that."

"It is fine, sir. With time, I hope to prove my worth for them to accept me."

"They will. It's just rough right now."

"And I do not blame them," Helga said.

"I won't keep you, unless you know how to make a weapon return to your hand or sheath after having thrown it."

"Like Mjolnir?"

"Oh, right. His hammer was supposed to do that," Sean said. "Kind of like that, yeah."

Helga frowned, turning back to the desk. "Mjolnir was made by the Dwergaz. It is inscribed with a number of runes... any of them could be the one that returns it to Thor's hand. I have seen it a few times. I can try drawing them for you."

Sean chuckled. "Better idea. Tonight, when we do the dream about the souls, we can also focus on Mjolnir. If I see it in the dream, I might be able to remember the runes better."

"Oh, that is a very good idea."

"And only possible because of you," Sean said. "If this works, Ryann will be very grateful. I have to ask: the Dwergaz— weren't they Dwarves?"

"Yes and no," Helga said. "Dwergaz are a branch of the Dwarf family that are divinely infused."

"Well, that explains some things," Sean said. "Okay, tonight, there will be a lot to do. Go ahead and head on back to the others, and thank you."

Helga brightened. "You are very welcome, sir."

"Sean. Please, Helga, call me Sean?"

"I will try, si... Sean. It feels disrespectful to call you by your name."

"It's a request, but I do prefer to be called Sean."

Helga bowed her head and left him to his work.

"Okay, throwing knives later, bows in a bit. Let's get the easy ones done first."

* * *

Sean looked up from his work when Fiona called to him. "Sparring time?"

"Yes, dear husband," Fiona smiled. "How has your work been going?"

"Pretty good," Sean smiled.

"How many have you finished?"

"A few," Sean said, picking up the ones he'd finished. "I'm trying different things for a couple of them. I'm hoping to get help tonight with the trickier ones."

"Helga did mention something about a dream and runes," Fiona said. "I thought you said a few?"

"This *is* a few," Sean chuckled, his hands full.

"That is several," Fiona sighed. "It's a good thing I take care of the finances if that's how you count."

"Probably right," Sean laughed.

Leaving the workshop, Sean watched everyone's faces as they approached. Myna was the first one to notice the weapons and her tail began to lash side to side.

"Okay, so I'm still working on finishing them all, but I do have some ready," Sean said. "You can see that, though. Let's start with the easiest two: Rosa and Rumia, if you'd like to grab yours? They are the pruners."

Rumia stepped forward and took the two mithril pruning shears. "Thank you, sir."

"They'll function for your regular work, but if you focus on them, they become short blades," Sean said. "This way, you always have your weapon at your side and no one will find it odd. Well, besides that they're made out of mithril. The extra is the black pearls infused with Camo. That will let you vanish without taking your own energy."

Rumia's eyes were wide as she handed one of the shears to her mother. "Thank you, sir. I'll treasure it always."

Rosa blinked, a tear slipping down her cheek. "Thank you, sir..."

Sean was a little surprised at the emotion Rosa showed, but didn't want to make her feel awkward or embarrassed, so he pushed on. "Tiska, Cali, Xenta, and Prita, I have these rods for you. They'll turn into short blades, and the diamonds in them will give you Mage Sight while you're touching one."

All four maids were shocked, speechless and frozen for a moment. Tiska was the first one to move, collecting the staves and handing them out to the others. "We are deeply honored, sir," Tiska said, and all of them curtsied deeply to him.

"Glorina, Lona, and Mona, these carving knives are yours. Like the others, they'll be short blades when needed, and the black pearls help you Camo."

Glorina collected them and handed them to the other two. "We are forever grateful, sir." All three of them curtsied just as deeply as the maids had.

Arliat looked eager and nervous when Sean turned to her.

"It's a spear like Helga's," Sean told Arliat. "Since you'll be on the wagon most of the time, it made sense to give you reach."

Arliat took the forearm-length piece of mithril reverently. "Thank you, sir. I'll train hard with it."

"Which brings me to Quilla and Quinna," Sean said, left with only the two hammers. "Hammers— useful for most of your work, but if you want them to be weapons, they'll become mauls. The rubies set in them will blast out flame when they hit something if you want them to."

Both of the sisters grabbed the hammers out of the air when he tossed them toward the pair. A moment later, they were both holding mauls. Weighing hers, Quilla frowned. "Heavy for mithril."

"That'd be the adamantine core," Sean grinned. "I wanted to make sure you can use your full strength with them."

Both of the Moonbound women stared at the hammers as they shrunk back down, clearly at a loss for words. Quinna spoke up in the sudden silence, "We'll be worthy of them, Sean."

"You already are. I'm still working on the rest," Sean told his wives. "I'm trying to work out some ideas."

"Of course, Master," Myna said, but there was disappointment edging her words.

"Silly kitty," Sean said. "Some of the best things take a little extra time, don't they?"

Myna's lips curled up at the edges. "Yes. I'm sorry. My emotions are a little wild right now."

"Okay," Sean said, going over to snag her for a hug. "It'll be worth it. Now, let's get sparring."

30

Sean didn't make great progress with the other weapons for his wives that night— he wanted to get a good look at Mjolnir before he did anything else. He'd sent Ven to let Fredrick and Mageeyes know that he'd be missing from the inn tonight, making sure they were aware he was just staying home.

Evening sparring, bathing, and dinner passed by without incident. The staff were all still buzzing about their new weapons, though Helga had barred them from using them during sparring. Quinna and Quilla, especially, could have seriously injured anyone hit by theirs.

Retiring to the bedroom as soon as dinner was over, Sean was followed by all of his wives and Helga. He headed for the dressing room, putting his clothing in the hamper, before going into the bedroom ahead of Fiona, Myna, Ryann, and Ida. He was just about to the bed when the other dressing room opened and Felora led Helga, Aria, and Andrea in.

His cheeks lightly heated when he felt all of their gazes on him until he got under the covers. Once he was in bed, his wives, all in their nightgowns, joined him. Helga was wearing a gown of black, and Felora had her lay next to Sean.

"It'll be Sean, Helga, and myself," Felora told the others. "We don't know what might happen, and Sean doesn't want to have more involved because of that."

"We understand," Fiona said. "We'll be beside you and watching, just in case."

"We don't know how long this might be subjectively, but I doubt it'll be longer than Sean normally is at the inn," Felora said. "The second part will just be Helga sharing some memories with Sean. I'll be stepping out at that point, and we can see if we can find Sean's demi-plane without Helga."

"I'm hoping it works," Andrea said.

"As am I, Andie," Felora smiled sadly.

Sean wondered if that would work, but there was no saying until they tried. "Good night. I love you, all of you," Sean said, looking past Helga to his wives.

"We love you, too," Fiona replied. "Best of luck on this."

"Once you're ready," Felora told Sean and Helga.

The two of them lay back, closed their eyes, and waited.

"Dream. Step between realities and find the place you need. Slip out of now, and into the time and place you desire," Felora's voice washed over them and Sean let it pull him into slumber.

* * *

Blinking, Sean found himself standing on the edge of a bog. He didn't know how he knew it was a bog, but he *knew* it. The area was being illuminated by a full moon that shone down only on the bog. Inky blackness surrounded them, the light cutting off at the edges. In the middle of the soft land, a giant yew tree with barren branches towered over the ground. Dotting the wetlands, heath and heather grew in patches.

Where are they? Sean thought, looking for Helga and Felora. A blink of an eye later and the two women were standing beside him. "There you are."

Both women looked around with surprise. "This is not what I had thought we would see," Helga said.

"Far from what I expected."

"Bogs are a place of death," Sean said softly. "The yew tree is an old Celtic symbol of death." He motioned to the giant tree, whose limbs looked like large skeletal hands reaching out to cover the area.

"It's also quiet," Felora shivered.

"Is someone there?" a male voice queried with hope.

"Someone's here?" another voice called out with a near frantic voice. "Help!"

Sean looked into the bog and, near one of the clumps of bushes, he saw where the voices had come from. Two heads rose just above the thick black moss that covered the majority of the ground.

"It is them," Helga told Sean. "The men who died. This isn't the frozen wastes of Hel, though."

"No. This is Sean's place for those who would be in your version of hell," Felora said. "As the manor is for those who believe, this is for those who have opposed him."

"Bogs are a place of death," Sean said again, staring at the two men who had nearly killed one of his family. "Yet things don't decay quickly in a bog."

"Help! Anyone?!"

"I can hear you. Where are you?" the first man called out, nearly as franticly as the second man had.

"They can't see us. How odd," Sean mused. "We might be able to help you," he called back to them, "but there's something you need to do first."

"What? Anything! Anything at all! Just get us out of here! Our hands and feet are bound by the plants. We can't get out on our own."

"Who sent you to kill my driver?" Sean said.

"Driver? What... driver? Oh, shit!"

"Yes," Sean agreed. "Shit is where you are, but it's not a creek—it's a lake. Now, who sent you to kill my driver?"

"We weren't sent to kill a driver!" the second man shouted. "We were sent to kill Jefferson or anyone who looked important near his shop. We had no idea that two winged women would chase us!"

"We're sorry, so sorry! Just get us out of here, please!" the first man pleaded.

"Who hired you?" Sean asked flatly.

"We can't. We're under an Agreement," the first man said.

"No, you're not," Sean said darkly. "Dead men don't hold Agreements."

"Dead?" The second man was on the verge of panic. "We're not dead...! W-we were running on the roofs to get away... a-and..."

The first man began to sob, "Dead! Dead because of some Moon-bound bitch!"

"I can still help you," Sean said, taking a step onto the bog without thinking. The ground felt firm under his foot, and he took another step. "You see, this is my world. Here, I can free someone or condemn them to an eternity of slow decay."

Both men looked up, finally seeing Sean as he walked slowly toward them. Eyes wide and panicked, they both failed to find words.

Stopping a few feet away from them, Sean squatted and stared at them. "If you tell me what I want to know, I'll see about freeing you. One of you will be stuck here forever. The other might leave. I don't know what'll happen to you, but at least you won't be condemned to this place."

"Darkfoam!" the second man shouted.

"Darkfoam!" the first man echoed a second behind him.

"It seems we have a winner," Sean said as he stood back up. "You were just a little too late, dead man."

"No, wait!" the first man screamed. "I can give you more, more than just a name! Please!"

Sean went back to his haunches, meeting the man's eyes. "Go ahead."

"You'll free me, too, right?"

"Maybe, maybe not. If I think you have something worthy, yes. If not, well... imagine if the plants started to tighten their hold."

With a startled yell, the man tried to thrash. "Call them off, call them off!"

Sean chuckled. "They react to my thoughts. I'll ease them back for now."

"Darkfoam... he let slip he was doing it on behalf of someone else. A favor owed, to give the real person distance from the deed."

"Is that it?" Sean asked, tsking. "A pity."

"No! As we were leaving, I heard him say something about a cleaver!"

"Cleaver?"

"Carver, Frank! It was Carver!" the second man called out, clearly trying to help his friend. "'Carver should be told it's started'. Sounded like he was telling a pest to deliver the message."

"Huh," Sean said, standing up. "Denmur used Carver, who was using Darkfoam? Yeah, that sounds twisted enough."

"That's enough, right?" the first man asked, eyes wide and pleading.

Sean walked back the way he came. As he went, the ground behind him rippled and became soft again. "Maybe. We'll see. What you both failed to ask was how long it would be until I freed you. You tried to kill my family, so you can suffer a bit longer."

"What?!"

"No, you—!"

Sean imagined vines wrapping around both men's mouths enough to silence them. Surprised grunts followed the thought, and he looked back to find out that they were covered by vines from under their noses down into the bog.

Felora and Helga stood waiting for him; Helga was wearing a grim smile and Felora was looking at him with a worried expression. Sean exhaled when he reached them. "So, we know that I have two worlds under me now. This one is pretty bleak."

"As it should be for your foes," Helga said.

"Sean... are you okay?" Felora asked, touching his cheek gently.

Sean leaned his head against her hand. Eyes closing, he took a deep breath. "Yeah, I'm fine."

"Sean?"

"Okay, I'm conflicted. I want them to stay here and suffer, but I also did promise them freedom."

"But as you said, you never said when," Helga reminded him. "You can hold your promise and still make them suffer for a while."

"Yeah, that is true," Sean said. "I don't even know if they can be freed or how. It makes me wonder... since they're here now, are you still carrying them?"

Helga paused, clearly thinking. "No. I think they are here and I shall be free of them. Though... Sean, may I take the one who answered first?"

"Huh?"

"Might I free the one who answered first? They will not be here if I am right."

"Yes."

Helga closed her eyes again and, after a moment, she smiled. "They are free."

Sean looked past her, and he could only see the second man's head. "What happened to him?"

"I took him back into me," Helga said. "I can resist death if I have a soul to offer up in my place."

"Ah, like how you survived the Bond? I approve of this," Sean said. "You may have them both."

"Thank you," Helga replied. "I also feel a connection to this place now. It is possible for me to open a path here while I sleep, much like your manor."

"Which will allow you to drop the souls off after you grab them," Sean nodded. "Okay."

"Are we done?" Felora asked.

"Yeah. Take us somewhere nicer so we can study Mjolnir, please?"

The world shimmered, and Sean smiled at Marjorie, who was having a cup of tea. "Evening, Marjorie."

"Sean!" Marjorie got to her feet. "Is something wrong?"

"No, just needed a place to do some studying."

There was a knock on the door, and Sean answered it. He let Helga in, but Felora stopped in the doorway. "Not coming in?"

"If I see her, I'll stay all night..." Felora said softly. "Tell her I love her, please?"

"I know you do, my dearest Fel," Lilly said from the archway into the hallway. "If you have to go, I understand. I'll be here for when you visit next. Maybe we can have some time to ourselves?"

Felora gave her a smile. "I'd like that, Lilly."

"Oh, and Fel? Chastity and I both think it's fine. If it's okay with you both, we'll do likewise."

Felora's eyes widened and she bowed her head. "As my mistress wishes. I need to go."

"Go on, and make sure Andie gives Chastity an answer."

"I will," Felora said before she vanished.

"I'm sorry for distracting you from what you came to do, Sean," Lilly said. "Your workshop is in order. We'd come up with a cleaning schedule for all of us to work on, but then we found out this place is always clean. Even the dishes vanish and end up clean and back in the cupboard."

"Must make things boring," Sean said.

"No. Not at all. The library... is different."

"Oh?"

"Yes. The books change every day. The majority of them seem to be from your other world. I'm currently reading one about a man sent to another world by the goddess of luck."

"Oh, yeah, that one," Sean said thinking about the one she was referring to. "It's a good series. The cliffhanger at the end of book two was a bit harsh, but I think the author made up for it in book three."

"I just finished book two," Lilly said. "I was very glad book three was there for me to grab right away. Let me not delay you further."

"You never could," Sean said. "Besides, I wanted to ask Marjorie and Omin something."

"What can I do for you?" Marjorie asked.

"I'm here," Omin said, landing on Marjorie's shoulder.

"I Soul Bonded Onim, Ven, Venn, Jutt, and Arla," Sean said. "I was wondering if you'd both like to try, as well?"

"Yes," Omin said without hesitation.

"What does that mean? It put bands on the fingers of your wives, but what about for the rest of us?"

"For the others, it was a tattoo on the back of their hands— the tree of life, same as the one on Helga's neck. As for what it means? I'm not sure. I get the feeling it ties your soul directly to me, but I'm not sure what it'll do eventually."

"I would like to," Marjorie said.

"Okay. I, Sean..."

* * *

Taking a seat in the workshop, Sean popped his neck. "Okay, Helga, you ready?"

"Yes, but I do not know what you need me to do," Helga said, standing beside the desk.

"Just focus on wanting a copy of Mjolnir, right here," Sean patted the desk.

Helga closed her eyes, her hand resting on the desk. Brow furrowing, she bent her entire being on doing as Sean asked.

"Nice," Sean said a second later.

Helga's eyes snapped open, and she saw Mjolnir beside her hand. Eyes widening, she felt the power radiating off it. "Sean... I do not know if this is a copy."

"It is," Sean said. "If you feel the energy, you'll note it doesn't feel like a dick."

Helga blinked, discovering that he was right. The energy radiating off the hammer felt like Sean, and nothing like Thor. "Thank goodness. I had feared he would come to reclaim it."

"That would be bad," Sean said. "Okay, now let's go over these runes." Sean knew what each rune did the moment that he saw them, and his smile widened. *Must be the Linguist gift from Oghma,* Sean thought. *I can understand even the magical languages.*

31

"I know all of you are probably wondering about last night," Sean said, taking his seat at the table.

Conversations cut off immediately and all eyes were on him. Before he could say any more, breakfast was brought in. Sean thanked the cooks and waited for everyone to have a seat.

"The dead that Helga collected ended up in a different plane of existence. They were in a bog where they were buried up to their necks in peat. The plant life had their arms and legs bound."

A few people at the table shuddered, but Rumia sat forward. "What kind of plants?"

"The yew tree at the center had heather and heath in clumps under its branches."

"Do you think I could see it?"

Sean's brow furrowed for a second. "Helga?"

"I can go when I sleep. The path is open," Helga replied.

"Take it up with Helga," Sean said. "Where was I?"

"The bog," Felora said. "Do you mind serving yourself so we can, husband?"

"Sorry," Sean said, forgetting that small bit of etiquette this world insisted on. He quickly served himself some of the eggs and bacon.

"Anyway, the two men who attacked Arliat were up to their necks in the bog."

Sean went on to describe the plane and his conversation with them. Finally finished talking, he started to eat while the others were already done with their meal.

"That's very interesting," Fiona said slowly, her eyes going to Helga. "You're sure that their souls can be used in place of yours to stave off your death?"

Helga paused before she said, "I am almost certain, mistress."

"Very well," Fiona said. "What if one of us dies? Will you collect our souls, as well?"

"Of that, I am certain, mistress. I can feel everyone in this room. Even when you are across the city, I know exactly where you are. I am certain that if you died, your soul would come to me." Everyone jerked slightly, and they stared at Helga.

"What would become of our souls, then?"

"I could deliver you to the manor," Helga said.

"Could you hold our souls for Sean?" Fiona asked.

"I do not understand."

"Our souls would reside inside of you until you took us to the manor?"

"Yes."

Sean could see what Fiona was saying and he sat forward. "You are to hold their souls until I can get you and their body in the same room."

Fiona nodded. "Exactly. You might be able to do what you've done before, as our souls would still be here."

"If she had collected Chas' soul..." Andrea whispered, her hand covering her mouth.

"Yes. Sean might've been able to reunite them," Fiona said sadly.

Andrea hiccupped as tears began to fall. "Oh, Chas...!"

Felora put her arms over Andrea's shoulders. "Yes. She was our enemy, then, though. There's no way to say she would've kept their souls and not spent them to keep her own life."

"I tossed aside my old ways on that field. As I told Sean, I would have held them and tried to give them to him," Helga said sadly. "I cannot change what came before, mistresses, but I will make sure that you are all safe for him."

Andrea sniffled and stood up, her eyes locked on Helga. "If you *ever* fail, I will kill you until you finally die."

Helga bowed her head. "If I fail, mistress, I will gladly give you my neck."

"Easy..." Sean said softly. "Andie, she's been trying to make amends. We all wish things were different, but none of us can change the past."

Wiping her cheeks, Andrea nodded. "I know Sean, and I'm trying. It just feels like a dagger every day."

"I know," Sean said. "I know..."

"We should get started for the day," Fiona said. "Helga, you're coming with us."

"As you wish, mistress," Helga said, getting to her feet with the others.

"I'll be here working on the weapons for you all," Sean said. "I'll skip midday training."

"Understood," Myna nodded. "What're you going to do with them?"

"Experiment," Sean grinned between bites of his nearly-cold breakfast.

* * *

Setting down the last throwing knife, he nodded happily. *Going to have to patent these runes. I can't let other people have access to them.*

When Myna entered the workshop, Sean gave her a knowing smirk. "Time for sparring, Myna?"

"Soon, Master. I came to check on what you've been doing. We were all curious, and your explanation at breakfast didn't give us a lot to work with."

"I found out something important," Sean said. "The runes do

have a limit. The smaller the weapon, the harder it is to get the rune to imprint and work correctly."

"Hmm... yes, I can see how that would be." Myna stopped beside the desk, taking in the vast collection of throwing knives and weapons. "Those would be mine?" She pointed to the two short swords that were identical in shape to her current swords.

"Someone wanted their gifts earlier, hmm?"

Myna sat on his lap, leaning into him. "I like it when you give me things. I'm appreciative, am I not?"

Sean kissed her cheek, as she was still staring at the swords. "Yes. Yes, you are. Those two and two of the throwing knives are for you."

Myna turned to face him. "Two of the throwing knives? Are they not all for Ryann?"

"No. There are two for each of you. Two for each of the staff, too," Sean said, "and two for me."

"Two throwing knives isn't nearly enough for Ryann," Myna said curiously.

"These will be enough," Sean smirked. "Come on. Let me up and we'll take them all out. I'm sure everyone is already gathering."

Myna pushed him back against the seat and kissed him passionately. Sean tightened his loose hold on her and returned the kiss. Suddenly, Myna broke it and rested her forehead against his.

"Thank you, Master. I would thank you in greater detail, but Felora and Andrea already claimed you for themselves."

Sean blinked, not having heard that before. "Hmm... that's still going to take some getting used to."

"If it bothers you—"

Sean put a finger over her lips. "No, it's fine. Probably for the best, actually. It does stop arguments among you, I bet."

Myna licked his finger and Sean removed it quickly. "Yes, it does," Myna giggled. "If you ever want to change those plans because you want one or more of us, instead, we've all agreed we accept that. Those who have had their night changed will just get you the following night."

Sean rubbed his finger on his shirt. "I guess that makes sense."

"The last two tendays of our term, we will all abstain from sex," Myna said. "Fiona insisted that we do so for the safety of the children. I argued against her, as my mother and grandmother were having sex until the last two days. The others agreed with her, but I'm betting they'll change their minds when the time comes."

Sean shook his head. "Can't say I disagree with Fiona. I don't know if it'd hurt the babies or not, but we can always keep an eye on it."

"Yes, we can," Myna agreed. "We have time before it becomes an issue." With a sigh, she slipped from his lap. "We should get going. May I take my blades now?"

"Yup. Do you want to know what they do now, or do you want to wait until I tell everyone?" Sean asked as he began collecting weapons.

"I'll wait, but you can tell me first," Myna said as she slipped the new blades into her sheaths, setting her old ones on his desk. "Will you keep these for me? I want to give them to my mother."

"I can improve them for you, if you want," Sean said.

Myna's hands slowed and she smiled before going back to collecting the weapons. "Please, Master? She'll be most pleased, and it will make things easier."

"I'll do it tomorrow," Sean said, "after I work with Giralt. I need to get back to that."

It took a couple of minutes before they had all the weapons gathered up in their arms and made it into the yard, where everyone was waiting. Sean moved to the middle of them, carrying the throwing knives.

"Okay, there are two knives for everyone," Sean said. "We'll start with this so I can hand off the rest of the weapons."

One by one, everyone took two of the knives, all of them curious about the rune etched into the blade. Ryann looked the most puzzled that she was only getting the same two as everyone else.

"The knives are special, and we should thank Helga for her help," Sean said. "If she hadn't been able to show me Mjolnir, I wouldn't have been able to make them."

All eyes went to Helga briefly, who was standing tall and looking straight ahead, her cheeks just starting to pink.

"I'll demonstrate," Sean said as he pulled one knife from the back of his belt. With a snap of his wrist, it flew across the yard and sank into the bale of hay that'd been set up for archery and knife practice. A second later, the knife vanished.

As everyone looked back to Sean, he grinned and turned his back to show them that he had two knives again. "They return to the sheaths they're bound to. I believe two should be enough for everyone. Ry, if you think you need more, I can make you more, but I have another weapon for you, too."

Ryann nodded as she put the new knives on her belt. "I'll test it later and let you know."

"Okay. As for weapons for my wives, we'll start with Myna's," Sean said, turning to Myna, who handed him the weapons she'd been holding before she drew both her swords. "The one in your left hand will help with Mage Sight. The one in your main hand will dampen your energy so you can become invisible to Mage Sight. With your innate control over your Talent, this will make you nearly impossible to find and help you find your enemies."

Myna's eyes lit up. "I will treasure them, Master."

"I'll do the same for your old swords," Sean told her.

"She'll be shocked," Myna grinned as she put her swords away.

"Fiona, this staff here is yours," Sean said.

Fiona took the forearm-length staff, looking over the craftsmanship with a soft smile. "Making it look like a tree limb? That's very sweet of you, Sean."

"It'll grow and shrink like Helga's spear," Sean smiled. "The rubies on this give you a lance of fire. The length of the flame is controlled by you."

Fiona let the staff grow to its full six-foot length and spun it through a simple attack sequence before letting loose a line of fire into the air. The sky brightened briefly as the six-foot flame was there and gone in an instant.

"You can concentrate on holding the flame, too," Sean added, "to make things even more dangerous for those against you."

Fiona was smiling as the weapon shrunk back down and she clipped it to her belt. "I do believe that no one will be prepared for us the first time we have to fight."

"Good," Sean said. "Next up, we have Andrea. The blade is a small belt knife, but will be equal to the small blade you normally use when you want it to be. The enchantment on it is a little different. It'll help with Camo, but its second enchantment is a bit of a *shock.*"

Andrea took the knife and attached the sheath to her belt. She drew it and let it turn into a short sword. "What do you mean shock?"

"See the sapphires?" Sean grinned. "Trigger one."

Andrea's fingers were in contact with the three gems, so she sent a thought to activate the gem. The blade was suddenly coated with electricity and her eyes went wide. "What?"

"There's enough juice in that to put down anyone. Even if you miss a clean hit, they'll still have problems. It'll be easier to show you — and this will suck— but you need to know what it can do."

"I will do it, Sean," Helga said.

Andrea gave Helga a nod and lightly touched the back of the knife to Helga's arm. Helga's muscles all locked up the moment the weapon touched her skin. Seeing her grimace, Andrea removed it and Helga fell over.

Sean was already kneeling next to Helga, his one free hand resting on her head. "She's fine. Just give her a moment for the juice to wear off."

Helga groaned as she started to move. "That was terrible. I could not move at all."

"Yeah, electricity can do that to the body," Sean said. "Just take a moment. It'll pass."

"Thank you, Sean," Andrea said, a touch breathless as she shrunk the weapon back down.

"You're welcome, Andie. That'll work in the smaller form, too, just so you know."

"Oh," Andrea's eyes widened slightly. "That'll be a nasty surprise, if needed."

"Next up, we have Ida's," Sean said, handing her a miniature hammer. "Same as the others— it'll grow when you want it to. This one has the same enchantment as Andie's and will return to you if you throw it, coming back to your hand."

Helga was just getting back to her feet and her jaw dropped. "You recreated Mjolnir?"

"No, just those two things. The hammer will hold the charge for a few seconds, but no longer than that if she isn't touching it," Sean said.

Ida checked her hammer before attaching it to her belt. "I'll treasure it, Sean."

Seeing her wide smile, Sean grinned in return. "I'm glad. Ry, this sword is yours."

Ryann took the sword that was the same length as Myna's with a questioning look. "What did you do for it?"

"The electricity, and it'll become a much bigger sword, depending on what you want," Sean said. "Give it a try."

Pulling the blade free of its sheath, Ryann let the blade glow with electricity for a few seconds before she imagined it growing. It was quickly the size of a regular sword, then grew until it was a zweihander.

"Oh," Ryann said with amazement. She gave the sword a few practice swings in the open middle area of the yard. "It's so light." She spun the big blade above her head with one hand.

"So you can wield it with ease, and that enchantment should conduct down another's sword if they clash," Sean grinned.

Ryann blinked at him as the sword reverted back to its small size. "Thank you..." Her words were soft and her eyes were a little damp.

"I'm glad you like it. I tried to make the throwing blades have both the returning and stun runes, but the knives don't hold a charge long enough to be useful."

"No, Sean, this is enough."

"Okay." Sean bowed his head to Ryann. "Fel," he said, turning to her, "I made something unique for you."

Felora took the coil of metal from him, looking over the handle. "A whip? It's a little small for that."

"Yes, a whip. It'll grow, and it has the same enchantment as the others," Sean grinned, "if you can use it. I'll make something else if you can't."

Felora laughed. Stepping into the open area, she snapped the whip open, letting the metal crack and the blue glow of the electricity light up the area. As she brought it above her head, the whip grew in length, giving her even more to work with, until she had nine feet of metal.

"My goodness, it's as flexible as leather," Felora grinned as the glow faded and the whip shrunk in size. "No one will expect this, Sean. I love it."

"I was a little worried, as you've only used small swords, but I had a feeling you could use it."

"Oh, yes. My family is well versed in whips," Felora smirked.

Sean rolled his eyes and turned to Aria. "I have a spear like Helga's for you. I figure she can help you get the feel for it, since you both have a similar skillset. I'm still working on your bows at the moment. I'm trying to get it to pass an enchantment to the arrows when they're fired."

Aria took the spear and clipped it to her belt. "I'll get used to it, Sean, and I'll be looking forward to what you can do with the bows."

"That's all of them," Sean said. "Now, who's ready for a bit of a fight?"

32

A rriving at the Oaken Glen that night, Sean took a deep breath. He was nervous about what he planned on doing. Once Aria had told him it was clear, Sean got out of the carriage.

"Still feels wrong to me..." Sean muttered.

"And yet it needs to be done this way," Aria countered.

"I'm not fighting it. It just feels wrong to me."

"Because you're a gentleman," Aria smiled. "We're thankful you don't fight us on it."

"After you," Sean said, motioning her to the door.

Leading him inside the inn, Aria looked over the room. The biggest table had people at it, but not the association. As they made their way to the hall beside the bar, Aria gave Allonen a nod.

Tabitha was just coming out of the private dining room when they approached the door. "Good evening," she smiled. "Can I get your drinks?"

"Hot cider," Aria said.

"Mulled wine?" Sean asked.

"Of course. I'll bring them with the refills."

"Thanks," Sean said, pulling out a coin.

"Blackhand already paid, sir."

"Okay," Sean said, putting the money on her tray. "Put it toward my driver's bill?"

"Yes, sir."

Aria motioned Sean into the open room before following him and closing the door.

"Sean, glad you could make it," Fredrick said.

"Thanks. Things have been busy for me. Winston, I should be by tomorrow, if that's okay?"

"That's fine," Giralt replied. "I've done all I can for the runes. I'm not sure what else I can do to help with your engine."

"We'll see what we can come up with," Sean said, taking his seat and saying hello to everyone else.

"Fredrick was telling us that Babbitt is pushing hard to get answers," Mageeyes said.

"The guard is split," Flamehair added, "and Babbitt being on the case is widening that rift."

"Makes it easy to know who to trust and who not to," Ryan said. "If they aren't with Babbitt, you can count them as in the pocket of the new commander."

"That's a gross generalization," Italice said calmly. "They might just be following orders. They should, regardless of how distasteful the order is. That's part of their job."

"True, but the new sergeant is bought and paid for," Eva sniffed. "He came into my shop today and informed me that the carriages out front have to be given a place to park off the street. If I can't provide the space, I will be fined."

"That law has never been enforced," Jefferson scoffed. "There's never been enough traffic for it to matter."

"I had my small friend go check— all of Denmur's associates had carriages out front. When I asked the sergeant about that, he just laughed and left."

"Wolen is an ass," Sean said flatly.

"He is, but he is an official ass," MacLenn sighed. "The gate guards are inspecting all of my wagons leaving and entering, eating hours of time at a go. They wave everyone else through as they do it, too."

"Add the gate guards to the list," Sean growled.

All eyes went to Sean, who held up a hand. A knock came a heartbeat later, and Tabitha entered with a tray of glasses. Once she had them handed out, she left them, feeling the tension in the room.

"Has Babbitt found anything?" Sean asked Fredrick.

"Nothing specific, but the scene of the murder was well disturbed, which is against the regulations," Fredrick said darkly. "When he inquired about it, the new commander got into a heated yelling match with him in the middle of the lobby of the magistrate's building over it. He tried to bar Babbitt from investigating, but Babbitt had been given a writ by Lady Sharpeyes, stating he was allowed to look into whatever he needed to in regards to a case he was working."

"I bet that went over well," Sean snorted.

Fredrick laughed mirthlessly. "Like a bar of adamantine."

"I was there at the time," Flamehair said. "Lomar almost tore the writ up— I could see his hands spasming on it. Instead, he shoved it back to Babbitt and said, 'We'll see about this,' before he stalked away like he was going to tell a parent."

"Lord Sharpeyes, no doubt," Eve sighed.

"Which will be interesting," Mageeyes said. "They are going to start coming into conflict in the open if this keeps up. The first one to make a move will lose a lot of influence."

Sean set down his mug after he had a swig of the heated wine. "I need to tell you all about last night."

"Is this really the time, Sean?" Knox asked with a waggle of his eyebrows.

Groans came from around the table, along with some sighs.

"Thank you, Knox," Sean said softly, his nervousness nearly gone with that line. "You'll never get that information, by the way, but I do have important news."

Everyone stared at Sean, waiting. Every time he'd thought something was important before, it ended up being so.

"The two men who attacked Arliat outside of Jefferson's shop died," Sean began. "What you don't know is that Helga collected their souls when they died."

A range of reactions came from the table— intrigue from Mageeyes and Flamehair, morbid curiosity from Jefferson, fear from Knox, puzzlement from Joseph, and more.

"If someone opposes me and dies doing so, she can collect their souls. They are then taken to a small plane of existence that I can access. The men were buried up to their necks in a bog. After some questioning, they told me who and why."

Jefferson sat up straighter. "And?"

"They were after anyone of importance who came to your shop, not my driver specifically."

"Damn them!" Jefferson spat.

"The who, though," Sean said slowly, "that was a surprise. Darkfoam."

Eva snorted. "He might be a prig, but he isn't bloodthirsty."

"He did it at the behest of Carver," Sean went on.

"Now *he* is," Italice said, "but he's just a toady."

"Exactly," Sean said. "The men only knew they were hired by Darkfoam and that he'd sent a message as they left to inform Carver it was done."

"Layers upon layers," Fredrick said tightly. "If Denmur is willing to go to those lengths to hide himself, then he was the one behind my brother's death, too."

"It solidified what I intend to do," Sean said, setting his mug down again after another long drink. "Does Babbitt know he's on a timeline?"

"I told him," Fredrick nodded. "He's doing the best he can, but with the lack of help from the guard..." Fredrick trailed off with a shrug. "I'm not sure he's going to find any real evidence."

Ven landed on the table before Fredrick. "He could find something if he checked the ruined guard tower near the warehouse."

"What?"

"The ruined guard tower, in the warehouse district," Ven said again. "The rope that bound your brother is there. Maybe he'll find other clues."

"How do you know that?" Fredrick asked, his gaze locked on Ven.

"One of the Fairies that hasn't sided with us saw a man come out of the warehouse that evening. Since the man was acting suspicious, the Fairy followed." Ven paused before continuing quickly, "Some of us might have stolen small items from criminals to survive in the past."

Fredrick shook his head. "I don't care why the man was followed. Did the Fairy follow the killer from there?"

"No. They went to see if they could get something from inside."

"Dammit," Fredrick hissed, his hands clenched tight.

"The Fairy is willing to speak with Babbitt and give him a description of the man. We haven't approached Babbitt directly yet. We aren't sure where we stand with him."

"I'll talk to him," Fredrick said, getting to his feet quickly.

"Get the carriage ready, please," Eva said softly.

"Right away," came the voice from above, accompanied by a flash of silver.

"Fredrick," Sean said, standing beside him, "either way, I'll end this. I'd just rather do it without us all feeling the blowback."

Fredrick's eyes closed and he took a deep breath. "If there's proof, Sean, I'll kill him myself." Opening his eyes, he met Sean's. "If not, I'll stand aside for you."

"If you need a champion…"

"I'll ask," Fredrick finished when Sean trailed off.

"Well, it seems we will be calling tonight short," Mageeyes said, her eyes going to the short spear attached to Aria's belt. "Aria, what is that? It glows so brightly."

"A weapon from Sean," Aria smiled softly. "This is what he's been working on the last few days. Weapons for all of his family. If we end up in a battle again, none of us will die."

Flamehair's eyebrows went up. "Is it that powerful?"

"More powerful than the sword Denmur crafted for Sharpeyes."

Everyone looked at the forearm-length shaft of mithril with wide eyes.

"And he made them for *all* of you?" Mageeyes asked with a touch of hesitation.

"Yes, but mine is far from the most powerful," Aria smiled. "He's working on my bow next. That will probably make this look like a toy."

"I don't know about that," Sean said slowly. "It'll be a real bitch to get it to do what I want it to do."

Joseph laughed, shaking his head. "Sean, if we've all learned one thing, it's that when you want something to work, it does."

That got the tension to break, and everyone began to laugh, agreeing with Joseph.

Mageeyes looked thoughtful for a moment. "Sean, may I speak with you alone for a minute?"

"Sure."

Goodbyes were said, but it was obvious most of them were curious over what Mageeyes wanted to talk with Sean about. Mageeyes relented and explained that it was personal. Everyone raised their eyebrows, but they stopped lingering.

When Sean, Mageeyes, and Aria were the last ones in the room, Mageeyes hesitated.

"Just say it, Amedee," Sean prompted her.

"How much to have you craft a sword to make the one Denmur made seem quaint?"

"Why?" Sean asked.

Mageeyes looked away and her cheeks took a hint of color. "For someone I know."

Sean's lips twitched at the corners. "I'd be glad to craft a blade for Bloodheart, if you provide the materials."

Mageeyes grimaced. "Is it that obvious?"

"He came to me a few days ago," Sean said, "wanting to make sure we weren't interested in each other. I didn't tell him your story, but Amedee, he's smitten. I had no idea you were thinking of moving forward."

"When he stepped forward at the party," Mageeyes said softly, "I felt a twitch in my chest. I worried for him. Afterward, when he flatly declared it was only to see me smile..." She turned away from them. "I'd thought I had pulled that part of me out and burned what was left. I must have failed, because I felt a spark."

"That might be my fault," Sean sighed.

Mageeyes turned back to him. "How?"

"From what I've been told, I change things, and—"

Mageeyes' laugh cut him off. She held up a hand for a moment so she could regain her composure. "Sorry. Such an understatement was too much."

"And those near me that want to can change, easily."

"I see. Well, I won't be easy to snare, but I will give him a chance. I have to make sure that this time, it is honest."

"It is," Sean said softly. "I'm as dense as a stone, and—"

This time, it was Aria's laughter that cut him off, and Sean rolled his eyes.

"As I was saying..." Sean went on as Aria tittered, "even I can see that he means it."

"I hope so."

"You want to give him an exquisite weapon," Aria said. "Why do you doubt yourself if you will go this far?"

"Solanice," Sean said.

"I want to see how he reacts to such a thing. The last time, I missed the first clue that things were not as they should be."

"Mithril and diamonds," Sean told her. "I need four pounds of mithril, a sapphire, and a diamond, the best you can get me."

"I'll have them delivered tomorrow."

"I'll bring the blade tomorrow, then," Sean said.

Blinking at him for a few heartbeats, Mageeyes just shook her head. "I shouldn't be surprised, but..."

"He still surprises us," Aria said lightly.

Clearing her throat, Mageeyes gave Sean a sad smile. "I want to be right."

"You will be," Sean said, putting a hand on her shoulder. "Your heart isn't wrong this time, Amedee."

33

"I must say, it's an interesting bit of machinery," Giralt said, puffing on his cigar.

"It'll work," Sean said. "It's not the best, but we're only working on the prototype, so it doesn't need to be perfect yet."

"And this will be enough to move a carriage?"

"Pretty sure it'll move a stripped-down carriage. The next part will be harder. Bronze and brass won't hold up to the strain needed, and iron isn't a thing here."

"It does exist," Giralt said slowly. "It's just restricted. For obvious reasons."

"Poisonous to the nobility," Sean snorted.

"Deadly toxic the closer they are to pure," Giralt corrected. "It can range from instant death to a long, slow, lingering death depending on how much pure noble blood they have."

"Good to know my world had something right," Sean said. "Anyway, I'm working on what I can do besides iron-based metals that won't cost what adamantine will. I'm thinking of trying an adamantine and copper mix to see if I can bring the cost down, at least."

Giralt picked up his cognac and considered the engine that was sitting on blocks above the floor. "I don't think you'll ever be able to produce it for the masses, Sean."

Sean started to object, but then he looked at the engine and thought about the work needed to make the one they had. "Maybe you're right..." Sean sighed and sat down on the floor. "That was my plan, but there's no industry here, no mass production of things. That's what really made them cheap enough for everyone to have a chance to own one."

"Mass production?"

Sean took a few minutes to explain the industrial revolution to Giralt, who was wide-eyed by the end of it.

"Your world sounds wonderful and terrifying all at once. What happened to all the crafters?"

"Mostly, they died off. Niche cases stayed around for hundreds of years, but a majority fell one by one to the rise of industry."

"I'd prefer to miss that," Giralt said as he set his mostly smoked cigar down to go out on its own.

"It would hurt my friends," Sean said. "Hell, it'd cause a massive shift in how things are done."

"You already push that to the breaking point with the items you produce," Giralt said. "Even Fredrick would never be able to match a quarter of what you do." He held up a hand when Sean started to object. "No, we've talked. All of us know better, Sean. You know it as well as we do."

"He has more experience than I do," Sean said.

"Yes, but you've shown him shortcuts he had not thought to even try."

"Huh... Well, if we can't make it cheap, we'll make it the best we can," Sean said. "It'll run and it'll keep running, making it a long-term investment. First, the easy one— a wagon for goods, both normal and cold. Augustus will pick them up. After that, we'll work on personal transport."

"What do we start on, then?"

The door to the shop opening stopped Sean from answering.

"It looks like they were at a stopping point," Clara said as she led Aria into the room.

"It's as good a place as any," Sean said. "Need to bring more adamantine over tomorrow."

"I can make sure I have more on hand, as well," Giralt added, getting to his feet.

"Is that it?" Clara asked, pointing to the engine.

"The engine is done, and yes, that's it. The hard part will be getting everything else around it. Need to get a wagon brought in."

"I'll tell Augustus," Giralt said. "I'm sure he has one that can be spared."

"It can be in less than great condition. Fixing it up will be easy," Sean added.

"Boys," Clara said, staring at Giralt, "enough for today."

"Yes, dearest," Giralt said quickly.

"I'm going," Sean chuckled.

Clara reached out and touched Sean's arm, making him pause. "Thank you, Sean. I've heard that you think all the strife going on is your fault, but it isn't. You probably worry about your friends, like us, going so far as providing a cuon and more Messenger Fairies to help keep us safer. I wanted you to know that I am grateful for what you've done for us, including being our child's guardfather."

Sean met her eyes. "I do worry, even with all that in place. And I was honored to be asked…" Sean trailed off and took her hand in his. "Can I check on the child?"

Clara blinked at him, then looked past him to Giralt before returning her gaze to Sean. "Will it hurt?"

"No."

"Okay," Clara said, raising her chin slightly.

Sean used his Flesh Shaping to look into her. Inside her womb, the new baby had started to grow. Sean focused on the child and smiled softly— even though it was only the size of a grain of rice, it had started to take form.

"You're pregnant, all right," Sean said. "The child is only this big," he held his thumb and forefinger apart, "but they're starting to grow."

Clara's hand went to her belly and tears started to fall from her eyes. "Oh... Winston..." she whispered, looking at Giralt.

Giralt was by her side instantly, placing his hand over hers gently. "Yes, and it's all thanks to Sean. I was surprised when he asked to get rid of any aches and pains all those tendays ago. Three days later, you were sure you'd caught, after all this time. Thank you, Sean."

Sean looked away clearly embarrassed. "Yeah, uh... no problem. I'll just get going."

Clara let out a small hiccupping laugh and grabbed Sean, hugging him, pushing her face into his chest briefly. "Thank you! So many times over...!"

Sean patted her back lightly. "It's okay. Really."

Pushing him away gently, Clara stepped back and leaned against Giralt, who put his arms around her. "So humble." Wiping at her tear-streaked face, she gave Sean a serious look. "We will help in any way we can, Sean."

"Best thing is to keep your child safe," Sean said.

"We will," Giralt replied.

* * *

The leather-wrapped package on his lap made Sean smile. *I wonder who will be more shocked— her or him?* Sean chuckled to himself.

"I can't believe you did that," Aria said.

"It makes the most sense for him," Sean replied.

"I guess that's true," Aria nodded.

"Did you have fun during sparring?" Sean asked.

"Not fun, but I did learn a lot."

"Going to have to be careful about it now," Sean said somberly. "If there had been people watching, they might try something during those moments."

"We know, and we'll be careful," Aria reminded him. When the carriage came to a halt, Aria got out. "It's safe, Sean."

Sean followed her out, the package in hand. "Arliat, are they taking care of you?"

"Yes, sir," Arliat replied. "The staff has been very welcoming. I've been sitting with the other drivers. It's been nice."

Something in her voice caught Sean's ear. "What's the problem?"

"They're worried, sir. What if it's them next time?"

"Oh."

"None of them blames you, sir. We all know who's to blame," Arliat clarified quickly. "It's just fear."

"Okay," Sean said, thinking about what he'd said he'd do if there'd been nothing by Tenday. "It should come to an end soon one way or another, Arliat."

"I know, sir," Arliat said. "Holding that to myself is a little tough, but I will never give away anything."

"Thank you," Sean said.

Sean followed Aria into the inn, but headed for the bar first. "Allonen, I have something for the Dame. Can you make sure it goes to her office?"

"I cannot, sir. She is, however, waiting for you in her office," Allonen replied.

Sean shook his head. "Of course she is. Very well."

"She said you know the way, sir," Allonen said.

"Okay, then," Sean said.

Aria followed Sean as he made his way for the staff hallway. Coming to Mageeyes' office, Sean knocked and waited for her to invite him in.

"Amedee, I... hello, Toivo," Sean said when he saw Bloodheart sitting across from Mageeyes.

"Mac... Sean," Bloodheart replied, his eyes going to the leather-wrapped package in Sean's hand. "You must be who we've been waiting for."

"Please come in, Sean and Aria," Mageeyes said.

"Didn't know you were doing this now," Sean said, moving to place the package on the desk.

"What is it that the smiths say? 'Best to strike while the metal is hot'?"

"Fair," Sean replied. "I did the best I could."

Mageeyes nodded, her hand moving to rest on the item. "I'll ask you to explain it in a moment." With a slow breath, she nudged it toward Bloodheart. "Toivo, you wanted to see me smile not long ago. Now, let me see something. This is my thanks for your dueling during the party."

Bloodheart's face fell slightly at her phrasing. "Ah, I see." Leaning forward, he picked up the package and his eyebrows rose. Untying the twine that held it closed, he folded the leather back and froze.

Seconds ticked by and he didn't move nor speak. After a long moment, he looked up from the sword to Mageeyes, who was watching him with a neutral expression.

"It is exquisite," he said softly, "but it is still a pale comparison to your smile." With that, he stood up. "I'm sorry, Amedee. While the blade looks like the work of a master, I have no desire for it."

He made it a single step away before Mageeyes spoke up, "Toivo?"

Bloodheart came to a sudden stop, not looking back at her. "Yes, Amedee?"

"Would the duel stand in place of a courting gift?" Her words were soft and trepidation laced them.

Sean was facing Bloodheart, and he watched the man's expression shift from sorrow to shock, then hope, before a radiant smile filled his face.

Turning back to Mageeyes, Bloodheart went back to the desk and knelt beside her chair. "That wouldn't be my first choice of courting gift for you. If that is your wish, though, it is mine."

Mageeyes stared into Bloodheart's eyes before she closed hers and took a shuddering breath. "Toivo... I..."

"All I want is a chance, Amedee. I will not press you. I can see the pain and hurt in you, and it pierces me deeply. Please, tell me what to do, and I will do it. All I wish is to see you smile and for the pain to go away."

"Sean," Mageeyes started, but her voice was tight with emotion and she had to clear her throat to continue. "Sean, please tell him about the sword I had you make for him."

"I made a mithril blade, but the cutting edges are adamantine.

The enchantment rune on them is new, something I'll be registering tomorrow. It's easiest to have you draw it."

Bloodheart looked at Mageeyes, who pulled the sword across the desk and held it out to him. "This is my first courting gift."

Bloodheart inhaled sharply and bowed his head to her. "I accept it as the first small step to your heart. I will wield this blade in your name alone. It will only be drawn when you have need."

"Draw it now," Mageeyes said.

Bloodheart rose smoothly to his feet and, accepting the scabbard from Mageeyes, he drew the blade. The two metals were clear to see, as was the sapphire set in the middle of the crossguard. The hilt only had the one ornamentation— a heart with a single eye in the center of it, the iris a sapphire. A small diamond was set in the end of the pommel, as well.

"When you will the sapphire to work, the blade will shock anyone it touches. That shock will also course down any blade it touches," Sean said. "I did test it against a blade with the same enchantment, and the two charges cancel each other out."

Bloodheart held the sword away from everyone and willed the enchantment to work. The blade was suddenly coated in a blue, crackling aura. "Goodness... This is going to cause many problems."

"She asked for the best sword I could make," Sean said. "This will devastate anyone it goes against because of that enchantment."

"Yes, it will," Bloodheart said softly. Shaking his head, he willed the enchantment to stop and after a second, the electricity faded. "Who knew that one could harness the power of storms?"

Sean blinked repeatedly before he exhaled, feeling like an idiot.

"Sean?" Mageeyes said.

"It's nothing for now," Sean said. "The other thing it does is give Mage Sight."

Both Mageeyes and Bloodheart looked at Sean with surprise.

Sean grinned. "It's a gift from her to you. It felt fitting."

Sheathing the blade, Bloodheart turned back to Mageeyes and knelt again, presenting her the sword. "Dame Mageeyes, I accept your gift, but I ask you to name me your champion, here in the presence of an Aspirant who can witness it."

Mageeyes inhaled slowly and took the sword from him. Drawing it, she held the blade before her. "Knight Toivo Bloodheart, I name you my champion. You will always be the one who fights on my behalf when required. It is by your request this pact is made." She took the blade and laid the flat of it along the left side of his neck, then raised it over his head and did the same on his right. Pulling the blade up again, she reversed it and set it point down in front of Bloodheart. "Your blade, champion."

Bloodheart's hand rose to cover the hilt. "I accept the charge, and will never fail in my duty to guard your life."

Sean was a little shocked, but didn't speak.

"Now rise, Toivo."

Bloodheart stood to his full height, his smile broad. "I will never fail you."

"Sean, I will join the association in a bit," Mageeyes said, not looking away from Bloodheart. "Please let them know."

"Of course," Sean said.

* * *

"Not the last one to show up for once," Fredrick said in greeting when Sean and Aria joined the others in the private dining room.

"Amedee will be along shortly," Sean said.

"Which means you know what she's up to?" Joseph asked.

"Her business if she wants to tell anyone," Sean said. "It's personal."

"Fine, fine," Joseph sighed.

"I wonder if we should wait for her," Fredrick said. "I have news, but wanted to wait for you, at least."

"I'm not sure how long she might be," Sean replied as he took his seat. "Maybe wait until we have drinks?"

"That would be for the best," Fredrick agreed, getting a groan from Joseph which, in turn, got laughter from the room.

Tabitha was there less than a minute later to take their drink order. Light chat carried the conversation until she returned and distributed their drinks. Just as she was leaving, Mageeyes entered the room, a drink already in her hand.

"Since we have drinks and we are all here now..." Fredrick nodded when Tabitha left. Seeing that he had everyone's attention, he cleared his throat. "Babbitt started to follow up on the bloody rope. He'd just gotten to the tower when Wolen showed up with a squad of men."

"Fucking hell," Sean said.

"Babbitt had the foresight to have a few other guards nearby— Ernest Carmady and his squad of men, who were supposed to be in that area, unlike Wolen," Fredrick went on. "The ensuing argument became street theater for everyone nearby."

"Bet Wolen hated that," Jefferson snickered.

"Especially when Carmady called him out for being out of his beat area," Fredrick nodded.

"What happened?" Saret asked.

"A compromise," Fredrick said. "Wolen, Carmady, and Babbitt entered the tower. The rope, along with cast-off clothing that was covered in blood, was found. Carmady started to set up a perimeter, following their regulations. Wolen left quickly at that point."

"He'll have another plan. Funny that he knew where to be," Sean said darkly.

"And that he was first on the scene when my brother was found," Fredrick said tightly.

"Was the evidence gathered?" MacLenn asked.

"Carmady collected all the evidence," Fredrick replied. "It'll be taken to the Magistrate's hall. I've requested Jasper handle the case, and he's agreed."

"Did he get another lead?" Italice asked.

Fredrick looked around the room, then looked up. "The room is secured?"

"Yes," Ven replied from above.

Nodding, Fredrick took a long drink of his ale before setting the mug down. "Babbitt acquired a scrap of the clothing. He'll be using a cuon tomorrow to start tracking the killer."

Sean sat forward. "Is he going to be prepared for where it'll take him?"

"I believe so. He had the forethought to bring Carmady with him for the tower."

"I wouldn't have thought to do that," Ryan said. "Babbitt is a smart man."

"He always has been," Flamehair nodded. "He wouldn't have been commander for so long if he wasn't."

"Does he need a cuon?" Sean asked.

"He advised me he had everything in hand, but did thank us for the clue," Fredrick said. "I believe the Fairy who informed us is now under an Agreement with him, as well."

"They are," Ven added from above.

"Maybe this will work," Sean said. "It'll be less bloody if it does."

"I want the man who killed him, and the one who ordered it," Fredrick said softly. "While we're fairly certain about the second, we have no idea on the first."

"That is valid," Sean nodded.

34

Sean followed Aria out of the carriage and into the building. The lobby felt strangely deserted as they approached the reception desk. Sean was surprised that Agatha wasn't the person behind it.

"Excuse me, miss," Sean said when they got to the desk, "I have patents to register."

The younger woman looked up and gave him a professional smile. "Of course, sir. Can I have your name?"

"Sean MacDougal."

The woman jerked slightly. "Ah, y-yes. Let me check if the registrar is available."

As the receptionist hurried away, Sean frowned. "I wonder what the current rumor is?"

"That you decapitate Knights who anger you," Aria said. "I'm sure she's terrified of what you might do to a commoner."

"Is it really?" Sean asked.

Aria shrugged. "I don't know, husband. I wouldn't be surprised if it was, though."

"That's fair."

The receptionist returned a couple of minutes later, moving

quickly, but not running. She slowed her pace when she saw them watching her. Clearing her throat, she patted her hair to make sure it was still in place. "If you'll follow me, please?"

"After you," Sean replied.

They went to Jackson's old office, and Sean felt his gut tighten. The woman knocked before opening the door. "Miss, MacDougal to see you."

"Thank you, Jenny. MacDougal, please come in."

Sean stared at Agatha before walking into the office. Aria shut the door behind them and stood beside it. Agatha glanced at Aria, then at Sean, her face paling.

"You came to register a new patent?" Agatha asked, her nervousness clear.

"A few," Sean said slowly. "When did you take over this position?"

Agatha's face cracked as she began to cry. "After... Jackson..."

"Did you have anything to do with that?" Sean asked flatly.

Agatha's eyes widened and she shook her head. "No! Never! Jackson and I..." She trailed off, clearly not wanting to say more.

Seeing her honesty and tears, Sean felt like an ass. "I'm sorry. I didn't know."

Agatha sniffled and wiped her cheeks. "We were always careful to not let it be known. I was going to meet with him after dinner... but then..." Tears began to fall again and she covered her face.

Aria moved over to her, gently patting her back. "We're sorry for your loss. Does Fredrick know?"

"No. No one knows. No one cares," Agatha sobbed, putting her head down on the desk and covering her head with her arms.

"That's not entirely true," Sean said. "We didn't know, and if we don't know, how can we show we care? Jackson's death is very much cared about. Babbitt is investigating it, outside of the guard."

Agatha sniffled, trying to regain control of her emotions as Aria continued to gently soothe her. "He is? Why?"

"Fredrick hired him," Aria said. "You should talk to Fredrick."

"No, I can't. Jackson was married. I won't tarnish his name,"

Agatha said, her head coming up off the desk. "That's the least I can do for him."

"Fredrick would rather know," Sean said. "I'm sure he won't be upset, and it might help them find the killer faster."

Agatha shook her head, but after a second, she hiccupped and scrubbed her cheeks. "You're right. I'll send him a message to see if he'll speak with me."

"Ven," Sean said, "let Fredrick know that Agatha would like to speak with him when he gets a moment, please."

"Yes, sir," Ven replied.

A silver blur left the room a second later. Agatha took a deep shaky breath and sniffled again, looking after the blur.

"I do actually have patents to register," Sean said softly.

Agatha jerked slightly. "Sorry. Of course. What do you have?"

Sean showed her the runes for the enchantments he had, as well as several diagrams and a glass bulb, which made Agatha frown. He took the time to explain each— she looked shocked about them all, but the bulb was the one that had her eyes wide.

"That's amazing. You can make them easily?"

"I need to work out a few minor kinks, but yeah," Sean said. "If people thought the taps were something, they haven't seen anything yet. You're actually the first person outside my family to see this."

Agatha's eyes began to tear up again and she touched the bulb gently. "Jackson would always go on about your patents. He idolized you, in his own way. Not at first, though— when Fredrick made the association, he thought his brother had gone a little mad, but he came around quickly when he saw your inventions. He always said, 'MacDougal is going to change the world', and he'd puff up a little before adding, 'and my family will help him.'"

Sean exhaled slowly. "Looks like I'm changing things, even if they are small things. Jackson was a good man."

Agatha nodded sadly before she jerked to her feet. "Now, let's do what he would've wanted. We'll get these listed and locked down to you."

"And the association," Sean added.

"Yes, of course," Agatha nodded.

* * *

Sean gave everyone a grin when he entered the private dining room. "Good evening."

"Sean," Fredrick said with an amused smile, "I had a message from the crafter's hall. New patents?"

"That's what I was working on all day," Sean said. "Sorry, Winston, the inspiration hit me last night. I'll be back tomorrow."

"Something conceived and finished in a single night?" Giralt asked, giving his mustache a smoothing pass with his fingers.

"Yeah, it's from my old world," Sean said as he set the lightbulb on the table for everyone to see. "Trick to this is that it takes a few Talents to really make."

"Of course it does," Ryan laughed. "Could we even make it if we pooled our resources? The rest of us, not you."

"It depends on if any of you can Shape sand into glass," Sean said. "If so, yeah. A Metal Shaper, a Sand Shaper, and you, Ryan."

Everyone sat forward a little to make sure they could hear him clearly.

"On my world, this was called a lightbulb. It replaced candles and lanterns as the source of lighting," Sean said. "As you can see, I made the bulb— the glass piece— from a few things."

"Which you got from me this morning, I bet," MacLenn chuckled.

"Thanks again," Sean said. "The glass can be altered some to provide different things, but I went for clear to make this easy for you all to see. Inside, you'll see the metal wires and filament. It's what will actually make this work. The base is the housing for the enchantments. I used cheap materials, with quartz being the most expensive part." He looked back to MacLenn. "Get as much of the materials as possible. Lock down all supply, if you can."

MacLenn nodded. "If you're that sure, then I will do so tomorrow."

"The association will," Fredrick said. "This is an association item, isn't it?"

"You are part of the patent," Sean said. "I hope one of you can make the glass. If you can, then I can hand all this off to Ryan and two others."

"Go on," Joseph said, eager to hear more.

"A couple of days ago, I made a new rune enchantment," Sean said. "This one creates electricity. Electricity is the key component to most of what my old world could do. The first, and most useful, arguably being this."

"But what does it do?" Joseph asked, clearly already on edge.

"The quartz at the base is the trigger point," Sean said. "I'm going to advise all of you to look away from it when I trigger it. It'll hurt your eyes, otherwise."

As one, everyone looked down at the table, and Sean triggered the quartz. Bright white light filled the room and everyone looked up instantly before cursing and looking away.

"Warned you not to look," Sean said as he turned the bulb off. "That's what it does. It creates light."

Fredrick was rubbing at his eyes. "That'll ruin the chandleries," he said, "if those *lightbulbs* can be made cheap enough. It was very bright."

"Yes, but the glass can be frosted to soften that, or you can do this." Sean put a small shade over the bulb and turned it back on.

"Oh, that is much better," Saret said.

Now, everyone was examining the bulb.

"How much do you think it will cost to make?" Fredrick asked Sean.

"How much were the glass components?" Sean asked MacLenn.

"A few copper," MacLenn replied.

"A large copper, maybe a little more," Sean said.

Fredrick shook his head. "Less than two large coppers? It'll ruin a whole section of crafters."

"Yeah," Sean said. "At most, they could start pushing for scented candles, but overall, they're done as soon as this goes public."

"This should take a little bit of thought," Mageeyes said. "Maybe a division of the association, a subgroup? We can give them the chance to buy into it— and it alone— splitting half of the profits for them and the other half for the greater association. They would be the sellers, and possibly the makers?"

"Yes. We'll need to move on this a little more slowly," Fredrick agreed.

"Did any of them side with us?" Sean asked bluntly. "*Any* of them?"

"No, but they didn't side against us, either," Fredrick said.

"I need one person for the Metal Shaping, one person who can Shape glass, and Ryan. I'm assuming your family would be okay with letting you move to something else, since we've stabilized the reservoir?"

"I'm almost certain," Ryan nodded.

"I'll leave the business up to you, Fredrick. When you have the other two positions, let me know. Ryan, come on over to Winston's tomorrow. Is that okay, Winston? I can work on other things while Ryan gets a hand on what I'm going to show him."

"I'm fine with that," Giralt said.

"I'll look into it, Sean," Fredrick said.

"I'll have that wagon over to your shop tomorrow, too, Winston," MacLenn said.

"So much going on," Mageeyes said. "Was there any news from Babbitt, Fredrick?"

Fredrick shook his head. "Hmm... No, and it bothered me. I'll be checking with him tomorrow."

"Might be for the best," Mageeyes said.

35

"Okay," Sean grinned as he set down a chest. "Let's get this going."

"I've been looking forward to it," Giralt said. "The... wagon." He motioned to the stripped-down frame of a wagon.

"Nice. That'll work great."

"It will?" Giralt asked. "It's barely got the important parts attached, and no bed or seat."

"Yup. It'll make this much easier."

"Okay... Where do we start?" Giralt asked.

"The brakes. We need to make sure it can stop. First thing we have to do is change out the wheels for new ones."

"Brakes? Interesting," Giralt said. "I would have thought that was the last problem."

"We already have the engine, which means we'll be going into the transmission after we get the brakes done."

"Before we get started, can you tell me what order things are going to be done in?"

"Brakes, engine, transmission and rest of the powertrain, then steering. We'll need adamantine for the gearing, but we can use bronze for the rest. We should probably use a little extra to harden it and make sure it can handle stress."

"Well, it looks like we'll have our hands full for a few tendays."

Sean chuckled. "Today, maybe tomorrow. That should be it."

"You're serious?" Giralt asked incredulously.

"Yup. Tomorrow, at the latest. It's why I had all the metal delivered this morning."

Giralt shook his head and set his cigar down. "Okay, I'm not sure how much I can help, but I'm more than willing to give it a good try."

Sean grinned as he moved over to the wagon. "As I was saying, wheels and brakes first."

* * *

A knock on the door got Sean and Giralt's attention.

"Come in!" Giralt yelled from where he was on the floor with Sean.

"Excuse me, Sean, I... what in the world?" Ryan Watercaller asked as he stepped into the workshop.

"Hey, Ryan. Give me a minute," Sean said. "We'll be at a stopping point soon."

"This is the horseless-wagon project?"

"Yup," Sean said. "First prototype."

With a grunt, Sean came into view, sliding on the mechanic creeper. He sat up when he cleared the vehicle. Giralt was a moment behind him, wearing a large grin.

"This is very interesting," Giralt said. "I'll gladly take a break, though."

"Go ahead. I need to show Ryan how to remove water, and hopefully, he can do it."

Ryan's eyebrows went up as he stood there, looking at the two men seated on small wheeled platforms. "Remove water from air?"

Sean got up and stretched. "Yes. It leaves nitrogen and other gases behind."

"Why is this important?" Ryan asked, following Sean over to the far side of the workshop.

"Because the inside of the bulb will blacken if there is any water. Technically, unless we remove all of the oxygen, it will anyway, but getting as much as we can out is important. It'll keep it going longer."

"Okay," Ryan said slowly, clearly not understanding.

"When the light is on, the filament superheats," Sean said, "the vapor from the filament combines with the oxygen and creates a sooty layer inside the glass."

"Why not just leave an opening in it?" Ryan asked.

"The filament is fragile," Sean said, "but honestly, I don't know for certain. I was a mechanic, not an electrician. I know lightbulbs were vacuum-sealed with inert gases, but I'm not going to work on a vacuum pump. It's not worth the investment right now."

Ryan didn't understand half of what Sean said. "Okay... I'm going to remove water from air. Got it."

"It was fairly simple once I tried it," Sean said.

"What isn't for you?" Ryan asked dryly.

"Understanding women."

Giralt laughed as he took a seat at his desk and lit up a cigar. "No one understands them. I'm not even certain they understand themselves most days."

Sean wisely kept his mouth shut, going off the theory that if he opined an opinion, that would be when Clara and Aria would show up. Instead, he stopped by the half-made lightbulbs he'd brought with him.

"Okay, we'll begin with this one. I'm going to start the process, and I want you to try following along."

"I'll do my best."

"Use this," Sean said, handing over a mithril monocle. "I made it last night. Mage Sight, and the diamond will fuel it so you can still be full for the work."

Ryan hesitated a moment before he took it. "This is worth a fortune... You know that, right?"

"Yeah, it doesn't matter," Sean said. "Now, focus on the energy and what I'm doing."

* * *

"It's so simple," Ryan laughed as he did the third bulb.

"It is, if the person working the glass can do what I am," Sean corrected him.

"That's a fair point," Ryan nodded. "I can do this easily, and it barely uses any of my energy."

"That's good, because these are going to be in high demand, even if we limit the number being sold to start with."

"I believe that. I know all of us in the association are first in line for a bunch of them."

"Don't blame you in the least," Sean said. "I'll be filling my home with them soon."

"A perk of being the inventor," Ryan chuckled.

"I hope Fredrick comes up with someone who can handle the glass and metal components," Sean said. "I'd like to hand this off completely— same with the truck, when I finish with it. Skilled Metal Shaping will be needed for it."

"Considering all you've given us," Ryan said seriously, "I'm sure he'll find someone. Might even be your apprentices."

"They could do the work," Sean agreed. "I'm sure they've had their skills refined by Fredrick and Eva."

"Is the break over?" Giralt asked, finishing his cigar and cognac.

"Yeah, time to get back to it," Sean said.

"I'll let Fredrick know that I can handle the removal part of the process," Ryan said.

"Thanks. I should have this done by tomorrow sometime. It'll really make people sit up and take notice."

"Horseless wagons, light without candles..." Ryan shook his head. "Everything is changing so fast."

"And as soon as I hand it off to the association, it'll pretty much seal Denmur's futility," Sean said with a dark smile.

"Glad we sided with you," Ryan chuckled. "I wish you good speed on your work."

"Thank you," Giralt said, sitting down on the creeper. "You don't want to see what we're doing?"

"I would, but Italice is waiting for me."

"Tell her hi for us," Sean said. "See you tonight."

"I can't wait to hear how things are coming along by then," Ryan laughed.

* * *

Sean apologized when he and Aria made it home. "Sorry for the delay."

"Well, sparring is over, and we're about to have our shower," Fiona said. "You stayed late, so did you finish it?"

"Nearly," Sean sighed. "The steering still has to be worked on. Maybe an hour of work, but Clara wasn't having any of it."

Fiona laughed. "She's a strong woman. You did the right thing to concede defeat to her."

"I wasn't given much choice. Giralt threw in with her right from the start," Sean snickered. "Man knows that a happy wife is important."

"As our husband does, too," Fiona smiled, kissing his cheek. "Come on, you can tell us all about it at dinner."

"Okay," Sean grinned. "I'll be doing a lot of patenting tomorrow, but even then, it'll be an early day."

"You're going to start on the lightbulbs?" Fiona asked as they went in the backdoor.

"And get them set up all over the house," Sean agreed.

"I do feel sorry for the chandleries," Fiona said as they entered the bathroom.

"I hope Fredrick was able to make a deal with them. It'll ripple out from here, though."

"Yes, I'm sure it will," Fiona nodded. "You'll be coming to the attention of the powerful houses quickly."

"Yeah," Sean said, taking a deep breath.

"There he is," Myna said from the tub. "We've been eager to hear about your work, Master."

"Okay," Sean smiled, taking a seat to get his boots off. "At dinner, so everyone can hear it all at once?"

"As it should be," Myna agreed.

* * *

Stepping into the private dining room, Sean laughed when Joseph greeted him. "Evening to you, too, Joseph. You sound a little impatient."

"My patience is legendary," Joseph said with a sniff.

"Legendarily *bad*," Knox said sotto voce, earning laughter from the others in the room.

"That's still a type of legend," Joseph said, rolling with the joke. "But enough about me. Sean, tell us— what did you manage today?"

"Ryan learned how to make one part of the lightbulbs," Sean said. "He's very adept at it."

"I've started negotiations with the chandleries," Fredrick said. "They don't believe me, yet."

"I know someone who can work with sand to make glass," Italice said. "Jeno."

"Jeno? Really?" Sean asked, thinking of his time teaching the younger Botrel.

"Had him and Maddox try today," Italice said. "Maddox wasn't able to manage it, but Jeno had some success."

"Hmm," Fredrick said. "Maybe we should spin the lightbulbs into a small subset of the association? Ryan, are you good with taking him under your wing to work on that?"

"Of course, if Sean will show him what to do first."

"Tomorrow, early morning," Sean said. "I'll do that, then go over to Winston's."

"Fredrick, since I'm going to be closing my shop, maybe we should let Derrin do the metalwork for them," Eva offered.

"Yes, an excellent suggestion," Fredrick said.

"Wait, you're closing your shop?" Joseph asked.

"I'm moving in with Fredrick, now that we're officially married. We're combining our businesses."

A round of congratulations went around the table. They were still talking about that when Tabitha came to get their drinks, then delivered them. Fredrick seemed a little subdued during the hubbub.

"Send Derrin over tomorrow, too, please?" Sean asked once the room had settled down again. "I'll get them both set up, and Ryan can start in on the work on Oneday."

"Everything is moving quickly," Giralt chuckled.

"Glad I managed to get more of the supplies for making glass," MacLenn nodded.

"Going to need more bronze and adamantine, as well," Sean said. "Tomorrow afternoon, right near midday, you should all be at the crafters hall."

Everyone sat forward, clearly waiting for him to continue.

"I will be getting the first prototype of the horseless wagon patented then," Sean said.

"Oh, this will spark something," Fredrick said. "Speaking of..." he exhaled. "Babbitt apologized— his one lead ended."

All eyes went to Fredrick as their excitement died instantly.

"What happened?" Sean asked.

"Babbitt managed to track down the killer," Fredrick said. "An ex-guard, who was outed during the purge. The man refused to come in and attacked Babbitt. He had no recourse but to cut him down."

"Fuck..." Sean said grimly.

"That isn't the worst of it. Wolen just *happened* to arrive with his squad. They arrested Babbitt for murder." Fredrick held up a hand as people began to speak. "He's already been released. The evidence pointed to him defending himself, and Jasper let him go, but it does kill our real leads."

"Wolen, again?" Sean asked.

"Old friends," Fredrick said tightly. "Was 'checking in on an old friend who was down on his luck,' he said."

"That seals his fate," Sean said darkly. "He's been at too many incidents for coincidence to be a thing."

"True, but without proof—" Fredrick began.

"Just give me time," Sean said. "Tomorrow, noon, guild hall. We rock the city then. After that, I start my war against Denmur."

"If you need—" Joseph started.

"I'll be fine," Sean cut him off. "You're all already at enough risk." Rising to his feet, Sean felt the weight of what he was going to do settle on his shoulders. "Just stand back, and be there if I need a hand to get back up."

"We'll be ready," Fredrick said.

36

J ust after breakfast, Sean met with Jeno and Derrin at his workshop. It took him a couple of hours to make sure they were able to do what was needed to make the lightbulbs. It took Jeno longer than it did Derrin to get the hang of it, but with Sean coaching him, he managed to make two before Sean called them good.

"Keep them. Consider them your journeyman pieces," Sean said. "You'll refine your work as you keep doing it."

"Sir—" Jeno started.

"Sean," Sean corrected him. "You're no longer an apprentice. You'll be one of three people who'll be making these."

"*Sean*," Jeno said, his smile wide, "we just wanted to thank you."

"We both know how lucky we've been," Derrin added in agreement.

"We'd have been smiths and proud of it. But to be able to Shape and work on projects like this..."

"It's been a blessing," Derrin said when Jeno trailed off. "We'll do it right. Don't you worry."

"I don't, because I know you will," Sean replied. "You both have the work ethic needed. Your fathers saw to that."

Both of the former smiths chuckled.

"Ryan will be the lead on this project, but you both bring vital work to it."

"We'll be the ones looked up to at the apprentice table," Jeno said, "along with Cartha."

Derrin glanced to Jeno. "Uh... about her, Jeno— did you have your eye on her?"

"She's pretty," Jeno grinned, "but no. I've seen you look at her, though."

Sean laughed. "Okay, we're done here." Shepherding them out of the shop and toward the gate, he nudged Derrin. "And you'll never know if you don't ask."

Derrin looked away from Sean. "That's true, but..."

"But?" Sean prompted.

"She used to be a Dame. I'm not sure if she'd even look at me."

"*Used* to be," Sean said softly. "Dame Loplis died. Cartha Somnia isn't that woman."

"True," Derrin said, though he was clearly uncertain.

"The worst that'll happen is she'll tell you no," Sean said, clapping him on the back. "At least then, you'll know where you stand."

"He's got you there," Jeno laughed.

"Fine. I'll see what she says."

"Good luck," Sean said, stopping at the gate.

* * *

Less than half an hour later, Sean was walking into Giralt's shop. "Sorry for the late start."

"As if I can fault you," Giralt laughed. "This is your project— I'm merely assisting. I still wonder if I'm doing that much to warrant it even being called assisting."

"You're doing a lot to help," Sean said. "That engine wouldn't be anywhere near as good as it is without you."

"I meant for the rest of it," Giralt said.

"I think you are, but if you don't think so, I don't know what to say."

"Ignore me. I'm just feeling a little underfoot today."

"Wife?" Sean asked.

Giralt looked to the door first. "A small argument... They happen with every relationship, especially one that has gone as long as ours has."

"I bet it's the hormones," Sean said. "Makes me wonder what my home is going to be like soon."

Giralt chuckled. "Well, you have how many expecting, now?"

"Six," Sean said.

"Aria is the only one not having a child?" Giralt asked.

"They wanted to keep one of them with me all the time."

"Ah, and since Ryann is no longer your shield, Aria is filling in."

"Yeah."

"Hmm. Dedicated, all of them."

"I'm a lucky man."

"Indeed, you are."

"Let's get to work," Sean said, moving over to the wagon. "We just need to finish up the steering. Two hours or less and we'll be good to go."

"Oh, this is going to be exciting," Giralt chuckled. "I can't wait to see the faces of the onlookers."

"You'll be patenting the engine with me," Sean said. "It's equal for us. The rest of this, I'll patent."

"The... oh, what did you call them? 'Shock absorbers'?" Giralt checked and got a nod. "Those are different."

"It'll make it so much smoother. I still need to add them to my carriage."

"Just those by themselves will be in high demand once people understand what they do," Giralt said. "Forged Bonds is going to be flooded with orders for so many things."

"Fredrick will figure it out," Sean said, getting onto the creeper. "Ready to get this done?"

"Ready to see what you do next," Giralt laughed as he got onto the second creeper and slid under the wagon.

Sean was having trouble not laughing as he watched the people he drove past. A pack of children ran alongside them, shouting questions to him and Giralt. Giralt sat beside him on the driver's bench, looking at the gaping crowd with an open smile. Aria was in the back, waving to the kids who called out to her.

Fredrick and the other members of the association stood outside the guild hall, staring at them with mild shock. Sean couldn't blame them— it was one thing to be told about a horseless vehicle, but it was another to see one.

Slowing the wagon, Sean engaged the parking brake before killing the engine. He used the release whistle to bring the pressure down quickly as the heating rune cooled off. The whistle made everyone nearby jump in shock, as only a few had heard a steam whistle before.

"This is it," Sean announced. "The horseless wagon. Since this one is for goods, I'm calling it a truck. The one for people will be a car."

"Can it still take the same load?" MacLenn asked.

"No," Sean replied with a straight face.

"How much less?" MacLenn asked, his excitement waning slightly.

"Less?" Sean laughed. "It's not less— it can take more weight now. The suspension is upgraded, and there are no horses to worry about. I'd say just short of double, but that's so it can travel as fast as it should."

MacLenn just blinked at Sean for a moment. "Double? I can move *double* the cargo?"

"Yeah, but you'll have to be careful about how you pack it in. Don't make this thing flip, as getting it back upright will be a real problem. I'd say cover the next one, insulate it, and you'd have an ice wagon."

Fredrick looked at the growing crowd and raised his voice to address them, "Ladies and gentlemen, this is a 'truck', and is the latest invention of Forged Bonds. It can move more goods, and without the need to care for horses or oxen. They won't be for sale for a while yet, but they will be in time. You can approach the new Forged Bonds shopfront tomorrow morning. It is located in Eva Silvertouch's old shop."

"How much will it cost?" a voice yelled from the back of the growing crowd.

"That's still being decided, but you'll need gold, and a fair bit of it," Fredrick replied. "I have it on good authority that it'll run for a long time before the enchantments need to be refreshed. The deposit cost to get put on the waiting list will start at five large golds. We'll have more known tomorrow."

"Is that another of MacDougal's inventions?"

"What gave it away?" Sean asked as he stood up, looking out over the crowd from the bench. "Yes, it is, but Forged Bonds will be making them exclusively."

"That'll tweak Denmur's nose!" another random person spoke up.

"Good," Sean said bluntly. "If you'll excuse me, I need to patent this. Fredrick, the seat is all yours to answer questions."

Sean jumped down, followed by Aria and Giralt. He turned around and took a large trunk from the back, hoisting it onto his shoulder. Entering the guild hall, he saw Jenny standing by the front door, her eyes wide. "Jenny, I need to see Agatha, please."

Jenny looked from him to the crowd outside, then back to him.

"I dare say you shocked her," Giralt chuckled.

Aria touched Jenny's arm softly. "Miss?"

Jenny jumped, her eyes focusing on Aria. "Yes, ma'am?"

"My husband and Magus Giralt need to see Agatha about patenting some things."

"Oh, uh... y-yes. Please, give me a moment," Jenny stammered before she hurried away, nearly running in her haste.

"People will remember this day," Giralt said with a proud grin.

Jenny returned not even a minute later, her steps just slightly slower than her retreat earlier. "If you'll follow me, please."

The three of them followed her down to Agatha's office. Sean was amused that the door was open. Agatha had started to say something, but upon seeing Giralt, she put on a business demeanor.

"Welcome, Magus Giralt and MacDougal. How might the guild help you?"

"Winston and I have a joint patent to file, and I have another dozen or so to file after that. I have the schematics of the devices, as well as smaller versions of them so they can be copied to the book. The size doesn't matter as much— they can be scaled up or down depending on the job. If you want to see the full devices, those are on the truck."

"Truck? Is that the horseless wagon that Jenny spoke of?" Agatha asked hesitantly.

"Yup. I'll give you a good look at it once we're done with the paperwork. I also have one more item to register, but I'll bring that one in after we do these."

"Of course," Agatha said slowly. "Shall we start with the joint patent, first?"

"Sure. Make sure to mark down Forged Bonds as being allowed full use of them."

Giralt nodded. "That includes this one."

"Okay," Agatha said, her hesitance fading. "What's first?"

"The engine," Sean grinned, "which includes all the new parts that aren't patented yet."

* * *

It was nearing evening when Sean, Aria, and Agatha left the guild hall— Giralt had gone back home after his patent was done. Sean was surprised to see the familiar faces near the wagon. The first was Babbitt, who was nearly nose to nose with a man in uniform that Sean had never seen. The second was Wolen and his squad of men.

The most shocking was Carver hanging out at the fringe of the crowd, watching the two men argue.

"Look here, *citizen* Babbitt!" the man snarled at Babbitt. "You are to clear off right now or I'll have you in chains!"

"Why does Babbitt need to leave?" Sean asked, putting the heavy trunk into the bed of the wagon.

"You!" the man in uniform seethed. "I'm Commander Lomar, the head of the Hearthglen guard. Is this your wagon?"

"I believe it belongs to Forged Bonds now," Sean said. "I merely invented and patented it."

"This wagon is in violation of a few laws. I'll be confiscating it."

Sean laughed and shook his head. "What laws?"

"Abandonment of a wagon on city streets!"

"It's not abandoned. I was *patenting* it," Sean rebuffed Lomar.

"Where are the horses, then?" Lomar asked snidely.

"It doesn't need them," Sean shrugged.

"Doesn't need them? Fine, where are the oxen, then?"

"Doesn't need them, either."

Lomar's eyes narrowed. "Are you trying to trick the guard, like the rest of these simpletons? Wagons do not move under their own power."

"It moves without horses or oxen. It moves because of the newly refined steam engine. Is that all, Captain?"

Lomar's eyes bulged, and he went red in the face. "Commander!"

"Oh right, sorry. I'm just used to Babbitt being the commander. He's got the right gravitas for it."

"Even if your *outlandish* claim was true," Lomar snarled, doing his best to ignore the jab, "leaving a wagon unattended on the streets—!"

"I told you, it isn't unattended," Babbitt said flatly. "I'm under the employ of Forged Bonds currently, and I am here with it."

"Even *attended*, it is a crime to have a wagon blocking a city street!" Lomar snapped.

Sean looked up and down the square, making it obvious he was doing so. "I'm sorry, blocking what? It's in the square. There's plenty of room for other wagons or carriages to get past it."

Lomar's face flushed a deeper red. "I've had enough of your lip, MacDougal!"

"I wasn't going to share it," Sean said, simply turning to Agatha, who was watching wide-eyed. "Agatha, you said you needed to verify that it works, right?"

"Umm... yes?" Agatha half-asked with a nervous glance to Lomar.

"Good, climb on. Aria, can you get in the back, please? Oh, and Babbitt, I'll be right back. Just going once around the block so she can verify it works."

"I'll be right here," Babbitt said.

"Now wait a damned minute!" Lomar growled. "No one is going anywhere."

"Are you interfering with guild business?" Babbitt asked with an amused grin. "He's clearly in the middle of a patent. The law on intentional interference on patenting is very clear."

Lomar paused, his mouth opening and closing before it snapped shut with an audible clack of his teeth. "Of course not."

"Good," Sean said, climbing onto the bench and starting the engine up. "If you can all move back, I don't want you to get injured."

The crowd backed away from the wagon as the noise of the engine, building pressure, started. Sean went through his checklist of brakes, and waited for the engine to get enough steam. Less than a minute later, he released the parking brake and the truck lurched forward, then began to move smoothly.

"And away we go," Sean grinned as he watched Carver and Lomar's mouths open in shock.

* * *

They were back at the guild hall after a couple of minutes, as Sean took a slightly longer route than he was going to at first. He was surprised to see the guard was gone, but the crowd had grown bigger.

"There you go, Agatha. Do I need to do anything else?"

"No," Agatha said breathlessly. "This is amazing."

"Thanks," Sean said. "Have a good night."

"You, too," Agatha said as she got down.

"Babbitt, what happened to the... commander?" Sean changed what he wanted to say after a short pause.

Babbitt's lips twitched, but he didn't comment. "He was convinced that none of the charges would stick. Lomar took his men and stalked off."

"Good. Can I offer you a ride home?"

"In that?"

"Yeah."

"I'd be glad to see what it can do," Babbitt said, climbing up.

37

Sean chuckled as he pulled the truck to a stop. "So, what do you all think?"

No one spoke up as they continued to stare, so Sean shrugged and pulled the release whistle. The noise made everyone jump, and Myna, Fiona, and Prita clutched at their ears, staring at him reproachfully.

"That hurt, Master!" Myna fussed.

"Sorry. It's the release for the engine so it can stop trying to move the truck," Sean said.

"You missed sparring again," Helga said.

"I had a small run-in with the guard commander," Sean said. "That took a lot of my time, and then I gave Babbitt a ride home."

"Which caused a lot of commotion," Aria said as she came around the building. "I shut the front gates."

"I had no idea they'd follow us all the way home," Sean shrugged.

"How many?" Fiona asked.

"Dozens, maybe even a hundred or more?" Aria replied.

Sean pulled the key out of the truck and put it into his pouch. "Not like they can steal it."

"But best to deter more problems," Fiona sighed. "Caleb, can you go bark at the front gate, please?"

A woof came from the back gate, and Caleb went trotting toward the front.

"I'll be dropping it off with MacLenn tonight," Sean said. "Arliat, I'll need you to follow me."

"Of course, sir."

"Are you still planning on confronting Denmur?" Fiona asked.

Meeting her eyes, he nodded. "Yup. I'm dropping this off, then going to the Golden Lion. I'll get something out of it, at least. I'm sure I can prod him into a duel, even if it is with champions."

"Sean," Aria said. "You should take Helga. She's the best fighter we have."

Myna's lips pursed, but she nodded. "Since the rest of us aren't fighting now, she's probably the best choice."

"I could," Sean said slowly. "Might also set him off more if he sees her there. Helga?"

"Yes, sir?"

"Do you want to go?"

Helga stared at him, then looked at Fiona questioningly.

"He's not the type to force you to do anything," Fiona said. "It's just the way he is."

Helga looked down for a moment. "I have a hard time trying to understand him. He is a god, but he does not act like any of them. He never yells, blames others, or lashes out at us for making mistakes."

"Yes, he is rather strange in that regard," Felora agreed.

"Those are some of the reasons we love him as much as we do," Andrea said.

"You all treat me well," Helga said. "None of you hurt me, physically or verbally. Do I not deserve your anger and pain? I am one of the reasons they are not with you anymore. Why do you not lash out at me?"

"Because you weren't there of your own will," Fiona said softly.

"And you opened the door for us to see them again," Andrea said.

"Sean doesn't want those he loves to fight," Felora added. "Hurting you would hurt him."

"You're family," Ida stated.

"Sean chose you to be here with us as he chose Aria and me," Ryann said. "All of us were against him before we were beside him. I shot him with a poisoned bolt, and he still forgave me."

"Master does as he feels is right, and he hasn't been wrong yet," Myna said as she advanced on Helga. "Or do you question his judgement?"

"Myna, she's just as upset as I was," Aria said, placing her hand on Myna's shoulder. "She isn't speaking against him."

"You all trust me to keep him safe?" Helga asked, her hands and voice trembling.

"Yes," Fiona said simply, and the others nodded.

"But it's your choice," Sean said. "You'll always have a choice, Helga. I'm not a drunken dick that'd use you and then toss you out. I'll leave that to the Thor-losers."

Aria snickered and gave Sean a grin at his pun.

Helga jerked at Thor's name, but when she understood what he'd said, her concern faded and a smile touched her lips. "You will never be like him. I know that, but at the same time, you do not act like *any* of the gods, even the decent ones like Loki or Tyr. They did not give choices, either— they just did not do as much wrong."

"Welcome to a new religion," Sean said. "We'll just have to find our own way. You'll be right here with us the whole time."

Helga's eyes swept the wives, and she bowed her head. "I would be honored to be your champion, Sean," she said a moment later, raising her head to meet his eyes. "My body shall be your shield."

"I'd prefer your shield to be my shield," Sean said. "We'll have to take one with us tonight, as Sam hasn't finished yours yet."

"I will make sure I am equipped," Helga said.

"Is it time for the bath?" Prita asked.

"Yes," Fiona said. "Here we are, keeping everyone in the yard."

Caleb suddenly started barking from the front of the manor and Sean tensed before remembering what Fiona had asked him to do.

"And that should take care of anyone foolish enough to think about coming inside the walls," Fiona said.

"I doubt anyone would have, anyway," Sean said. "It's common knowledge we have a cuon or two in the yard."

* * *

Sean pulled into the Oaken Glen's yard and gave the slack-jawed stable boys a smile. "Where am I parking it?"

"Uh... over there?" one of the two boys asked hesitantly.

"Sure thing," Sean said, driving to where they'd pointed and parking it.

The two stable boys started to get closer to the truck only to stumble backward when Sean pulled the release whistle.

"Sorry about that. It's fine now," Sean said, pulling the key. "You can look at it, but don't go messing around with it, okay?"

"Y-yes, sir."

Arliat pulled into the yard, turning the carriage around and parking it off to the side. Getting down, she gave the two boys a wave. "Just keep them here. I'll be back shortly."

"Yes, ma'am," one of them said, hurrying over to her.

"We are going inside?" Helga asked.

"To see the others, then we'll be heading out," Sean told her. "Come on."

Stepping into the inn from the stable door, Sean found every eye in the building on him. "Sorry about the whistle. I'll probably have to tone that down for the next one."

"Is that the horseless wagon?" someone asked him.

"Truck," Sean corrected, "and yes. I have eyes on it, so if anyone tries to touch it, I'll know."

Everyone looked away from him, clearly not wanting to anger the man who'd killed a noble outside the inn not that long ago.

Sean led the way to the private dining room. Knocking, he entered right afterward. "Sorry for the delay. You've all seen or met Helga, right?"

Everyone in the room agreed that they had, and the majority of them welcomed her to the table.

"We're used to you being last," Joseph laughed, "but Sam isn't here yet, so you're not last tonight."

Sean got worried, but before he could do anything, there was a knock, and Sam Bronzeshield entered the room. "Sorry for being so late... I must be really late, because Sean beat me here."

Laughter went up at her words and Sean exhaled, glad she was okay.

"Didn't mean to worry you, Sean," Sam said, seeing him relax. "I was just putting the finishing touches on the armor."

Sean looked to Helga, his lips turning up. "That'll be good."

Helga stood up and bowed to Sam. "You have my deepest thanks, crafter."

Everyone looked surprised at her actions, but Sam smiled. "You're welcome, Helga. I did my very best, as Sean said it was important to him. I hope that it's everything you hope it could be."

"How did the patents go?" Joseph cut in, wanting to know. "The crowd was still huge when we went back to work."

"Smooth," Sean said, "and they were still there when I came out."

"There was trouble afterward," Fredrick said.

"That's true," Sean sighed.

A knock stopped him from elaborating as Tabitha came into the room. "Drinks?"

A call for refills went around the table, and Eve handed over the money for the drinks. Sam ordered Serumtrutous to celebrate her job being done. When it was Sean's turn, he ordered a mulled wine. Helga started to shake her head, but Sean touched her arm.

"A small one is okay, as long as you aren't hindered by it," Sean told her. "Ryann and Aria usually go with the hot cider."

"I shall try the hot cider, then," Helga said.

As Tabitha stepped out, Sean went back to explaining Commander Lomar's attempt to stir up trouble. He was just finishing when Tabitha came back with the drinks.

"So the guards are all in Sharpeyes' pocket, then?" Knox grumbled. "That's not going to go well for us."

"Indeed, it's not," Ryan said.

"I'm concerned as to what they might do in the 'name of the law,'" Joseph said.

"Means I'm going to need a few people nearby for tonight," Sean said.

The room went quiet.

"You're planning on going after him tonight?" Fredrick asked.

"Yes— I'm done with this idiocy, though I am worried about what the guard might try to pull if there's no one there to speak for me."

"Is that why you brought her?" Mageeyes asked.

"My wives prefer that someone else champion for me if possible, and Helga is the best fighter. That armor was done in perfect time, Sam. Is it at your shop?"

"Yes."

"We'll swing by there on the way to the Golden Lion."

"I think we could all use a change of scenery for the evening," Mageeyes said. "I'm sure we have enough carriages to go around."

"Oh, before I forget," Sean suddenly said, pulling the key from his pouch and sliding it to MacLenn. "One truck in the yard. Just slot the key in and it'll connect the enchantments to get the engine running. Close the whistle valve first, though."

MacLenn picked up the key and studied the plain-looking item. "And this is what is needed to make it run?"

"Yup. Can't make it work without that in place."

"Wouldn't any piece of metal work, then?" Joseph asked.

"This one has a thin vein of ruby in it," MacLenn said, turning the key so Joseph could see it. "I'm assuming this triggers the enchantment?"

"Yup."

"When do we go?" Knox asked.

"As soon as we finish our drinks," Sean said.

* * *

The ride from the Oaken Glen to Sam's was swift, as it was only down the street. Sean was still thinking about the expressions on everyone's faces in the taproom when the entirety of Forged Bonds left.

"They all know something's up," Sean said. "With the majority of them going to the Golden Lion, it'll pull more eyes that way."

"The... truck?" Sam hesitated on the word Sean had used earlier, continuing when he nodded, "Will do that all by itself."

"That's true enough," Sean snorted. "The new and fantastic does that."

The carriage came to a stop, and Helga was the first one out. After scanning the area, she stepped aside. "It is clear."

Sean got out next, helping Sam out last. "After you?" he told her.

"Brendis will want to know what is happ—"

The shop door opened, and Brendis was standing there, looking a little worried. "Sean, you need the armor tonight?"

"I'll explain while Sam helps Helga," Sean said.

"Hmm... Should we be prepared for an attack?"

"Not you, but someone should be," Sean said.

Sam led Helga and Sean into the shop, closing the door behind them. "Helga, follow me. We can check that everything fits. Sean can alter anything that needs it."

"Why the rush on the armor tonight?" Brendis asked as the two women went into the back.

"Denmur," Sean said. "I'm going to start pressing him. We're going over to the Golden Lion as soon as she's kitted out."

"You're going to attack him?" Brendis asked.

"No, I'm going to challenge him, and keep doing it until he breaks. I'll either drive all of his supporters away from him or kill him. I'm done letting them dictate what happens."

Brendis nodded. "I'll be right back."

Sean was left alone in the front of the shop, wondering where Brendis was going.

Sam and Helga returned first, and Sean's breath caught for a moment. The single lantern in the front room lit up the mithril armor and made it shine. Sean's gaze went from breastplate to the pauldrons, upper arm guards, vambraces, gauntlets, cuisses, greaves, and sabatons. Pulling his eyes back up, he saw that Helga was holding her helm and shield, watching him.

"Sam, you did marvelous work," Sean said. "How does it feel, Helga?"

"Extremely light," Helga replied. "Much lighter than my old armor. I would ask you to touch up a few minor spots on the way to the confrontation, please."

"Easily."

"Ah, good, I'm not late," Brendis said.

"Husband?" Sam asked when she saw him. "What're you planning?"

"I'm going with them," Brendis told her. "They attacked us in our home. I want to be there to see it repaid."

"But our son?" Sam asked tightly.

"Asleep. Esmerelda is with him, along with Ang and the Fairies," Brendis said.

Sam hesitated and stepped back. "Then go and represent us. I will stay here."

Brendis took a slow breath. "You don't want to be there?"

"I do," Sam replied, "but I'd rather one of us stay here."

Brendis shook his head and stepped back behind the counter, shutting it. "Then I will stay. Make sure to tell me about it when you get home? I won't sleep until you are safely back here."

Sam met his eyes for a long moment before she moved forward and kissed him softly. "I'll be fine, dear husband. Sean won't let anything happen to me. I'll bring home good news."

Sean watched them with a heavy heart. His friends wanted to be there, but also felt they had to stay and protect their family, as well.

"Sean, I'm ready," Sam said, pulling away from Brendis.

"Let's go. I'll touch it up in the carriage, Helga."

"As you wish, sir," Helga said, opening the door.

"Look, you," an irate voice was saying, "it's clearly after business hours, and—!"

"Is there a problem?" Helga asked the two guards bluntly, who were speaking to Arliat.

"Is this your carriage?" one of the guards snapped at Helga.

"No. It's mine," Sean said flatly as he came out behind her. "Oh, it's you," Sean snorted at the guard who'd given him problems outside of Jefferson's.

"MacDougal? We should've known," the guard sneered. "It's illeg—"

"Is there a problem?" Sam asked, coming out behind Sean with Brendis in the doorway behind her. "Can I not have customers? Is that against the law now?"

The guard's jaw clenched. "No, it's not, but having a carriage parked for an inordinate length of time is."

"Do you know how long it takes to fit armor?" Sam asked.

"Then you need to have a place off the road for them to park," the guard said triumphantly.

"Because the traffic *sure* is busy right now," Sean added sardonically, looking at the street bereft of other vehicles. "I'm pretty sure it had something to do with impeding traffic..." Sean paused and looked up and down the road again. "Huh, doesn't seem to be happening."

The second guard looked embarrassed. "Avarn, come on. He's right. You know it as well as I do."

"Pax, *who* is the senior of us?!" Avarn snapped.

"You, but he's right about the law."

"Pax," Sean said, turning his attention to the other guard, "is Avarn one of the guards who listens to Wolen?"

"We are both part of Wolen's command," Pax said, looking unhappy.

"And the guard stations just rotated?" Sean asked.

"That's not your concern!" Avarn snarled, turning back to Sean. "Stay out of guard business."

Pax didn't speak, but he nodded his head behind Avarn's back.

"Yeah, thought so. Pax, there might be a time later when the orders go against what you believe. If that happens, I hope you listen to your gut," Sean said. "Now, Avarn, since there is no traffic being impeded, we aren't committing a crime. Bronzeshield herself has said we were here on business. So, are we done?"

Avarn's jaw clenched, his teeth grinding before he spun on his heel and stormed away from them. Pax gave an apologetic shrug and moved to follow his partner.

"I'll be locking up," Brendis told Sam. "Send word when you are coming back, please? I'll be hunkered down and prepared, just in case."

"Yes. It might be as bad as the last major rift in the city," Sam said sadly. "And all because of Denmur."

Sean looked at Arliat. "Are you okay?"

"The one was talking of arresting me if I didn't move the carriage," Arliat said. "I was trying to explain when you came out. They were being unreasonable."

"Yeah... Let's hope that tonight might fix a few things."

38

Sean felt his heart speed up slightly when they arrived at the Golden Lion. Stepping out of the carriage, he took a deep breath and helped Sam out behind him. Sean then looked at Arliat.

"I don't know how long we might be. I'm sure they'll have something to help warm you up, though. Do you have money to—"

"More than enough, sir," Arliat said, her face serious. "Please be careful?"

"I will."

"Think they're all inside already?" Sam asked.

"Should be," Sean said. "Helga?"

"Actually, if it's okay, I'd like to slip in first," Sam said.

"Okay."

As Sam went in, Sean caught dim voices, but no actual words before the door shut behind her. A gust of cold wind blew by and Sean looked up— he could see that the stars were mostly occluded by the dark clouds. Sean counted in his head, wanting to give Sam time to find a seat.

"Sean, I will keep you safe," Helga said, "even if it costs my life or soul. This is what I am made for."

"I won't try to coddle you," Sean replied, "but I also won't put you into needless danger. You are family, not some nameless pawn to be used in some cosmic game. There's also the chance that you won't be able to fight for me. If it comes to that, watch the others. I don't trust Denmur to play fair."

"I will protect you, even if it is in that small way."

"I know you will. I can get hints of your feelings at times. You don't feel afraid of combat, but you are terrified of failing."

Helga swallowed, her eyes closing for a moment. "I was wondering what that was on the edge of my mind. It is comforting to know you are there."

"I think we're good," Sean said. "Lead us in, Chooser."

Helga gave him a smile. Touching the sword and small spear on her hip, she reached back to check her shield before nodding. She stepped forward and opened the door, walking inside the building.

The conversation in the room dropped to nothing as the statuesque woman in mithril came inside. Eyebrows went up, jaws dropped, and everyone was shocked.

"You fucking bitch!" Those three words echoed in the silence. Denmur shot to his feet, his chair going over behind him. Eyes locked on Helga, his face contorted in anger. "You *dare* come near me? I'll have your head!"

Helga stared Denmur down, her lip curling up in distaste. "You don't even know how to hold a sword properly."

"But my friends do!" Denmur nodded to the two richly-dressed men flanking him.

"Life Bonded, isn't she?" one of the men asked. "She's just property, so it's not even murder."

"Are you threatening my Bonded?" Sean asked, coming in behind Helga.

Denmur's already flushed face darkened further. Nostrils flaring, his hands curled into fists. "MacDougal... That explains why the *roaches* came in."

Sean looked to where his friends were sitting at two of the tables.

"Did you just call Dames Flamehair and Mageeyes roaches? I think I'm going to take offense to that."

The same richly-dressed man laughed. "And Denmur will have a champion stand in for him."

"And Helga will stand in for me," Sean shrugged, "if Denmur even knows how to back up any of his bark. I mean, his son didn't know how to, so maybe it runs in the family."

Denmur's face lost all color and he stood up straighter. "You'd insult my son after your *whores* cut him down?"

"My wives aren't whores," Sean said flatly. "Not like your son, who'd kneel for Evan whenever he needed to."

Denmur lurched, but the two men got to their feet and grabbed him. "Easy, easy— he's baiting you. You have to let one of us defend the insult against the Dames, as it is. If you attack him, he'll have the right to fight you himself."

Sean laughed— it was dark and had nothing to do with humor. "Yes, Denmur, listen to your protectors. That'll let you live maybe a little bit longer. You should have stopped, but you kept pushing, kept attacking my friends and family. All I wanted was to craft and love my wives, but you woke the dragon. Now, you'll reap your folly."

"You damned Outsider! You think you're so special?!" Denmur spat, still being held back by the two men. "My son was destined for great things! If you'd just bent your knee as you should have, you would have been left alone!"

"Pick champions or meet me outside yourself," Sean said. "I'll defend the Dame's honor. Then, if you have a set of balls, you can challenge me over calling your son a disgrace and insulting your house." Turning on his heel, Sean walked back outside.

Helga watched everyone for a moment longer before she followed him. She went over to Sean, who had walked into the street, and whispered softly, "Sean, I will kill him quickly."

"I know you will," Sean said softly, his voice shaking. "I just want this over."

One of the two men came out and walked into the street. "Mac-

Dougal, I am Knight Mithrilarm, heir to the Mithrilarm house. I have never lost a duel in my life."

"You've never faced my Chooser," Sean said flatly, having recovered his mask.

A crowd of people came out of the inn, consisting mostly of Denmur's group, including Denmur, and all of Forged Bonds. The windows and doorway were packed with people, and Sean caught snippets of conversation, mostly about people betting on the outcome.

"We need a neutral moderator," Sean said. "Is there even one here?"

"I will—" the second rich man began.

"What is all this?" Bloodheart asked as he came walking around the building.

"A duel, Knight Bloodheart," Mithrilarm snorted. "One that will be over with quickly."

"Mithrilarm, you are a competent swordsman," Bloodheart said, "but MacDougal is going to surprise you."

Mithrilarm snorted. "I very much doubt it, but he's already opted for his... *woman*... to fight for him."

"We never stated rules, and I hadn't yet stated that she'd face you," Sean said with a smile. "You've said you are Denmur's champion. He lacks the balls even his son had." Denmur had to be restrained again and Sean snorted. "What are the weapons, Denmur?"

"Swords!" Denmur snarled. "Only swords."

Mithrilarm turned to Denmur. "I'll end this quickly."

Helga drew her sword, which was still only a short blade, and Mithrilarm laughed as he pulled his arming sword. The onlookers skewed the odds even further in Mithrilarm's favor. Helga looked at the onlookers and smiled as her sword grew to match Mithrilarm's.

"It's just swords, not Talents!" Mithrilarm snapped.

"We haven't started yet," Sean said pointedly. "Still need a moderator."

"Why is there even a duel?" Bloodheart asked.

"Denmur referred to Dames Flamehair and Mageeyes as 'roaches,'" Sean said.

Bloodheart's eyes narrowed, but he didn't respond to the insult. "I'll moderate."

"I accept," Mithrilarm said. "I know that you would never tarnish your family name."

"Acceptable," Sean said. "Helga Oathsworn will be my champion, since Denmur refuses to face me himself."

"Knight Mithrilarm and Helga Oathsworn will fight for Aspirant Otis Denmur and Aspirant Sean MacDougal. The duel is with swords alone, with no Talents to be used. To the blood, as all duels of slight are."

"MacDougal," Mithrilarm asked snidely, "since you keep insulting people's courage, you wouldn't be opposed to this duel going to the death, would you?"

"Helga?" Sean asked.

"I will cut him down if you desire it, Sean."

"Death is fine," Sean said casually.

Bloodheart's lips pursed and he looked at the crowd. "I do not have a barrier to prevent outside interference, but I will say this—anyone who interferes will face me."

Sean could hear the increased babble over the news that the duel was to the death. He ignored the voices as he locked eyes with Denmur, who looked triumphant.

"MacDougal, please step back. Oathsworn and Mithrilarm, please take your places twenty feet apart."

Sean went to stand on the edge of his group, which was only feet from Denmur's collective. Helga and Mithrilarm moved to the center of the street and Helga took her shield off her back.

"Need a shield to fight me? I should have suspected you would," Mithrilarm laughed. With a look over his shoulder, he motioned the other noble, who moved forward and presented his sword to Mithrilarm. "There. That should even things up."

"Are you both ready?" Bloodheart asked.

"Yes, though I doubt this will last long enough to matter," Mithrilarm replied.

"Ready," Helga said simply.

Bloodheart moved to stand opposite the group by the Golden Lion, so he could watch the fighters and the onlookers at the same time. "Begin!"

Mithrilarm charged forward, being aggressive and using both of his blades in a tandem attack. He aimed one for Helga's legs— it would make her use her shield to deflect it— and aimed the other high to pull her sword up.

Helga didn't follow the script that Mithrilarm seemed to have planned. Instead of lowering her shield and blocking the attack to her legs, she waited, then lunged forward. The resounding slap of her shield against flesh filled the air.

Helga didn't hesitate— she pushed off with her shield, shoving the slightly stunned noble backward. Her blade whipped down and across, and Mithrilarm screamed. The noble stumbled back, his left leg nearly buckling as he lashed out to keep Helga away. Helga didn't let up, blocking one strike while another bounced off her greaves.

Helga's blade came down again, twisting as it connected with Mithrilarm's sword and slid down into his arm. The noble let out another scream as one of his swords fell to the ground. Helga's face was expressionless as she kept her attack going, driving Mithrilarm back.

"No, no, no!" Denmur yelled. "Not again!"

Sean felt a moment of satisfaction as Helga continued to take Mithrilarm apart. *You've gone after my friends and family... now, it's time for you to pay for that,* Sean thought.

Helga's sword nearly hummed as she swept Mithrilarm's head from his shoulders. Nodding, she turned back to Bloodheart, to be proclaimed the winner.

Sean moved up to congratulate her, glad that she'd won so easily. There was a scream of surprise from behind Sean, and that was all the warning he got before pain hit him from behind. Sharp, stabbing pain radiated through him as a dagger buried itself in his back.

"Kill them! Kill them now, and Sharpeyes will pardon us!" Denmur shouted from directly behind Sean.

Pandemonium reigned in the next few seconds as the majority of Forged Bonds scrambled to get away and Denmur's group drew weapons, rushing them. Not many from Forged Bonds carried weapons on them, but it turned out the unarmed ones wouldn't need to worry about it.

Flamehair stepped in front of the entire group and extended her arms wide. A blazing heat grew out from her and washed over their attackers. Pained screams pierced the air as she held the flame on them.

The onlookers inside the Golden Lion scrambled to get away from the door and windows as the panes cracked and the door began to burn. Screams of fear echoed from inside the building.

The noble that'd been standing near Denmur came out of the flames and plunged his sword through Flamehair's chest. Face a blistered mess as his sightless eyes wept a thick film, the man yanked his sword free and struck again.

Sean kicked out with his foot, flinging Denmur away from him. He poured his energy into healing his wounds as Helga and Bloodheart moved to kill the attackers. Denmur screamed out once before he was suddenly silenced just as Sean's wounds closed.

Looking back, he saw Helga standing over Denmur's headless corpse, and Bloodheart helping Flamehair to the ground, her attacker having been run through.

Sean rushed to kneel next to Flamehair, who had blood bubbling from her mouth. Placing both of his hands on her bleeding wounds, he spoke softly, "Easy, Charie... easy. I've got you." Infusing her body with healing, he fixed her heart first, followed by her lung, then the rest of the injuries.

Flamehair watched him with wide eyes as the pain faded and she could suddenly breathe again without drowning in her own blood. Mageeyes was kneeling on Flamehair's other side, holding her friend's hand.

"Charie...?" Mageeyes whispered, worried even as she watched the wounds close.

"Alive," Flamehair managed a moment later. "Sean... thank you."

"Thank Bloodheart. He's the one who got the man off you," Sean said, angry at himself that his simple plan had come undone so easily. "I got you injured."

"No, you healed her," Bloodheart said simply.

The whistles grew louder, and Sean looked down the street to where a large number of guards were running toward them.

A few whimpered whispers came from the nearly cooked group. Sean looked at them and shook his head. He didn't know if they all had gone to attack or if some of them were innocent. The only ones moving were those furthest away, making it likely that they'd been innocent and hadn't tried to attack.

Kneeling beside one of them, he gave them enough healing to put them to sleep, making sure they'd live to see a healer.

"Sean, what are you doing?" Bloodheart asked with incredulity.

"Healing them, at least a little," Sean replied. "They were furthest away— they might not have attacked. They deserve the chance to learn."

"He is far too kind," Bloodheart said from Mageeyes' side.

"Yes, but that is one of the things that sets him apart," Helga said.

The whistles grew louder as the guard came to find out what had caused the commotion.

"Well, this is certainly going to be a problem," Fredrick sighed, looking down the street at two dozen men running toward them.

"It is fairly open and shut," Bloodheart said.

"It should be, but with the new commander..." Fredrick said, trailing off.

39

"What in Winter's name?!" the shocked exclamation came from the first guard on the scene.

"A bit of a disagreement," Bloodheart said.

"More like a blatant attack on people peacefully enjoying a drink," Wolen said, striding to the front of the contingent of guards

"I'd think a Knight would speak the truth," another authoritative voice said.

Wolen glared at Eugene Carmady, who was advancing with a smaller group of guards. "We were here first, Sergeant."

"True, and interesting in the fact that this is no longer your beat," Carmady said. "We saw the flash of light and the whistles and came running. I find it odd that nearly your entire patrol group is here and not in the crafter's quarter, where it should be. Or did you get lost and just *happen* to return to your old route?"

Wolen's eye twitched, his nostrils flaring as he stared at Carmady. "I'm sure the *commander* won't care about triviality, considering the serious nature of this event."

"Hmm, interesting. I think a whole patrol not being in their assigned area is a serious problem on its own," Carmady said. "Be that as it may, as the most senior sergeant in the area, and the sergeant in his actual area of command, I'll take this from here."

"Whichever of you is in charge, can someone get these five to healers?" Sean asked, kneeling by the last of the living burn victims.

"Of course," Carmady said. "Sergeant Wolen, you and your men can get these people to the healers before you head back to your patrol."

"Belay that order!" another man barked as he walked out of the growing group of guards.

"Captain," Wolen smiled, "I'm glad you're here."

Carmady's expression became stony. "Captain? I'm surprised to see you here."

"This is my area of command, Sergeant!" Fokler snapped. "Now, you and your men return to your patrol. I'll use Sergeant Wolen and his men for handling this mess."

"That goes against six different regulations, sir," Carmady said tightly, "including the most important one— a beat not having the minimum number of guards walking it."

Fokler advanced on Carmady. "Are *you* telling *me* what the regulations are, *Sergeant*?"

"No, sir," Carmady replied. "I just want it noted that my men and I are here, in our assigned area, and have already started handling the incident."

Fokler's eyes narrowed. "Noted? *Noted*, you say? I note some insubordination, Sergeant."

"Not at all, sir," Carmady said. "I'll take my men back on patrol, as you command."

"First, you'll take the injured to healers!" Fokler snapped. "I want the reports of their healing on my desk before sunrise, Sergeant."

Carmady snapped a salute and motioned to his men. "Get some wagons and let's see to the burned."

Fokler snorted and turned back to the group with a slight smirk. "Forged Bonds. You're a little farther away from your usual stomping grounds."

"Are we not allowed to have drinks in different places?" Saret asked.

Fokler's eyes went to Saret, taking a moment to look her up and down. "No one said anything of the kind. However, it is odd that the first time you do, a major incident occurs. Adding on to the fact that I see three nobles dead along with a dozen others, it looks like a deliberate attack."

"Most of us are unarmed," Ryan said stiffly, "while most of them have weapons."

"Still in their sheaths," Fokler pointed out, looking at the burnt bodies. "Dame Flamehair, you are under arrest for the wanton murders of a dozen people."

Flamehair, who'd just gotten to her feet with Mageeyes' help, looked at Fokler like a parent looking at a petulant child. She glanced at her blood-soaked clothing, then back to him. "*I* was the one attacked, Captain."

"Is that right? Yet you seem to only have some blood on you. That could have come from any number of the unburned bodies."

"If you're arresting her, I will be going with her," Mageeyes said flatly. "Considering someone died alone in your cells not that long ago, I won't let a wounded friend of mine go alone."

"You do *not* dictate to us, Dame Mageeyes," Fokler growled.

Bloodheart stepped forward, placing himself between the Dames and Fokler. "Captain Fokler, surely you know that any noble arrested can request to have up to two companions with them while they wait to see a high magistrate. With that still being the law, myself and Dame Mageeyes will accompany Dame Flamehair into custody."

Fokler stared at Bloodheart with frustration. "I see. Fine. Sergeant Wolen, take the Dames and Knight Bloodheart into custody. There might be more charges after we investigate the incident."

The three nobles moved to where Wolen and his men stood, ready to be arrested.

"What about us?" Joseph asked.

Fokler turned to Joseph with a smirk. "Tackett, at the moment, you are a person of interest. Some of the men here will be watching you while we speak to those inside the Golden Lion. I think Denmur will have a lot to tell us."

"Not unless you can speak to the dead," Sean said, moving away from the wounded. Carmady had sent his men for wagons and was now checking on the five burn victims.

"*Dead*?" Fokler asked.

Sean pointed to Denmur's body, then toward the alley beside the building. "His head went rolling that way."

The entire group of guards suddenly looked uneasy. The majority of them drew their weapons, causing Bloodheart to touch his own sword hilt. Sean looked at them with cold, flat, eyes.

"Who killed Denmur?"

"I did," Helga said. "After my duel, he attacked Sean, stabbing him in the back. When Sean flung him off, I engaged and dispatched him."

"Sergeant, arrest this woman for murder," Fokler said.

"Defense of her Holder," Sean said flatly, staring at the guards. "The dagger is still in a death grip in his hand. My blood is still on the blade, and my clothing has tears and blood on it, even if I am healed. How do you get to murder, *Captain*?" The disdain in that last word was clear.

"Lacking evidence to the contrary. At the moment, I am having her arrested for the murder of a noble," Fokler said with a sneer. "Do you want to be arrested for interfering with the guard?"

"Yes," Sean said. "As a noble myself, I'll have my accused Bonded, and if she's willing, Saret Somnia, accompany me."

Saret blinked, then bowed her head. "I am willing."

"Take them away," Fokler said with a triumphant smile.

"Sean?" Fredrick called out worriedly.

"I'll be fine," Sean said. "This has to happen so this idiocy ends."

Fredrick nodded. "We'll be at the hall come morning."

"Or you'll still be being questioned," Fokler snorted. "Sergeant, take those six away."

Wolen grinned as he advanced on Sean. "I'll need your sword."

"No," Bloodheart said flatly. "He is a noble. He'll turn it over to the custodian, as I will."

Sean gave Wolen a sardonic smile. "Seems the Knight knows the laws. Helga, give me your weapons, please. I'll make sure those get handed over, as well."

Helga handed over her sword, which had been cleaned and sheathed, along with the spear. "As you wish, Sean."

Wolen's lips puckered, as he had just been about to take Helga's weapons from her. Saret spread her arms, showing that she had no weapons on her person, when Wolen turned to her. Grumbling under his breath, he motioned them toward the other three.

Sean was tempted to call the sergeant out on what he was mumbling, but instead, he just walked to the others. "At least I'm in good company," he said when he came even with the other three.

"Good company, indeed," Bloodheart nodded. "You fought well, Oathsworn, though I might have had to call you on the technicality of using your shield as a weapon."

"Would it have been different if I had punched him instead?" Helga asked.

"No, which is why I didn't call you on it. The shield is part of your armor, and therefore, not a weapon any more than your greaves or gauntlets are."

"Quiet!" one of the guards snapped. "No talking!"

Mageeyes pinned the guard with a firm stare. "I shall remember that, Corporal."

The man wilted under her gaze, going to a different part of the encircling ring of guards walking them down the street. Silence fell among the group as they continued heading to the magistrate hall.

Flamehair's steps became a little less steady as they got closer to the hall, and Sean steadied her. "Easy, Charie. I healed you, but you're still missing a lot of blood. Get some rest as soon as you can."

"I said no talking!" the previous guard snapped.

Sean glanced at the guard and snorted. "I'm caring for a friend who was stabbed twice not even an hour ago, Corporal. Have you been stabbed twice, arrested, and then made to walk to the magistrate's hall without aid?"

The guard's mouth snapped shut, and he looked at the other guards. None of them said anything, as they'd all seen the bloody clothing Flamehair was wearing and remembered the burnt bodies.

"Just keep it down..." the guard muttered.

They were taken to the holding area while one of the guards split off toward the desk in the reception hall. Going down the stairs, Sean saw the older guards he remembered from the last time he'd been arrested.

Gaoler Henik looked up from the game of cards he was playing with the other two guards and his eyes went wide. All three old men got to their feet and waited for the group to reach them.

The angry guard was the one who spoke up first, "Dame Flamehair— charges of murder a dozen times over. Dame Mageeyes and Knight Bloodheart are with her as support. Aspirant MacDougal— interfering with a guard investigation. His Bonded is arrested for the murder of Aspirant Otis Denmur. MacDougal insisted on his right to two people accompanying him to include the Bonded and Madam Somnia."

Henik nearly choked on his own spit when he heard the charges. "What in Winter's name happened?"

"That is being investigated," the guard snapped.

"Ah... weapons?" the old guard with the waxed mustache asked.

"Here is my sword and dagger," Bloodheart said, laying them on the table that the cards were on. "My name is Knight Toivo Bloodheart."

"We know who you are," the mustachioed-guard said faintly. "You trained us years ago. I'm not surprised you don't recall us, though."

Bloodheart stared at the older man for a moment before his lip twitched. "Corporal Collin Machar? The mustache was not as grand back then. Did you fix your drifting guard problem?"

"No, he didn't," the second of the older guards snickered. "Cost him a few fingers and landed him here."

"Corporal Ramos Stein," Bloodheart smiled. "I bet your dagger work has slowed down."

"Along with the rest of me," Stein guffawed.

"And that means you are Corporal Dale Henik," Bloodheart finished. "You three were promising swordsmen."

"But we age faster than a noble," Stein said somberly, the humor gone. "I need your valuables, as well, please."

"I need the other weapons, first," Machar said.

Sean handed over Helga's weapons. He watched Machar's eyes get wide when he saw how much mithril had been used on them, and coughed when Dark Cutter's adamantine blade was added to them.

"MacDougal, I remember the sword, but now you have a mithril sword, and this... club?"

"Spear," Sean said. "It can become a spear. It's just compact at the moment."

"He can Shape them in combat," Stein said. "Remember what was said of the fight outside the walls?"

"Oh, right," Machar nodded. He bent his head to fill out some forms, intent on getting everything down correctly.

"And as I was saying. I'll need your valuables, including that armor," Stein said, nodding to Helga. "I don't know when you became an Aspirant, MacDougal, but most of them don't have that kind of armor for themselves, much less their Bonded."

"She's my shield," Sean said as he turned to help Helga with the buckles and straps of the armor. "Her safety is my safety."

"They didn't make shields like that when I was younger," Machar said under his breath when he glanced up to see Helga stripped out of her armor.

Stein nudged Machar and gave him a stare as all four women there turned their gazes on Machar. Machar went stone-faced and quickly went back to his paperwork.

"We'll take them from here," Henik told the lingering guards.

"If it's not too much trouble, we'd like some tea once we are celled," Mageeyes said. "Our friend lost a lot of blood and will be sleeping, but Bloodheart and I will be staying awake the entire night."

"I'll see what I can do, Dame," Henik said as he watched the guards leave.

Once they had handed over their valuables, Henik pulled out the keys and opened the thickly-banded door that led to the cells. "If you will follow me, I'll get you put into your rooms."

"Cells," Sean said. "I remember them."

Henik snorted. "Not those. The nobles have different cells."

They were led down the hall past the cells Sean recalled until they came up to a half-dozen thick doors. All of them stood ajar, and Henik entered the first one. "Dame Flamehair and associates, this is your room until the high magistrate can see you."

Sean looked at the room and shook his head. It looked like a well-appointed inn room, not a cell. The furniture was all well-made, and a divider looked like it separated the room from what was likely a sleeping area. Golden lanterns hung from the ceiling, giving the room light.

"Thank you, Gaoler," Mageeyes said.

"I'll bring some tea after I get the others settled."

"That'll be fine. Thank you."

"Follow me, please," Henik said, leading Sean, Helga, and Saret to the room across the hall. "This is your room."

It looked identical to the other room, so Sean nodded. "Thank you, Henik."

Henik hesitated and looked down the hall, staying in the doorway. "Denmur's dead?"

"Yes," Helga said. "I removed his head."

"Well, that means that your feud with each other is settled," Henik sighed. "It won't be as bad as others we've seen."

"It's not over," Sean said softly. "Someone else has a grudge with me."

Henik winced. "Bloody hell. Not Lord Sharpeyes?"

"His son is dead," Saret said. "That's normally enough reason, even if they did it to themselves."

"Summer, help us," Henik sighed. "I'll see you for breakfast."

"Good night, sir," Sean said. "Hopefully, this will end soon."

"The Queens willing," Henik said as he shut and locked the door.

40

"I've never been arrested before, but I think this is better than the other cells we passed," Saret said as she moved over to take a seat. "Why did you request me to come along, Sean?"

"I wanted to speak with you about different planes of existence, and maybe about your power of voice?"

"Felora has been telling me about what you've been doing. She's asked me to do a lot of research," Saret smiled. "As for my Talents, I know why you're interested. You apparently collect them, and you *did* marry my eldest of this world."

"So that's a yes, then?"

"If you will do one thing for me."

"I'm listening," Sean said slowly.

Lips curling up and eyes glittering, Saret giggled. "Wise to ask what the price is first. I don't think it's too onerous, though— I wish to go with you to see these small planes you've created."

"I'm not positive I can take you," Sean said. "I promise to try?"

"I'll accept that," Saret replied.

Sean felt the deal settle over him and nodded.

"Helga, did you reap the souls of those who died?" Saret asked, not wasting any time.

Helga just met Saret's gaze for a few awkward seconds before looking at Sean.

"Go ahead," Sean prompted her.

"The dead all came to me, for they opposed Sean, and since their souls were not already bound to another god, I took them... no, that is not entirely accurate. It is more as though they got pulled into me."

"Intriguing. And what of his wives, who are now all Soul Bonded? Would you collect them, as well?"

Helga glanced to Sean, who nodded. "I believe that if any of them die, their soul would come to me."

"Hmm, interesting. I've not read of another case where a Valkyrie left your old pantheon. It makes me wonder what powers get lost or changed because of it."

"I have not noticed any losses," Helga replied. "My choosing of souls is vastly different, though. Speaking of, Sean, I sent them all on. I have a conduit now, so I no longer need to go and release them myself."

"Make sure you don't do that to those we love," Sean said quickly.

"I will hold those until you tell me otherwise," Helga replied.

Saret watched the byplay with interest. Seeing them lapse into silence after their brief exchange, she cleared her throat. "About my Talents, Sean... what were you hoping for?"

"I've heard your voice before, so I think I can replicate that, I just haven't tried it yet. You hold power in two other locations inside of you."

"Hmm... Mage Sight is troublesome that way. Maybe I shouldn't say that, as that is what got Amedee and myself speaking to begin with. Which did you wish to talk about first?"

"Your eyes?"

"My kind can project our power out to ensnare the mind of someone foolish enough to meet our gaze. If we push, we can dominate their thoughts and make them do things for us. I'm not positive you can do this, though. Our eyes are different from a normal Human's, though I guess you aren't a normal Human, either."

"Yeah, definitely not," Sean snorted. Taking a deep breath, he licked his lips and met Saret's gaze. "Use it on me, please?"

Saret's eyebrows rose. "You trust me that far?"

"Huh?"

"If I do ensnare your mind, you would be powerless to refuse my requests," Saret said.

"I'll be fine," Sean said. "I trust you."

Gaze flickering to Helga briefly, Saret sighed. "Sean, if you weren't an ally and married to my daughter, I would gladly do as you ask. You are a temptation... a sinfully delicious temptation." Meeting his eyes, she smiled sadly. "I love my daughter and value our alliance, and so I must decline your request."

"Oh, Okay. I didn't think it was that bad."

Saret gave him a searching gaze. "You really don't understand, do you?"

"I guess not," Sean said. "Can you explain it?"

"You used to be someone touched by the divine," Saret said. "Such a being is delicious to my kind, but now, you've gone past that. You are divine in your own right. A fledgling god with a growing powerbase and fervent followers... If someone like me could get their claws into you, we'd rise high. I could rival the Queens themselves, if not surpass them, as you keep growing."

"'As beautiful and as terrible as the dawn,'" Sean murmured, thinking back to a favorite movie.

"Yes," Saret agreed, not knowing the movie, but understanding the subtext. "My daughter has tempered that desire with her love of you and your wives, as I once did for love." Saret's eyes closed and a single tear slipped free. Exhaling slowly, she opened her eyes, a sad smile on her lips. "My daughter will not suffer the same fate as me, not with you as her husband. For that, I am grateful."

"Is there any way to resist the mind-fuckery?" Sean asked, wanting to help shift the topic away from what was clearly painful to her.

"What?" Saret asked, having been lost in her thoughts for a

moment. "Oh, no special tricks. It just takes willpower. The stronger the person trying to ensnare you, the harder it is to resist."

"Felora can do this, right?"

"Yes. She can do everything I can. Before, I would have said not as effectively as me, but she is growing powerful quickly."

"I'll ask her to show me, then."

"Probably for the best," Saret said. "As for my other point of power, well, surely you can figure that out."

"Addictive, and used to pull more energy from a person than they would otherwise intend?"

"Very good," Saret nodded. "'Addictive' is one way of putting it. If used, that person would be in a state of constant stimulation until we stop using the power. They also wish nothing more than to continue being used in such a manner."

"Yeah... that lines up with the stories of Succubi that I know of," Sean said. "I'm glad Felora never used it on me."

"My daughters won't use that power unless they are being forced, against their will, into such acts," Saret said primly. "We are not animals, after all. We can sup without gorging ourselves."

"Something you enforce along with the power of your voice, I take it," Sean said, thinking of Felora's words during the party when Delia died.

Saret looked down. "Yes, even if I failed my own restrictions briefly."

"Why didn't it work when Felora tried to sway the Einherjar?"

"It did," Helga said. "I had to expend a lot of energy to clear their minds, but they were still not prepared to leap the sudden hole."

"Except the captain," Sean said.

"He was a berserker," Helga said. "A functional one, at that. His mind would be hard to influence once his blood was up. Her interference is what caught as many of them as it did. Felora is a truly frightening opponent in that regard."

"Few born of this world would be able to resist as they did," Saret agreed. "Did that answer your questions, Sean?"

"About your powers," Sean agreed. "What did you learn about the two planes of existence that I seem to be in charge of?"

"Those are born of your divinity," Saret said.

A knock came on the door, interrupting her before she could continue, and opened to reveal Henik. "I have some tea for you."

"So different from the first time I was here," Sean said.

"We don't get nobles in the cells often," Henik said, "and now, we have four of the nobility."

Helga accepted the pot and cups from Henik. "Thank you."

"Just leave them here and we'll get them when we bring breakfast. If you need something, the bell pull there," he pointed to a red rope, "will alert us. We'll be with you as soon as we can."

"We won't need anything else tonight, Henik," Sean said. "Hopefully, we'll be gone after we see High Magistrate Jasper in the morning."

Henik's smile became strained. "You're slated to see him after Dame Flamehair. Your Bonded is going before Magistrate Amerut, though."

Sean's heart paused and he stood up. "What? Why?"

"He claimed the case as soon as the paperwork was filed," Henik said a little stiffly. "He tried to take your case, and Flamehair's, as well."

"Tried to?" Sean asked.

"High Magistrate Jasper was just leaving for the day and heard Magistrate Amerut arguing with the clerk. He claimed them, as nobles are supposed to be seen by high magistrates or the chief magistrate only."

"I'm betting Amerut didn't take that well?"

"I wasn't there," Henik said, then looked into the hall. Lowering his voice, he said, "Furious, from what the clerk said. Nearly came to blows."

"That would've been priceless," Sean sighed. "Fine. When do I see Jasper, and when does Helga see Amerut?"

"Unknown yet. We'll know when we get breakfast."

"Please let me know once you do?" Sean asked. "Maybe Jasper

will put my appearance off until after Amerut is done. As her Holder, I am allowed to be there, right?"

"Yes, sir. It's the law."

"Never stopped Amerut before," Sean snorted.

Henik's face went frozen, and Sean held up a hand. "I apologize, Henik. Thank you for the tea. Please have a good night."

"You, as well, sir."

The door shut, and Sean sighed. "I can't wait for tomorrow."

"It will be different," Saret said. "What tea is that, Helga?"

"Peppermint," Helga said, having carried the pot to the table they'd been sitting at.

"Hmm... pass," Saret said. "Now, as I was saying, those planes exist because you brought them into existence. Planes come and go at a god's whim. How big or complex they are is partially up to the deity, but also limited to their power. As you grow, the planes will expand."

"Okay. So they won't be stuck in a manor forever?"

"If you continue to grow those who believe in you. If you do not, then they will be."

"Thank you, Saret."

"My pleasure, Sean," Saret said. "Can you tell me about these planes you have created?"

"Helga?"

"I can cross over, and you can, but I do not know if she can," Helga said. "If she can initiate a dream like Felora, it should be easy enough."

"That I can do," Saret nodded.

None of them were interested in the tea, so Sean went to check on sleeping arrangements. The alcove area off the main room held three beds, just large enough for a single person each. Stripping the bedding, he made up a sleeping area on the floor.

"I have something rigged up, if you're both ready," he told them when he went back to the front room.

"As you wish, Sean."

Saret didn't say anything, but did go past him into the alcove. She stopped at the foot of the bedding and her lips tweaked up. "I see."

Sitting on one of the beds, she stripped her shoes off and set them aside before laying down on the floor. "It's been some time since a man was brazen enough to have me lie on a floor."

Sean covered his face with one hand for a moment. "At least your daughter comes by it naturally."

"Of course. What else is a mother for?"

Sean just shook his head and took his own boots off. Helga copied him, laying on the other side of Saret. Once they were all on the floor, Sean placed his hand on Saret's beside him.

"Ready," Sean said.

"As am I."

"Very well," Saret said. Taking a deep breath, she exhaled slowly. "Dream. Dream the dreams of your planes, and open the way."

* * *

Sean looked around the moon-bathed bog and nodded. Voices echoed in the still night air, and the heads of multiple people dotted the ground. A second after he got his bearings, Helga and Saret appeared on either side of him.

"What a delightful place," Saret said, looking at the landscape. "These are your foes?"

"These are the people who just died," Helga said.

The voices, hearing someone new speaking, started calling out for help. Sean ignored them all as he spotted the only person that mattered. Stepping forward, the ground became solid as he moved across it.

Denmur glared at Sean, even while he tried to get free of the roots entangling him and the soft ground engulfing him. "MacDougal! I'll see you dead!"

"Too late for that, Denmur. You already died, and this is your hell. Welcome to my own special hell for those who anger me."

Denmur's eyes went wide. "Klein! Klein, are you here?!"

Sean's laughter was soft and decidedly unfriendly. "Klein isn't here. Helga spent his soul to keep her own."

Denmur's eyes went wild, and he started thrashing even more.

"Squeeze him," Sean commanded, watching as Denmur's struggles slowed when the roots did what he said. "I can send you to him."

Denmur's struggles stopped entirely, and he stared at Sean. "No. You're just trying to hurt me more."

"I can release you from this hell," Sean said, meeting Denmur's eyes. "That would send you on your way to find your son."

"What will it cost?" Denmur spat, breathing hard.

"A few answers," Sean said, squatting down to see Denmur better. "Why? All I wanted was to have a quiet life."

Denmur sneered. "So high and mighty. You mocked me, and spat in the face of all Shapers! If you'd just known your place, this would have been avoided."

Sean's eyelid twitched. "Why did you attack my loved ones?"

"Are you *seriously* so dumb to not know how society works?"

Hands curling into fists, Sean had trouble not punching Denmur's fat face. "Answer the question, or you'll stay here for eternity."

Denmur bit his lip hard enough that it began to bleed. "Because you undermine, then destroy. You use cat's paws and stay at distance, you damnable Outsider! That first attack should have killed Ida to hurt you and to teach her mother a lesson!"

Sean's fist lashed out and Denmur's head exploded. Breathing hard, Sean was pissed— not just with Denmur, but for losing it before he'd finished. As he started to calm down, Denmur's head reappeared on his body, and Sean blinked at him stupidly for a moment.

Denmur wasn't much better— he had felt a brief moment of extreme pain, then it had all gone dark. Now he was back in the bog, still being held down and stared at by Sean.

"Insult any of them again and I won't be as merciful next time," Sean said, his voice trembling with rage. "You can't die here; I can torture you for eons."

Denmur met Sean's eyes and his own rage was snuffed out almost entirely. Sean's eyes were wide and burning with a white-black flame, and Sean's words echoed with truth. He didn't speak, as he tried to think of any way out of his situation besides doing exactly what Sean wanted.

"Why did you go that far, after having her injured at the Dominguez's?"

"I *didn't* have her injured there," Denmur said flatly.

Sean hesitated— Denmur's words were tinged with truth, and Sean knew they were truthful. He was certain of it, as certain as he was that he could threaten and torture Denmur for eons.

"Carver?"

Denmur didn't answer, and Sean sent a mental command to the plants, which constricted tightly enough to sever Denmur's hands.

"Carver! Carver did that on his own!" Denmur hissed a few seconds later.

"The attacks on my friends and family," Sean asked as he started to regain control of his anger, "how many of them were you?"

"None."

Sean just stared at Denmur, his shock showing.

"Moron! Fool! What did I say?" Demur began to laugh, his laughter tinged with madness. "I set up many plans, all of them to hinder and anger, but I didn't try to kill anyone except Ida for spurning me!"

"The attacks on the Bronzeshield's, my driver, on Rebecca Angusson, and Jackson Gertihs' death?"

Denmur laughed longer and harder as he watched Sean. "You will *never* survive if you can't even figure out who's been doing what!"

Sean had planned to torment Denmur for years regardless of what he said during their conversation, but now, he had to rethink his plans. *Denmur only sent attackers once... his words have been truthful. That means it has to be Carver and Lord Sharpeyes. Carver, though? How? Why?*

"Now, free me! Free me to see my son!" Denmur snapped, his laughter cutting off abruptly.

Sean stood up and began to walk away. "I will. In time. You still tried to kill one of my wives, and for that, you'll have to pay."

Denmur started to yell, but vines lashed around his face and he sank beneath the bog.

"Well?" Saret asked when Sean returned to them at the edge of the bog, one of her shoes covered in black soil.

"You didn't hear him?" Sean asked.

"Only his laughter, and that shows he was mad," Saret replied.

"Mad enough," Sean said. "His only attack was on Ida and Ryann. All the others, he didn't set into motion."

"And you believe him?" Saret asked, surprised.

"I know he spoke the truth. I can feel it here," Sean said, looking at the bog.

Saret nodded slowly. "This is your field of judgement and repayment." She looked at the other heads, which had all gone quiet during Sean's talk with Denmur. "What of them?"

"Right now, they will stay. If they act up, they will be pulled under for a time. I might free them after they pay for standing in the way."

"Are we going to the manor now, Sean?" Helga asked.

"Yes, to complete my deal with Saret," Sean said.

41

Sean was sitting in the front area of the cell, sipping cold peppermint tea alone. Both Saret and Helga were still asleep. Sean didn't know why he'd woken so early, but he felt refreshed, so he didn't fight it. The knock on the door got him up and to it quickly so the women wouldn't get disturbed.

"Sir?" Sean asked when the door opened.

Henik and the same Moonbound that Sean recalled from his previous time were there with a cart. "Breakfast," Henik said. "Can we put it out?"

"It's your place. I'm just a guest," Sean chuckled as he stepped aside.

Henik shook his head as the Moonbound wheeled the silent cart into the room. "MacDougal, you're a headache at times. I almost want to talk normally to you, but as a noble, that wouldn't work out."

"I prefer that, honestly," Sean said. "I just became an Aspirant, and honestly, I have no love for most of the nobility or the way they act."

Henik gave him a sidelong glance. "You're an odd one, but you've been pleasant to deal with. And I still appreciate the cart no longer squealing."

"Me, too," the Moonbound added.

"Henik, I'm just a crafter. Lady Sharpeyes might have granted me a title, but I'll always just be a crafter."

Henik snorted. "Just? Nothing *just* about your crafting. Hair clips, kettles, faucets, heating and cooling torcs, iceboxes, and rumor says a horseless carriage now? Calling you *just* a crafter is like saying the Queens are *just* minor nobles."

Sean shrugged, a little uncomfortable with the comparison. "That might be a bit too much."

"Not to this old man, it isn't," Henik said. "High Magistrate Jasper said he'll wait for your case until after your Bonded has been seen by Magistrate Amerut. Amerut wants to see her as soon as the day begins, so you only have half an hour before being taken up."

"I'll wake them, then," Sean said. "Thanks again for everything you do, Henik."

Henik nodded and stepped aside for the Moonbound to get out of the room. "I hope the meal is satisfactory."

The door shut and Sean exhaled. "Well, at least he's civil, which means he isn't in the new commander's or Lord Sharpeyes' pocket."

"Is that breakfast?" Saret asked from behind Sean.

Looking over his shoulder, he gave her a nod. "Just dropped off. I need to wake Helga. We only have half an hour before her trial."

"I'll be right out," Helga said from the alcove.

"I'll have some food set aside for you," Sean called back.

Their breakfast consisted of boiled eggs, cheeses, fruits, and warm bread with butter and jam. Yet again, it pushed the difference between nobility law and common law to the forefront of Sean's mind as they ate.

* * *

They had finished breakfast and were making sure they were ready to go when a knock came on the door. A moment later, it opened to reveal Henik and another guard. Henik looked serious and the other guard wore a smirk.

"Oathsworn, Corporal Venim will be taking you up to Magistrate Amerut."

"I'll be going with her," Sean said, standing by Helga's side.

"Magistrate didn't call for you," Venim sneered.

"As her Holder, I *will* be going," Sean said flatly, staring the man down, "unless you want to break laws yourself."

Venim's lips compressed and he hesitated. "You're under arrest for a different charge. Unless the other Magistrate allows it, you have to stay here," he finally said.

"High Magistrate Jasper already sent word that MacDougal is allowed to attend his Bonded's appearance first," Henik said idly.

Venim turned an angry gaze to Henik before snorting. "Well, it seems like you'll be allowed to go, after all."

"I will be going, as well," Saret said, her voice drifting over the two guards.

Venim blinked slowly. "That's fine, miss."

"Thank you," Saret replied. "If you are ready to lead us."

Venim gave her a long look up and down, a smile growing. "Gladly. This way."

Henik shook his head, as if clearing cobwebs away. The others were already heading for the exit, and he sighed. Moving a little quicker than normal, he caught up to them as they exited the cells.

They had to pause for Saret to be given her things back, as she wasn't in custody. When she had all of her things and was ready, Venim led them up the stairs and into the main room of the building.

Sean was very aware of the crowd in the room as they were brought toward Amerut's courtroom. There were more people than he'd expect for early in the morning on a Oneday.

"MacDougal? They say he attacked the entire…"

"Tore Denmur's head off with his bare…!"

"Heard Denmur attacked him first…"

"Who's the looker?"

"Is that the madam of the Den? Why would she…?"

"That's the one he claimed after…"

"She's the one who killed…"

The snippets of conversation were heavily slanted against him, and Sean had to wonder about that. Things had been starting to even out for him in the rumor category just a few days before.

Venim led them into the empty courtroom, motioning Helga to the front and the others to stay back, before he took up position by the doors. He'd only just settled in when the doors opened and a mass of people entered the room.

"There they are," Joseph's voice cut through the conversation. "Sean, have you seen—?"

"What is this?!" Venim demanded, cutting Joseph off.

"We're here to see the trial and to give testimony," Fredrick replied.

"No!" Venim snapped, having put himself in their way. "This is a closed court today."

"Is it?" Fredrick asked with disbelief. "Why?"

"Because it is my court and I have said so," Amerut said condescendingly as he entered the room from his chambers. "Now, you will leave!"

"But we have testimony to give," Knox said.

Amerut scoffed as he moved behind his desk. "I determine who has evidence and who does not."

"Considering it's my Bonded on trial and I can call witnesses on her behalf, I don't know why you're trying this," Sean said.

Amerut's gaze swiveled to Sean, and the hatred in his eyes was obvious to everyone. "MacDougal? I didn't call for you. You shall return to your cell, and—!"

"High Magistrate Jasper saw fit to let me attend this trial," Sean said, coming to stand behind Helga. "As her Holder, it is my right and duty to be here, unless a law has changed."

Amerut's lips thinned. "You do have the right to stay. They, however, will wait outside the room unless they are called upon."

"Sure, if that'll help your ego," Sean shrugged. "Fredrick, can you all wait outside for a moment? As soon as we get to call witnesses, I'll be calling for you."

Fredrick was watching Amerut with disdain. "Very well, Sean. We'll be just outside the door."

"Oh, and someone send word to High Magistrate Jasper, please? Tell him I'll likely need to appeal a judgement," Sean said, his eyes still locked on Amerut's.

Face going red, Amerut hammered his gavel onto the desk. "Contempt, MacDougal!"

"Add it to the false charges already leveled against me," Sean said flatly. "I never said you were an unfair and biased judge. All I said was that I'd likely appeal it."

Eye twitching, Amerut's hand was white as it clutched his gavel. "One more unasked for word and you will be held in contempt. See? I'm giving you a chance."

Sean didn't speak— he just stared Amerut down.

"Better," Amerut snapped as he took his seat. Looking up, he saw everyone still in the room. "Leave, or contempt for all of you!"

Fredrick nodded slowly. "We're leaving, Magistrate."

The door snicked shut a moment later, leaving just Venim, Amerut, Helga, and Sean in the room. Amerut took a slow breath and set his gavel on his desk, flexing his stiff hand. "The charge is murder of a noble. The defendant is Helga Oathsworn, Life Bonded to Sean MacDougal. Since a Bonded committed the crime, that puts the crime on your shoulders, MacDougal."

Sean just looked at him impassively.

"I have numerous eyewitness accounts from patrons of the Golden Lion describing the attack," Amerut went on. "Before we go any further, how do you plead?"

"Innocent. It was in defense of me," Sean said flatly, "as any Life Bonded should defend their Holder."

The door opened briefly, and Captain Fokler stepped in, shutting the door on Fredrick's face. The commotion of the hall was cut off when the door shut.

"Sorry for the delay, sir. There's a lot of rubbish in the hall," Fokler said.

"Indeed, there is," Amerut agreed. "I forgive your tardiness.

Please step forward, and tell the court what your investigation uncovered. Oh, and Corporal? Secure the door. There's no reason to give them a chance to interrupt the court until they are called for."

"Yes, sir," Venim said, throwing the bolt on the door. "Door is secured, sir."

Fokler went to stand in front of Amerut's desk. "Sir, the guard was notified last night of a disturbance at the Golden Lion. Upon arrival, the first sergeant on the scene, Sergeant Wolen, was witness to a massacre of horrific proportions. The one who slaughtered most of the dead is being seen by High Magistrate Jasper. During questioning, the defendant admitted to killing Aspirant Denmur."

"Ah, the defendant admitted guilt," Amerut nodded sagely.

"Objection," Sean said. "Helga admitted to *defending* me, not admitting guilt, for there wasn't any to admit to."

Amerut fixed Sean with a hard stare. "I did not give you leave to speak."

"I'm sorry, your honor, but when hearing false facts, I felt you'd prefer to have corrected ones."

Fokler turned to smirk at Sean. "Are you saying the guard is lying?"

"No," Sean replied. "I'm not saying that you're misstating facts to try misleading the court at all. I was only suggesting that someone misunderstood what was said."

"Enough," Amerut said, giving his gavel a tap on his desk. "Captain, what did the evidence show?"

"That Aspirant Denmur died with his blade in hand, trying to defend himself when he was decapitated. According to eyewitnesses inside the Golden Lion, after Dame Flamehair incinerated Denmur's friends, he attacked to defend himself and was cut down for his efforts."

Sean coughed, his hand raised, giving Amerut a blank stare.

"MacDougal?"

"How did I end up stabbed in the back, then?" Sean turned around to show his bloody clothing with tears in the fabric.

"You were injured?" Fokler asked with a smirk. "You never reported it to the guard."

"I healed it myself. Why let the guard take me to a healer and cost the courts needlessly? Henik, Machar, and Stein can testify that my clothing was in this state when I was brought in, and that the blood was fresher at that time."

Amerut's lips thinned. "Order. This has no bearing on this case."

"Yes, it does," Sean said, his anger rising at them trying to railroad him. "Denmur stabbed me in the back, and Helga killed him for it. Self-defense, for those who don't understand the concept, is preserving oneself from harm. In this case, it was my Soul Bonded that defended me, hence self-defense."

"Contempt, MacDougal!" Amerut snarled, banging his gavel. "You were warned multiple times."

"I'll add it to the list of false charges against me, shall I?!" Sean snapped back.

"How dare you?!" Fokler snarled. "That is a direct attack on the guard's honor!"

"That died when Babbitt was removed as Commander," Sean said flatly.

Gavel banging, Amerut shot to his feet. "Enough! I'll add the charges once we find your Bonded guilty. Not that it will matter, as you'll join her in death."

Sean nodded, his blood going cold. "So you admit that you just want a verdict of guilty and not a fair trial?"

"Enough! Do it!" Amerut snapped.

Sean's brow furrowed, not understanding, until he heard a muffled scream of pain. Spinning, he saw Venim's hand covering Helga's mouth and his dagger buried in her back. He reacted without thought, his clothing hardening as far as he could get them to, which saved him from being run through by Fokler.

Sean had no plan for what happened next. Energy was suddenly encasing him, freezing him in place. Sean strained— he'd seen Jasper use it on Lord Sharpeyes during Helga's trial.

"We'll claim he attacked us and had to defend ourselves," Amerut sighed. "This isn't what we wanted, but it will do. Kill him, then we'll injure ourselves and set the stage before calling for help."

The sound of small twangs filled the room. All three men let out muffled hisses of pain as small slivers of metal hit them. A dozen small crossbow bolts were distributed among them— none had hit their eyes, but a few were very close to having taken one out.

"Damned pests!" Amerut hissed as he raised the amber rod again, and a wave of energy flashed through the room. "Well, that helps stage them attacking us." Picking up a second rod, he pointed it at Venim and Fokler. "Take care of him, then squash the bugs."

"Understood," Fokler said as he walked around Sean so he could see his face. "You crossed the wrong people."

Sean's lips twitched as he pushed against the energy. "I'll kill you!" Sean managed to get out through gritted teeth.

"No, you won't," Fokler snorted.

Sean's arm moved with the speed of a sloth, but that made Fokler's eyes go wide.

"What?! How is that possible?" Fokler gasped.

Amerut's face went white. "Kill him! Quickly!"

Fokler cut hard, slicing through Sean's neck, severing both arteries and just missing his spine. Sean was still reaching for Fokler when darkness grabbed him and pulled him under.

42

Sean felt himself being pulled away, rising above his body and the courtroom. A silver thread connected him to his body, but it was fraying and about to snap.

No! Sean hissed, throwing everything in him at the silver thread. *Fuck these assholes! You think I'm just going to roll over and die for you? Aed blessed me, you stupid fuckers!*

The thread pulsed brightly and Sean felt it start to repair itself. He floated closer to his body and saw the gash in his neck knitting together. If he'd had a body, he'd be grinning wolfishly and flexing his hands in anticipation.

That anticipation turned to rage when he watched Venim and Fokler both smash a Fairy underfoot. *No, you slimy, fucking bastards!* Sean raged.

His awareness went to Helga, who was blinking as she came back to life. *Helga, move! Quick! Stop them!* Sean yelled spiritually, as he was still outside his body.

Helga jolted as if slapped and jerked to her feet, surprising the men in the room. Amerut had moved to look down at Sean gloatingly while the other two were near the door. With no one next to her, Helga glanced at Sean and her face went white.

She said something before launching herself at Amerut. The magistrate stumbled back, sprawling onto his ass as he did. Helga reached him and picked him up, an evil smile on her face as she spun to face the two others, who were charging her.

Amerut's eyes went wide and he tried to speak, but Venim's sword had punched into his chest and Fokler's ended up hacking at his arm, neither of them able to check their attacks in time.

Helga shoved Amerut toward Venim, further impaling the magistrate, and backed away from Fokler, who was wild-eyed. She was speaking as she backed toward Amerut's desk.

"—cannot stop me!" Helga's shout echoed in Sean's ears.

Back in his body and feeling drained, Sean lurched to his feet. Venim was kneeling next to Amerut, having freed his sword, and was trying to staunch the wound. Sean grabbed the guard from behind and snapped his neck, nearly tearing it free of the body in the process.

Amerut's eyes went wide and he tried to speak, but blood bubbled up from his mouth instead. Eyes rolling up, Amerut either passed out or died.

Helga had been thrown over Amerut's desk, and she pushed herself up the far wall, sporting a deep gash in her arm. Fokler was rounding the desk to finish her off, and Sean knew he wouldn't make it in time to save her.

Helga just grinned as her other hand, which had been hidden behind her, came up, an amber rod in her hand. "It is your turn," she said.

Fokler started to lunge, but his muscles locked up and he toppled to the floor, instead.

"The crystal rod to free the Fairies!" Sean told her as he went to see about the two who'd been crushed under boots.

Helga blinked, not having seen Sean get back to his feet. Shaking her head, she looked for the other rod on the floor.

Onim and another Fairy that Sean didn't know had both been crushed. Kneeling beside them, he reached out to heal them, but found their bodies lifeless. He rubbed at his face— he knew he couldn't save both of them, and he wasn't even certain he could save one of them. Drawing on his Bonds to his wives, Sean pulled energy from them, trying to get enough to bring at least one of them back to life.

Sean was reaching for Onim when Ven was suddenly in his way. "Ven?"

"Can you bring them both back, Sean? If not, let it be Mak? Onim told me they'd be fine if they were with Omin again."

Sean hesitated, then bowed his head. "Mak first, then."

Reaching out to the body, Sean pushed healing into it first, as it'd have to be healed for the spirit to reside in it. Helga moved to Sean's side as he restored the Fairies. She knelt beside him and rested her hand on his back. Sean felt the rush of energy as she fed him more.

"I have their souls, Sean," Helga said softly. "Maybe it'll be easier than having to call them back yourself?"

Sean fervently hoped so, but didn't speak as he finished healing the Fairy. Taking a deep breath, he felt for a way to reunite Mak with their body. A snapped silver thread appeared, and he touched it. Another emerged from Helga's breastbone and he touched that one, too. Moving on instinct, he brought the two threads together and imagined them reuniting.

The flood of energy made Sean rock in place as his energy pool began to empty rapidly. Faster than he expected, and for less energy than he feared, the flow stopped and Mak suddenly gasped for air. Shifting to the side, Sean reached out for Onim and repeated the process. A moment later, Onim also rejoined the land of the living.

The doors suddenly flung open, and Fiona and the rest of Sean's wives were at the front of the group. Everyone stopped at the doorway, taking in the blood-drenched floor and the dead guards and magistrate.

"Stop!" Sean croaked out. "I'm alive. We're alive, but we need this to be seen by an impartial person. I pray that one of the Carmady brothers is in the building."

"I'll go," Ven said, flashing away.

Fiona rocked in place, wanting to go to Sean, but also knowing he was right— they couldn't go in until Carmady arrived. "We felt the Bonds shiver, and then you were pulling on them," Fiona whispered, her voice trembling. "We feared...!"

Sean looked up at her, his eyes sunken and tired. "With good reason. It's okay now. Hah, Jasper is going to be pissed at me," he added with a wan smile.

"You won't be seeing him," Fredrick said from the doorway. "Killing a magistrate sends you straight to the chief magistrate."

"Chief magistrate?" Sean asked, puzzled. "Didn't know there was one."

"He doesn't normally take cases," Saret said softly. "Excuse me." With that, she slipped away from the group.

Raised voices came from the hallway and Sean picked out Ernest Carmady's among them. "Let them through," Sean said.

The people in the hall made way for Carmady and a small group of guards. Carmady looked grim when he made it to the door and stepped inside. That grim look shifted to one of surprise. "Winter's pale tits..." Carmady breathed out.

"Self-defense," Sean croaked, his throat dry. "My Bonded and I were attacked by Amerut and the guards."

Carmady's eyes went to Sean, and he took a half-step back involuntarily. Sean was a grizzly sight— the wound on his neck was healed, but a thick ugly scab covered it, and his entire front was covered in blood. With the sunken eyes and his dry voice, he nearly resembled a zombie.

"Yo... you're under arrest, MacDougal," Carmady stammered to start with, but got his voice under control.

"I figured, but self-defense," Sean replied as he got to his feet slowly. "Venim attacked Helga from behind, Amerut immobilized me, and Fokler cut my throat. My Messenger Fairies tried to help defend me, but they were ineffective. As they plotted to make it look like we attacked them, Helga and I healed and then defended ourselves."

Carmady took in the scene and nodded slowly, noting where everyone was in the room. "Men, take note of everything. MacDougal, we'll need to shackle you. Will you and your Bonded come willingly?"

"Yes," Sean said. "Helga, don't resist them. I trust Carmady."

"As you command, Sean."

Carmady looked at the crowded hallway. "Everyone, move back to the lobby and give us a wide berth. I will not tolerate any interference." His gaze went to Fiona and Sean's other wives. "Ladies, I understand you are distraught and that you likely have a low opinion of the guards at the moment, but I vow that I will make sure he is safe."

"My husband trusts you," Fiona said. "We will do so, as well. This never would have happened under Babbitt."

Carmady didn't rebuke her, merely nodding instead. "Please give us room to put together the facts and know that he will be under protective detail." Turning to one of the men, Carmady gave an order. "Call for the rest of the squad. My name rides on this, and the reputation of the guards has already been tarnished today."

"Sir!" one of the men said before rushing off.

"Sean, we'll be waiting to go to the chief magistrate's court," Fredrick said. "We'll do as we've been told until then."

Sean nodded weakly. A bit of the scab flaked away from his neck and a small trickle of blood trailed from it. "Thanks."

"And get a healer!" Carmady yelled into the hall.

Sean held out his hands to the guard who approached him slowly. "As long as you don't slit my throat or stab my Bonded, you won't get trouble from me."

The guard nodded, but was still leery of getting close enough to put the manacles on Sean. "Turn around and put your arms behind you, please."

Sean, hearing the tremor of fear in the man's voice, sighed and did as requested. It wasn't as if he couldn't Shape the things off if he wanted, anyway. Once they were locked in place, the guard gingerly took Sean's arm by the elbow, leading him toward the door.

"Watch your step," the guard told Sean.

As the guard was reaching the door with Sean, an older woman was being escorted to the room. "How is he not dead?" the woman asked, shocked to see Sean moving. "His throat was cut recently?! Move, move! Let me see him," the woman said, pushing the guard with Sean aside and taking Sean's face in her hands.

Sean tried to place her, as she looked familiar, but he couldn't remember her.

The feeling of energy touched Sean and he felt her checking his wounds. "Hmm... healed enough to live, but there is still damage. Who healed you?" Her eyes, a dark brown almost to the point of being black, locked on Sean's.

"I did," Sean croaked.

"That can't be right. You're a crafter, MacDougal, not a healer. Otherwise, I wouldn't have seen you and your wives before."

That placed her for Sean— she was the healer who'd seen him the last time he'd been arrested. "I can heal, as well. I was depleted then, if you recall."

"That is true, and you look nearly the same now...that isn't surprising, considering the wound." The old healer sighed, looking tired when she removed her hands. "You'll be fine. I don't have much left, but I'll see the other one now."

"Thank you," Sean said.

"This is twice I've healed you, both times at the request of the guard, MacDougal. Thank me by not making me heal you again."

Sean snorted, as the acerbic woman didn't hate him, but was just generally crotchety. "I'll do my best, ma'am."

The older woman gave him a glance before she reached Helga. "We'll see, won't we?"

Taking a minute with Helga, the healer sighed and swayed on her feet. "It's closed and healing, but make sure you don't reopen it or it could go bad," she told Helga as firmly as she could.

"I understand," Helga replied, her arms still manacled behind her back.

"Thank you, healer," the corporal holding Sean's arm said.

"I'll leave a bill at the front," she replied, moving slowly down the hall. "And MacDougal, I did as much as I could for you. If you think I deserve more, I wouldn't turn down a kettle or faucet."

Sean chuckled. "If I'm not executed later today, I'll see what I can do."

She slowed and looked back. "Executed? What is the charge?"

"Murder of guards and a magistrate," the corporal told her.

Shaking her head, the healer sighed. "Ah, well then it seems unlikely."

The lobby was packed with people, many wanting to get a glimpse at the "magistrate murderer." The voices were white noise to Sean as he let the guard lead him toward the stairs down to the cells. He met the eyes of his wives and gave them an apologetic smile.

Once they reached the processing room, Sean felt Henik, Machar, and Stein all staring at him. All three older men eyed him warily, as if he were a dog that had slipped its leash and attacked someone.

"Triple murder; two guards and one magistrate," the guard holding his arm informed the trio. "Ernest ordered them kept under protective guard."

"We'll keep someone with him," Henik said. "Paperwork is ready."

Machar handed paperwork up to the guards. "We'll unchain them once we have them in their cells. Take a different set of manacles with you."

"Understood," the corporal said, taking the paperwork and snatching a set of manacles as he left with his fellow guard.

"I'll have your Agreement not to cause trouble or attack us," Henik said, standing in front of Sean and staring into his eyes.

"I agree that I will not act up or cause trouble for you," Sean stated and felt the weight land on his shoulders.

"As you're under protective guard, I'll be with you the entire time until the chief magistrate calls for you."

Sean nodded. "We're in your hands, Henik."

Stein unlocked the manacles and set them aside, then looked at them. "They used normal...?" He trailed off with a sigh. "When we take you up, we'll be using the heavy manacles. No offense, but you have a reputation." He pointed to the adamantine manacles hanging next to the bronze ones.

"Understood," Sean said. "I don't hold any ill will to you three. I know you're only doing your job."

"This way," Henik said, unlocking the door to the cells before tossing Stein his keys. "You're the doorman until this is over."

"Oh, the keys of honor and duty," Stein said with mock reverence. "I'll try to walk in your footsteps, but perhaps with a manly gait instead?"

Henik rolled his eyes and started toward the cells. "Follow me, MacDougal."

43

Sean groaned as he sat up. "Is it time?"

"You were asleep for a couple of hours," Helga told him. "Stein is here. The chief magistrate is ready to see us."

Sean got out of bed and stretched. *I feel a little better, at least, but still well under normal.* Pushing the thought aside, Sean followed Helga back to where Henik and Stein were waiting for him. Seeing the adamantine manacles, Sean walked to Stein and turned his back, presenting his arms.

"Thank you for not fighting," Stein said.

"I don't break Agreements," Sean said.

Neither of the guards said anything, and soon, they were back in the processing room, Sean gave Ernest Carmady a nod. The sergeant gave him a level look, but didn't react otherwise.

"Has he given you any trouble?" Carmady asked.

"Agreed not to," Henik replied.

Carmady sighed. "MacDougal, you're a headache and a half."

"Sorry. I don't mean to be. All I wanted was to craft in peace."

"I wish you'd been able to," Carmady said. "Henik, please help me get Oathsworn up to the chief magistrate."

"Bed, finally," Stein sighed as he signed off a form and gave it to Carmady. "See you at the bar, Dale?"

"Be along when I can," Henik replied.

"First round is on us if you bring the verdict," Machar said.

Sean realized that three other guards were in the processing room, clearly in the midst of shift change. All of them were staring at him with fear. Shaking his head, Sean waited for Henik and Carmady to lead them away.

Sean felt the eyes of the crowd in the lobby on him as he was led to the stairs going up, his face grim.

"Killed a whole squad..."

"Snapped the magistrate's neck like...!"

"His Bonded seduced..."

"Bathed the room in blood..."

"Tore his head clean off and shi..."

"...down his neck? Really?"

Following Carmady, Sean did his best to ignore the conversations, wondering how this trial would go. *Magistrates have been split half-and-half on fair and biased... this one will tip that one way or the other.*

Sean was surprised that the décor was the same as it had been all the way throughout the building, even up to the top floor. The double doors were open and Sean could hear the hubbub of voices coming from inside.

As soon as he entered the room, conversation fell off. Looking around, Sean spotted his wives at the front and gave them a strained smile. All around them sat the association members. The other side of the aisle held Wolen and his squad, along with a group of people from the Golden Lion. The rest of the room was filled up with others Sean didn't know. Around the edge of the room at regular intervals, guards stood, armed with loaded crossbows.

Carmady and Henik took Sean and Helga to stand before the magistrate's desk. Henik took a few steps back, but stayed within arm's reach of the pair. Carmady stood directly to Sean's side, his hand still on Sean's elbow.

Conversation had just started up again when the door at the back of the room opened, and the room went silent as the old man walked in. Dignified and composed, the magistrate looked over the room as he went to his desk.

Taking a seat, he cleared his throat before talking. "There will be order in this room or I will have it cleared. If anyone makes me use my gavel, they will be held in contempt, regardless of who they are. The room is for civil discourse and judgment."

He looked over the room and, seeing everyone had understood what he'd said, nodded and turned his attention to Carmady. "Sergeant, this is Sean MacDougal?"

"It is, and his Bonded, Helga Oathsworn."

"MacDougal, you are here because you are accused of having murdered Magistrate Amerut, Captain Fokler, and Corporal Venim. How do you plead?"

"Innocent. I defended myself and my Bonded, sir."

The chief magistrate nodded. "Innocent. Very well. Let's get to the facts and determine if you are indeed innocent or guilty." Turning his attention to Carmady, he motioned the sergeant to begin.

"Sir, I was called to Magistrate Amerut's courtroom by a Messenger Fairy. The Fairy stated that three were dead and that I was needed to see the scene."

"One of the Fairies employed by the guard?"

"No, sir. It was one of MacDougal's."

"Hmm. A man accused of murder sent his own messenger for you?"

"That is a valid point, and one of a few things that cast doubt."

"Continue," the magistrate said.

"There was a crowd in the hall that slowed us from getting there as quickly as we could have. None of them had entered the room, even with the doors open. As I got to the doorway, I was shocked to see what had become of the room— Magistrate Amerut had been run through and Corporal Venim's sword was bloody and laying next to the body. The corporal lay next to the magistrate, but his head had been nearly ripped from his body. Near the magistrate's desk,

Captain Fokler lay with his throat open and his sword on the ground beside him."

"Just those weapons to be seen?"

"No, sir. Venim's dagger held traces of fresh blood, but was in its sheath."

"Henik," the magistrate began, "when MacDougal was taken to Amerut's room, was he weaponless?"

"They both were, sir."

"Hmm. Yes, a good point to make."

"Sir?" Sergeant Wolen had his hand raised.

"I normally do not let others interrupt, but considering who the dead are, I will make an exception. Go ahead, Sergeant."

"Sir, it should be noted that MacDougal is an exceptional Shaper who is known to Shape weapons in combat. It isn't beyond the pale to imagine he made a weapon, killed them with it, and then reverted it."

The chief magistrate nodded slowly. "Duly noted. Carmady, were you able to rule out that possibility?"

"No, sir, but we didn't find evidence of it happening, either."

"Very well. Continue."

"The floor had a lot of blood, and in positions away from where the bodies were. There was no discernible cause for them until I laid eyes on MacDougal. He looked like he was a half breath away from death. He bore a ragged, ugly scab that reached completely across his neck. Oathsworn's clothing was coated in fresh blood, as well."

"How fresh was the scab?"

"I have the report from the healer who saw MacDougal before he was taken down to the cells," Carmady said, moving to hand it to the chief magistrate. "As you can see, Chief Magistrate, she was surprised he'd survived and notes that he admits to being able to heal. According to her, his neck had been cut wide open from ear to ear, and nearly deep enough to reach his spine."

The magistrate read over the report slowly before setting it aside. "MacDougal, did you heal yourself?"

"As much as I needed to, but not as much as I could, because I had to save my Bonded."

"Is there anything else you need to note, Sergeant?" the chief magistrate asked.

"There were a dozen tiny crossbow bolts distributed among the three dead."

"Explain."

Carmady approached the desk again and placed a few items on it from his pouch. "The bolts and what we believe is one of the crossbows that fired them."

"Hmm... I've never seen the like before. Sized for a Messenger Fairy, are they?"

"That is our guess."

"Sir," Sean said and waited.

"MacDougal, you wish to add something?"

"That belongs to one of my Messenger Fairies, and yes, they are sized for them."

"You admit, then, that the Fairies under your employ attacked?"

"They were trying to save me. They attacked in self-defense."

"Self-defense?"

"Some of them are Life Bonded to me," Sean explained, not wanting to give the actual number.

A small commotion started in the gallery, and the chief magistrate grabbed his gavel. The room went silent again before he could bang it. "I will remind you all that you are here at my whim." Taking a moment to eye the crowd, he nodded. "You Life Bonded Messenger Fairies?"

"Yes, sir."

"I would like to hear your side of things, MacDougal. Explain it to me from the moment you entered the room."

"Yes, sir," Sean replied. "Helga and I..."

* * *

"Preposterous!" Wolen spat. "Fokler was a decorated member of the guard, and Amerut had been a magistrate for a decade!"

"Order!" the chief magistrate banged his gavel, as the room had all started talking when Sean said that the dead had attacked him and Helga.

The room went quiet, and the old man glared at everyone before turning an angry face toward Wolen. "Sergeant, did you not hear me at the start of this trial? Anyone and everyone will be held in contempt. Given the accusation that was just leveled, I will give you a chance. You will not interrupt again, no matter what the provocation. Understood?"

"Yes, sir," Wolen said stiffly.

"And you," his gaze went to the audience, "another outburst will clear this room." No one spoke, and he nodded. "Now, MacDougal, that was a very serious charge. Please continue so we can hear about how they died."

Sean finished telling the story, but left out that Onim and Mak had died— he'd changed that to them being badly injured. "That is when I asked one of my Bonded Messenger Fairies to inform a sergeant."

"Where is the Messenger Fairy?" the chief magistrate asked.

"Here, sir," Ven said, landing on Sean's shoulder. "I am Ven, paired to Venn, Life Bonded to Sean MacDougal."

"Did your Holder command you to go find a sergeant to report the scene?"

"He did, sir."

"And you found Ernest Carmady first?"

"He is the first one I found," Ven replied.

"Very well. You may go."

Ven flew up to the rafters again and all eyes followed them. A small ripple of shock came when the crowd realized that the rafters were filled with Messenger Fairies.

"You will all behave, right?" the chief magistrate asked.

"We are just here to support our Holder, sir," Ven said.

"All of you?"

"We all owe our status to him, sir."

"That coincides with the rumor of him being covered in Fairies after the trial by combat," the chief magistrate said. "The rules apply to you all, as well."

"We understand, sir, and will abide."

"Good. Now, Oathsworn, MacDougal didn't know how Fokler died. Can you enlighten us?"

"He drove me back over the magistrate's desk," Helga said evenly. "After a brief struggle, I took his sword from him. The resulting attack carved deeply into his neck."

"Sergeant Carmady, does that coincide with your investigation of the scene?"

Carmady was looking into space for a moment before he nodded. "Yes. The bloody footprints and other evidence would give this credence."

"What?!" Wolen erupted, on his feet in indignation. "You're going to ignore evidence and let a self-confessed guard-killer walk?!"

The other guards with Wolen, except for one, were also on their feet. That last one rose slowly, looking uncomfortable.

"Order!" the chief magistrate snapped, banging his gavel. "Guards, report yourselves to the cells for contempt. Right now!"

Wolen stood there, glaring at Carmady, before he turned his gaze to the magistrate. Giving the stiffest salute he could, he turned and marched out of the room, his entire squad following him.

"Now, as you were saying, Sergeant Carmady, you believe the defendant has told us the truth?"

"Yes, sir."

"Is there anything that might cause you to think the deaths were not self-defense?"

"I have no evidence that it was anything but. The records show that the magistrate had tried to go out of his way to hurt the defendant before in regards to his Bonded, and that MacDougal was the catalyst for the guard being investigated for corruption. Fokler might have been lucky to avoid the sweep and been angry about it."

The chief magistrate considered Carmady's words before sighing. "If there is no evidence that it was anything but self-defense, it behooves me to clear MacDougal of the charges of murder of Amerut, Fokler, and Venim. There is also the charge of the murder of Aspirant Denmur. That was why you were originally brought before Amerut."

"Sir," Carmady said.

"Go ahead, Sergeant."

"I was on the scene until Captain Fokler ordered my men to leave. He turned the scene over to Sergeant Wolen, even though his beat was meant to be the crafter's quarter. I would wonder if the reports from that scene can be accurate. High Magistrate Jasper just exonerated Dame Flamehair of the murders of the others involved in that incident."

"Hmm," the chief magistrate said before he looked up. "One of you, go tell Jasper that I need him to attend the court." A streak of silver flashed from the ceiling and through the floor. "We will have a moment to wait. You may talk quietly until he arrives."

Muted conversation sprang up behind Sean, and he did his best to ignore it. Staring straight ahead, he was aware that the chief magistrate kept looking toward his wives. He wondered what was happening and looked back to the group— all of his wives were staring at him. The oddity was Saret, who was smiling slightly, a gleam in her eye as she looked past Sean.

Sean looked back to the magistrate and his lips pursed. *Okay, so Saret and the chief magistrate know each other? Huh. Maybe I owe her for him being so understanding? He hasn't gone out of his way or anything... he's just been open to the possibility of me being innocent. That by itself is probably going to cost him with Lord Sharpeyes.*

Ven flashed back into being, landing on Sean's shoulder. "Sir, High Magistrate Jasper is on his way. He had been half-expecting to be called."

"Good. Thank you."

"We live to serve," Ven replied before zipping back up to the rafters.

A minute later, Jasper walked into the room, and the gallery went silent. Jasper gave the room an appraising glance, then moved to stand near Carmady. "I was called, sir?"

"Did you hear the case against Dame Flamehair?"

"I did, sir."

"How did you find the evidence?"

Jasper took a moment before he spoke slowly, "I exonerated Dame Flamehair, as a percentage of the evidence was flimsy and unsustainable."

"How much was flimsy?"

Jasper hesitated and cleared his throat before answering, "The majority of it. I'd go so far to say over three-quarters."

"Was there evidence about how Aspirant Denmur died?"

"Decapitation."

"MacDougal?" The chief magistrate looked to him for an explanation.

"Helga killed him, sir. After the duel, he stabbed me in the back. Helga drove him off and killed him."

"Hmm... Carmady, did you see anything to support that claim?"

"Denmur had a bloody dagger clutched in a death grip, sir."

"I take the word of a guard seriously. Considering the other evidence was thrown out by High Magistrate Jasper, I'll rule it as self-defense."

"MacDougal was supposed to be seen by me for obstruction of the guard during their duties, as well," Jasper said. "Considering how today went, I was going to toss the charge out."

"Very well. I take the case against MacDougal from High Magistrate Jasper and exonerate him of it."

"Thank you," Jasper said, a little surprised.

"That clears all charges," the magistrate said. "This session is over." With a single bang of his gavel, he nodded, rose, and left the room.

Conversation sprang up immediately, filling the room with noise. Carmady pulled a key and began to unshackle Sean and Helga. Jasper, seeing he wasn't needed anymore, left without a word to anyone else.

Free from the shackles, Sean rolled his shoulders. "Thank you, Sergeant."

"Just doing my job and obeying the laws," Carmady replied. "I have a bad feeling about this though."

"Because of the new commander?" Sean asked.

Carmady looked from Sean to the full room. "Have a good day, MacDougal. Please, for the love of my sanity, give me a few days' rest?"

Sean extended his hand. "I'll do my best."

Carmady shook his hand and headed for the door, the guards in the room following him out. The room began to slowly empty and his wives went to his side once the guards were past.

"Sean, thank goodness!" Fiona cried out, the first one to hug him.

The others echoed her in various ways, and he was completely surrounded and hugged on all sides when they got to him. He hugged them back, kissing each one briefly as the knot of worry in his chest finally dissolved.

"He was extraordinarily open about the case," Fredrick said. "Normally, he sides with the guards and has a very harsh record on assaults against them."

Sean's eyes went to Saret. "Guess I got lucky."

Saret's lips twitched, but she didn't show any more than that. "Lucky, indeed. This will likely give him trouble."

"Sharpeyes will be furious," Mageeyes nodded. "You and Flamehair were both cleared."

"And with so many crafters dead, the city just took a hard hit," Italice said.

"Darkfoam is dead," Eva said. "Along with several others you've probably never heard of, Sean."

"No more Dark Delights for anyone," Sean said before pushing into a different topic. "I have news about... things... but privacy would be best."

"The private room," Mageeyes said. "Say... in two hours?"

"Enough time to go home, bathe, and have a good meal," Flamehair nodded. "I would like that."

"Okay," Sean said. "Two hours. Be ready to hear what we're really up against."

CHARACTER INFORMATION

Sean Aragorn MacDougal
Godling
Age: 33

Gifts:
Metal Bones, Viney Muscles, Mithril Blood, Magic Bond, Mending Body, Death
Ward, Linguist, Hunter's Blood, Infinite Possibilities

Spells:
Summon Water
Fireball
Flame Arc
Steam Cloud

Talents:
Shaper- (Wood, Metal, Flesh)
Mage Sight
Camouflage
Targeter
Elemental Manipulation (Water, Earth)
Enchanting
Beast Tamer
Energy Wings
Battle Magic

Bonded:
Fiona Mithrilsoul- Soul Bonded/Wife
Myna Mooncaller- Soul Bonded /Wife
Ryann Cullin- Soul Bonded /Wife
Ida Bronzeshield- Soul Bonded /Wife
Andrea Brandt- Soul Bonded /Wife
Felora Somnia- Soul Bonded /Wife
Aria Swiftwing- Soul Bonded /Wife
Chastity Bisset- (Deceased)- Soul Bonded/ Wife
Lilliana Lunatis- (Deceased)- Soul Bonded/ Wife
Helga Oathsworn- Soul Bonded

Ven- Soul Bonded
Venn- Soul Bonded
Onim- Soul Bonded
Jutt- Soul Bonded
Arla- Soul Bonded
Omin- (Deceased)- Soul Bonded
Marjorie Bisset- (Deceased)- Soul Bonded
Rosa Rington- Life Bond
Rumia Rington- Life Bond
Glorina Coit- Life Bond
Lona Lenik- Life Bond
Mona Lenik- Life Bond
Quinna Denna- Life Bond
Quilla Denna- Life Bond
Tiska Trech- Life Bond
Cali Ornia- Life Bond
Xenta Smurm- Life Bond
Prita Funder- Life Bond
Arliat Afreghan- Life Bond

Metal Bones- Your bones are not ordinary calcium, but Adamant and Iron. (Crafted by Goibniu.)
Viney Muscles- Your musculature is built of Iron Vine, reinforced with traces of Adamant. (Crafted by Luchta.)
Mithril Blood- Your blood is not the red watery stuff of normal people, but Mithril blended with Iron. (Crafted by Credne.)
Magic Bond- Able to learn and wield the magic of the world. (Gift of Beag.)
Mending Body- Your body will repair any damage with time and energy. (Gift of Dian Cecht.)
Death Ward- Force death away if enough energy is present. (Gift of Aed.)
Linguist- Know and speak every language. (Gift of Oghma.)
Hunter's Blood- Master of woodcraft. (Gift of Cernunnos.)
Infinite Possibilities- Blessed to be able to learn all Talents. (Gift of Dagda.)

AUTHOR'S NOTE

Please consider leaving a review for the book, feedback is imperative for an indie author. If you don't want to review it then think about leaving a comment or even just a quick message. Remember, positive feedback is always welcome.

If you want to keep up on the latest updates, or the one stop shop for all the links, my website is the best place for that. Remember to subscribe to the mailing list to know when I publish a new book, and you get an exclusive short when you sign up.
http://schinhofenbooks.com/

Other places you can keep up to date on me and my works:
https://www.patreon.com/DJSchinhofen
https://twitter.com/DJSchinhofen
Fan group on Facebook for Daniel Schinhofen
https://schinhofenbooks.blogspot.com/

A big thank you to my editors, Samantha Bishop, and Sarinia Phelps. Also props to Geno Ferrarini, and Sean Hickinbotham for being my Alpha Readers. I'd be remiss if I didn't include my beta readers, in no particular order: Ian McAdams, Dame, A.J. Bishop, Jay Taylor, Zee, Scott Brown, Kevin Kollman, Justin Johanson, Kenneth Darlin, Rob Bunting, Aoife Grimm, Peter LaFemina, Tanner Lovelace, Tim?, Carl Gheradi, Shiafu, Dimitri Shadow, Matt Case, Richard G Stahl, Cheyene Adams, A Madsen, MrNyxt, J. Stone, D Smith.

The cover for Lost Bonds is brought to you by Anthony Bishop, a very talented artist. You can find him at https://grimmhelm.artstation.com/

A big thanks to my Patreon supporters who have gone above and beyond in their support:

Scott Hank, Christina Dammyr, Jeffrey Buchanan, Daniel Lynch, David Peers, Lgikito, Erraticcyprus, Wesley, Prosailor22, Seth Martinez, Shawn Meade, Vaeld, Bpgt64, Zachery, General Raith, Christi Stanley, Brendon Quinn, Zachary Johnson, Larry the Emu, Johannes Müller, Jascha Weiss, Dragonkain, Magnus Gammal, Brett Hudson, Pheonixblue, Dane Smith, Robert Knight, Benjamin J Russel, Matthew, Winston Smith, Aryan Eimermacher, Michael Jackson, Tom Richards, Jose Caudillo, Rey T Nufable, Eli Page, William Merrick, Southern Celt, Abraham Madsen, Chris Cannon, Masta Matna, Kevin Harris, Don Jinkins, J. Patrick Walker, T3iain, Jeff Morris, Joshua McCane, Berry Dirickson, Robert Owen, Matthew Malkin, EthanK, Chace Corso, Robse, Jeremy Cox, Jacob Lawlor, Malcolm White, Derek Raines, Aaron Blue, Allderin, Nathan Goforth, Tristitan, Seto Kyba, Robert Shofner, David Taylor-Fuller, Forrest Hansen, Joshua Towns, Kurt Bodenstedt, Thomas Smith, Tyller James, Matthew Zarember, Kevin McKinney, Kenneth Freeman, Xiao, Travis Btmb, Deme A, Clinton Wertzbaugher, Michael Erwin, Ryan Luttinger, James Parker, Spencer Jefferson, Stephan Caperton, Eliseo Rios, Kyle Gravelle, Dedalus Inventor, Matthew Parikka, BobsNemesis, Tetsu-nii, Matthew Myers, Michael Hyde Jr., Scott Hank, Justin Cox, Loyd Hockersmith, Eric Jaschen, Emil

Thoren, Michael Shearer, Christopher B., IntheRaccon, Mark Kewer, Kevin Clark, Zachariah Miller, Cole Depuy, Joshua Stusek, MattMick-222, Shakekiller, Michael S Pellman, Paul Mallon, Chanh Pham, Craig Mather, Gregory Sanders, James Murphy, Gabe Olah, Chris Guerrero, Susan Lofböm, Michael Mooney, Red Phoenix, Charles Henggeler, Wesley, Alexander Rodriguez, Dwayne Bullock, Brandon Haag, Khamla Khongloth, Matthew Kelly, Jessie Redd, Ori Shifrin, Tara C Mulkey, Ashley Scott, Hill44, James Domec, Eric Hutinson, Stephen Juba, Mike Durie, Matt, Jeff Kollada, Eric Hontz, Alarinnise, Christopher Cales, NooneSpecial, Ronald C Abitz, Sean Fitzpatrick, Jeff Gaebler, Adam, Jeremy Patrick, Kori Prins, James Breaux, Exempt Pie, Chase G Harstad, Brian Biggers, Arthur Cuelho, Scott Baxter, Ian Weatherly, Charles Demarest, Tyler Scheibe, Matthew Paulin, Bret Cole, Zachary Nahstadt, Dwinald Lint III, Frankie Gouge, Christopher Edstrom, Mike Brown, Tim Nielsen, Matthew Richardson, Jason Davis, M. Ahles, Patrick Glass, Michael Moneymaker, Dameon Cornish, B Liz, Jon Bryant, Top Cat 269, TheRou, Ken Giles, Sith, Robert Howden, Robert McCoard, Roman Smith, Joel Wilkinson, Stefan Holze, Tyler Clifton, Cody Carter, Christopher Gross, Ben Foard, DeseriDan, Tanner Lovelace, Richard Papst, Corran Horn, Jenn Bean, David Florish, Jason Moore, J. Sullies, Randall Kemper, David Hoerner, Brad Schultz, Rafnar Caldon, Travis Hilliard, Caleb Bear, Matthias Meilahn, Pamela J Smith, David Morrissey, Damien Osborne, Lui Adecer, Choike Nelson, Terry Wood-Davies, Thomas Lindsay, Malcolm Wade, Kenneth Darlin, Andre Durkalec, Morgan C Williams, William Simmons, Ryan A Larkey, Dreamon, Brandon Lai, Thomas Corbin, Andrew Nevis, Jeff Ford, Daniel Glasson, Gregory Lamberta, Daniel Jones, Zachary Johnson, Logan Cochrane, Shadowsteppez, Brian O., Kevin Kollman, Robert Whittaker, Riley Dunn, Kurt Borek, SpartanGER, Paul Barron, Gslice100, Robert Jacobs, MrNyxt, Philippe Bruneau, Alkon Rameriz, Bryon Gobert, Samuel DeBoard, Carl Alston, Yo Dude, Ryan Phelps, Jjstone, ItWasIDIO!!, J.G. Patton, LordStabbers, Robert Michael Barfield, Jerrod, Chad Arrington, MadManLoose, Edward P Warmouth, Sawyer Williams, Jose Ibarra, Cheyene Adams, subVersion, JakeTylerPsn, Korbin

Wilson, Gregory Johnson, Aristo, John Cothrin, Otis Coley, Justin "Johnist" Johanson, Brian Sutton, Gianfranco Marmolino, John Curtis, Josh Holmes, David Simmons, Kyle Pettay, Blake Cawthon, Adam Setzco, Setret, Cory Miller, John, Joshua Morris, Noel Kurtz, Matthew Caro, James Scacco, Timithy Klesick, Brian McDonald, Bradley White, Jason Broderick, Bob, Jason Bryant, Michael Browningkoelper, Derek Morgan, Cody Creager, Randall Randall, Garrett, Zifferix, Alan Spector, Cody Givan, Thomas Belcher, Ryan Williamson, Matt Sensenig, Council Of Nine, Lord Shackleford, Erin Jordan, Matt Thompson, Terry Carter, Theodore Ursa, Eloren Koori, Miguel E Rameriz, Drew Williams, PantherTheory, Mizu Damen, Calidia, Influenza, Tishane McFarlane, Curtis Allan Sayles, Allen Deck, Robert Norwood, Daniel Shimek, Marty, Mars Ultor, Taylor Tilbury, Angelina Ward, Zane Brannon, Myles Beyl, Dante, Fermin Rodriguez II, Robert Yarber, Garrett, Robin Lee, Jens Nordin, Evil-Zetti, Tanner Sealock, Alan McLoughlin, Taefox, Dominic Harrold, Mankey, Samantha K., Barry Drickson, Joshua Border, Andy Overcash, CosmicOrange.

My last big thank you goes out to Nick Kuhns who formatted this book for paperback. If it weren't for him you wouldn't be holding this book in your hands.

Made in the USA
Coppell, TX
22 October 2024

39047824R00225